BLOODY BOUGAINVILLE

A WWII NOVEL

CHRIS GLATTE

Created with Vellum

THIS IS A WORK OF FICTION

Though based on an actual campaign during the second world war, none of the characters or events depicted follow an accurate historic account. Characters are products of the author's imagination and any resemblance to persons living or dead is coincidental.

Thank You

Enjoy

PROLOGUE

December 28th 1943, North of the Crown Prince Mountain Range

~

General Hyakutake didn't like venturing far from the command headquarters at Buin, but getting out with the troops was good for morale, and he wanted to see first-hand the work being done to push the Imperialist American's off the beach-head at Empress Augusta Bay.

The jungle was thick, making the air humid and sticky. It clung to the general like a wet rag. His staff clustered around him, their khaki colored tunics dark with sweat. The journey to the hills surrounding Empress Bay took most of the day. At some points, the road, which seemed more like a dirt track, was so choked they measured progress in meters rather than kilometers. They finally came to the end, and met a group of officers from the 17th Army. They braced and saluted their commander.

They walked General Hyakutake and his entourage of officers and soldiers through the thick jungle for five kilometers.

General Hyakutake had been on Bougainville for months. He'd

retreated there after leading his men in defeat at Guadalcanal. He'd been ready to commit suicide for his failure, but his superiors ordered him not to take his life. They had a new assignment for him in the northern Solomon Islands. Bougainville, the largest of the Solomons and strategically important, needed a combat veteran for the coming clash with the allies.

The five-kilometer walk reminded him what his soldiers had to put up with everyday. The bugs were almost as thick as the jungle, and they all seemed to bite or sting. During his short walk he'd seen more snakes than he could count on two hands. His men hacked through the jungle making it easier for his old body, but it was still hard walking.

The officers assured him there were no Americans past the mountain range, but they still traveled as quietly as they could while hacking a path with machetes.

After two hours they stopped, and the sweating Captain Shigeo gestured to the wall of jungle that started to angle up towards the mountain range. "This is the pass our men go through to the foothills surrounding the Americans. It's impossible to see from the air. Our men, along with many," he smiled a crooked grin showing straight white teeth, "native volunteers, cut a path that passes through the mountain range. It is not ready for heavy vehicles but will be soon. Once in place, we will no longer need to haul our guns through the jungle." He indicated the denseness surrounding them. "Just as you've stated in your plan, the foothills around Empress Bay are perfect staging zones for artillery. We can hit all three of their airfields."

General Hyakutake nodded, "Yes, It will allow our forces to mass and push them back into the sea." The old general didn't smile. He'd been in almost constant combat for a decade and knew the vagaries of war. He'd seen too many officers exaggerate their successes. It was the reason he'd insisted on coming to see the roads for himself. "I want to see this road through the pass, Captain."

Captain Shigeo bowed slightly, "Yes, sir. We have motorcycles with side cars. We can travel most of the way through, but there are some tight sections. As we speak, work parties are widening the road. You'll see them as we pass."

True to his word, when they'd gotten halfway through the mountain pass they came across a large group of men, women and children hacking and pounding the jungle back by hand. Their black bodies glistened with sweat as they swung hatchets and machetes. General Hyakutake stood in his sidecar and held up his hand. The small motorcade stopped, their engines ticking at idle. He got out of the car and stood watching the work. Captain Shigeo hustled up beside him. General Hyakutake said, "The natives use weapons. Has there been any trouble?"

Captain Shigeo nodded and called to a lieutenant who was overseeing a group of heavily armed soldiers. The Lieutenant ran up and went into an impossibly stiff salute. General Hyakutake returned the salute. Captain Shigeo said, "General, this is Lieutenant Hiromi. Tell the general how you deal with security issues."

Lieutenant Hiromi bowed and pointed to a machine gun crew aiming their gun at penned natives. They were mostly young children, too young to work. Some held the bamboo bars and watched their families toil. "We have armed guards on constant watch, but if someone tries to escape or attacks, my men have orders to kill the children."

General Hyakutake nodded. "Have you had trouble?"

The young Lieutenant nodded eagerly. "Yes, sir. The workers tried to overpower us a few weeks ago. My soldiers did their duty and gunned the children then we killed the attackers while the others watched. They did not die slow. There hasn't been any trouble since."

General Hyakutake nodded and said, "Keep up the good work, Lieutenant." The man beamed, saluted and went back to watching the natives hacking at the jungle.

Satisfied, General Hyakutake ordered the motorcade back the way they'd come. Before motoring away he said to Captain Shigeo, "We will attack the Americans in a few months. This road is vital to our plans. Can you keep it hidden from the Americans?"

Captain Shigeo braced and with the confidence born of a man who'd never known defeat said, "Absolutely, sir."

1

On February 9th, 1943, hostilities ceased on Guadalcanal. American blood from every branch of the military had been shed to secure its beaches. The men of the 164th Infantry Regiment had fought a bloody battle lasting from October 1942 through to the day the Japanese forces were defeated. They won the battle, but the war was just beginning.

The men of the 1st Marine Division went back to the states, but the grunts of the Americal Division were sent to the Fiji Islands to defend against Japanese aggression and to rest, recuperate and train.

The second platoon of Able Company had just finished a grueling ten-mile hike with full gear. The humid heat of the island drained their energy, pulling their bodily fluids from every pore like a carnivorous sponge. The men had been on the lush island for the past eight months.

Sergeant Carver made sure all the soldiers drank their canteens and refilled and drank again before he let them sit. They sprawled, turning their loose rank into an unorganized mass of sweating soldiers. Sergeant Carver kneeled.

Corporal O'Connor shucked his heavy pack, wiped his brow and spit. He wiped his mouth and looked sideways at Sergeant Carver. "Hell of a way to celebrate our anniversary."

Sergeant Carver spit out the weed he was chewing. "Anniversary of what?"

"It's October 13th. One year ago today we landed on the canal."

Carver looked at the men surrounding him. There was only a handful from the original Guadalcanal force. Many had died, but most had been rotated home with debilitating wounds. He pulled a cigar from his pack. It was short and coming apart, but he pushed it into his mouth and shuffled it to the corner. "Seems like a lifetime ago."

Corporal O'Connor nodded, thinking the same thing. "We were green as grass back then."

Carver thought back to the men he'd served with, the soldiers who'd died. The image of Private Dunphy skewered on the end of a Japanese bayonet always popped into his head. *Will the memory ever fade?* It still woke him from a dead sleep at least three times a week. The face would change, but it always ended with Dunphy's vacant death stare.

The men lay around like vagabonds, but Sergeant Carver was proud of them. They'd been training almost constantly since arriving in late March. As replacements came in and filled the ranks, the old hands at first tolerated, then actively helped them assimilate into the unit. The constant training had pulled the men together. They'd gripe and complain, but the work became an enemy they could all hate together. The men were in the best shape of their lives and ready for action. Even the old hands, like Corporal O'Connor, who'd seen enough combat for six lifetimes was antsy to get back in the war.

Sergeant Carver stood and put his fists on his hips. He pulled his helmet low and moved his wet cigar to the other side of his mouth. O'Connor stood beside him; his red hair was black with sweat, his cheeks rosy red. He still looked like a kid until you looked at his eyes; they belonged to a man three times his age.

O'Connor asked, "You know where they're sending us next?"

"What makes you think they're sending us somewhere? You ain't comfortable on this island paradise?"

He shook his head and shuffled his feet, "We've been training like madmen. Don't think they're getting us ready for a parade."

Sergeant Carver said, "Thought they'd send us to the New Georgia Campaign, but that hell hole's all but finished. I overheard the brass going over a map of New Guinea. The Japs have a stronghold on the northern tip. Place called Rabaul; be a tough nut to crack by the sounds of it."

Corporal O'Connor nodded and reached for his pack. "That sounds about right. Get us toughened up for a tough fight." He put his back-pack on and adjusted the straps. The men noticed and started rising from their prone positions. O'Connor was proud to see none of their rifles in the dirt. The GIs were filthy, but their weapons were clean. "The men are ready, Sarge. Ready for anything."

DECEMBER 25TH, 1943 0100 HOURS

~

Sergeant Carver gripped the side of the troop ship as it swayed on the gentle sea. He felt in his pocket for a cigar but came up empty. He cussed, remembering he'd chewed his last one the night before. *How am I supposed to go into combat without a cigar?* He'd taken a liking to a particular kind of stogie the Fijian Islanders rolled. He used to smoke cigarettes but gave them up for the better tasting and longer lasting cigars.

He thought of the village elder he'd bartered with for the cigar. The old man had more wrinkles than any man he'd ever met. His nose was flat and wide taking up most of his face. He couldn't remember his name, something unpronounceable to his mid-western mind. He'd offered the old man the last Japanese flag he had from Guadalcanal, a hard earned souvenir, but the man shook his head and handed him a box of the cigars and shooed him away with a toothless smile. *His way of thanking us, I guess.*

The night was warm, not sweltering like the days. Sweat still beaded on his skin, but it didn't run off in rivulets like during the day.

A sentry walked by with his M1 rifle slung over his shoulder. His steps were slow and deliberate. Carver eyed him as he got closer trying to figure out if he knew him. He decided he didn't and spat into the black sea.

He looked to the beach a mile off the bow. It was mostly dark, but he thought he could see a dim light past the beach in the palms. He squinted, *great way to get strafed*. The thought took his gaze to the sky. It was moonless, and the stars were brilliant. He wondered what would happen if a Japanese Zero appeared. He instinctively felt for the stock of his Thompson sub-machine gun.

He heard steps coming behind him. He turned and saw his commanding officer, Lieutenant Jeffery Swan approaching. He pushed off the gunwale and came to attention, snapping off a salute. Lieutenant Swan returned the salute. It was quick and half-assed like he was embarrassed to be in charge. Carver frowned remembering the Lieutenant was just a kid straight out of his second year of college. Having Sergeant Carver salute him was like having his father salute him. "How are things, sir?" Lieutenant Swan reached for the gunwales, tripped and would have fallen at Carver's feet if he hadn't caught him. "Whoa, you okay, sir?" Even in the darkness, Sergeant Carver could see the man's face was a crimson red.

He shook off Carver's hand and looked for the culprit that tripped him. "Fine, fine. Tripped a little." He leaned over the rail looking down at the black water. Carver tensed, ready to save him if he started to fall overboard. "Sure is dark out here." Carver relaxed as Swan stood upright. He nodded. "How are the men?"

"They're fine, sir. Ready to get off this rust bucket."

Lieutenant Swan laughed too hard. "Yes, it is rusty, a rust bucket as you say." Silence followed. Swan started to speak but stopped himself.

"Something on your mind, Lieutenant?"

Swan started picking his fingernails. The clicking sound grated on Carver, but he didn't speak, waiting for Swan to get whatever was bothering him out. Swan finally spoke. "These past months have been tough. I'm proud of the men. All of them."

Carver nodded, and when there was no more said, "Yessir, they gutted it out." He spit over the side.

Lieutenant Swan tried to mimic it, but his spit barely cleared his chin and splatted on the deck between them. He brought his sleeved arm across his mouth. *Christ, this kid is an infant.*

The Lieutenant finally got around to what he wanted to say. "You've been in combat. You and a bunch of the other men." Carver looked out over the sea, *here it comes.*

There was a long pause, and Carver was about to fill the gap telling him, 'he'll be okay if he remembers his training, it's okay to be scared as long as you do your job…' the standard response he'd given countless times to green, scared soldiers. But instead, Lieutenant Swan said, "What do you do if you have to take a shit?" he looked at the stunned Sergeant. "I mean I've got an irritable bowel, sometimes I just have to go, and there's nothing I can do to stop it. What if I'm leading an attack? Or giving an after action report in front of the brass?" he continued to pick his fingernails. He tore off a long thin piece causing his finger to bleed.

Sergeant Carver stared at his officer, a smile creeping across his face. Finally, he gave a hearty laugh and slapped Lieutenant Swan on the back. Between laughing and breathing, he said, "Well, shit Lieutenant, if that's the least of your worries you'll do fine out there." He shook his head letting the laughter roll over him. He couldn't remember the last time he'd laughed. It felt good, the worry seemed to roll off his shoulders.

The Lieutenant smiled but didn't laugh. Carver got control of himself. "If you gotta shit, then shit. I'm sure the brass'll understand." He broke out laughing again picturing the skinny lieutenant squatting in front of the brass. He couldn't contain himself. The image sent him into a fit.

Lieutenant Swan moved to leave, but Carver wiped his eyes and put his hand on his shoulder. He got control. He turned serious. "Look, I'll cover for you whenever I can, okay? I'm sure the brass would rather you didn't shit your pants in front of them and if you're leading an attack? Well, you won't be the only one. Hell, you'll probably get dysentery anyway. Probably cure your irritable bowel."

Lieutenant Swan smiled and nodded. "Thanks, Sarge." He turned to leave then spun back around, "Oh, one more thing." Carver lifted his eyebrow wondering what it would be this time. Lieutenant Swan looked at the luminous dials on his watch. “Merry Christmas.”

2

Before the sun rose, the men of the 164th Infantry Regiment were on the landing craft shuttling to the beach of another Japanese-held island. The similarity to their landing on Guadalcanal over a year before was hard to ignore. Like Guadalcanal, they were landing after the Marine's had already established a beachhead the month before, and like Guadalcanal, they were landing unopposed.

The Marine's Third Division had landed on November 1st and lost nearly 100 men before finally securing a beachhead and clearing Empress Augusta Bay of Japanese soldiers. They immediately pushed out into the jungle to secure a wider defensive zone. The going was tough; there was swamp just beyond the beach that bogged them down. Unlike Guadalcanal, the U.S. Navy was up to the task of defending the beachhead from marauding Japanese warships.

The allied generals wanted Bougainville in order to build airstrips that were close enough to bomb the heavily defended city of Rabaul. It was the last Japanese stronghold in the Solomon Islands.

The Japanese tried to dislodge the Marines with multiple counterattacks staged from landing craft on beaches north of the beachhead. The Marines repelled them each time, but casualties mounted.

When the airfield at Torokina Point was complete, the Marines considered the job done. They would be pulled off the island to be replaced by the well-rested Americal Division.

Sergeant Carver and his men didn't know the bigger strategy; they only knew they were going into combat on Christmas morning. The gentle bay waves slapped against the landing craft as they sped toward the beach's white sand. Sergeant Carver looked over his men in the dim light. They hunched under their steel pots, rifles pointing to the sky, prophylactics covering the barrels to protect from sea water. Most of the second platoon were replacements but there were still a few old hands. Of course, Corporal O'Connor, the crazy woodsman from Oregon was there, staring at the back of the man in front of him.

To his left was Private First Class Blake. He'd joined them in January and seen a lot of combat on the canal. He was reliable and had become one of the best BAR men in the company. He could accurately shoot the big gun from his hip. He'd seen him hit enemy troops while running too, an unheard of feat with the unwieldy weapon.

A few rows up, he recognized the sloped shoulders of Private Willy. He was the greasiest kid he'd ever met. His complexion was mostly black-heads. Whenever he smiled, which was damned rare, his face would erupt with mini-volcanoes of puss. He'd seen him scrub himself until his skin was raw and still he'd come out with a greasy sheen. But what he lacked in hygiene he made up for in fighting intensity. The kid seemed to slip into another zone when the bullets started flying. He seemed to be charmed. Multiple times, Carver had seen him bolt from a foxhole and charge headlong into a Jap attack, or into the withering fire of a Nambu machine gun, but he never got a scratch. He hoped his luck would last, but he wasn't holding his breath.

He found the other veteran, Sergeant Milo grinning at him from the second row. Carver spat and scowled until the man turned away. He was a quiet, competent son-of-a-bitch that could wield his Thompson submachine gun almost as well as he could. He liked Milo, but found his chumminess with the enlisted men annoying and dangerous. He was a good man under pressure, and he was glad to have him in his platoon, leading first and second squad.

He looked to his right and gave Lieutenant Swan a once over. He was a new addition, joining Able Company after Guadalcanal. From what he'd seen during the endless training on Fiji, he made mostly good decisions. He could read a map, but he was unsure of himself, often giving orders that sounded more like questions. He needed to toughen up if he hoped to survive in the jungles of the northern Solomon Islands. Carver wondered if the kid had to take a shit.

The driver of the LCVP leaned down and tapped Lieutenant Swan's shoulder. He jumped and stifled a yell. He turned to the helmeted Navy man, "Land in five minutes, sir."

Swan nodded and looked to Sergeant Carver. "Tell the men?"

Carver shook his head and bellowed above the engine noise. "Five minutes! Check weapons and gear. There's not supposed to be any opposition, but I want to see an organized landing. Let's show these dandy boy Marines how to hit a beach." The men grinned and looked over their weapons. Sergeant Carver always had a way of cutting through tension.

The LCVP lurched, and the front gate smashed onto the beach. It was just getting light. The men ran as one onto the beach, went halfway up, spread out and crouched with their M1s ready. Captain Tom Flannigan walked off the LCVP beside Carver's and sauntered to the crouched men. He put his hands on his hips, his right hand near the handle of his service issued .45 caliber. He tilted his helmet back and looked behind at the approaching Lieutenant Swan and Sergeant Carver.

He turned his broad shoulders square to the men who snapped to attention. Lieutenant Swan saluted, Sergeant Carver hesitated not wanting to draw attention from unwanted snipers, a lesson he'd learned on the canal. He snapped off a salute, pulling it down as soon as Captain Flannigan returned it. Carver took a half step back trying to take himself out of the line of fire, but Flannigan didn't notice. He only had eyes for the diminutive Lieutenant. He looked him up and down then leaned in. "These your men, son?"

Lieutenant Swan looked at the men as if he'd never seen them. "Uh, yessir. My men, sir."

"Well, they look like shit. That the way you assault a beach? Good thing the Marines have already cleared the way or you'd be chowder, cut to ribbons like confetti."

Sergeant Carver gritted his teeth. His men looked sharp; Captain Flannigan never had anything good to say about anyone except his 4th platoon. Carver didn't know how Flannigan got mixed up with his men, but the sooner he could get him shuffled back to command the better. Sergeant Carver thought Lieutenant Swan was going to cry.

"I, I'm sorry, sir. No excuse, no excuse," he stuttered.

"You're damned right there's no excuse. How are these men going to fight the Japanese? How are they going to keep our proud tradition from becoming a laughing stock of the whole damned division?"

Sergeant Carver saw Corporal O'Connor start to move from his position on the flank. He thought he better intervene before his Corporal got his stripe pulled. Carver snapped to attention. "My fault, sir. I'll drill them harder. We'll whip 'em into shape, I've been too easy on 'em, sir."

Captain Flannigan spun to the Sergeant looming behind him. Lieutenant Swan looked at Carver like he was a lifeboat to a drowning man. He was grateful, but he felt heat pulse up his neck with rising anger at the captain. "See that you do, Sergeant." Lieutenant Swan tried to look into Carver's eyes, but he looked at his own feet instead.

Carver glanced at O'Connor who was still getting to his feet. He gave him a quick head shake. "All right you men, on your feet and double time it up to the edge of the beach." The men sprang up and ran to the thick jungle and crouched.

Their weapons were leveled at the jungle. They were all breathing hard, but being this close to the jungle gave them pause. It wasn't Fiji; this was an enemy jungle full of hidden death. O'Connor nodded. "This is the real deal, men. Stay sharp, and don't listen to that asshole, Captain Flannigan. We look good."

~

THE REST OF CHRISTMAS DAY, 1943 was spent moving the division's gear from the ships to the beach. The Third Marines were starting to move their gear to the beach as well in preparation for their departure on the same ships the Americal Division arrived on. A smooth transition of forces was the goal.

Captain Flannigan and Lieutenant Swan went to a briefing by the departing Marine General, Turnage. They entered the open air tent swatting at flies and mosquitos that seemed to feast on the fresh meat. Lieutenant Swan slapped at the bugs in a hopeless attempt to remain unbit, but his skin already looked like a moonscape.

The Marines clustered in front of their General. The flies and mosquitos seemed to leave them alone. Lieutenant Swan hoped he'd eventually adjust, or would be able to ignore the constant buzzing and biting, but he doubted it.

He found himself a folding chair and sat down as General Hal Turnage entered. He was a handsome man with perfectly combed hair and piercing blue eyes. Despite the heat and dirt of Bougainville, he looked freshly showered and shaved. The men braced at attention, Lt. Swan knocked the folding chair over making a racket that earned him a glare from the Marine General.

"At ease, men." He stood behind a makeshift podium, gripping the sides with tree trunk hands. An aide stepped behind him and placed a map of the island. General Turnage extended a pointer and smacked the area of Empress Augusta Bay. "As you know, we are here. The Third Marines along with the 37th Infantry Division landed here on November 1st to light resistance. Our objective was to push inland a few miles, set up a secure beachhead and build an airstrip here." He smacked the map again indicating the finger of land poking into the sea. "Torokina Airfield. In early December with almost constant Japanese harassment, we succeeded. The airstrip went operational earlier this month and is currently used by both Navy and Marine squadrons." He paused to look the men over. "They've successfully used Torokina to hit deeper than they've ever been able to before. The Nips have brought artillery pieces to the surrounding hills and have struck the airfield a number of times.

"My Marines have been able to hunt down and kill most of these guns but make no mistake; this jungle is thicker than anything you've seen on the canal or that tropical paradise you grew so attached to, Fiji."

The Marines in front looked back and sneered. General Turnage continued. "We've pushed into the hills to deny the Japs the high ground. This hill here," he smacked the map again, "is Hill 700. It's dotted with bunkers occupied by the 37th Infantry. It's the key to this whole operation. If the Japs own it, they can rain artillery fire on any part of the beachhead including Torokina. The smaller hills to the south are also key and defended, but we expect the Japs to make a push for Hill 700." He paced away from the podium and clasped his hands behind his back.

The pointer extended above his head like an antenna. "The nips we're facing are the 17th Army led by General Hyakutake. The same General that lost on Guadalcanal. So far, his forces have been smart and tough. They use the thick jungle to their advantage and can bring artillery pieces to bear despite it. There are no roads, only footpaths, so they're hauling these pieces by hand." He looked at the attentive faces, "These are tough hombres with an ax to grind. The main force we're fighting is the 6th Division. These sons-of-bitches have been fighting since the '30s. They're brutal and professional soldiers. They're the same troops that fought in Nanking, China." He stopped pacing and stared hard at the fidgeting army officers. "Don't underestimate these soldiers. They'll make you pay if you do."

He returned to the podium and let out a sigh. "My Marines are needed elsewhere, so it's up to you men to continue what we started. You'll occupy our outposts and headquarters tomorrow. I'll expect a smooth transition.

"Reconnaissance patrols haven't picked up any unusual activity, so we're not expecting an imminent attack. You can be sure they're watching us, but I don't think they have a sizable force in the area to take advantage of our transition.

"Some of my men will hang back with you for a day or two until you get the lay of the land. They'll show you defenses, trails, problem areas, that sort of thing. Listen to them; it's information that's come at a price, believe me."

3

Corporal O'Connor didn't sleep well his first night on Bougainville. The incessant buzzing and biting of millions of insects wouldn't allow it, so he got up from his cot and with bleary eyes went out to take a leak. He wore his skivvies; his rifle slung over his shoulder. The night was black. He squinted into the jungle as his stream made a puddle in the dirt. *There could be a Jap right in front of me, and I'd never know it.* The thought made him cut his stream short and unsling his rifle. He held it at the ready and tried to pierce the night. All his senses were firing, but the only sound was the buzz of insect life.

There was a sudden brightening of the sky, he crouched waiting for the boom of artillery, but it never came. The brightness flared then dimmed. He wondered if he was seeing Mount Bagana acting up. The massive volcano was always spewing white smoke and could be seen from every corner of the island. O'Connor watched the light disappear. He shrugged, *if that thing blows it's top everyone on this island will cook.*

He went back to the tent he shared with the other six men and sat on the edge of his cot. It creaked like an old rocking chair. The deep breathing of sleeping men surrounded him. He envied them. He was desperate for sleep, but knew he wasn't going to get any tonight. A voice cut through the darkness in a whisper. "You can't sleep either." It was a statement more than a question.

O'Connor laid on the cot pulling the thin sheet over his body as an ineffective barrier to the biting insects. His cot protested in loud squeaks. "That you Blake?" A grunt from PFC Blake. "Nah, can't sleep. You seen that volcano? Looks about ready to blow."

"Yeah, that would shorten this little operation. We could make a break for the ships, but the Japs wouldn't be able to escape." He sat up on his cot. "That's not a bad idea, wonder if our bombers could drop a stick of bombs through the top and cause it to blow?"

O'Connor smiled picturing the scene. "That'd be a neat trick alright, but I don't think it works like that."

Blake said, "Oh really, you a professor of volcanic activity or something? I think it'd work. I read about it somewhere. It's worked before."

"Really? Where?" O'Connor was suddenly interested; he didn't think Private First Class Blake could read well and doubted he'd be reading about volcanos if he could.

Blake continued, "I saw it in a comic book my little brother had I think."

O'Connor sat up and laughed, "A fucking comic book? Does that mean you think there's a Superman living somewhere in the States?" he didn't wait for a reply. "You know that's all made up, right?"

Blake said, "Fuck you, Corporal."

From across the tent a gruff sleepy voice, "would you two shut the fuck up?"

Blake said, "Sorry Sarge." Sergeant Carver grunted, and his breathing returned to deep sleep.

O'Connor slapped at a large insect that smacked into the side of his face, closed his eyes and tried to sleep.

IT WAS STILL DARK when Sergeant Carver's internal alarm clock went off, and he swung his legs from under the dirty sheet and sat on the side of his cot. He rubbed his stubbled chin. *Gotta shave this morning.* It would be a busy day moving the men and material to the Marine's positions. He doubted he'd get another chance over the next few days.

He pulled on his pants, shirt and laced his boots. He'd gotten new boots right before shipping out from Fiji. They still looked new, but the mud and grime of the Bougainville jungle would take care of that soon enough.

He stood and stretched. He felt good. He'd slept better than he normally did on a hostile beach. He could feel his muscles relaxing. He'd packed on all the weight he'd lost fighting on Guadalcanal. He'd lost 20 pounds during that campaign. He wondered what he'd look like after being on this shit-hole for a couple of weeks. He slapped at a fat mosquito, and a smudge of his blood stained his arm. *Damned bugs will drain a couple pounds of blood before the end of the day.*

He'd been in the tropics for two years now, first on New Caledonia, then Guadalcanal, then Fiji and now Bougainville, but he'd never seen the insects as thick as they were here and they hadn't even ventured into the jungle yet.

Most of his veterans had been afflicted with some kind of ailment from the terrible conditions on the Canal. Many had cases of malaria, dysentery and various forms of foot rot. Many had combinations of all those and some were incapacitated and had to be evacuated. He wondered how many men he'd lose to insects and jungle during this campaign.

A CHOW HALL was set up to accommodate the extra men in the headquarters area. There was a group of Marines standing in line when Sergeant Carver and members of Able Company arrived. The Marines gave them scathing looks and the soldiers returned them.

The Marines looked bedraggled and skinny, much the same way they'd looked after fighting on the canal. The veteran soldiers could tell the Marines standing in front of them had been in combat. The way they carried themselves, the way they looked at green soldiers was a sure giveaway, but the green soldiers only saw men who looked like shit.

Sergeant Carver saw one of his bigger soldiers lean down and whisper something to the man behind him. They snickered, obviously talking about the Marines. His men were tough, even the ones that hadn't faced a Japanese soldier yet. They'd been training nonstop for months, their bodies highly tuned killing machines, but Carver was sure the Marine vets would make short work of them if they brawled. The vets wouldn't hold back. As he knew all too well, the only way to stay alive in combat is to show no mercy; to come at the enemy relentlessly until either they're dead or you're dead.

The Marine in front of the soldier turned around and looked up at the man sneering down at him. He looked him up and down then nudged his buddy and said, "Looks like this one stayed on his momma's tit too long don't it, Lee?"

The other Marine, who looked to weigh all of one hundred pounds soaking wet, laughed, "Didn't know they stacked shit that high."

Sergeant Carver stepped forward as his soldier, Private Bennett, was about to lunge. Carver stepped in front, and even though he was six inches shorter, his presence was giant. He thrust his thick finger into Bennett's face. "Stop right there soldier. Don't do something you may not live to regret."

Private Bennett scrunched his head in confusion. He pointed at the smiling Marines. "They're jar-heads, Sarge, talking shit about my momma. No one gets away with that."

Sergeant Carver's finger stayed in Bennett's face, which turned from confused to angry as he saw the Marines snickering. Sergeant Carver raised his voice so all the men could hear. "There will be no fighting. Any man caught fighting will have to face me, and God help you." The mess hall went silent. Every man in the unit knew of Carver's fighting prowess. He'd received the Silver Star for gallantry on the battlefield on Guadalcanal. He was one of two men that survived a twelve man patrol and by sheer force of will completed an impossible mission. Even the Marines knew who he was. He wasn't a man to be trifled with and every man knew he'd follow through on his promise.

Private Bennett, the big farm boy from North Dakota, looked crestfallen. He wanted to beat the puny Marines into the ground. He couldn't understand why his hero sergeant wasn't letting him. From what he heard Sergeant Carver wasn't a big fan of the Marines. One of their pilots had killed some of his men on that patrol.

The Marines turned back around and slapped one another on the back. Sergeant Carver pushed Private Bennett to the back of the line like the big oaf was in middle school.

Carver joined him at a long table full of Able Company soldiers. Sergeant Milo was beside him. He looked pissed as he shoveled food into his mouth. Between bites, he leaned close to Carver and said, "Why didn't you let Bennett get his ass whooped? A little brawl might be just what the men need to shake off some steam."

Bennett dropped his spoon splattering the brown gravy like substance onto his shirt. Sergeant Milo looked at him and squinted, "Those are combat vets, they'd have killed you if the rest of us weren't here." Bennett shook his head not believing any ten Marines, veterans or not could take him.

Sergeant Carver looked hard at Sergeant Milo. "Those men beat back a Jap assault just a few days ago. They were on Hill 260, where we're headed. They were attacked by a large force. I heard over 1000 men to their 200, and they kicked their asses." He looked up and down the long table at his rapt audience. "If they hadn't held, our reception wouldn't have been near as friendly. We'd most likely be fighting the little yellow bastards as we speak. We owe them gratitude and respect, not some small town bullshit." He stared at Private Bennett who lowered his head and pushed his food around his plate.

4

By midday, the men of the fighting elements of the Americal Division were formed up and ready to take over the Marine positions. The narrow strip of beach they stood on was inadequate for their numbers. Carver squinted into the perfectly blue sky searching for the tell-tale engine noise of an approaching Japanese Zero. *If they catch us on the beach, it'll be a massacre.*

He knew the Japanese Air units had been thinned out over the past months, but they were still a threat. He would've felt better if there was some air cover. He wiped his brow then heard the deep rumble of an engine. He scanned the sky, but the noise was coming from behind him, from the sea. He turned to watch a pair of speeding PT boats weaving in and out of the transport ships they'd abandoned the day before. Nearly the entire Third Marine Division was on those ships now, heading off to another piece of shit island, no doubt.

The PT boats were small in comparison, but they looked deadly with their black torpedo tubes and front and back mounted machine guns. The throaty engines propelled them along at a moderate clip amongst the larger ships, but once they were clear the engines opened up, and they surged to their top speed.

Sergeant Carver whistled his admiration. Corporal O'Connor was beside him nodding. Carver said, "If I ever had to be a squid, I'd want to be on one of those sexy things."

O'Connor added, "They're fast and quick striking, but heaven help you if one of them Jap destroyers gets you in her sights." He watched Sergeant Carver staring as they went around the Torokina Airfield and out of sight. O'Connor thought he looked like a kid staring into the front window of a toy store. "Too bad were heading inland, there's a whole fleet of 'em sitting on Puruata Island." He pointed at the small island off the coast a quarter mile. "They're on the other side in a little bay. If we had more time, we could've borrowed one."

Sergeant Carver shook his head and came back from his daydream of captaining a PT boat. "Shaddup, Corporal." O'Connor smiled and gave him a mock salute.

There was a shout from the front of the column. Sergeant Carver heard Lieutenant Swan order them forward. Carver boomed, "all right, let's get a move on. Single file, keep it tight, don't want anyone getting lost."

Soon they were entering the jungle along a track they called a road. It was hardly wide enough for a side by side column, let alone a truck. The men had their rifles slung. A squad of Marines dressed in mottled camouflage led the way. Their rifles were at the ready, but they were relaxed. Carver decided the recent battle had chased off any enemy soldiers. He gritted his teeth, *don't assume anything with these bastards.* He unslung his Thompson and checked his magazine was firmly locked in place.

They'd only walked a hundred yards when the road turned muddy. The smell of decay stung his nose and forced him to breathe with an open mouth. So many feet pounding the already sloppy road made it worse, and by the time his platoon got through, they were muddy up to their knees. *So much for new boots.* Each step made a sucking sound as the mud clung to them like grasping hands from the grave.

The trail started sloping upwards, and the mud turned to hard pack dirt. The jungle was oppressive and looked impenetrable to either side. Carver didn't think any jungle could be as thick as Guadalcanal, but this place made it look like a parking lot.

An hour passed before they halted and were told to break into individual platoons. Lieutenant Swan called up Sgt. Carver and Milo. In his squeaky voice, he said, "This is Corporal Phinney," he gestured at a dirty marine holding an M1. "He's going to guide us to the bunkers we'll occupy on the top of Hill 260." Sergeant Carver gave his Lieutenant a once over; the kid looked like he was sweating buckets. His greasy face was glistening like a glazed donut.

Corporal Phinney waved them off the main path, onto a smaller one leading south. "It's not far, but be ready there's sometimes Jap snipers that creep around in here." He pointed to the tree tops. "Sneaky bastards like to sit in the trees, keep your eye's peeled."

Without being told, the platoon unslung their M1s and held them at the ready giving nervous glances to the trees. Carver waved them forward, shuffling Lieutenant Swan to the middle of the column. Carver raised an eyebrow, and Swan gave him an awkward grin and shrug. "So far so good." Carver wondered if he was carrying extra toilet paper. Dysentery or the shitty K-rations would probably take care of the wiping issue.

The Marine Corporal moved well along the path. The jungle was still thick, but the path widened slightly allowing the men to spread out.

They'd been walking for ten minutes when the unmistakable signs of battle emerged. The jungle thinned, not from anything natural but countless artillery tree bursts. The blazing sun streamed through the thinned jungle canopy. If it weren't for the smell of rotting flesh, it would have been a beautiful scene.

Corporal Phinney held up a fist and went to his knee. Sergeant Carver slunk forward. Phinney pointed to the base of a hill thirty yards ahead. "That's the bottom of Hill 260. Japs tried to flank us and come up this side, but our boys got wind of it and called in an artillery strike. Even with the thick canopy, it laid waste to the fuckers."

Carver nodded as his eyes started seeing Japanese corpses. Their tan and greenish uniforms blended in well, but once he saw one, he started picking out more until he realized it was a slaughterhouse. He guessed there were forty or fifty dead Japanese soldiers rotting in the sun. "Why haven't these bodies been buried?" he asked as he pulled his t-shirt over his nose.

The Corporal smiled, "We killed 'em, you boys get to bury 'em."

Carver and the men surrounding him scowled, but kept their mouths shut. Lieutenant Swan came up beside them and crouched. He scanned the carnage, realized what he was seeing and smelling and before he could get a word out, threw up his breakfast. More soldiers joined him as the smell and sights assaulted their senses. Corporal Phinney grinned, delighting in the officer's discomfort. "Careful as we walk through, sometimes they like to play possum until they have a chance to pop up from the dead and kill you."

Sergeant Carver put his hand on Swan's shoulder and said, "I'll pass it along. Better get back to the middle, sir." Swan wiped his mouth and nodded. His skin was the color of the maggots crawling amongst the bodies.

They walked through the killing field. Most were torn apart. There were body parts littering the ground like confetti after a parade. Walking without stepping on pieces was difficult. Carver could hear more men adding their vomit to the lieutenant's.

Once they were through the killing zone, they climbed the hill. It was only 260 feet, but the heat and the smell of rot made it seem higher. As they neared the crest, the smell of cordite and charred wood mixed with the smell of decomposition. The hill looked empty but upon closer inspection, they could see the tops of Marine's heads here and there dotting the area.

As they approached one such hole, a jubilant Marine Captain sprang up and rushed to them. Carver and the men around him sprang to attention but knew better than to salute in a hostile area. The Captain extended his hand to the white faced Lieutenant Swan, who took the proffered hand. His grip was rough and strong. "Am I ever glad to see you dogfaces."

The Marine corporal introduced him, "This is Captain Hanson. Captain, this is…" he gestured to Swan.

Lieutenant Swan stared into the Captain's face, the silence getting uncomfortable. Carver jumped in. "Lieutenant Swan and I'm Sergeant Carver; this is Sergeant Milo and Corporal O'Connor." He saw the Captain giving Lieutenant Swan the once over. "Lieutenant Swan's not used to dead bodies. The Japs at the bottom of the hill shook him a little. He'll be fine after some water, sir."

Captain Hanson smiled, "Don't worry about them, Lieutenant. Those are the good kind of Nips...dead. You gotta worry about the other kind." Lieutenant Swan nodded. "Don't worry; you get used to the smell." Lieutenant Swan looked around at the moonscape of his new home and thought, *God, I hope not.*

CAPTAIN HANSON WANTED to get off Hill 260 as quickly as he could, and it was evident by the way he showed Lieutenant Swan, and his sergeant's the stronghold. The once lush hill had been bombed incessantly for the past weeks. The top of the hill by the Japanese and the rest by the Marines and Naval units. There were large craters down the hill which had to have come from the big 152mm naval guns. Closer to the top, the craters were smaller, mostly from mortars with a few bigger ones from some of the artillery the Imperial Japanese Army was able to get into range.

Lieutenant Swan noticed the difference and asked, "Are there roads into this area?" Captain Hanson shook his head, no. "How are the Japs able to get their artillery pieces close enough? Are they cutting their way through the jungle?"

Captain Hanson stopped and pointed to a ridge to the north; it was denuded much like the top of the hill they stood on. "That's Hill 700. The Army 37th has been holding off Jap attacks, but the Japs owned it for awhile. They had all sorts of artillery up there. Not just small mortars but big guns. They even managed to get an anti-aircraft gun up there, used it to knock the shit out of a couple of our tanks. Cut through them like butter."

He shook his head and placed his hands on his hips. "They're resourceful make no mistake, and they'll keep going until they're dead." He looked Lt. Swan in the eye. "There's no roads, only dirt tracks through the thickest jungle I've ever seen. I don't know how they get those guns an inch let alone miles upon miles." He frowned and looked at the distant hill. "They're like little fucking ants. Thousands of 'em. You kill one there's ten more right behind. It's unnatural."

They continued touring the hill. They had an escort of five other Marines, Corporal Phinney included. They kept a sharp eye on the areas that still had trees.

The hill's defenses were a series of bunkers laid out on the top of the ridge supporting other bunkers further down the hill. They were hastily built fortifications started by the Marines, added to by the Japanese, then finished by the Marines. Each attack had left the bunkers scarred and some destroyed, but with the help of the Navy Seabees, they were able to rebuild and reinforce them with sandbags and downed trees.

They'd held up well to the most recent attack, although the Japanese had managed to get close enough to one to lob in a satchel charge. The explosion completely destroyed it and the men inside. There was nothing left of the six Marines, not even their dogtags. Lieutenant Swan made replacing the bunker a priority once they got settled.

The tour took an hour. Captain Hanson was eager to get he and his men off the mountain. "I think I've covered all the defenses you've got. If you don't have any more questions, I'll hand over the radio codes and leave you with a few men to show you around the patrol area." Sergeant Carver noticed Corporal Phinney tense up and take a step back.

Lieutenant Swan rubbed his chin and looked at his boots, "Seems like we're exposed out here on this knob. We're what, 800 yards from the northern knob, separated by the saddle?"

Hanson nodded, "Yep, that's correct, but there's plenty of fire support from the main area."

Lieutenant Swan continued, "Those dead Japs at the bottom of the hill can attest to that, but it seems to me they were able to cut you off from the main line. Correct?"

Captain Hanson nodded. "This position's temporary, at least that's what we were told. By being here, we deny the Japs another hill to fire from. If the Japs come in force, you'll have to retreat or be cut off."

"You didn't retreat when they came." He grinned at the Captain.

"We were told to hold, so we held, but if they'd dug in on the saddle, we would've been in a world of hurt."

Swan nodded, not liking the position, but not wanting to show his fear to the Marine captain. "I guess that's all the questions I've got for you, sir."

Hanson looked around at the Marines guarding them. "I'll leave you these men here. They've been here since the start and know this area better than anyone. They'll show you around, but I want 'em back by dark tomorrow."

"Yessir. That should be no problem." Carver didn't think it was enough time but understood the Captain's desire to get his men to the transports in one piece.

Hanson nodded. "The rest of us will be leaving within the hour." Without waiting for a reply, he told the sulking Corporal Phinney to inform the men of their imminent departure. Phinney turned to give the news, mumbling under his breath.

TRUE TO HIS WORD, ten minutes later the only Marines still on the hill were the six guards. They slinked off together and found a hole to bitch and complain about their bad luck.

Lieutenant Swan, his two sergeants and a couple of Corporals were checking out the main command bunker. It was the largest and had the best view of the hill and the North Knob. It was a good vantage point and equidistant from the other bunkers.

Swan called them together and laid out a map of their surrounding area. It was an old German map from before the turn of the century, but it got most of the bigger features correct including their hill. Using a short pencil he pulled from behind his ear, he pointed. "We're here with bunkers here, here, here and here." He circled their locations. "Downslope bunkers are marked with the Xs." He drew circles dotting the hillside. "These are the foxholes the Marines were using, there are others, but these are the best. They're linked by this trench system."

He looked from man to man. Carver was impressed with the Lieutenant's grasp of his surroundings. "The mortar pit is here with another here." He drew slits near the bunker they sat in. "I want the 61mm mortar pit moved to here. They can cover further down the slope. I don't think we need to worry about our flanks, seems the naval guns and beach artillery are enough to stop any attacks." Everyone thought about the carnage they'd walked through. "I want two more mortar pits dug here and here. They'll be protected by the slight defilade, but won't lose any range." He paused, "The thirty caliber machine guns will obviously be best suited for the bunkers, but I want a few more placed here, here and here. That'll cover any withdrawals from the bunkers if anything goes wrong."

Sergeant Carver looked at the map trying to envision the defenses. He nodded, pleased with the changes. It would make the hill more defensible without too much extra work. *This rookie might just work out after all.*

Lieutenant Swan looked at Sergeant Milo. "Take six men to the base of the hill and bury those stinking bodies. Four working, two watching for Japs, got it?" Sergeant Milo nodded. He'd be sending Corporal Dunlop on that particular duty. "I don't like being out here on a limb like this. It's too easy to be cut off. I'll need to think about that and maybe..." Lieutenant Swan suddenly stood up, stiffened and put his pencil behind his ear. He turned for the back door, made from bamboo thatch and said, "that'll be all, men. Dismissed."

The others were surprised at the abrupt end to the briefing, everyone except Sergeant Carver. He yelled at the retreating officer, "Shitter's to the right, sir." He didn't get a reply.

5

The 164th Regiment's first night on Hill 260 was uneventful but terrifying. The new men weren't able to sleep, kept awake by the constant sounds of the jungle. Every shape looked like an enemy soldier, every sound impending death. The blackness surrounding them was complete. There was no moon and clouds skittered across the stars. Even without the thick jungle canopy above, it was dark as ink.

O'Connor was at the bottom of his hole sleeping soundly when Private Bennett, the big BAR man called out, "Who's there? I'll shoot, I swear I'll shoot."

O'Connor opened his eyes and saw the big man's silhouette against the dark sky. His huge head looked like something from outer space. He kicked the back of Bennett's calf. "Shut the fuck up, Bennett. I'm trying to sleep, goddammit."

The kick surprised Bennett, and he fired off a long stream of thirty caliber rounds into the night. O'Connor sprang up with his rifle ready and leveled it towards the jungle, but knew Bennett didn't have a target. He pulled the weapon away from Bennett's iron grip with a hard yank that pulled the skin from Bennett's trigger finger. He was breathing hard, reaching for his weapon. "Give it back; they're out there, they're everywhere."

Corporal O'Connor kept the weapon from him. "Shut the fuck up, Private, there's nothing out there but jungle. Knock it off!"

Private Bennett lunged again, but O'Connor dropped the BAR into the bottom of the hole and landed a hard right cross to Bennett's chin. The blow knocked him back. He hit the side of the hole, stumbled and fell to the bottom, cussing and holding his chin. Rage filled his eyes, and he tried to lunge at O'Connor's legs, but before he could, O'Connor kicked him in the chest and stepped on him, pinning him to the ground. "Pull yourself together Bennett, or I'll bury you out here."

Bennett struggled against O'Connor's foot but before he could break free Sergeant Carver slithered into the hole and stood beside Corporal O'Connor. He looked down at his BAR man. "What the hell's all the racket, Private?"

Bennett spluttered, "there's, there's a shitload..." he realized there was no return fire, no screaming Japanese soldiers on a banzai attack. "I, I thought I saw something, saw a Jap coming at me then O'Connor kicked me and..."

"Shoulda kicked you in the damned head. You woke up the entire Company with your chickenshit."

Private Bennett looked down and shook his head, "Sorry, Sarge. I fucked up."

Sergeant Carver slapped O'Connor on the shoulder. He removed his boot from Bennett's chest. Carver said, "The next time he does that you've got my permission to kill him."

Even in the darkness, Bennett could see the evil grin spreading across O'Connor's freckled face. He pulled out his K-bar knife. "Haven't had a chance to use this in awhile."

Carver nodded. "Now get some sleep, we're patrolling in the morning."

THE JUNGLE LIGHTENED with the morning in a slow, colorful dance. The dark jungle which had seemed so forbidding and close only an hour before was green and distant, almost welcoming. Beyond the barren shelled area it thickened and looked forbidding but the morning light even made that look inviting.

O'Connor kicked the sleeping giant beside him. Bennett had finally fallen asleep sometime in the early morning, and now he was snoring. O'Connor shook his head, *looks like a big fucking teddy bear.* He kicked him again, and the big man's eyes shot open, remembering where he was. "Japs?"

O'Connor shook his head and dropped a can of K-rations on his chest, "Nope, breakfast." O'Connor hopped out of the hole. "We muster at 0530, don't be late."

Private Bennett nodded and sat up to open his K-rat. "I won't be late." He looked up, "Wait. Late for what?" O'Connor kept walking, shaking his head, *guy's dumber'n a stump.*

All of second platoon was milling around the command bunker talking about what little sleep they'd gotten. When they found out who'd fired the rounds, they cussed and threw dirt clods at Private Bennett who took his lumps with a sheepish grin.

Lieutenant Swan came out of the bunker with Sergeant Carver and Sergeant Milo on either side of him. He didn't look like he'd gotten much sleep either. He tried to make his voice sound deep and authoritarian, but instead it came out high and squeaking. "Men we're patrolling today. The Marines will be leading squads around the perimeter. We don't expect any trouble, but you never know. Stay sharp and pay attention." The six Marines stood behind the platoon with their arms crossed. "Break up into squads. I want third and fourth squads out first. We'll swap the whole thing around midday when they return." He thought he should say more, maybe something to ease any nerves, but instead he put his arms behind his back and nodded, "Good luck, stay sharp."

SERGEANT MILO and Carver stood in front of their squads. The men had their weapons slung. Carver and Milo gripped they're Thompson's the stubby barrels pointing at the sky. The Marines sauntered over and stood in front.

Corporal Phinney went to Sergeant Carver. "I'll take you guys out along with Private Flynn," he indicated a tall skinny Marine with one of the longest necks Sergeant Carver had ever seen. "And Private Skinner, PFC Stanton, and Private Watkins," The Marines looked bored, not happy with their assignment. With the three Marines, the squad would have thirteen men.

Sergeant Carver nodded and turned to face the men. "The Marines have been on this hill awhile and know the surrounding area. This is not a combat patrol, we're only getting the lay of the land, but that doesn't mean there aren't Japs out there. The battle was only a couple of days ago; there could be wounded or even snipers. Stay alert and keep your interval just like training."

He turned back to Phinney, "lead on, Corporal."

Phinney unslung his M1 and moved off the top of the hill and past the command bunker. The squad made their way around the bomb craters and foxholes. The slope was gentle all the way to the bottom. The ground was littered with splintered wood and jungle debris. As they neared the bottom, they came across more rotting Japanese. They'd been there a long time and were now more a part of the jungle floor than the human race.

As the jungle closed around them, they slowed and spread out. Corporal Phinney went into a crouch keeping his weapon at the ready. The other five Marines watched the trees for movement. Sergeant Carver noticed and did the same. He was the ranking man; Lieutenant Swan would be heading out on the evening patrol.

The jungle pressed closer and closer the deeper they went. After twenty minutes they were slowed to a shuffle. Corporal Phinney stopped and motioned Sergeant Carver forward. He stood beside him, and Phinney said, "The east-west trail's just in front of us. It's the most used trail, by them and us. We'll patrol along it a quarter mile to give you a feel for it."

Sergeant Carver nodded and signaled the men to move forward.

They pushed through the impenetrable green and came out onto a relatively open space. There was a trail running through the center of the greenery. Carver immediately felt exposed. He searched the area for anything out of the ordinary. He swept the area with his Thompson. Corporal Phinney said, "We'll move up either side. We're definitely in Indian country, but they took a beating the other day and are probably off licking their wounds."

Carver nodded and waved them forward. The men moved slowly getting the feel of the jungle they'd be living and fighting in for the foreseeable future.

They'd gone an eighth of a mile when there was a sharp crack, and Private Bennett yelled out and fell to the ground. The men dove to the ground. Corporal Phinney yelled, "Sniper!" Another crack and a bullet slammed into the ground beside Phinney. He low crawled to his right finding cover behind a downed palm tree.

The green troops fired. The din of fire was deafening and despite Sergeant Carver yelling "Cease fire," it continued, unabated. The jungle shredded in front of them as bullets tore into the greenery.

Sergeant Carver scanned, but with all the bullets flying he couldn't tell where the sniper was hiding. When he started hearing the distinctive "ping's" of M1 clips running out, he yelled again, "Cease fire, goddamit! Cease fire!" The shooting stopped and Private Bennett's agonized screams filled the void.

Another crack and someone near the back of the two squads yelled out in panic, "I, I'm hit, I'm hit!"

Corporal Phinney and Sergeant Carver made eye contact. Carver said, "See him?" Phinney shook his head. "I'm coming to you, watch for the shot." Phinney nodded and leaned out from behind his cover, bringing his rifle to his shoulder. Carver took a deep breath *what the hell am I doing?* He jumped up and ran the ten steps and leaped for cover. He felt the bullet graze past his head the same time he heard the shot. He crashed into the jungle behind Corporal Phinney.

He heard Phinney's rifle bark three times. "Got you, you sneaky slant-eyed shit."

Carver rolled up and pulled his helmet off. There was a crease across the side. He put it back on and felt goosebumps spread across his body. The sound of Bennett and the other wounded soldier brought him back to the present. "Stay down, watch for more. Get a medic to the wounded." He saw the medic, Corporal Dawkins jump up and weave back and forth like a football running back. He dove next to the BAR man and went to work. There were no more shots.

The men spread out in a perimeter protecting the medic as he worked. Private Bennett was hit in the upper right chest. His chest bubbled red from his punctured lung. He gasped for breath his eyes darting side to side looking for relief from the pain. Corporal Dawkins pulled his bandages out and pressed them against the wound. The sucking sound stopped, and he secured the bandage, wrapping it tightly around the big man's chest. The bullet hadn't passed through his body, so there wasn't an exit wound.

Dawkins laid him on his back and called to a nearby soldier. "Come here and keep pressure on the wound. I need to check the other man."

The soldier, Private Denn kneeled over Bennett. Denn's face was white as a sheet as he took in the scene. He'd never seen so much blood. He froze in place. Dawkins grabbed his hands and forced them onto the bloody bandages. "Hold pressure. Don't release it for anything. He's got a collapsed lung, gotta keep pressure so he can breathe…got it?" When there was no response, Dawkins yelled, "Got it!"

Private Denn snapped out of it and nodded, "Yeah, yeah, I've got it. Go help the other guy."

Corporal Dawkins ran off and slid next to Private First Class Henry. Henry laid on his back, his belly was open, and his guts were visible. "Jesus Christ." There was a ring of crouched soldiers around him, guns pointing outward but they couldn't help looking at PFC Henry's still body. Dawkins felt for a pulse and listened for breathing, but there was nothing. Private First Class Henry from Wilmington North Dakota was gone. "Shit," he said. He ran back to Private Bennett. A group of men watched the struggling soldier.

Sergeant Carver yelled, "Corporal Phinney, lead two men back and get two stretchers." Phinney nodded and grabbed two Marines. Carver said, "The rest of you watch for more Japs. We'll move out soon."

Sergeant Carver pointed at Private Willy, then the remains of

Private Henry. "Wrap him in your poncho. Use your rope to tie him in tight. You and Denn take him back."

Private Willy cursed under his breath as he pulled out his poncho, "Gonna get guts and blood all over my new poncho." He shook his head as kneeled beside the gray face of Private Henry.

6

The evening patrol went better than the first. There were no enemy encounters. Lieutenant Swan and Sergeant Milo got a good idea about the terrain surrounding Hill 260.

Upon their return, Lieutenant Swan thanked the Marines for their help. Corporal Phinney found Sergeant Carver before leaving. "Wanted to wish you dogfaces luck. I don't usually give a rat's ass for grunts and yesterdays cluster fuck didn't help my attitude, but you guys'll do alright out here. You're not Marines, but your men move well and besides some fire discipline issues. Well, they'll come around."

Sergeant Carver wasn't sure if he should ring the cocky Marine's neck or thank him, so he scowled. "Don't recall asking for your opinion, Corporal." He emphasized his rank.

Corporal Phinney held up his hands in surrender. "Don't mean nothing by it. I'm glad to be leaving this hill. It's too exposed and too easily cut off. I don't envy your job, but I think you and your men are up to it."

Carver shoved a half chewed cigar into the side of his mouth. "Course we're up to the job. Now get the hell outta here before I ring your scrawny neck."

He leaned into the Corporal who smiled and turned to leave. "Sorry about your man. How's that big fella, Bennett?"

"He's stable. You'll be escorting him and the medics back to the beach. You can ask him yourself." Corporal Phinney nodded and waved goodbye.

Corporal O'Connor came up beside Sergeant Carver. "Why didn't you kick that cocky son-of-a-bitches ass?"

Carver spit a piece of tobacco onto the ground. "He killed the sniper that nearly punched my ticket this morning." He took off his helmet and showed the crease where the bullet had nearly killed him. O'Connor let out a whistle and went back to cleaning his M1.

Just before nightfall, Lieutenant Swan called the sergeants and corporals into the bunker. The air inside felt like an oven, and the smell of rot and men in need of showers could make a man gag. Lieutenant Swan stood over a table with the same map he'd had out before. He had a red x marking the spot where they'd encountered the sniper.

"Good job today men. I know we lost two good men." His voice cracked, "But I'm proud of the way you handled it. Getting Bennett and Henry out of there without more casualties is a testament to your skill." He looked up from the map. His eyes went from sad to hard like a light switch had been turned on. "Those men didn't die in vain, and we'll avenge them." Lieutenant Swan's eyes went to each of them. Sergeant Carver had never seen his lieutenant look so angry. The timid soldier had disappeared, replaced by a man who wanted vengeance. It made him nervous.

Lieutenant Swan smashed his finger on the red x. "This is where the sniper was that got our guys. At 2300 I'm sending out a squad to set up an ambush in that spot. You'll stay until noon then return here." The men looked at one another; this wasn't a tactic they'd ever done in real life. They'd trained for it, but even on Guadalcanal setting and springing ambushes wasn't something they'd done. Swan, sensing their apprehension asked, "Questions?"

Sergeant Carver asked. "Sir, we just got here, the men barely know where they're sleeping. Do you think tonight is a good time?"

Swan paced, "The men are fine. We need to make our presence known. The Japs need to know were not standing by letting them make all the moves. I want to make them pay for sneaking in snipers."

Carver nodded, not agreeing but knowing he wasn't going to change his mind. "What about support if the shit hits the fan?"

"I've already plotted the coordinates for our mortar team, and I've alerted base of my intentions and have set up artillery coordinates." He leaned forward and with his pencil, marked spots in front of the red x. "This is fire-mission Albert, this one's fire-mission Zulu. I'll only bring in the heavy stuff if you encounter a sizable force. A squad or two, we'll deal with ourselves."

Carver crossed his arms. "Who's going, sir?"

"I want you and third squad out there. Take Corporal O'Connor too." He looked at the two men whose faces were masks of stony silence. "Chances are you won't encounter anything, but if the Japs come to pick up their dead sniper or insert another one, we'll be ready and take them out. Understood?"

The men snapped to attention and saluted, "Yes sir."

"Inform your men and get some chow and some shuteye. There's no guard duty for third squad tonight. I'll be there to see you off."

Sergeant Carver couldn't sleep. After the men had eaten, he gathered them and made sure their weapons were clean, and they had plenty of ammo. He went over their gear making sure there was nothing shiny and nothing that would make noise as they moved through the jungle. The men acted subdued getting used to the fact that they'd soon be beyond the immediate safety of their comrades.

"I know this is a sudden and unexpected mission, but we trained for it. When we get to the trail, we'll set up the ambush, with the thirty caliber as the crux.

"The LT isn't expecting trouble, but you never know. If Japs come into the area we'll wait until the majority are in the kill box. No one shoots until I give the command. No one shoots until I do...understand?" The men responded, "yessir," in unison. "I don't want the fire discipline breakdown like we had last night. We're better than that. Let's be professional out there."

He dismissed them. Everyone went off to their holes or bunkers to try to sleep through jitters. O'Connor stayed back and when the men were gone said, "Do you think this is a good idea, Sarge?"

Carver watched the squad leave and shook his head. "We're gonna have to be on our toes. This isn't our mission. The men know how to set up and execute it, but these are front line troops. We're not guerrillas." O'Connor raised a red eyebrow. "Well, not really. You and I have been out there, but most of these men are green as grass. I don't trust 'em not to open fire if they hear so much as a monkey howl."

O'Connor nodded. "Well if someone does open up, we'll have to end the mission. Can't risk staying out there once we're compromised."

Sergeant Carver grinned, "then we'd have to come back here hours before our guys will be expecting us and probably get shot up by our troops." He shook his head, "I don't like it one bit. What's gotten into the LT?"

Sergeant Milo had been standing in the back of the group. He heard Carver's question. He stepped forward. "I was here when Lieutenant Swan saw Bennett and Henry come out of the jungle. His face went white like he'd seen a ghost or something. He looked physically ill. Thought for sure he'd lose his lunch any second. Then something happened. I don't know what, but suddenly he changed." Milo looked down at his boots remembering. "It was like he aged twenty years in two seconds. He went from white to red, and his eyes went from teary to hard as stone."

He looked from Carver to O'Connor. He'd been through the hell of Guadalcanal with them. He'd seen men die and killed plenty himself. He'd seen both these men kill, sometimes with their bare hands. He'd also seen them mourn many fallen friends and comrades. "I've seen it before. The lieutenant wants revenge. He took those two casualties personally, and he wants payback."

Sergeant Carver nodded. "That's what it seems like to me, but this is no place for personal vendettas."

~

THE TOP of Hill 260 was pitch dark. There was cloud cover, and it looked like it might rain. True to his word Lieutenant Swan was there to see them off. He spoke quietly to Sergeant Carver and Corporal O'Connor. His attitude seemed to have mellowed with the darkness. "I want you to be careful out there. If you see anything that seems out of place, don't push. Use your judgment and good sense."

Carver gritted his teeth. *Now that this shit is real he's losing his nerve.* "Yes, sir. As careful as we can be considering were patrolling in enemy territory."

Lieutenant Swan nodded, "Good luck, Sergeant." He stepped aside, and Carver led the fourteen man squad down the slope. As they passed the other platoon members in their holes, they nodded, wishing them luck. They were happy they weren't going with them.

When they entered the jungle line, it seemed like the blackness swallowed them. To Corporal O'Connor it seemed they'd entered a nightmare of vines, snakes, and insects. Sweat wet his shirt making him sticky. He wanted to scratch every inch of his body. Even though he'd been in the tropics almost two years, his fair skin never adjusted. His skin had burned countless times, but instead of becoming dark tan like Sergeant Carver, he only turned deeper shades of red.

They moved at a snail's pace. O'Connor was on point, as usual, his upbringing in the Oregon woods had groomed him perfectly for the job. He took careful steps in the unfamiliar jungle, trying to come to terms with the wildness all around him.

Every forest was slightly different, and the same held true for jungles. The jungle on Guadalcanal had become like a second home to him, then the more paradise like jungles of Fiji had become the same, and now he was in another jungle and felt like a visitor from another planet.

Things were the same, but there were differences. The night birds were different, the soft eerie glow of Mount Bagana, was different, even the soft ground felt different. O'Connor used every sense trying to come to terms with the newness. His progress was slow.

It took almost two hours to travel less than a quarter mile, but they arrived safely and quietly. Corporal O'Connor stopped at the point where the sniper had killed Henry and sent Bennett home with a sucking chest wound. He crouched and heard Sergeant Carver come up beside him. He put a hand on O'Connor's shoulder. He nodded, indicating he agreed they were in the correct position.

Carver signaled to the men, and they silently spread out. Sergeant Carver helped the two men with the thirty caliber find and set up in a spot with good cover and a clear shot down the trail. It took only minutes for the rest of the men to set up.

O'Connor put himself in the center of the ambush next to Private Willy and Denn. Private Willy had been with the 164th Regiment since they landed on Guadalcanal. He was a veteran who'd seen as much combat as O'Connor and Carver. Private Denn, on the other hand, was a replacement. He'd joined the regiment on Fiji. He'd proved himself a good soldier but he was still young and green, and O'Connor wanted to stay close to him in case he decided to shoot at ghosts and give away their position.

The night seemed to have weight as they laid there waiting for something to happen. They'd been keyed up when they first arrived, but after an hour, the newness and even some of the terror had worn off. Some of the men's eyes were getting heavy.

O'Connor noticed Private Denn start to nod off and he nudged him in the ribs. He leaned close and whispered in his ear, "It's a dereliction of duty to fall asleep during an ambush."

Private Denn jolted and repositioned himself. "What's that word mean?"

"It means I'll kick your skinny ass if you fall asleep out here. Stay alert."

The jungle went quiet then suddenly the sky opened up like a faucet, and within seconds every member of the squad was soaked. They scrambled to open their packs and pulled out ponchos. O'Connor shivered despite having been in a lathering sweat only a minute before. *This is a damned cluster-fuck.*

The rain hammered them for an hour then tapered to a slow soaking drizzle. The ground beneath their prone bodies started to feel more like a marsh than ground, and they slowly sank into the stink.

The ponchos kept most of the water out, but they also kept the wetness and heat trapped inside creating a mini-weather system. Instead of shivering they were now sweltering. O'Connor felt like he was being broiled alive.

Staying alert and vigilant was difficult. The darkness and the rain made it impossible to see more than a few feet in front of them. O'Connor thought a whole company of Japs could be walking by them and unless they stepped on him, he'd never know. He glanced over at Private Denn. His eyes were drooping, and he was trying his best to stay awake, but it looked like a losing battle. He decided to let it slide. One more set of eyes in this gloom wouldn't help much. *At least someone should get some shuteye.*

Fifteen minutes later the rain stopped, and the only sound was the dripping of water off palm fronds. Even the animals hadn't come out from cover, the night was quiet and calm. O'Connor thought it beautiful the way the jungle seemed to cleanse itself. Slowly, one by one, sounds of insects, then animals started to come alive again.

He strained to see into the night. Without the rain, he could make out shapes twenty yards down the trail, trees, and thick foliage. The trail itself seemed to glisten with a slight sheen of wetness. He glanced at Denn, who was obviously asleep. He looked to Private Willy on his other side. It was hard to see his eyes, he had his helmet and poncho pulled so far down, but he figured the veteran was aware, if not wholly awake.

He was about to nudge him when he heard a different sound, a splash, like a boot in water. He saw Private Willy tense and his head moved to look down the trail, towards the sound. O'Connor followed his gaze, moving his head slow, careful not to attract attention.

As far as he could see down the trail, there was nothing new. Then a black shape appeared, stepping onto the shimmering path. O'Connor knew it was an enemy soldier and he was only twenty yards away moving towards him. He brought his M1 to his shoulder and put the iron sights where he thought the man's chest should be. He licked his lips in anticipation.

Sergeant Carver was off to his left and further forward, near the thirty caliber machine gun. He knew the old veteran would be lining up his shot, keeping the nervous machine gun crew from firing too early. O'Connor kept his sights on the front soldier, but out of the corner of his eye tried to count how many more soldiers stepped onto the trail.

He figured he'd seen at least ten when the night erupted in sound and fire. Long tongues of flame lanced out from the thirty caliber, sending tracer fire into the Japanese soldiers at almost point blank range. The man in O'Connor's sights was no longer there, blown down with withering fire but he fired on the spot anyway, knowing there were more soldiers behind him. His eyes burned from the sudden light show. He couldn't see targets, only blurry outlines of darting soldiers. He shot at them until he couldn't find anymore.

The firing all around him continued. Private Denn had woken from his slumber and was waving his rifle around with wild eyes. O'Connor reached out and grabbed the weapon, keeping it from swinging into friendly troops. It took only a second for Denn to get control of himself. He ripped the gun from O'Connor's grasp and looked at him with saucer eyes. O'Connor didn't think the human eye could have so much white.

He heard Sergeant Carver yelling, "Cease fire! Cease fire!" The men got control of themselves, and the onslaught of sound and fire stopped.

The night's darkness swept back in shutting out the light like a thick blanket covering a candle's delicate flame. The night sounds were absent, but all the men could hear was the ringing in their ears. The first sound Corporal O'Connor heard was the moaning of a wounded enemy soldier. He hadn't heard the sound since Guadalcanal where it had been as common as the rain. That sound, a dying man, was as unique to combat as crying babies were to nurseries. O'Connor suppressed a chill running up his spine as he reacquainted himself with the ugliness of his job.

He gave Private Denn a scathing look which he doubted he could see. He went to his knees holding his M1 at the ready. He'd instinctively closed one eye when the shooting started preserving some of his night vision. He could see blobs in the darkness covering the trail. He stood and looked where he knew the rest of the squad were still prone. He could see the dim orange outline of the thirty caliber's hot barrel. It looked like a branding iron.

He stepped forward. "I'm checking the bodies, nobody shoot." He didn't wait for a response. He went to the first body and kicked them onto their back, ready to shoot if he was alive. He'd learned not to trust dead Japanese soldiers until he'd proved they were really dead. He'd seen too many GIs blown up by Japs playing possum. This one was obviously not faking. There was nothing but glistening gray matter where his face should have been. The next man was dead too, riddled with bullets that had severed one leg at the knee.

The third man was the wounded soldier. O'Connor bent down to get a closer look. The man was facing upright. He could see both his hands were at his sides and they were empty. The Japanese soldier was swallowing over and over like he couldn't get his throat wet. His mouth opened and closed making him seem to be gulping air like it was food. O'Connor stepped back and aimed at the man's head. The soldier stared into the muzzle of his death. When O'Connor hesitated, the man looked him in the eye and gave a slight nod. O'Connor's M1 jumped in his hand, and the thirty caliber round put a neat hole in the soldier's head, ending his misery.

O'Connor hadn't noticed Private Denn beside him and flinched when he squawked, "What'd you do that for? You murdered him."

He turned to the young private and in a menacing voice said, "He was suffering."

Private Denn didn't notice the menace in O'Connor's voice and continued. "He's not a dog; he's a human being. You killed him in cold blood. You're a murderer!"

O'Connor moved in a flash, smashing his left fist into Private Denn's jaw. He went down hard, and O'Connor jumped onto his chest pinning him there. He leaned close, nose to nose. "If things were reversed and that was you down there they'd be cutting your balls off about now. Then they'd cut off your pathetic little cock and shove it down your throat until you choked." He let his words sink in. He leaned back a few inches. "I've seen it myself, so shut the fuck up until you've been around longer than a few days." He pushed off Denn's chest and went to the next dead soldier.

Private Denn laid in the mud as the adrenaline from the ambush washed over him in waves. He felt sick to his stomach, and he rolled onto his knees and puked. Hot tears came to his eyes, and before he could stop, he was sobbing.

Sergeant Carver was beside him. Without leaning down he said, "Get off your knees and clean yourself up, boy. You're not sucking on momma's tits anymore. This is the real deal and make no mistake."

7

Carver was proud of the way his men had handled themselves during the ambush. They'd waited for his order to open fire, and they'd ceased fire when ordered. He wasn't able to see the men in the dark, but he could hear their excited whispers as they went over the battle amongst themselves.

They'd retreated to Hill 260 after the ambush, not wanting to stick around the area in case there was a larger force nearby. The rest of second platoon had heard the brief firefight from their positions on the hill and were confident it was the GIs guns they'd heard, so were ready for the squad to return early. Coming back through the lines had gone off without a hitch, and the men were sitting around waiting for the debrief.

The jungle was lightening as dawn approached. Lieutenant Swan came out of the bunker and addressed the squad. "Good job, men." He paced with his arms clasped behind his back. Sergeant Carver thought he looked like a kid play-acting at war. "The Japanese felt our presence and won't be inserting snipers anytime soon."

Carver folded his arms across his chest. *Doubt one ambush will deter those sons-of-bitches.*

"You men rest until this evening. Get some chow and some sleep. Once again, good job." He gestured to Sergeant Carver and Corporal O'Connor to follow him into the command bunker.

He leaned over the map and put his finger on the spot of the ambush. "This seems to be a hot spot. Any reason either of you can see?"

Sergeant Carver spoke. "Other than it being the main trail into and out of here, no."

Swan continued. "And you didn't find anything on the bodies?" he looked at Corporal O'Connor who'd searched the Japanese soldiers.

"Just the normal shit, sir. You know, pictures of family, girlfriends, that sort of thing. The highest rank I saw was a sergeant, but I'm sure some got away, sir."

Carver continued. "They were armed with Arisaka rifles. One guy had one of those knee mortars. We put it all in a hole and blew it with a grenade, sir."

Lieutenant Swan unfolded the rest of the map showing the entire island. He pointed to their beachhead on the western shore almost in the center of Bougainville. "The question is: where are the Japs coming from? There's no roads, only overgrown dirt tracks, yet they continue to attack us in force and fire artillery from the hills around us onto our airfields and beach." He pointed to the southern end of the map. "The main Jap force is here at Buin," he moved his finger to the northern end, "And here at Buka. That's a hell of a long journey on foot with heavy equipment." He put his hands behind his back and paced. "I know the Nips are sneaky and resilient, but it seems like they're getting to us too easily. There has to be a road somewhere, some jumping off point to get close with those heavy guns and troops."

Sergeant Carver didn't like where this was going. "Sir, haven't they landed men and supplies onto the beaches north and south of here?"

Swan nodded, "they did that successfully once and attacked the Marines by surprise. From what I hear they had a hard fight. But that was months ago and every attempt since, at least as far as we know, has been stopped by our Navy.

"Those PT boats patrol the area constantly, and they've run off more than one ship trying to get in close, presumably to offload troops." He shook his head. "I think something else is happening. I think they're building roads and the thick jungle doesn't allow our air forces to see them building."

Sergeant Carver and Corporal O'Connor looked at one another with grim faces, knowing what was coming.

"We need to have eyes on the ground out there. We need to find out how the Japs are getting to us and stop it. Once we locate the road we can attack it by air and artillery and cut off the artery that's feeding their troops."

Silence filled the bunker as Lieutenant Swan looked at Carver. Finally Sergeant Carver broke the silence. "You want a patrol to find this road, sir? A patrol from Hill 260?"

He nodded. "We can work out the details later, but yes. I want an experienced patrol out there with eyes on the Japs." Carver and O'Connor stared into the lieutenant's eyes. He continued, "I want you two to lead the patrol. You're the most qualified with your experiences on Guadalcanal. You can pick whatever men you think you need, whatever equipment. I'll leave the specifics up to you."

Sergeant Carver intensified his stare, drilling holes. "When you want this to happen, sir?"

Lieutenant Swan looked at the floor then back at Carver. "Sooner the better. I don't like not knowing where the enemy is. The sooner we know, the better we can stop another attack and save American lives." Carver stared, wanting a more specific answer. Swan shrugged. "In a couple of days at the earliest. You men need rest, and we'll need to come up with a plan and a list of men you want with you. You can take whoever you want from the platoon. We're getting first platoon from Baker Company tomorrow. I'm thinking a squad-sized force of twelve men?"

Sergeant Carver asked, "You asking or telling, sir?"

"I'm asking your opinion. Isn't that about the size of the force you took behind the lines at Guadalcanal?"

Carver gritted his teeth, remembering the ill-fated mission. He'd started with twelve men and ended with two, just himself and

Corporal O'Connor made it out alive. Sergeant Carver nodded. "We had twelve men, but we lost most of them, sir." He put his hands behind his back and asked, "Permission to speak freely, sir?" Lieutenant Swan nodded. "The mission on the Canal was a complete cluster-fuck. Sending us behind enemy lines is a good way to get good men killed. We only pulled that mission off by sheer luck, and even then we had over a ninety percent casualty rate. Why doesn't Regiment send out a large force if they're so bent on finding the Jap road?"

Carver knew he was pushing it questioning orders, but he hoped he had a good enough rapport with the young Lieutenant to get away with it. Lieutenant Swan's face turned a shade of red. "I haven't passed this by Regiment." Sergeant Carver exchanged a look with Corporal O'Connor who sneered back. Before Carver could speak, the lieutenant continued. "I have orders to hold this hill any way I see fit." He started pacing again. "If I can find the Jap's supply routes I can stop them from attacking."

Sergeant Carver stared, stunned at the news. "Are you telling me we'll be out on our own without even the support of the Regiment?"

Swan's face went from red to pale. "You'll have any support you need. You'll be in radio contact with me the whole time. If you need artillery support or air cover, you can relay it to me, and I'll pass it along."

Carver frowned. "Radios don't work too well from the top of this here hill, let alone down there in the jungle. It's thick, thicker than any I've ever seen."

Despite his pale features and obvious discomfort, The lieutenant stuck to his orders. "You've faced adversity before, Sergeant. I'm sure you're the man for the job. You and Corporal O'Connor. I want it done. It's," he braced himself like he was getting ready for an ocean wave to slam into him. "It's an order."

Sergeant Carver's spine stiffened as he threw up his hand in a tight salute. Corporal O'Connor was slower and not as stiff, but he saluted as well.

"Get some rest; I'll have a search area mapped out for you by tomorrow. I've got some ideas about where I think the roads probably are." He returned their salutes and bent over the map.

Carver and O'Connor turned and left the bunker. When they were out of earshot, O'Connor said, "This shit's starting to become a habit."

Carver snorted, "Yeah a bad habit. I don't like it, not one bit. Maybe he'll come to his senses after we've been here a day or two."

O'Connor shook his head, "Doubt it. He's got one successful mission under his belt; now he thinks he's goddamned MacArthur."

8

The two days Lieutenant Swan had given Sergeant Carver to assemble his patrol members passed. Carver kept it simple, choosing men from his platoon. He'd picked as many seasoned soldiers as he could, but was forced to use some green troopers. He felt he had a strong mix. The green troopers were solid soldiers. He'd trained with them on Fiji, but he had no idea how they'd react when the bullets started flying. Some had been on the ambush patrol, but that was an unfair fight.

Including himself and O'Connor he had twelve men picked out. They stood around awaiting orders to move off the hill. Lieutenant Swan stood before them. He pulled Sergeant Carver aside. "Remember, if you run into trouble it's okay to come back without finding the road. I want you back here no more than four days from now. You'll run out of food after that."

Sergeant Carver clenched his teeth making his jawline ripple. He nodded, "Yessir." The lieutenant nodded at the men and disappeared back into the bunker.

Corporal O'Connor had heard the exchange. "What's he mean, *run into trouble*?" he shook his head as he stared at the entrance to the bunker. "He wants it both ways. Wants us to complete the mission, but also doesn't want any more casualties on his conscience."

Sergeant Carver normally wouldn't allow a soldier to badmouth an officer, but he and O'Connor had a long history. He spit and said, "Yeah, when the chips are down, he's losing his nerve."

Carver turned to the men who were sweating in the evening sun. "All right, make sure your gear's good and tight, nothing dangling, nothing making noise. Two full canteens, full ammo load."

He found Private First Class Timothy with the bulky radio on his back. He pointed at him, "You stay close with that radio, never more than a few feet." Timothy was green, but he'd performed well in training and was a magician with the radio. PFC Timothy nodded. "I want Corporal O'Connor on point."

The men marched down the side of the hill and entered the jungle. The platoon had thinned out the jungle in front of the hill for a better field of fire, but it was still thick.

Once off the hill, the ground softened, and soon their feet were caked with a heavy layer of mud. Each step was difficult; their legs burdened with the extra weight. Carver tried to avoid the mud holes from the previous men's feet, but it hardly mattered. Anywhere he stepped he sank up to his ankle. It was impossible to move quietly with all the sucking and slurping sounds.

They walked until the evening turned to darkness. They were exhausted and had travelled less than two miles. Corporal O'Connor found themselves a dry spot amongst an assortment of volcanic boulders. It was better than sitting in the mud, but the pointed rocks weren't comfortable by any means.

Sergeant Carver set out security, each man taking two hour watches. Carver hoped leaving Hill 260 from the side would make it more unlikely for a Japanese patrol to find their trail. If they did, it would lead directly to them. Even as tired as they all were, few slept well.

WITH DAWN STILL AN HOUR AWAY, the men were up eating a light breakfast of K-rations and getting ready for another grueling day of patrolling.

Sergeant Carver put his poncho over his head and with a red lensed flashlight found their position on the map. They'd recently gotten new maps from G2 which were much more accurate than anything they'd previously had. He found the closest area Lieutenant Swan wanted them to reconnoiter. It was another three miles due north to the base of the Crown Prince Range where a steep canyon cut into the nine thousand foot peaks. Judging by their slow progress thus far, he figured they'd reach it by the evening. He wasn't going to push the patrol and end up walking into the middle of a Japanese patrol.

He showed Corporal O'Connor the route he thought they should take, not direct but following a small spine that looked to be off the muddy jungle floor by a few yards. O'Connor thought he could find it and turned to get his gear together. He'd tried to sleep on the outer edge of the rocks. He'd found a comfortable spot but only got a few hours of sleep. He never slept well on an overnight patrol.

He was rolling his poncho when he heard something out of place in the jungle. He froze, his senses going into overdrive. He couldn't place what he'd heard, but he strained to hear it again. He was about to chalk it up to nerves when he heard a dull sucking sound, like a boot being slowly pulled from mud.

He knew none of his squad would move that far away to take a shit. Someone was out there. Keeping low and making sure he made no noise he scampered back to Carver's side. "There's something out there following our trail. They're close, maybe thirty yards."

Carver trusted O'Connor and didn't hesitate. "Tell the men; we engage as they approach. It's too late to leave this cover." Carver moved to PFC Timothy and got on the radio. He needed to get fire support in case things got out of hand.

O'Connor nodded and told the first man he found to pass along the order. He went back to his spot and laid out two clips and two grenades and set them on the rock beside him. He heard movement to his right and was relieved to see PFC Willy aiming his M1 into the night. They'd need his shooting skills if this were anything more than a few men.

The darkness was giving way to light, but the jungle was dense to O'Connor's front. He'd only have a second to see and kill an enemy soldier before they'd be on top of him. He wished he had a Thompson like Sergeant Carver's, for this close in fighting. What you lost in accuracy you gained in fire suppression and the pure havoc the .45 caliber bullets created.

He took a deep breath and let it out, listening. He thought he heard another squelch of a muddy step. They were just a few yards away. It would happen any second. He pulled the rifle tight to his shoulder and looked over the sights. The seconds passed like cooling lava meandering down the side of Mt. Bagana. Then there was a sudden yell. It startled him nearly causing his bowels to loosen.

The empty jungle suddenly was full of targets bursting forth only feet away. O'Connor didn't need to use the sights, he fired point blank into the nearest man then shifted to the next and the next.

Willy's M1 barked as he swept the gun across the front. Every man was firing as fast as they could pull the trigger, but the enemy had gotten too close. They'd be amongst the rocks in seconds.

O'Connor's weapon 'pinged' as his clip ran out. Instead of reloading he palmed a grenade pulled the pin, released the handle and threw it into the jungle yelling, "Grenade!" Everyone who heard him instinctively ducked but kept firing. The explosion sounded muffled in the mud and jungle, but the flash from the explosion highlighted Japanese being shredded by shrapnel. In a smooth motion, he hurled his second grenade and palmed another clip into his M1. He waited for the explosion then rose and continued firing at anything that moved.

He felt, rather than saw movement to his left. There were no friendlies that way. He swung his rifle, but the khaki-clad soldier was too close. The soldier grabbed the M1 and ripped it out of O'Connor's hand, sending it flying into the jungle. *I've lost my weapon.* The thought enraged him. He'd committed the ultimate sin, the one thing the drill sergeants had pounded into his head over and over, *take care of your weapon.*

He pulled the K-bar knife from his belt without consciously thinking to do so. The weapon seemed to appear in his hand.

The enemy soldier was screaming and thrusting down with the

bayonet attached to his Arisaka rifle. O'Connor's only chance was to attack and get inside the deadly blade's arc.

From his crouched position he launched into the Japanese as the blade missed his back by a fraction. He slammed into the soldier like a linebacker leveling a quarterback. At the same time, he brought the K-bar around and plunged it into the soldier's back. With speed born from adrenaline, he pulled the knife out and thrust it back in over and over until the soldier's body went limp.

O'Connor jumped off the body and looked for more targets. There weren't many left, but they were in amongst the rocks fighting hand to hand. He drew his sidearm, a Webley he'd bought off a Brit in Fiji. It didn't carry as many rounds as a service .45, but he liked the way it felt in his hand.

He pulled back the hammer and aimed at a soldier who'd just been pushed back by Private Willy. The soldier was trying to get his balance as he toppled on top of a rock. O'Connor pulled the trigger, and the pistol bucked in his hand. Through the smoke, he could see the hole it created in the back of the Japanese soldier's back. The soldier spun off the rock and landed at Willy's feet.

O'Connor moved forward searching for more targets. The last struggle was happening where he'd left Sergeant Carver. He ran forward with his pistol extended. He couldn't see what was happening, the struggle was partially hidden by a boulder, but he could tell it wasn't decided.

He ran around the boulder at the same time he saw the Japanese soldier falling backward with Sergeant Carver's K-bar planted in his eye socket. The stricken soldier fell to the ground, smashing his head against a rock. His body convulsed and shook as the life left him. Carver leaned forward and pulled the knife from the man's eye socket, and the convulsing stopped.

O'Connor looked around for more enemy soldiers, but all he saw were men breathing hard with wide eyes. He yelled, "Anyone hit?" They were in too much shock to answer. He repeated the question as he scanned the area. Everyone seemed to be okay until he saw the radio man holding his arm and rocking back and forth. Blood seeped between his fingers. "You hit, Timothy?"

O'Connor holstered his pistol and ran to him. He pulled the white faced Timothy's hand away and could see a bloody mess of bone and muscle mixed with the green of his uniform. Carver saw the wound and called the medic. "Dawkins, we need a medic!"

Corporal Dawkins came around the corner his M1 still smoking. He dropped it and pulled out his medical kit as he looked at the wound. "Cut his sleeve off so I can see it," he said as he pulled out bandages and an ampule of morphine. O'Connor drew his K-bar which was still dark red and sticky with blood. He cut away Timothy's sleeve.

Dawkins was about to stick the morphine into his arm when Carver stopped him. "Hold off on the morphine, Doc. We gotta get the hell outta here in a hurry."

He stepped in front of his radio man's face and tilted his chin so he was staring him in the eye. "We can't carry you, Private. You have to walk, or we'll never make it out of here. The morphine will put you into la-la land, and you won't be able to walk, okay?" when he got no response Carver slapped him across the cheek. The slap focused his eyes. "You understand? You've gotta stay with us until we get to a more secure area. The Japs'll be all over us after the ruckus we just made." Timothy nodded and slurred through the pain. "I'm okay, Sarge. I can make it."

Carver nodded. "I know you can. Doc'll slap a bandage on you, we'll give the radio to Private Willy, and we'll get the fuck outta here."

Sergeant Carver backed away to allow Corporal Dawkins to work. Private Willy was already hefting the radio. The contents of his pack were divvied up to the rest of the men, and they were ready to move inside of ten minutes.

O'Connor asked, "Where we going Sarge?"

Carver checked his Thompson's magazine and slapped it into place. "I'd say this qualifies as, 'running into trouble.' We're getting our asses back to Hill 260."

9

Sergeant Carver didn't need to tell the men they had to hurry. They knew any Japanese troops within hearing distance would be on them within the hour. "We'll go east; it looks like the ground is firm. We can cover our tracks easier." He looked at O'Connor who nodded. Carver looked around for a point man. Normally he would've given the job to Private Willy, but he wanted his experienced man in charge of the radio. "I'll take point until we're out of the area," he said.

Carver moved to the front and took them east along the spur of volcanic rock. He moved fast, jumping from rock to rock, trying to leave no tracks.

The rocks ran out thirty yards from their bivouac site. He stepped onto the jungle floor. It was hard, like normal ground. He hunched over and moved into the denseness of the jungle.

He led them due east for what he figured was about a quarter mile. The jungle was dense, but by staying low, they could move through it faster. He stopped and held up his hand. They stopped and pointed their weapons in a defensive posture.

O'Connor moved through the column until he was beside Sergeant Carver. The sweat on his brow dripped like a faucet. He nodded at

Carver. "This seems like a better route. Better than that shitty mess." He pointed with his thumb the way they'd come in.

Carver nodded. "I want you to lead us south now. We'll come up to the east of Hill 260 if we go due south from here." O'Connor nodded and moved off to the right. Carver let the men move past him until he saw Private Willy, and the radio. He took his place in front of him. Willy nodded, his black eyes unreadable behind his greasy eyebrows. Carver wondered what the man did before the war. *Probably a mafia hit-man.*

The image of Willy back at the rocks flashed across his mind. The man had taken on three Japs hand to hand. He'd killed all three with his knife before they knew what hit them. He was the most skilled knife fighter he'd ever seen, above and beyond anything the Army taught.

The scary thing, was the way he seemed to relish the fight. He'd lick his lips in anticipation like he was getting ready for a turkey dinner. Carver was glad he was on his side but didn't doubt that if he crossed Willy in peacetime, he'd carve him up the way he did those Japs without a second thought.

They moved for a half hour before O'Connor stopped, and held up his hand, then signaled to take cover. Like silent snakes, the men lowered themselves prone, and watched and waited. The wounded PFC Timothy was glad for the rest. It was all he could do not to cry out with every jarring step.

A minute passed. Sergeant Carver trusted O'Connor more than any other man alive. He'd stay down until signaled. O'Connor didn't spook easily. If he wanted them down, Japs were close.

Carver could feel insects moving beneath him, edging their way into his pants and shirt front, but he ignored them. He listened for any unnatural sound and soon heard the shuffling of feet through the jungle, then the low murmur of unintelligible voices. He moved only his eyeballs, but couldn't see the soldiers he knew were there. Suddenly there was a Japanese boot in front of his nose. The distinctive notched toe gave no doubt it belonged to a Japanese infantryman. Carver stopped breathing. He tried to calm his heart, but it felt like it would pound out of his chest. He watched as the boot hesitated. *Have they seen me?* He thought sure he'd feel a bayonet in his back any second. The boot picked up and stepped forward. The Jap was being quiet, hunting him and his men.

No more soldiers came that close, but he could hear more passing all around him. When he didn't sense more, he waited another five minutes. None of his men moved a muscle. O'Connor was the first to move. He faded back to the first man in line, and the signal went back for Carver to come forward.

He took a deep breath and let it out slow. *That was too close.* He low crawled forward to O'Connor who seemed unfazed.

O'Connor grinned, "Thought I was gonna get stepped on."

Carver nodded trying not to show his fear. "Guess we got lucky. Take us forward, doubt they'll be another patrol, but stay focused."

O'Connor nodded and turned to take the lead. Sergeant Carver went back to his spot looking each man in the eye. They all looked like they'd seen a ghost. When he got to his spot, Private Willy showed him his knife. He whispered, "If that nip would've seen you, I would've skewered him, Sarge." Carver nodded and flashed him the thumbs up. *Crazy fucker looks disappointed.*

THEY DIDN'T COME across more patrols, but they did see signs of them. There were boot tracks on the muddy ground, and they found a trampled area only a half mile from Hill 260. The area seemed to be swarming with the enemy. Carver marked the spot on his map as a possible artillery target.

O'Connor took a grenade from Private Willy, who wasn't happy about it, and set a booby trap. He scraped a small depression in the middle of the clearing, and after pulling the pin placed the grenade with the handle facing up. He reached into his ammo pouch, and pulled out a clip for his M1. He pulled a jungle leaf, and shredded it into strips. When he found the correct sized leaf strand, he threaded it through the M1 clip, then tied a loop at the other end of the strand, and looped it over the handle of the grenade.

He concealed the grenade, and set the clip on top. The shiny brass of the thirty caliber bullets would catch the eye of anyone coming through, and when they picked up the clip the tension would pull the handle of the grenade, and maim or kill anyone nearby.

Sergeant Carver wasn't happy about the delay, but was satisfied with the trap. He recognized it from some they'd seen on Guadalcanal. The Japanese killed and maimed more than a few of his men that way. They'd learned through hard lessons not to pick up strange items that didn't seem to belong in the jungle.

When O'Connor finished he picked up his rifle, and as he walked past Carver said, "A little payback."

Carver grunted and nodded. O'Connor took point, and they used every bit of caution for the next two hours. The men were tiring when they came to a small clearing, and could see Hill 260 poking up from the jungle floor. It looked like it had gotten a shave from a lazy barber. The sparse trees shredded by artillery looked like stubble. They were still too far away to see their platoon members, but the sight gave them hope that they'd make it back.

THEY ENTERED their perimeter in the same spot they'd left. It heartened Carver when he was stopped and asked the password long before an enemy soldier could've caused damage.

Private Denn sounded scared as he challenged them, but Carver had radioed ahead telling Lt. Swan about his early arrival, and his need of medical care for PFC Timothy, so they were expecting his squad.

As Carver passed him, he slapped his shoulder, "Good job, Denn. If I were a Jap, I'd be hightailing it out of here."

Denn gave him an 'aw gee' smile. "Thanks, Sarge." Sergeant Carver shook his head, and trudged up the hill.

Their squad was met halfway up by another set of medics who put PFC Timothy onto a stretcher, and walked him the rest of the way.

Lieutenant Swan was waiting on top; his face went white as he saw the bloody bandage on Timothy's shoulder. Sergeant Carver gave him a quick salute. "Doc Dawkins says he'll be fine, but out of action for awhile."

Lieutenant Swan got his color back and said, "Get your men settled then brief me in the bunker in ten minutes."

Carver said, "Yessir." He was exhausted, and wanted to lay down and sleep, but the lieutenant wouldn't wait. He splashed some water on his face, opened a can of spaghetti from a K-rat, and got a few spoonfuls before it was time to debrief.

Swan was waiting for him inside the dim bunker. It was evening, the sun still a few hours from setting. It was sweltering inside. He wondered how Swan could stand staying in here all the time. There was a radio in the corner manned by a sweating corporal who looked ready to pass out.

"Ah, Sergeant Carver, come in." Carver was already inside, and took off his helmet. "Have a seat, and tell me what you found."

Instead of sitting, he went to the map on the table. "I'll retrace our steps for you, sir." He put his dirty index finger on Hill 260 then found the spot they started. "We left here and went due south for about an eighth of a mile then veered east. When we'd thought we'd gone far enough to line up with the pass we turned north…" he went through the day, describing the mud, the terrain, anything he thought important.

He compared his map with the rocky bivouac site, and found it on the lieutenant's map. He told him of the night, and the morning attack. "They found our tracks. A blind man could've found us. The mud's no good." He relayed the battle, then their run back. He marked the areas they found sign of the enemy, and told him of the booby-trapped camp. He circled an approximation on the map.

"The long and the short of it, there's Japs all over the area. I don't know where they're coming from, but it's too dangerous to have patrols out there. We were lucky to get back, sir."

Lieutenant Swan nodded, then slammed his hand down on the map, "Dammit!" He shook his head. "I know there's a road out there, and if we could find it we could seal it off and…" he didn't finish.

Carver wondered, "And what, sir?"

"And hit them before they hit us. We're hanging in the wind out here. Our main lines are behind us. We're exposed out here, and the only way to keep from being overrun, is stopping an attack before it happens." He pointed out the bunker slits at the vast green carpet of jungle. "They're out there, and all we can do is sit here and wait to get hit. Wait for more men to die."

The radio man looked up at Swan then quickly made himself look busy when he caught Sergeant Carver's scowl.

He pulled Lt. Swan away a few feet. "You want some advice, sir?" he didn't wait for a response, "This is war, and in war, men die. That's an unavoidable fact. Men die. *Your* men will die. Men you've trained with for months, men you like, men you respect. It's gonna happen again and again, and the only way to deal with it is to accept it. If you try to save everyone, you'll only get more men killed."

Lieutenant Swan looked up at him sharply, and Carver held up his hands. "I'm not saying sending us out to find the enemy road's a bad idea. In fact, the more I think about it the more I agree with you, but even if we find it, and bomb the hell out them, we're still gonna lose men.

"I've fought the Japs; they don't stop until they're dead, and even then they can be deadly with their goddamned booby-traps." Lieutenant Swan looked at his boots. Carver put his hand on his shoulder. "You're doing good, sir, but don't start over thinking shit."

Swan moved to his makeshift desk and sat down. He put his head in his hands and said, "I want to find that road, Sergeant. How we gonna get a patrol past all those Japs? You have anything in mind?"

Sergeant Carver smiled. "I've been thinking about that, and I think I have a solution that just might work."

10

Purata Island sat off the coast of Empress Augustus Bay beachhead like a tiny pimple. It was mainly used as a holding area for supplies and equipment for the Army Divisions protecting the airfields, but it was also home to the Navy's venerable PT boats. Eight of the seventy-seven foot, low profile vessels lay at anchor on the southwestern side of the small island.

Commander Hawkins was the officer in charge of them. He sat hunched over a map of Bougainville Island. Beads of sweat dripped off his nose, and pooled on the map. He was shirtless, as were all the men around him. He slammed his fist down, and in a gruff Texas twang said, "These damned maps are next to useless. We were just here last night," he punched a spot on the coast to the north of Purata Island, "But this map shows nothing about the bay we found." He took out his pencil, and drew the small bay he'd discovered. "Guess I'm a damned cartographer now, eh Smitty?" he slugged the man to his right Bosun's Mate, Smith.

Smitty grinned, and rubbed his hands together like he was looking at a freshly baked pie. "Yes, sir. That bay's a perfect spot to lay up and watch for Jap cruisers. We could dart out, hit 'em with the mark 13s and scurry back before they knew what happened."

Commander Hawkins leaned back and stared at him with a sneer. "We haven't seen a Jap heavy for weeks. We're barge hunters now. You know that Smitty."

Bosun's Mate Smith looked down, and nodded. "I know. I long for the old days though. Remember the Canal, sir? Darting out to a real target, a cruiser or frigate, putting fish in the water, and watching 'em run true. Damn, I miss that."

"You've forgotten more than you remember, Smitty. Half the time those damned torpedos failed to detonate, or ran in circles chasing us out there."

Smitty took the few steps to the dock, and put his arm around a Mark 13 torpedo. "Now we've got these new fish. That won't happen anymore. They're as reliable as the sun."

Commander Hawkins guffawed. "Not quite, but damned better than the Mark 8s, that's for sure. Only problem is, we got no more targets for 'em"

Smith lit up, "We should shoot one at the next barge we come across." He gazed longingly at the torpedo under his arm. "Oh my, I'd sure love to see that." He lifted his hands, and made a mock explosion sound.

Commander Hawkins grinned, imagining it. "That would be a sight to see, but getting close enough would be a formidable task. That's what we have those for." He gestured at the big 40mm gun on the back, the mounted twin fifty calibers on both sides, and the 20mm gun on the front. "Those babies do plenty damage, and we don't need to get too close to the little bastards."

The welcome addition of the heavy deck guns was made possible by switching out the large Mark 8 torpedos with the smaller and lighter Mark 13s. The firing tubes of the Mark 8s were also switched out for the lighter launching racks, simple devices that dumped the torpedos over the side where they're engines would kick on, and swim them to target. The mark 13s were smaller, but packed a bigger punch than the mark 8s. Their only drawback was their shorter range.

Over the past month their mission had changed, forcing them into the different gun configuration. No longer were they hunting the big capital ships of the Imperial Japanese Navy. Indeed, none had been spotted in these waters for weeks. Now their primary objectives were finding and sinking the large force of Japanese barges used to transport men and material to the increasingly cut-off forces on Bougainville.

At first, they thought the barges were anomalies, something they'd stumbled upon accidentally, but soon they were finding them night after night. Increasingly, they'd become more deadly as the Japanese mounted machine guns, and even mortar tubes.

"Gather the men, Smitty. We're going out tonight, and G2 seems to think we're gonna find some barges."

In minutes the open sided thatch hut attached to the dock was clustered with forty men. Most were shirtless, squinting in the midday sun. Some had been sleeping from last night's mission. Four of the boats had gone out just after dark. Standard operating procedure was to stick together loosely. Typically they'd be within a half mile of one another, checking in every half hour by radio.

Each boat had three, 12-cylinder Packard engines. They'd proved reliable but in combat conditions, they weren't serviced as often as they should have been, and crews often found themselves stranded. Often having to use only one engine to get themselves home. Working in teams kept the casualty lists lower.

Commander Hawkins stood before the men. He'd donned his shirt, which was already soaked through with sweat. "Boats 360, 345, 334 and 423 are patrolling tonight since you had the night off last night. The rest of you don't need to stick around."

He waited as officers and petty officers filed out. When things had settled down, he continued. "G2 thinks the Japs will try to drop troops off barges tonight to the north of us. Seems they had some spotters report movement.

"We don't know numbers, but the spotters are on high alert, and will relay any sightings as soon as they see them. Like always, we'll be johnny on the spot, and intercept and destroy them." With a bamboo stick, he pointed to the map he'd hung on the back wall of the thatch hut. "Despite what the map shows us, this area has a nice little bay we can use for cover. We'll patrol the coastline in pairs. If we run into trouble, this will be the rally point. We'll call it 'victor.'" The men scribbled on their sheets of paper with nubs of pencils. "We shove off at 1930 hours. Any questions?"

Lieutenant Mankowitz raised his hand. "We expecting any shore activity in that cove, sir?"

Commander Hawkins shook his head. "I was there last night with boat 345. It's unoccupied as of last night, but we'll use caution when approaching, just in case. We didn't head far back into it, but it was good deep water, don't think we need to worry about beaching." The man sat, and there were no more questions. "Be sure you have a full load of ammunition and top off your tanks. See you at 1930."

AT 1930 THE PT boats backed out of their moorings on Purata Island and made their way to deep water. They were side by side; the low profile boats looked menacing in the darkness. Their silhouettes bristled with weapons.

Once they were in deep water, they opened up the throbbing Packard engines, and the wooden boats accelerated and were on smooth planes within seconds. A PT boat in top condition could make forty knots, but the boats of Squadron 32 were well past their six hundred hour engine overhaul requirement, so were lucky to get thirty knots. They wouldn't be able to outrun a Japanese cruiser, but aside from that, they were the fastest boat on the water.

Commander Hawkins had piloted PT boats countless times, but he never failed to feel his pulse pound when he pushed the throttles and felt the boat get up to speed. He could've had command of a Cruiser or maybe something bigger, but there was nothing like the exhilaration he felt behind the wheel of a PT boat. They were small but deadly, packing more punch than any surface craft, pound for pound, in the US Navy.

The traditional navy men looked down on PT boats. To them, they were glorified speed boats. They referred to them derisively as the 'mosquito navy,' more a nuisance than a threat. Rather than take offense, the tightly knit crews took to the name with affection. They were small but caused endless irritation and if you were bitten by the wrong mosquito, fatal.

When they were a mile from Purata Island the commander said, "Signal the others we'll break into twos from here."

The signalman, Gramly, whose five-foot tall frame allowed him to move around the boat like a monkey, said, "Aye aye," and flash signaled the other boats. Soon PT 345 and PT 360 were in echelon moving closer to the coastline. PT 334 and 423 would stay further out looking for any Japanese naval boats. Commander Hawkins and Lieutenant Mankowitz would be barge hunting.

An hour passed without any contacts. Commander Hawkins found the cove from the night before. He cut his speed and nosed his way in. His men were ready on the guns. Bosun's mate Smith was on the rear 40mm cannon, Petty Officer Cutler on the forward 20mm. Smith kept his eyes on the starry night searching for enemy fighters. It was unlikely a fighter would find them at night. The fifty caliber gunner on the starboard side, Seaman Russell, kept his twin muzzles pointed into the jungle.

Hawkins had been piloting PT boat 345 for two months. He got along well with the crew while maintaining tight discipline. They worked well together. They'd seen plenty of action since getting their base on Pruata Island set up. Hawkins trusted every man with his life.

The engine was idling as they slipped into the cove. Hawkins turned the boat, bringing the 40mm to bear. Smith shifted his sights and waited for the flash of a rifle, but it never came. Hawkins didn't like coming to a spot he'd been to only the night before, but it was a good place to lay low and see if any Japanese barges passed. Boat 360 was also faced outward searching for targets. If something did pass by, they'd be able to see them, but the blackness behind them would make the PT boats invisible.

The men kept vigil on the guns while the rest of the crew used binoculars and searched the sea. Besides the constant tittering of night animals and insects from the jungle, the sea was quiet. The soft lapping of small waves rocking the boat was soothing, threatening to dull their senses.

Commander Hawkins called up his second in command, Ensign

Hanks. Hanks let the binoculars dangle and walked to Commander Hawkins's side. "Sir?" He was a thick man with tree trunk sized thighs from playing football at Ohio State. He'd been the leading rusher as a full-back when he quit school to join the fight against the Japanese. "If anything comes by be sure the men know we'll be letting them pass. I don't want to start a fight pinned against the jungle. Once they're past, we'll sneak out beyond them, then stick it to 'em."

"Aye, sir." He went off to relay the plan. Commander Hawkins watched him go. Hanks was a good second in command. He'd made a good showing of himself up to now. He had a good head for tactics and knew these boats like the back of his hand. By all rights, he should be in command of a boat of his own, but there weren't enough to go around. Even with near constant manufacturing, it was a daunting task to get the boats from stateside to the Solomon Islands.

He'd decided he'd let the Ensign take the wheel when they returned to base when Signalman Gramly whispered. "I see something." Keeping his binoculars to his eyes he pointed, and Ensign Hanks shuffled over to him, and following his finger brought his own binoculars to his eyes. At first, he didn't see anything, then there was a white flash from a boat's wake. He leaned forward, his heart rate doubling, causing his mouth to go dry. He scanned forward looking for another but didn't find anything. He went back to the barge; it looked to be a sixty footer bristling with what had to be machine guns. He thought he could also see helmets sticking up from the high walls.

He scanned back when Gramly whispered, "Another one behind," he paused, "make that two, no, three."

Hanks nodded as he confirmed the sightings. He waited for more, but after a minute decided there were only three. He made his report to Commander Hawkins. "Tell Gramly to signal boat 360. We leave in 3 minutes. We'll get to open water then attack them broadside with everything we've got."

"Aye aye, Commander."

The air seemed to turn electric as the men scrambled, readying the boat but mostly themselves, for impending action. Seaman Floyd on the port-side twin fifty pulled back the charging handle and took a deep breath. He'd be facing the enemy. He pictured himself raking the barge. There were three of them, which meant he needed to make quick work of the first boat. He doubted they'd have any trouble, particularly with the added firepower of the 40 and 20mm cannons.

The three minutes had passed before anyone was ready. Commander Hawkins nudged the throttles forward. The increase in the Packard engine's throb was barely noticeable, but to him it sounded like fireworks. *The Japs engines will mask the sound.* He knew there was no way they'd be heard; they'd have complete surprise.

Ensign Hanks had his binoculars up. "I've still got them in sight, at least the tail end charlie. They haven't altered course, still hugging the bank making eight to ten knots, sir."

Hawkins didn't respond but put more power to the engines. Now they were gliding along at ten knots. When they passed the cove inlet, the gunners instinctively shifted their muzzles to starboard in case there was another group of barges they hadn't seen. To be caught between two barge forces could prove disastrous. Once away from the cove they shifted their weapons back to the three enemy barges. They couldn't see them in the gloom, but they knew they were out there, close.

Hawkins led PT 360 out until he figured they were two hundred yards from shore then he turned to parallel the barges' course. Lieutenant Mankowitz would be closer to shore on PT 345's port-side and a little back, assuring both boats had clear fields of fire.

Without being asked, Ensign Hanks kept Hawkins appraised. "I've still got their wakes; we're gaining slowly. They haven't changed course or speed. We'll be broadside to them in approximately six minutes, sir."

Hawkins nodded his head, then had a thought. *Wonder where they're headed?* "Any sign they've spotted us, Ensign?"

Hanks kept scanning them, "No sir. We'll take 'em by surprise."

Commander Hawkins made his decision. "Tell Gramly to signal 360. We're tailing them to wherever they're going. Follow my lead."

Hanks took the glasses from his eyes and looked back at his commander. He hesitated for an instant then said, "Aye aye, sir." He ran forward and relayed the message to Gramly who quickly flashed the message. Lieutenant Mankowitz had the sense not to flash back but decreased speed acknowledging his intent to follow.

Ensign Hanks resumed his post at the commander's side and brought the binoculars up. Commander Hawkins said, "The instant you see anything that looks like they've seen us, we'll open fire." He brought the throttle down to match the barges speed.

"Aye aye, sir." Despite the pleasant sea breeze, Ensign Hanks started to sweat. He concentrated on the barges, trying to distinguish individuals, but they were invisible against the jungle. All he could see were the wakes. The first sign of being spotted would be tracer rounds lancing towards them.

~

THE CREW DIDN'T MAKE a sound as they traveled along the coast. Every gun muzzle aimed towards the barges except the starboard side twin fifty manned by Seaman Russell. He kept watch out to sea scanning for any enemy ships. He couldn't help glancing over his shoulder though.

Ten long minutes passed, and it seemed they were invisible to the barges. They were within 10 miles of the beachhead at Empress Augustus Bay. Commander Hawkins knew the barges would be at their final destination soon. They wouldn't have enough time to get the barges back to safe water before daylight unless they turned around soon. Traveling by day would almost certainly end with American planes strafing them.

He glanced at his watch and pulled his sleeve back to expose the luminescent dials when the world exploded in sound and light. He instinctively ducked.

"Open fire, open fire!" yelled Ensign Hanks. The streaking tracers lancing towards them were met with their own tracers. They met in the middle, and for an instant it looked like they were connected by a light bridge.

Seaman Floyd had been waiting for the barges to open fire, but when they did, he was taken by surprise. It only took an instant to recover. He depressed the top triggers and felt the satisfying chug of both barrels sending hot metal at the Japs. The tracers blinded him, but he kept the barrels steady and walked them through the first barge. Every fifth .50 caliber round was a tracer, making it easy to adjust fire. The barge was being torn apart with the massive firepower bearing down. Suddenly it flashed, and a yellow explosion lit up everything around it for a hundred feet. He saw debris flying through the air.

He kept the trigger depressed and moved to the next barge. This one had all guns blazing, and he could see the big tracer rounds coming at him. They looked like glowing beach balls. He hunched his shoulders as he heard the thumping sound of bullets hitting the metal combing of his turret. He gritted his teeth and depressed the trigger harder as if that would give his bullets more power.

For an instant he felt he was battling alone, trying to suppress and kill the Japanese all by himself. Soon he could see the 20 and 40mm cannons were tearing huge chunks out of the side of the barge. The Japanese must have added steel siding to this one. It sparked, and ricochets buzzed straight up like flaming turtles. He kept sweeping past the doomed barge and engaged the third and final one, but as his bullets started to hit, it exploded, obliterating everything inside. The concussion of the blast swept over the water making waves and slammed into PT 345 knocking the wind from several men.

Seaman Floyd felt the concussion through his eyeballs. He ducked down, the barrel pointing skyward sending a short stream of tracer fire into the black sky. Through the ringing in his ears, he could hear the cease fire order. A quiet passed through, only the sound of the engines purring at five knots. Ensign Hanks yelled, "Sound off." When no one responded he yelled louder, "Sound off, Goddamit!"

He listened for voices and was just about to call out again when he heard, "Cutler here."

"Russell here."

"Floyd here."

"Smitty here."

Hanks kept a running list in his head. The men tending the engines were all accounted for as Machinist 1st mate Calvin poked his head up and said, "All accounted for below decks."

With himself and the Commander, thirteen men had chimed in. He shook his head. *Where's the fourteenth man?* He went through the names in his head seeing each man's face. He was missing their signalman, Gramly. Nausea suddenly gripped his gut. He yelled. "Gramly, where's Gramly." No answer.

Beside him, Commander Hawkins tensed, and ordered, "Find Gramly! If he's on this ship, I want him found now." They searched all eighty feet, but there was no sign of Signalman Gramly. He got on the radio. "Boat 360 we're missing a man, cut power and circle back with spotlights."

Both boats turned lazily back the way they'd come. The powerful spotlights swept the sea. One of the biggest hazards on a PT boat during combat was getting thrown when the boat made a sudden turn. Commander Hawkins prayed that was what happened. He pictured finding the diminutive man cursing as he bobbed with his life preserver. He'd never hear the end of the ribbing.

Five minutes later his fantasy was squashed. Petty Officer Cutler yelled out pointing, "There, something's over there floating."

Commander Hawkins followed the light beam and saw a body bobbing in a green life preserver. He was facedown. When they were ten feet away, Bosun's Mate Smith dove in and came up beside Gramly. In the white light, he turned the man onto his back, hoping he was only unconscious. There was nothing left of Gramly's face except an eyeball floating at the end of a ligament. Smith reared back and vomited into the sea, the bile quickly spread like a drop of oil.

He recovered and put his arm under Gramly's armpits and stroked for the boat. The men were there, and they carefully lifted him onto the deck and laid him beside a Mark 13 torpedo. Smith was pulled in a second later. He stood dripping wet, staring down at Gramly. Petty Officer Cutler found a wool blanket and covered the man's body, hiding the gruesome wound. The men stood around staring.

Commander Hawkins gave the controls to Ensign Hanks who took them without looking him in the eye. Hawkins gritted his teeth. *I should've engaged them first.* There was little doubt based on where they found him, that he'd died within the first few seconds of the firefight.

Hawkins went to the body and kneeled beside him. He took his helmet off and dropped it at his side. He put his hand on Gramly's shoulder and whispered, “I’m sorry, so sorry.” His shoulders slumped and he bit his knuckle. “Dammit,” he said.

The men stared at their commander. He was tough as nails, and that’s the way they liked him. He’d lost men before but he hadn’t shown outward emotion. The crew shifted and looked one another in the eye. Petty Officer Cutler barked, “Back to your stations.” When they hesitated, he yelled, “Now!”

11

When Sergeant Carver told Lt. Swan about using the PT boats to insert them far enough south to get behind the Japanese lines, he discounted it as too complicated. But the more he banged his head against the problem without a solution, the more he warmed to the idea.

Sending the men south on foot would add days to the mission, days he didn't have. Lieutenant Swan liked the idea, but didn't know if the brass would. Nor did he know if the PT boats were even available. They were part of the Navy, what business did the Army have with them? *Guess it can't hurt to ask.*

Asking brought up another hurdle. Swan hadn't told Regiment about sending the squad out the first time. He had the freedom to do what he thought best for his position, but now he'd need to run the whole thing by them. He doubted they'd interfere, in fact they'd be thrilled with the information, but it was another step out of his control.

He'd sent a runner with a detailed note of his intentions. He'd received a reply the same day. They'd look into it and let him know. Lieutenant Swan's shoulders slumped when he read the reply. They might as well have said, 'don't call us we'll call you,' like an unwanted salesman. He decided to move onto other projects, like making his defenses stronger. In the morning he organized work teams and would have the men digging new holes and improving old ones with more sandbags. He had two platoons now, which would make defending Hill 260 more manageable.

Around noon a runner came from Regiment. Swan was surprised he got an answer at all, or maybe this was about something else. The corporal said the brass wanted his men assembled and on the beach by the end of the day. More good news, four Sherman tanks would arrive to help shore up his defenses.

Swan called Sergeant Carver, who was overseeing a group of sweating soldiers filling sandbags. He was covered in a thick layer of dust and grime. Swan gave him the news. The corner of Carver's mouth turned down, and he nodded. "When do we leave, sir?"

Swan slapped his back, and a dust cloud erupted like from a dirty rug. "Right now. Assemble the team you chose and gather your gear. We leave in an hour. The corporal there," he pointed at the runner who was looking around the base as if an attack would happen any second, "Has some drivers with jeeps to take us to the beach."

Sergeant Carver nodded and turned to tell the men. Despite Lt. Swan's obvious delight, Carver felt a heavy doom settle over him. *Another damned patrol. Thought I was in a line company, not recon.* He found Corporal O'Connor who was holding a bag while Private Denn scooped dirt. "Give it a rest you guys." The men slumped to the ground and guzzled water from canteens. "O'Connor, follow me." He walked ten paces away and thumbed towards the command bunker. "Looks like MacArthur, AKA Lieutenant Swan got the recon mission approved."

O'Connor spit a chunk of dirt off his tongue. "No shit? When we leave?"

"An hour. Get the men we decided on and make sure they get their shit packed tight. I have no idea how long we'll be out there. We've got jeeps waiting at the base of the hill for us."

~

THEY PULLED into regimental headquarters a few minutes past three.

The jeep ride left them jarred to the core. The mud made for interesting driving. The drivers were forced to find harder ground and would fish-tail and bounce along from side to side along the narrow track. The tanks that were at the base of Hill 260 had chewed up the road, making it look like chocolate pudding.

Carver was impressed though. Even with the mud and mauled road, the drivers were skilled enough to get them to the beachhead without getting stuck. The last thing the men wanted to do was get out in the slop and push.

Lieutenant Swan was in the lead jeep, and when it swung in front of a faded green tent at HQ, he stepped out a second too early and had to run to keep from falling on his face. He almost recovered, but he tripped on a rope holding the tent secure and sprawled out in front of the entrance.

Feet appeared at his nose, and he looked up to see Captain Flannigan looking down at him in disgust. He had his hands in fists against his hips. "Still as athletic as always, I see. Get out of the dirt Lieutenant."

Swan leaped up and saluted his company commander. "Sorry, sir."

Captain Flannigan ignored him and looked at the men piling out of the jeeps. They hadn't had time to clean up after the work detail, and even if they had their second sets of fatigues were just as filthy. "Jesus Christ, Swan. This is the crack unit you wanna send behind enemy lines?" he took a step closer and recognized Sergeant Carver, Corporal O'Connor and a few of the others. They put up crisp salutes despite their uniforms. He saluted back and spun around to face Lt. Swan. "Would've thought you'd pick Sergeant Milo to lead it."

Lieutenant Swan squinted and shook his head. "Sergeant Carver's got a lot of experience doing this sort of thing on…"

He was interrupted, "I know all about the canal and the silver stars, Swan. How much you think a man can take? Carver's tough, but Milo's fresh. Carver could be one casualty away from the nut-house." He spoke as if Carver wasn't five feet behind him. Carver didn't flinch just stared at the back of his head and concentrated on his breathing. "You've heard of battle fatigue, no doubt?" without waiting for an answer he spun back around to look directly into the Carver's dark eyes. "You got battle fatigue Sergeant?"

Sergeant Carver extended his chest and bellowed, "No sir."

Captain Flannigan put his hands behind his back and walked around the men, who stood in loose formation. O'Connor rolled his eyes. He didn't like being treated like some raw recruit, particularly by this Ivy League asshole. O'Connor looked sideways at Sergeant Carver beside him. He could tell by his rippling jaw line that he didn't like it either.

Lieutenant Swan spoke up in a nervous voice, "I need to be excused, sir."

Captain Flannigan looked at him like he was out of his mind. "What's so urgent, Lieutenant?" He said lieutenant like the word tasted like dog shit.

Swan bounced from foot to foot. "Where's the latrine?" Captain Flannigan saw the beads of sweat forming on Swan's forehead. He pointed, and Swan ran around the corner with clenched butt cheeks.

There was a moment of silence while the men watched their officer running like a stiff flagpole. Captain Flannigan turned back to them and shook his head. O'Connor's face was turning purple, and Private Willy was shaking his head side to side with a crooked grin. Flannigan threw up his hands and walked back into the tent. The squad burst into laughter.

THE SQUAD of twelve men plus Lieutenant Swan were put up in an unoccupied tent. The cots felt like luxury after sleeping in foxholes. For the first time in many nights, the men slept soundly in the comfort that came with life in the rear.

At 0600 they woke to the sounds of a blaring horn over a loudspeaker. They sat up looking confused; then they heard the distant 'whump' of enemy artillery landing on Piva Airfield to the north. They were up and scrambling out the barracks tent running towards the slit trenches they'd found before going to bed. They slid in half dressed clutching their M1s.

The artillery stopped after a few more explosions. They waited for the all clear signal. It came a few minutes later, and the men went back to the barracks to finish dressing. A corporal poked his head in, "You fellas sleep okay?" The corporal had a face that wouldn't need a razor for another five years.

Corporal O'Connor was closest to the tent entrance. "Yeah, until the rude wakeup call." The corporal looked confused. O'Connor pointed east, "You know the artillery strike?" the corporal nodded suddenly understanding. "How often does that happen?"

"Everyday at least once but usually more. They're shooting from the high mountains to the north. They can't see what they're shooting at, but sometimes they get lucky and hit a parked plane. It was worse when the Marines first got here. They cleaned them out a little, but now they're coming back I guess."

Lieutenant Swan stood up and approached the corporal who was surprised to find an officer bunking with the enlisted men. He snapped off a sloppy salute. Swan said, "You here to take us to the PT boats?"

The corporal looked confused, "No sir. You're to report to HQ for a briefing." Lieutenant Swan dismissed the corporal. He turned to Sergeant Carver. "You and O'Connor come with me, the rest of you find the chow line but be ready to roll soon."

They walked across the muddy ground to the headquarters tent. A sentry was standing outside with his M1 slung over his shoulder. He eyed the three men. "Lieutenant Swan?" Swan nodded. The soldier stepped aside and let them enter.

The sides of the tent were pulled up, but even with the added air flow, it was stifling inside. They started sweating.

Standing with his back to them was a tall officer looking at a large map of Bougainville Island. Beside him was the bullish figure of Captain Flannigan.

Lieutenant Swan cleared his throat, and they both turned. The three visitors saluted smartly. The tall man had graying hair and light blue eyes with deep creases at the edges, and the silver eagle on his shoulders of a full colonel. He returned the salute and gave them a once over. "So, you're the men going to find the enemy road?"

Lieutenant Swan swallowed, but his mouth was too dry. Standing in front of the regimental commander had him speechless. Colonel Canfield was a legend amongst the troops. Swan squeaked, "These men are going, I'm just along to help with logistics." He stammered, "It was my idea. I sent them off Hill 260 first, but the Japs are too thick."

The colonel glanced at the captain standing beside him. He stood with his meaty arms across his chest.

The colonel continued. "It's a good idea, lieutenant and I think you're onto something sending them with the PT boys. They've been busy busting up enemy barges most nights." He paced a step to his right. "Using them for this type of insertion is risky. It'll have to be at night, and they'll have to get close enough to drop you off. They don't pull much draft, but there are shallow rocks and reefs all around this island. The risk is grounding them. You don't want to be stuck when the sun comes up. We've thinned out the Jap Navy, but there are enough troops around to still be dangerous."

Lieutenant Swan nodded, wondering why the colonel was telling him all this. If he didn't think it was worth the risk, why were they here?

The colonel continued. "I've passed it by the PT commander, a good officer named, Hawkins. He's in command of the eight boats we've got, and he thinks he can pull it off. He'll get as close as he can then send you off with a crewman and a rubber boat." He looked squarely at Sergeant Carver, "You have any small boat maneuvering training?"

Carver stood straighter and shook his head, "No sir. But I've paddled around a lot of lakes with my father. I can handle a boat, sir."

Corporal O'Connor chimed in. "Me too, sir. Canoes and some row boats, mostly on rivers."

Colonel Canfield nodded. "Well the PT men'll be able to put that experience to work." He pointed at the map behind him. "The PT base is on the other side of Puruata Island." He pointed to the small island off the coast from where they were standing. "They run patrols most nights and usually come in contact with Jap barges trying to reinforce their stranded troops."

Carver looked confused. "Barges sir?"

The Colonel looked him in the eye. "That's right. The Japs are cut off from their main supply lines. Our main forces have bypassed this island cutting off one hundred thousand front line troops. They're slowly starving over there." He gestured east. "They'll wither and hopefully surrender." He shook his head. "That probably won't happen, but at least we've taken them out of the fight." He paused letting it sink in. "So the Japs are trying to resupply their troops on this side of the mountain range with barges from Biak Island to the north and Buin from the south."

The three soldiers listened with interest. They knew the basic strategy, but it coming from the colonel shed new light on why they were there.

Colonel Canfield squinted and crossed his arms. "I think inserting you men to the south is our best option. I don't think getting there undetected will be a problem. I'm more worried about getting you back. The only way I can see is set a date and approximate time for pickup. The PT boats can't sit in one place night after night waiting for you."

Carver and O'Connor exchanged worried glances. Lieutenant Swan raised his hand, and Colonel Canfield nodded to him like he was a student. "Sir, the men could return to Hill 260 directly." He pointed to the map and approached. "If we dropped them off here and they traveled northeast to the mountains then cut north until they find the road, they'd be closer to our line than the coast." He motioned to Carver. "They did it once before."

The colonel nodded. "That sound okay to you, Sergeant?"

Carver looked the map over thinking about the mud, the thick jungle, the enemy soldiers. The distance to the mountains was only eight miles, they could walk that in less than an hour in ideal conditions, but things were far from ideal. He figured the round trip, assuming they found the road where Swan thought it would be, would cover nearly twenty miles. It might as well be a hundred. "That's a lot of ground to cover, sir, but I think going to Hill 260 instead of back to the coast is the better option."

Colonel Canfield heard the hesitation in Carver's voice. Lieutenant

Swan did too. He blurted, "They've done it before on Guadalcanal, with worse circumstances."

The Colonel ignored him. "It's up to you, Sergeant. I'm not ordering you to do it; this'll be volunteer only."

Lieutenant Swan started to speak but thought better of it when he caught the colonel's withering glance. Carver looked at O'Connor who shrugged. Carver said, "Yeah we can do it, but I want enough control to scrub the mission if it's not working out."

Colonel Canfield nodded and without looking to Swan said, "Absolutely. You're in charge."

~

THE PARTICULARS of the mission were worked out by noon. They'd be leaving the following night. They had the rest of the day to consolidate their gear and rest.

At 1500, the squad went down to the beach and met a small motor barge. Carver wanted to meet the PT boat crews before the mission, and Captain Flannigan had arranged for transport to Puruata Island.

They waded out to the barge through warm crystal clear water that lapped against their legs. Sergeant Carver thought what a nice place this part of the world would be if it wasn't full of Japanese soldiers trying to kill him.

The boat driver was a grimy sailor who gave him a half-assed salute. Normally he would have put the man in his place, but he wasn't in the mood. He saw Private Willy standing in ankle deep water with his gun over his shoulder.

He gestured for him to hurry up, but Willy shook his head, "Sorry, Sarge. Go without me. I forgot to pack something, and I don't wanna forget it." The entire squad looked back at him. He waved, "See you tonight." He turned and splashed back to shore.

Carver looked at O'Connor who shrugged, and said, "Beats the shit outta me."

The boat ride took a few minutes. Carver could see the cigar-shaped island was bigger than it looked on a map. They motored around the east side, giving him a good view of Cape Torokina, and it's vital airfield. There weren't any air activities happening at the moment but he could see the outlines of fighters parked in the shade of the palm trees. He tried to find Hill 260 to the north but couldn't pick it out from all the other low hills.

The barge chugged around the corner and soon sidled up to a large docking area filled with PT boats. Carver was awed by the long lethal looking boats. Their low profile, bristling with machine guns and long torpedoes along the side was impressive. The boats looked to be in good shape. The Navy crews obviously took good care of them. At the moment there were no sailors in sight. *Must be ducking the heat of the day,* he thought.

The barge bumped against the dock between two PTs, and O'Connor hopped out and held the barge in place as the sailor shut off the engine and tied the stern and bow to the dock. The squad hopped out onto the dock. They'd brought their weapons with them, but nothing else.

The sailor led them to the small buildings just off the dock. They were wood structures with Army green canvas covers. The sailor pulled a flap aside and gestured for the squad to enter. Carver ducked down and paused to let his eyes adjust to the darker interior. There were folding chairs set in a line facing a large chalkboard with indecipherable drawings. It reminded him of the highschool locker room he'd sat in before football games back in South Dakota. The sailor waited until they were all inside then said, "Have a seat, I'll let the C.O. know you're here."

Sergeant Carver didn't sit, but the rest of the men found chairs, unslung rifles and talked amongst themselves.

A minute passed then the front flap opened, and in came Ensign Hanks followed by Commander Hawkins. Sergeant Carver barked, "Ten-hut!" and the men snapped to attention.

Commander Hawkins stepped past Ensign Hanks and stepped in front of the chalkboard with his hands clasped behind his back. He wore a faded brown top with a frayed collar tucked into pants with a pleat that had lost its crispness a long time before. "At ease, soldiers." The men sat on the metal folding chairs. "I'm Commander Hawkins, and this is Ensign Hanks. I've seen the plans for your insertion. I'll be honest with you, we've never done anything like this." He paused and looked the men over. "I don't see any reason it won't work, but I want to do a reconnaissance of the drop off point first. The maps of this place aren't too good as I'm sure you're aware, and the reefs surrounding the island are even less well marked. Since we're not dropping you off until tomorrow night, we'll do the recon tonight."

Sergeant Carver asked, "Is it a good idea to go to the same area twice in a row? Basic patrolling procedure is to vary your movements. I'm not a boat captain, but I'd think the same would apply."

Hawkins exchanged a glance with Ensign Hanks. Hawkins answered. "That's certainly true for foot patrols, and normally I'd say the same about boat patrols, but in this case, I think the information we'll get outweighs the risks. If we come under fire or see the enemy, we may have to reconsider the drop-off point anyway." Sergeant Carver nodded his understanding.

Commander Hawkins continued. "One of my men has come down with a nasty bug, can't stay off the toilet. He won't be able to patrol with us tonight." Carver and O'Connor exchanged glances. "Every boat's going out tonight, so I can't pull from the other crews. Any of you men willing to fill in? It'd be in a gunner's position. I assume you've trained on the fifty?"

O'Connor shot to his feet. "I'll go." He looked down at Carver, "Unless you wanted to Sarge."

Carver looked up at O'Connor who looked like a school boy on Christmas morning. "Fine with me." He shook his head and addressed Commander Hawkins, "He can shoot the fifty."

Hawkins gestured to Ensign Hanks. "The Ensign will show you around the boat. It'll be tight quarters tomorrow night. It'll be important for you men to know where to be and what to do if we make contact. Mostly you'll just stay out of the way." He looked over the men and focused on O'Connor. "You may as well stay here, Corporal. We'll be shoving off at 1700 and be gone most of the night."

12

O'Connor reported to PT boat 345 at 1600. The day's heat was stifling but would start turning more manageable as the sun descended towards the sea. He was on the starboard side twin fifty caliber machine gun. It took a few minutes to become familiar with the weapon, particularly how to move it within the mount. He rotated the wheel feeling the ease of movement.

He met the crew. They were scruffy but had a way of going about their jobs that gave him confidence. He knew they were veterans even if he hadn't seen the eight barges and half a destroyer painted on the side of the pilot's cabin, marking kills. He felt comfortable going into combat with them, but nervous at the prospect of meeting the enemy in such an exposed craft.

He sat inside the metal cupola behind the fifty, but he felt exposed and naked not being able to dive behind a tree or into a foxhole.

The throaty sound of all eight PT boat's engines starting filled the evening air. He could smell the one hundred octane fuel as it heated and burned moving the pistons in their chambers.

O'Connor sat in the worn seat of the gun mount with his hands on the gun handles. As the boat edged away from the dock, he saw Sergeant Carver watching. His arms crossed his chest and a half chewed stogie was on the side of his mouth. O'Connor waved, and Carver nodded.

Soon PT boat 345 was in open water, and Commander Hawkins pushed the throttles. O'Connor couldn't help grinning at the sensation of power and speed as the boat went up on a plane and started to glide across the light chopped sea. He'd been on lumbering transports and landing crafts plenty of times. He wanted off them as soon as he was on, but the PT boat was a thrill. He let out a whoop before he could contain himself. He looked back at the commander who grinned and gave him a thumbs up. Ensign Hanks shook his head and leaned in to say something to the commander.

O'Connor went back to searching the horizon. *What the hell am I looking for anyway?* He decided he'd man his post and do what they told him to do, nothing more.

They went out to sea and waited for evening. As the boat drifted at idle, O'Connor watched the sun melt into the sea. The orange color seemed to dissipate and become a part of the water, like butter melting in a heated pan. The warm breeze and the view made him forget there was a war on. As darkness descended, the short-lived fantasy came to an end.

Ensign Hanks growled, "Alright men stay sharp were heading down the coast." The engines pushed the boat along at a steady 10 knots. The darkness was complete, and stars shone brilliantly above as the PT boat made it's way east a half mile from the Bougainville coastline. They zigzagged to throw off any enemy subs. There hadn't been a sub sighting for months but there was no point taking chances.

An hour passed before the commander turned the boat toward the coast line. O'Connor saw the signalman flash a message to the trailing PT and they turned in unison. Ensign Hanks said, "Stay sharp, watch for barges." When the island seemed to be right in front of them, Hanks said, "Smitty get to the bow with the sounding line."

"Aye." Bosun's mate Smith went to the bow of the boat with a coil of rope with a 30-pound weight dangling from the end. Once there, he strung the line through an anchor point and ran the rope down with the weight leading. He counted in his head as each fathom marker on the rope passed the anchor point. The weight hit bottom after three marks. The water was eighteen feet deep.

He whispered to Petty Officer Cutler, "We're at three fathoms." The information was relayed back to Commander Hawkins and Ensign Hanks. As they moved forward, BM Smith continued to call out the depth. When they were twenty yards from the shoreline, he called out, "All stop."

Commander Hawkins idled the engine and added power to the reverse engine bringing the boat to a full stop. "Take over, Ensign."

Hanks took the controls. "I have her, sir." He turned the rudder and goosed the engine a touch turning the boat parallel to the shoreline. He kept his hands on the throttles ready to put in full power if they came under attack. The other PT boat had stopped to cover their approach and was loitering 50 yards off their stern searching for targets.

They sat at idle as Commander Hawkins walked to the bow. Bosun's mate Smith still kneeled, the coil of rope in his leathery hands. Hawkins put a hand on his shoulder. "Figure we're twenty yards out?" He could see Smith's head nod, but he didn't take his eyes off the coastline. "I'll mark this spot on the map, looks like as good a place as any to drop off the ground pounders."

Commander Hawkins could feel Smith's tense shoulders. "I don't like being this close to shore any more than you do." He turned to move back to the pilot's seat. Without turning, Smitty backed up pulling the rope with him. He secured it and went back to his station beside the signalman. His sidearm was on his belt, but he felt better feeling the snub nose of his M3 grease gun.

The engines went a decibel higher as they made slow progress away from the shore. The blackness of the island was still ominous. They'd only gone thirty yards when the night behind them lit up with tracer fire. The sound came a second later, the ripping of a Japanese Nambu machine gun.

Everyone aboard ducked. Corporal O'Connor knew the distinctive sound immediately and swung his fifty caliber machine gun around to face the line of tracers. His breathing came in short bursts, thinking the tracers would find him in his lightly armored cupola.

An instant later, he realized the tracers weren't directed at him, but the other PT boat. He could see sparks as the rounds found metal. Some of the tracers bounced straight up in ricochet, but most sliced into the mahogany side planks of PT 278. They were catching hell.

It wasn't long before PT 278 recovered and started returning fire. The tracer fire increased from both sides, the light-show meeting in the middle. The fire was thick, and it lit up the ocean.

O'Connor couldn't tell what was firing, but he knew it wasn't coming from the island. The Japanese had sneaked up on them in a boat. He saw white water around PT 278's bow and realized they'd put the hammer down and were speeding away from the threat with guns blazing.

O'Connor had a bead on the Japanese muzzle fire but hadn't received an order to fire. He caressed the trigger and licked his dry lips.

He fell to the side when the PT's engines went to full power. He struggled to keep his position, but when the order to open fire came, he wasn't ready. He struggled to right himself. They were still heading straight out to sea. He figured they'd turn towards the injured PT any second.

He steadied himself and depressed the trigger. The flash from the fifty was intense. He squinted and continued hammering the big shells out. His fire was low, he could see great geysers of whitewater erupting, obscuring his view of the Japanese. He adjusted his aim slightly, walking the rounds into the yellow flashes.

A second later the PT boat swung to starboard directly at the enemy boat. O'Connor swung the fifty, but the cupola wouldn't let him swing the muzzle into the boat. As the target went out of his muzzle sight, he released the trigger. The twin muzzles glowed a red hot orange.

He raised his head to watch as the big twenty-millimeter gun opened up. Petty Officer Cutler was standing behind the gun, braced and hammering rounds into the now visible Japanese Barge. He expertly walked the rounds up and down the length of the vessel. The barge came apart like a cookie jar hitting a concrete floor. O'Connor watched as silhouettes of helmeted Japanese troops were shredded and flung into the sea. It was over in seconds. Commander

Hawkins yelled for a cease-fire and the thumping twenty-millimeter stopped.

They kept their speed, still aiming straight for the sinking barge. O'Connor thought they were going to ram it, but at the last instant, Hawkins made a high speed ninety-degree turn to port. Seaman Floyd on the port-side fifty swept the smoldering remains of the barge. Tiny fires lit up floating debris and bodies.

They flashed by then turned back to sea. The faint phosphorescence from the fleeing PT 278 was like a trail in the dark. They soon came up alongside PT 278 and hailed them. Both vessels slowed and in the calm seas were able to tie to one another.

PT 278 had been hit hard in the first few seconds of the firefight and had suffered damage to the engine room. The hull had large holes in the planks. The lower holes had already been caulked stopping more sea water from coming in, but the reverse engine had taken multiple hits and didn't function. It wasn't vital for forward operations, but it would need at least a couple of days for repair.

None of the engine room crew were hit; they'd been near the bow in their makeshift chairs. If they'd been fussing over the engines as they normally were, there would have been casualties.

Once PT 278 was squared away, they continued patrolling. It was unusual for Japanese barges to be traveling alone. It was also unusual for a barge to take on a PT boat's superior firepower and maneuverability. Either they'd thought they could disable PT 278 before they knew what was happening or someone on the barge had opened fire in a panic.

They patrolled for two hours before turning back for home. O'Connor was tired. Being on constant vigil through the night was exhausting. He was far more on edge than he would have been in the jungle, an environment he was on intimate terms with. The wide open sea with its unknown dangers and sparse cover made him nervous.

The ride back was uneventful. They pulled into the docks of Puruata Island at 0400. The sky was still dark, but there was a hint of the coming day on the horizon. When the boat docked, he came out of the cupola he'd been sitting in for the past few hours and stepped onto the dock.

An immense feeling of relief swept through him, and he knew why sailors sometimes kissed the ground after being at sea for long periods of time. He'd only been out a couple of hours, and it was all he could do not to drop and give mother earth a sloppy kiss.

He stretched from side to side. He groaned as his stiff muscles protested. Commander Hawkins came up beside him. "You did well out there, Corporal."

O'Connor cringed not used to praise from the brass. He stammered, "Thank you, sir."

"We'll make a sailor out of you yet."

O'Connor gave him an exaggerated head shake, "No sir, no way." He thumbed towards the docked PT, "The boat's great, but I felt like I had a target painted on my chest. Give me the jungle with plenty of stuff to hide behind over that any day, sir."

Commander Hawkins laughed and slapped him on the back. "To each his own I guess."

Hawkins went past him grinning. O'Connor watched him go wondering at the commander's approach to enlisted men. O'Connor heard someone approaching from behind; he turned in time to see Ensign Hanks. O'Connor came to attention and snapped off a salute. He sneered back at him and saluted as he walked by without a word. O'Connor wondered at the different styles of leadership. He shrugged, *guess they sort of even each other out.*

13

O'Connor slept most of the day away. Private Willy woke him up at 1500. O'Connor hadn't slept that much since being on the island. He felt disoriented but rested. As he was wiping the sleep from his eyes, Private Willy asked, "So what're the boats like? They look fast."

He nodded, "They are. Faster than any boat I've ever been on by a long shot." Willy hung at the entrance of the tent fidgeting from foot to foot. "Something bothering you, Willy?"

He looked at O'Connor and tilted his helmet back. O'Connor thought he was the dirtiest human he'd ever come across. He kept his hygiene up the same as the other soldiers, but he was the kind of guy that always looked dirty even after showering. Private Willy shrugged, "They just seem kinda on the smallish side."

O'Connor stared. If he wasn't mistaken he thought Willy looked scared, but that couldn't be, he'd seen Private Willy charge Japanese machine gun nests like it was nothing. O'Connor thought he had a death wish, in fact.

He probed, "Well yeah, smaller than anything we've been on I guess, but that's kinda the point. They're harder for the Japs to find and they pack quite a wallop."

Before he could find out what was bothering him, Private Willy spun on his heel and left the tent. He called back, "Briefing in an hour at the docks."

O'Connor nodded and continued lacing up his jungle boots. He'd been on the island less than a month, and already they were faded and starting to come apart at the seams. The constant mud and wetness wreaked havoc on all their gear.

~

THE SQUAD SAT on the rickety folding chairs while Commander Hawkins went over how the insertion would go. "We'll leave here at our normal time of 1700 and head out to sea where we'll split up.

"Boat 278 isn't ready for duty so will stay in dock along with boat 304. Boats 291 and 300 will patrol together to the west. The rest of us, that's four boats, will patrol east to the insertion point.

"We'll split the GIs up amongst boat 345 and 360. We'll have the others cover us while we slip in close then ferry them in the rubber boats." He paused looking around at the intently listening men.

The Navy men were in the back, most standing with their arms crossed. "We'll be cramped with the extra men, so we'll stay in the middle. If we encounter any Jap barges, we'll let them go unless we can't avoid them."

Voices rose from the back. Commander Hawkins held up his hands. "I know, I know. I don't want to let any of the little bastards get away either, but getting these men to shore undetected is our mission." He stared the Navy men down. "Once that's done, it's business as usual.

"If we're compromised on the way in we'll have to abort and find another suitable spot tomorrow night, so let's get it done tonight and get back to what we all want to be doing…killing Japs."

The men nodded their understanding and when there were no questions the Navy men dispersed. The soldiers remained seated as Lieutenant Swan took the front.

Commander Hawkins gestured that he had the floor. Swan nodded and fixed his already combed hair. In his best rendition of a hardened combat soldier, he addressed them. "Men," he squeaked, "this is an important mission. One which, if successful, will go a long way to saving many of your fellow soldier's lives." He paused looking to see if his words had any effect. Most of the men were staring at their boots, or running their hands through their hair, or inspecting their weapons. "I have no doubt you'll do your duties and perform admirably."

He coughed then stood up straighter. "I will be tagging along for the insertion but won't be going ashore with you." Sergeant Carver sat up straight; this was news to him; unwelcome news. "As much as I'd like to join you inland my duties back on Hill 260 are more pressing." He looked the men over; they were watching now. "I'll see you when you return." He nodded and moved off to the side.

Sergeant Carver got to his feet and in an angry growl said, "Dismissed."

~

AT 1700 THE men were crammed onto the two PT boats. O'Connor crouched beside Private Willy who looked white as a sheet. "You okay? You look like you're gonna be sick."

Private Willy squinted and spat onto the deck. In his Midwestern nasal tone, he said, "This fucking boat's too damned small. What's to keep a guy from falling off?"

"What the hell Willy? You've been on plenty of boats, hell you crossed most of the world in one. What's the matter with you?"

Private Willy looked nervously over the port side towards the water. He leaned in close to O'Connor's ear and whispered, "I, I can't swim."

O'Connor thought he hadn't heard correctly. "What? Can't swim? Can't swim?" he shook his head. "How'd you deal with all the boat rides we've been on?"

Willy grabbed his arm and squeezed, "Not so loud, asshole." He looked around, but no one was paying any attention. "Those boats were big, hardly felt like we were on one at all. I could deal with that, but these little tin cans are like toys. The wind could tip 'em over for chrissakes."

O'Connor wiped the smile that kept trying to creep onto his face.

He'd never seen Willy scared, even during the most harrowing firefights, he was as cool a soldier as he'd ever met. He leaned in, "Look, I was on this same boat last night. They're solid. The crew's solid too, really know their business."

Willy scowled and interrupted, "They're squids, swabbies. They can't be trusted. They'll get us all killed, me especially."

"Just stay close to the center and keep your head down. In the dark, you won't even notice the size. Just think about something else."

He sneered. "Easy for you to say, you can swim. If you go out, you'll just bob along until someone picks you up, me?"

O'Connor patted the life preserver he was wearing. "That's what this thing's for, as long as you're wearing it, you can't sink. It'll float you."

Private Willy guffawed, "This thing? It doesn't look like much and what if it gets ripped off me? What then?"

O'Connor shrugged. "Then be glad you're not live shark bait."

Willy's face turned another shade of white. "Jesus, Corporal, you're a real help. A real ray of sunshine."

O'Connor cinched up Willy's life jacket. "There, you're good to go."

PT 345 WAS TRAILING PT 314 at a comfortable one hundred yards. The two other boats were in echelon behind them. They were a mile off the coast moving at a steady twelve knots to the east.

The sea wasn't as calm as the day before and with each swell, boat 314 went out of sight until they crested the next wave. The constant up and down sent sprays of warm sea water into the faces of the soldiers. Their helmets kept most of their heads dry, but the rest of their bodies were soaked. The breeze was warm, but in combination with the water, they were starting to shiver.

To make matters worse Private Palmer got sick and spewed his guts onto the deck. The vomit was swept away quickly with the next wave but not before the smell assaulted their noses. Soon every soldier was adding their guts to the growing pile.

Sergeant Carver was not pleased. His men were taking a beating before they'd even gotten to the insertion point. He'd have a group of sick, dehydrated soldiers when he needed them to be at their best.

He stood from his crouching position and in the dark found his way to the commander's seat. He expected Commander Hawkins but instead found Ensign Hanks. "How long til we head in?"

The dark silhouette of Ensign Hanks said, "We'll turn in about ten minutes, then we'll slow and get you in close after we clear the shoreline." Hanks looked towards the dark shapes of the soldiers. "How're they holding up?"

Carver shook his head, "Not well. Most are sick."

Ensign Hanks nodded. "Yeah, I can smell that. Tell them to take breaths in through their mouths and out through their noses."

"Does that help?"

"Not really, but it'll take their minds off the smell."

Ten minutes later the engines quieted, and the boats turned towards the dark shape of the island. Sergeant Carver had no idea how far they'd come, but it seemed like many miles.

PT boat 345 and 360 hung back while the two escort boats went ahead to scout the shoreline. The bobbing of the boat was somewhat better, and the men weren't throwing up anymore. *Probably nothing left.*

Time inched along. The warm night air soon had the men sweating again. The smell of vomit mixed with sweat, and he breathed through his mouth.

Carver forced each man to drink water from the boat stores. Dehydration could be as deadly as the Japanese forces lingering in the jungle.

A flash of light from the shore caught his attention. He watched as the signalman reported something to Ensign Hanks, who passed it along to someone Carver presumed to be Commander Hawkins. The engines increased, and they started in towards the island.

Lieutenant Swan stumbled towards him. "Shore's all clear. We're heading in to drop you off. Be a couple minutes. Get the men ready to enter the boats."

He nodded and passed it along. There was nothing to be done except move closer to the edge of the boat. The men checked their weapons, careful their muzzles were protected from the corrosive seawater by condoms slipped over and secured with rubber bands.

The swabbies unstrapped the rubber boat and moved it to the edge. After a few minutes, the engines went to idle, and the gentle sea lapped the side.

At a whispered word from Ensign Hanks, the rubber boat was sent over the side. One of the sailors went with it and landed in the bottom. He reached up as two more sailors handed down seven paddles. He bundled and stowed them by shoving the blades under the crease between the tubes and the floor.

Sergeant Carver moved beside the sailors still on the PT boat and helped his men pass their packs and weapons. The process went smoothly despite the swell lifting and dropping the boats. Carver helped each man over the side until it was his turn.

He was about to slide off when a hand gripped his shoulder. It was Lieutenant Swan. "Good luck, Sergeant. See you in a few days." He said it like he didn't believe it.

Sergeant Carver nodded and let himself fall into the bottom of the boat where his men steadied him. He moved to the rear, and sat next to the sailor who would act as the rudder man. He passed out the paddles and grabbed his own. The sailor said, "Ready? Stroke."

The men had some training in small rubber boats when they were training back on Fiji, but none of them had spent a lot of time in them. Their strokes were erratic and out of sync but soon the sailor had them paddling in cadence. The boat skimmed along the sea, the sailor steering, the soldiers providing power.

The other rubber boat came out the darkness like an apparition. The occupants of both boats were surprised, and the sailors flashed grins at one another.

They paddled in side by side. When the looming jungle seemed only feet away, they stopped paddling and swapped paddles for rifles and submachine guns. The boats drifted, the sailors kept them straight.

There was no beach. The sea ran up against the jungle like moving from desert to forest. There was nothing in between, no transition point.

The branches and vines reached out over the water, and they

passed beneath them. Carver thought about snakes that no doubt lived in these trees and vines waiting to drop onto unsuspecting prey.

He took a deep breath, scanning the jungle for sign of the enemy. *It's so thick, there could be a regiment in front of me and I'd never see them.*

The boats nudged up against the island, and the two men in front of each boat went over the side. The water came up to their waists, and they made a lot of noise as they struggled to get to shore. Once there, they crouched and searched for any movement then reached back for the ropes. They pulled the boats in close and held them secure as the squad scrambled to shore.

Sergeant Carver was the last man out. He hefted his pack onto his broad shoulders. Once on shore, he looked back at the sailor who was already pulling the boat away with a backstroke. He watched the boat go, the squads last chance to get home the easy way was leaving.

After five minutes Sergeant Carver combined the two groups. He found Corporal O'Connor. "We need to move away while we've got darkness on our side. Find us a good spot to lay up until daylight."

O'Connor nodded and took point. As he passed Private Willy he punched him in the arm and whispered in his ear. "You can take off the life jacket now."

14

Colonel Araki listened to his officer explaining why he'd failed to complete his mission. He gripped the bamboo cane he was forced to use until his hand ached. He'd sent him and a small squad on a simple mission to insert snipers around the American lines. Now, this fat, groveling lieutenant was giving him excuses. He'd been ambushed and lost most of his ten-man patrol.

Before he finished explaining, Colonel Araki smacked the cane down on the wooden table separating them. It sounded like a gunshot, and the lieutenant nearly jumped out of his boots. He bowed his head and waited for the verbal bombardment that was sure to follow.

With barely suppressed rage Colonel Araki seethed, "It was a simple mission, Lieutenant. How is it possible you failed? How could you lose eight men on a mission of stealth? How could you walk into an ambush?" He'd already heard the excuses. "I'll tell you how. You're incompetent. You're an incompetent, fat buffoon." He stepped from behind the table wincing at the pain in his right leg.

It was a lasting gift from the Americans on Guadalcanal. Most of the front of his leg had been shredded by an artillery shell. He'd been in a group of four other officers trying to organize a fighting retreat.

He'd been the only survivor when the shell exploded only yards from them. He'd been thrown twenty feet backward into a burning tank.

When he came to, he realized he'd been left for dead. Through sheer force of will, he'd crawled into the jungle back towards his lines. It had taken three days before he finally came across a friendly patrol. He was whisked off the island and spent long months in a jungle hospital on Bougainville. The pain was constant. He used it to fuel his hatred for the round-eyed Yankees.

He stood in front of the cowed junior officer. He gnashed his teeth. He was short on officers and couldn't afford to relieve him. *Who'd I replace him with?* The impossible situation brought his anger close to boiling over.

He took a deep breath thinking of his Sensei back in Tokyo. He tried to center himself, get control of his feelings. In a calm voice, he said. "You have disgraced your unit and yourself. I'm taking you off the line and sending you to Major Kotani's unit in the rear. He's in charge of our prison camp. Maybe seeing Americans on a daily basis will teach you to loath them as I do and fight harder." The lieutenant kept his head bowed, staring at Colonel Araki's polished leather boots. "Do you think you can perform your duties for Major Kotani, Lieutenant?"

He bowed deeper and said, "Hai, sir."

"You'll leave tomorrow. I'll send you with a squad from Alpha Company." He reached behind him and held up a leather bag. "This is a courier bag." He waited until Lieutenant Taro looked at the bag and nodded. "You'll deliver this to Major Kotani. It's important that its contents get there, do you understand?"

He reached out for the bag, but Colonel Araki kept it. "I'll give it to you tomorrow, the less time it's in your incompetent hands, the better. The POW camp is two miles to the rear. We don't have any trucks available at the moment, so you'll have to walk. You'll have a full squad with you." He eyed him, "You think you can deliver it without getting those men killed and losing my bag?"

The lieutenant gulped and nodded. "Hai, sir."

~

Lieutenant Taro entered Colonel Araki's tent the next morning and bowed until the colonel acknowledged him. He had great respect for the tough combat veteran, but also fear. He thought sure the colonel was either going to relieve him or put a bullet between his eyes last evening. Colonel Araki's acid temper was legendary amongst the junior officers. No one wanted to be on his bad side, and that's exactly where Lieutenant Taro found himself.

"Lieutenant Taro, good morning. Are you ready to move to the POW camp?"

Lieutenant Taro snapped his heels and bowed deeper. "Yessir. The squad from Able Company is assembled and ready to escort me and the satchel to Major Kotani."

Colonel Araki smiled and nodded. His demeanor was opposite from the evening before. "Good, you will leave immediately. Once there, deliver the satchel to Major Kotani only, then send the squad back here."

He paused and looked him over. His distaste for Taro's pudgy body was obvious. "Major Kotani is a tough soldier; you can learn a lot from him. I'll expect you to be much improved when I see you again." He leaned into Taro's space. "Don't let me down again, Lieutenant. I assure you it will be the last time."

Lieutenant Taro snapped his heels again and saluted. "I will not let you down, sir. I will die first."

Colonel Araki handed him the satchel. "Good. Dismissed."

When he left the tent, Lieutenant Taro let out a long breath he hadn't realized he'd been holding. His legs felt heavy like they were made of cement. He approached the squad of men formed up in line with a surly looking sergeant standing to the side.

As Lieutenant Taro approached, the sergeant snapped off a salute. "First squad ready for departure, sir."

Taro returned the salute. "We leave immediately." He realized he didn't know exactly how to get where he was going. "Lead on Sergeant."

The sergeant nodded and barked, "Echelon formation. Forward." The men staggered themselves and moved off at an easy pace. Lieutenant Taro waited until half the soldiers had passed then put himself in the middle of the group. He clutched the satchel to his chest like it was the most precious item in the world. The enemy would have to pry it from his dead arms if they wanted it.

THEY MOVED CAUTIOUSLY along the road, but kept up a good pace. The road was well used and mostly mud. The constant slurp and suck slowed them down, but they didn't stop to rest. They came to the gates of the POW camp at noon. Mud encrusted their legs up to their knees.

The camp was well hidden in a particularly dense section of jungle. It would be invisible to any allied air, and enemy ground troops would have to stumble upon it accidentally.

The front was defended by a ten-foot fence topped with barbed wire. On the corners, guard towers manned by sentries with machine guns. The back of the camp was pushed up against the steep hills of the Crown Prince Range. An enemy approaching from there would need ropes and considerable climbing skills, and they'd be exposed.

Lieutenant Taro was impressed. He hadn't heard anything about the camp and assumed it would be a temporary, ramshackle prison, but this camp looked more permanent and built to last. The guards looked well fed and disciplined. He assumed all the derelicts and deadbeats would be sent here as punishment, as he'd been, but these were professional troops.

As he stood at the front gate waiting to be let in, he thought things might be looking up in his world. He'd assumed he'd be treated even worse here than in his old unit, but maybe he was wrong.

As an officer, he received more food rations than ordinary enlisted men, but even so, he was always hungry. He was quietly optimistic about his new unit with the well-fed soldiers.

The squad stood at attention at the front gate, sweating. A guard had scurried off when they'd approached. Taro saw him returning with an officer in tow, a major.

The major stepped to the gate and stood with his hands on his waist. He was tall for a Japanese and looked like an athlete. Taro guessed his age to be early forties. At twice Taro's age, he looked like he could outdo him in any athletic endeavor. Taro was by no means an athletic man, but he respected those that were and was in awe of the major.

Lieutenant Taro snapped to attention, clicking his heels and presenting a stiff salute. He hoped to make a good impression. The major had a seemingly permanent downturn to his mouth. He returned the salute and pointed at the satchel he was carrying. "I've been waiting for that." He spoke to the guards and they unlatched the wooden gate and opened it inward. "Welcome to Camp Honsu, Lieutenant. I'm Major Kotani."

Taro bowed and ordered the squad forward. He entered the gate, and it was shut and latched behind him. Major Kotani reached for the satchel, and Lieutenant Taro handed it to him. Relief flooded through him; he'd completed his mission for the colonel. It felt good to succeed after so many failures. He couldn't help smiling.

"Something amusing, Lieutenant?"

Lieutenant Taro's smile disappeared when he heard the menace in the major's voice. "No sir, just happy to be in this fine camp."

Major Kotani looked at the surroundings. "I suppose you thought you were being sent to a hovel, somewhere disgraceful." Lieutenant Taro shook his head no. "I can assure you our prisoners aren't as pleased with the surroundings." He turned to the bamboo and thatch hut he'd come from and called to someone. A lieutenant appeared as if by magic awaiting the Major's orders. "Lieutenant Shibata, show our colleague what we do here."

Lieutenant Shibata nodded and gestured for Taro to follow. He gave a last salute to the major and shuffled off to follow Lt. Shibata. When he was beside him Lt. Shibata said, "Do you have a strong stomach, Lieutenant?"

Taro looked at him; they were the same rank, equals. "What do you mean?"

"I mean do you get queasy easily? You will see things here that might upset a delicate stomach."

Lieutenant Taro didn't answer. As they approached the center of the camp, a smell assaulted Lt. Taro's nostrils. He put up his hand to block the overpowering stench. "Wha, what is that smell?"

Lieutenant Shibata smiled, showing off teeth that didn't seem to fit in his mouth. They went in every direction at once. "The prisoners of course." He pointed to a long wood building. It was off the ground, supported by stones and logs. It was well built and clean on the outside. The smell was coming from the inside.

There were two hard looking guards at the front door. When they approached, they saluted and gave Lieutenant Taro a long look. "He's our new officer, come to relieve me. This is Lieutenant Taro." Lt. Taro wondered how he knew his name and decided Colonel Araki must have radioed ahead. The guards nodded.

Lieutenant Shibata gestured for them to open the doors. They did so and entered the darkness to hold the doors open. Lieutenant Shibata gestured for Taro to enter. He went up the two steps and peered into the darkness of the long room. The smell was overpowering, but Taro kept his hand away from his face. He didn't want to show weakness.

He stepped in past the guards and waited for his eyes to adjust to the dim light. He could tell there were people in front of him; he could smell their fetid humanity and sense their movements. The smell was like an open sewer mixed with the tanginess of yeast, or was it blood? He thought he might pass out if he stayed a second longer, but he closed his eyes and calmed himself. He would not let the colonel down again, no matter what. He steeled himself.

A guard lit a gas lantern and Lt. Taro almost fell over when he saw the gaunt faces of men staring at him with bloodshot eyes. The prisoners were mostly white men, Americans he assumed, or possibly British colonists that hadn't left when the war began. There were a few dark faces, obviously natives.

He stared back at their tortured faces. Their tattered clothes were filthy and hung off their skeletal frames, as if hanging from closet hangers. He wondered how long they'd been here, and how long since their last meal. Their faces said years, but they'd only landed a few months before. They must have been captured early in the battle.

He figured he should say something, rather than staring like an idiot. "How, how many prisoners are here?"

He jumped when Lieutenant Shibata spoke next to him. "We have twelve Marines and three natives." He corrected himself, "Excuse me, eleven Marines. One died this morning in a pool of his own shit." Lieutenant Taro nodded, maybe that explained the smell. "They all have weak systems; they die of dysentery quite frequently. We used to have fifteen Marines. The natives are a hardier bunch. They only seem to die when you kill them."

Lieutenant Taro didn't know what to say. Was he supposed to inspect them? Make them stand at attention as he walked down their barracks? He wanted to get out of the hell hole as soon as possible. He turned to Lt. Shibata, "What time do the prisoners eat?"

Shibata looked at his watch. "They dine in the mess hall at 1500 hours. They have one hour to eat then they form up for final inspection before retiring back here." Hearing Lt. Shibata talk about dining and retiring made it sound like the men were on a resort vacation. The contrast repulsed him and that combined with the smell almost sent him over the edge.

He swallowed the bile threatening to disgrace him and turned to leave. "Very well, I've seen enough." He took long strides and stepped into the relatively fresh air.

Lieutenant Shibata stood beside him. He slapped his shoulder with a scarred hand. "You did well, Lieutenant. Most aren't able to keep their stomach contents contained when they first meet our guests."

Lieutenant Taro looked at him with disgust. "You tried to disgrace me in front of them?" he didn't wait for a response. "What is the purpose here? Are we interrogating them?"

Lieutenant Shibata smiled his crooked smile, "Purpose? There is no purpose. We aren't trying to rehabilitate these cowards. These men surrendered, they are lower than the lowest mongrel dog. I have more respect for the natives than these weak Americans." He rubbed his chin contemplating the question like some dime store philosopher. "I suppose the purpose is to make them suffer as much as possible before they die."

15

Sergeant Carver had the men up and moving before light. No one had slept. The night had passed without incident. They hadn't heard anything that could have been the enemy. The jungle was thick. It pressed in on them like something alive. Even laying down on their ponchos was no relief. Their bodies slowly sank into the mud, and soon the jungle wetness seeped into their clothes making them cold, despite the muggy air.

O'Connor didn't think he could get more uncomfortable as he stood and shook the mud off his boots. He looked around in the darkness trying to figure out which way was north. He always had a good sense of direction, but in this jungle, his skills were hard pressed.

This was nothing like the forests he'd grown up hunting in Oregon. He'd spent the better part of two years in the jungles of the South Pacific, and he'd never seen a more miserable place than Bougainville. *We should let the damned Japs have it; it'll kill everyone on it eventually.*

The squad tried to find dry spots while they ate their K-ration breakfasts but ended up standing. No one felt hungry, but they all knew they needed the calories.

O'Connor shoveled a spoonful of what was supposed to be spaghetti. It had a vague ketchup taste, but spaghetti was not what his taste buds told him it was. He wondered when he'd get another chance to eat, not for the sake of calories but the sake of taste. His sparse upbringing wasn't big on culinary delights, but when something was labeled spaghetti, he expected it to at least be in the same ballpark.

Ten minutes later he was at the front of the squad on point. While it was still dark, the men stayed close. It was too dark and too easy to get separated. He moved slowly, careful not to make excess noise. He doubted there were Japs anywhere close but he'd led a squad into an ambush once before, and he wasn't going to let that happen again.

A half hour passed and the jungle started lightening up with the rising sun. Back in Oregon the rising sun always dropped the temperature a degree or two, but out here the only temperature change was hot and hotter.

With the daylight, O'Connor realized he was heading northwest instead of due north. He adjusted his course and moved further ahead. If he ran into an ambush, he wanted plenty of separation between himself and the squad.

A point man's job was to get the squad through the jungle safely, but if the shit hit the fan, it was also to die. He didn't intend to die, so he moved with caution and trusted his senses. Right now his senses were telling him there was nothing in front of him but jungle and mud. He increased his pace.

The jungle was seemingly impenetrable, but O'Connor's woodland sense found the tiny creases between the vines. The rest of the squad wasn't as skilled, but they could easily follow his boot tracks in the mud.

They were making good time. O'Connor had been on point for two hours when he stopped and waited for the rest of the men to catch up.

Private First Class Daniels moved forward. Corporal O'Connor signaled for Sergeant Carver to come to him. The PFC nodded, and went back through the clinging wet vines. He disappeared from O'Connor's view like he'd been swallowed by a huge green mass of vegetation.

Soon Carver was beside him. O'Connor pointed. The land was starting to rise, leading up to a low hill. It looked like a good spot to lay up for a rest and possibly see some of their surroundings. Sergeant

Carver liked it and sent O'Connor, PFC Daniels, and Private Gomez up to investigate.

Minutes later Carver could see O'Connor giving him the all clear. The squad moved up the hill. As soon as they started up, the mud gave way to more solid ground. They went to the top of the hill, and Sergeant Carver told them to take ten. With the exception of two men posted to the perimeter on guard duty, the men sat down. The absence of mud was like a minor miracle.

Corporal O'Connor and Sergeant Carver huddled together looking over an antiquated map. They guessed their position. They'd covered nearly half the distance to the foot of the Crown Prince Range. Carver said. "We've come farther than I thought we would by now. The ground's not quite as shitty as the last patrol."

O'Connor ran his finger over the map, Studying it closely. "It seems like the ground should rise as we head towards the mountains, but who knows. These maps are shit. I may lead us directly into an uncrossable swamp."

"Well, if that happens we'll backtrack." He slapped O'Connor's shoulder. "You holding up? You need a break?"

O'Connor shook his head. "I'm okay, Sarge." He glanced at his watch "I've gotta take a piss before we go."

Carver nodded and noticed Private Gomez. "Gomez, how you at climbing trees?"

Private Gomez pulled himself off the ground and trotted over to Sergeant Carver. He had a Mexican accent left over from his first ten years living south of the border. His parents had legally emigrated from Mexico, and their first order of business was getting their ten-year-old son his American citizenship. He was a short man with dark skin. His black hair complimented his deep brown eyes. He didn't look like much, but the man could shoot the ass off a gnat at two hundred feet with his M1. "I climbed many trees, Sergeant, yes, many trees."

Sergeant Carver pointed at a thick trunked tree whose top couldn't be seen through the canopy. "Get up there and see what you can see."

Without missing a beat, Private Gomez trotted over to the tree. He looked up from the base for a few seconds, unslung his rifle and laid it against the trunk. He spit on each hand, and rubbed them together, and launched his small body up to the first limb. He went up the tree like a monkey. Sergeant Carver smiled remembering another soldier who'd been a good tree climber, Private Caldwell. His smile faded when he recalled that soldier's fate.

Sergeant Carver watched Gomez climb until he was into the jungle canopy and out of sight. He kept thinking the little man would look down and swoon when he saw how high he was, but he never looked down except to secure a foothold. He shook his head, *crazy sumbitch.*

Minutes passed, and Carver sat and leaned against a tree trunk. He angled his head up watching for Private Gomez. He hoped he wouldn't see him falling from limb to limb all the way to the ground. He was starting to worry that he'd been taken by a jaguar or some other tree-dwelling creature when he saw him coming down the tree almost as fast as he'd gone up.

He watched as Gomez got to the last branch pushed off and landed softly in a crouch. He looked up at the tree and slapped his hands together. He was grinning like a schoolboy.

He looked around for Sergeant Carver and saw him shaking his head. Gomez lost his grin. "Is something wrong, Sarge?"

Carver pulled himself up and readjusted the Thompson on his back. He shook his head. "No, nothing's wrong, just can't believe how fast you moved up and down that tree."

Private Gomez smiled showing off perfectly straight teeth. "I climbed a lot of trees when I was a child."

Carver expected more of an explanation, but when there wasn't one forthcoming, he moved on. "Well? What'd you see?"

Gomez dropped to his knee and cleared leaves and sticks from a piece of ground. He smoothed it out and put his finger in the dirt. "This is our location." Carver stopped him and waved Corporal O'Connor over. When he was there, Gomez continued. "We're on this little hill. To the north, about three miles is the base of the mountain range. The jungle looks like a carpet all the way there. I can't see anything except the tops of trees. It's the same in all directions. I think I could see Hill 260 and also Hill 700." He pointed northwest. "About three-quarters of the way to the mountains I saw smoke coming through the trees. At first, I thought it was fog, but it moved more like smoke." He put another point on the dirt. "I'd guess it would be about here, maybe two miles."

Carver nodded and cuffed Gomez's shoulder. "All right, good job. We'll be moving out soon, pass it along." Gomez beamed and spun away. Carver called, "Gomez," he stopped, and Carver pointed back to the tree he'd climbed, "you'll need that." Gomez's dark features turned pale. He went to the tree and scooped up his M1. He looked back and nodded to Carver, who watched him retreat.

He spoke to O'Connor. "He's a damned good tree climber." O'Connor nodded but didn't comment. "You okay on point still? Sounds like there's something in front of us, could be Japs."

O'Connor shrugged. "Our mission's to find that road. If we find Japs we go around 'em, right?"

Carver nodded. "Doubt natives would be stupid enough to show smoke. From what I've heard, they've gotten the hell out of the way and moved to the other side of the island. Be careful out there. We get in a firefight there's no help coming."

O'Connor nodded. "Seems familiar, don't it?" he slapped Carver's back, "Don't worry, Sarge, I'll be careful, always am. The men are moving well, I think they understand our situation. We'll probably have to hunker down another night though, this jungle's thicker'n snot."

Carver nodded. "Let's move out."

WHEN THEY CAME off the hill, the ground once again became a muddy mess. They'd hoped things would dry out with the gradual elevation gain towards the mountains, but it wasn't happening. The going was tough, and their pace slowed.

O'Connor was out front trying to find the best route through tough terrain. He had to backtrack once when he led the squad into a swamp. He wondered for the thousandth time why the hell they didn't just leave the Japs this piece of shit island.

As the daylight was fading, a storm cloud opened up and hit them with a deluge of rain. It happened suddenly and unexpectedly. They were soaked to the skin by the time they pulled out their tattered ponchos. Carver made the decision to stop for the night. O'Connor found a tiny rise that was slightly less muddy and they set up for the night.

The rain lasted an hour and a half. They filled their canteens, then sat hunched under ponchos waiting for it to end. Finally, it stopped.

It wasn't like the rainstorms O'Connor was used to in Oregon where the rain started slowly, gained momentum then slackened and stopped. This rain stopped like someone had shut off a spigot. It was raining hard one second, the next it wasn't raining at all. The trees dripped, and the rain water hissed as the warm air turned it to mist.

The men opened cans of K-rations and ate until they were gone, scraping the bottoms. The hard patrolling took everything out of them and the foul tasting meals were full of life-sustaining calories.

Sergeant Carver had two men on guard duty pulling hour long shifts. O'Connor's turn came at 0100. He was nudged, and he was awake and alert instantly. His body needed sleep, but he didn't allow himself a deep sleep. He teetered between the dream world and the real world, always ready for a fight. There'd be plenty of time for real sleep when they got back to their lines.

He grabbed his rifle and followed Private Denn back to the spot he'd been on watch. He pointed, and O'Connor nodded and slid into the shallow foxhole. It wasn't deep enough to cover his body, and he could see why they hadn't dug it deeper, they'd hit rock. The bottom of the hole was covered in six inches of water. He cursed and decided he'd be better off out of the hole. He sat on the edge of it trying to get comfortable. There was thick brush he leaned against. He did so slowly, making no noise.

He scanned the dark canopy over his head. It was sparser here, and he thought he could actually see stars. The cloud burst had moved on leaving clear skies. The blackness around him was complete. The air was warm and muggy, but tolerable. He sighed. *The jungle can be a beautiful place.*

He stared into the nothingness. He was watching the trail they'd come in on. The rain had done a number on their trail. The sticky mud had turned to liquid and their tracks simply washed away.

He thought about the last time they'd been out here. They'd been followed and the Japs attacked. The superior cover was the only reason they weren't all killed. If something similar happened here, they wouldn't have a chance. The only cover was the jungle itself which didn't stop bullets as well as rocks.

His hour passed quickly and without incident. He was about to move back the ten yards to wake Private Willy, when he heard something out of place. He froze and tried to see through the darkness. He felt the weight of his M1 in his hand. He aimed the muzzle toward the sound. His heart rate increased making him feel warm all over. He could hear it pounding in his ears. Something was out there, something big, like a soldier.

He tried to control his breathing. The sound was not a normal jungle sound, something was coming and would be on him in a second. He was about to pull the trigger, but he wasn't confident he was aiming in the correct spot. As soon as he shot he'd be lit up like times square on New Year's Eve, and targeted. He had to make the shot count.

The noise stopped. O'Connor doubted whatever it was could see him, he was a part of the bushes he leaned against, but he had the distinct feeling something was watching him. He strained to see into the gloom for some shape, something that didn't fit. A minuscule movement caught his eye. It was low to the ground, lower than he'd been looking. He adjusted his aim and focused every fiber of his being at the spot. Another movement, only feet away. Sweat poured off his forehead and threatened to blind him.

Then he saw eyes, glowing eyes nearly on the ground. He realized he wasn't dealing with a soldier but a jungle animal. The thought didn't make him feel better. The eyes stared straight at him. The beast looked ready to spring. O'Connor had his finger on the trigger and was applying gentle pressure.

The eyes blinked and were suddenly gone. The shape in the dark disappeared as if it had never been there. He strained to see where it had gone. A hand pushed on his shoulder, and it was all O'Connor could do not fire. With a conscious effort, he released the trigger, and let out a long breath.

Private Willy tensed and whispered, "What's wrong? Japs?" he pulled his M1 to his shoulder and scanned the jungle, kneeling at the same time. His eyes were wide as he swept the area.

O'Connor wiped his brow. "Shit, you scared the hell out of me, almost made me fire." He shook his head and reached out to lower Willy's muzzle. "There was something out there, something wild, not a Jap, but something more deadly." Private Willy gave him a confused look and continued to stare into the jungle. "I think it must have been a Jaguar or maybe a panther." He leaned back into the bush and let out another long breath. He tilted his head side to side, loosening his taut neck muscles. "Maybe a tiger. They have that kind of shit out here?"

Private Willy shook his head, "I don't know. Whatever it was is gone now. I'm here to relieve you. It's my turn."

O'Connor shook his head, "I'll stay here with you." Willy looked at him like he was crazy. "If that thing comes back it's better if there's two of us." He hugged his rifle and went prone onto his back. "Wake me if it shows up again, I'm gonna get some sleep."

16

The night passed without further incident. O'Connor slept but was never deep. The guard changed and now Corporal Dawkins, the unit medic tapped his foot. "Starting to get light. Reckon we'll be leaving soon, O'Connor?"

Corporal O'Connor nodded and sat up and stretched. His back cracked as he moved it side to side. He rubbed his neck; he felt like he'd slept on a boulder garden. He stood and looked to where he'd seen the animal. He leveled his rifle and walked to the bushes that were beginning to glow a vibrant green with the morning light. He hunkered into a squat and slung his rifle. He pushed back the bushes looking for tracks. There was nothing there. He pushed his way further into the brush, but he could see nothing that would suggest a large animal.

"Hey, what you looking for?" Dawkins whispered.

O'Connor shook his head, "Nothing," and moved back to the half dug foxhole. He looked back at the spot. *Am I losing my mind? Was it some kind of jungle ghost?* He decided he wouldn't bring the incident up to anyone. He hoped Private Willy wouldn't either.

Over a K-ration breakfast of rice and beans, Carver and O'Connor pored over the map. It was old and suspect, but they both decided they had another mile and a half before they butted up against the Crown Prince Range. "Don't forget about that smoke, Gomez saw. Should come across that area this morning." O'Connor nodded. It wasn't like him to be this quiet. "Something bothering you?"

O'Connor looked up and shook his head. "Nope." He unslung his rifle, "I'll head out when you're ready."

Sergeant Carver nodded. "We're right behind you."

O'Connor went to the front of the line. They fidgeted and finished eating, and buried their K-rat garbage. O'Connor doubted the Japanese would be able to miss the fact that a force of American soldiers was in the area if they happened upon the spot; there were boot prints everywhere in the soft ground.

O'Connor got to the front man, Private Willy, who grabbed his arm as he passed. "You find any tracks from that animal?"

O'Connor sneered and shook his hand off. "Forget about it, my mind playing tricks."

Willy watched him pass and muttered just loud enough for him to hear, "Who shit in your soup?" O'Connor ignored him and pressed into the jungle.

When he'd gotten twenty yards in front of the squad, he looked back. Nothing but jungle. He took a deep breath and thought about the yellow eyes he'd seen. He felt goose bumps on his neck and scalp. He shook his head, *get your damned head in the game, slick.*

He tried to push the image from his mind, but it kept coming back to him every couple minutes. He thought he could feel the eyes piercing into his back, and he turned to catch it looking, but there was nothing there. He licked his lips, and swallowed against a dry throat. He crouched and wiped his brow. He'd come about a half mile and seen no sign of the enemy or the beast.

He felt parched; he needed water. He looked back, he had time for a quick sip from his canteen. He pulled it out of his combat belt. He unscrewed the lid quickly and dropped it. The string holding the lid to the canteen kept it from falling to the ground but the metal lid smacked against the metal of the canteen. The chirps and clicks of the ever-present insects stopped for an instant. In the lull, O'Connor heard the distinct sound of humanity.

He froze, the canteen halfway to his cracked lips. Moving only his eyes, he scanned the area. All he could see was jungle, but he could still hear the sound. Not voices, but activity, like a work crew, or an incautious foot patrol.

He felt the presence of Private Willy coming through the jungle. Without looking back, O'Connor signaled him to stop and take cover. Willy sent the signal back and went prone with his M1 sticking out from his shoulder.

O'Connor was still crouched trying to pinpoint the sound. Moving like a sloth, he put the canteen on the ground and eased himself onto his stomach. Every muscle ached with his slow movement, but he ignored the pain.

When he was down, he stayed that way for over a minute. He looked back at Willy and signaled that he was moving forward to get a better look. Willy relayed the message and looked down the sights of the rifle.

O'Connor pushed his way forward inch by inch until he was ten yards further into the bush. He could tell there was something ahead. He almost yelled out when there was a voice only yards from where he lay. It spoke Japanese. His bowels threatened to loose, and all color drained from his face. The enemy was right on top of him, but he still couldn't see anyone.

The voice came again, and this time he was able to pinpoint the source better. It was above him. There was a small cluster of tree trunks to his front. *There must be a sniper in the tree.*

He waited for the bullet that would sever his spine. When it didn't come, he moved his head until he was looking up. There was something different about the trees. He pushed a vine out of the way and realized what he was seeing. The trees weren't trees at all, but part of a fence. The sniper in the tree was actually a soldier in a tower. He could just make out the barrel of a mounted machine gun barrel sticking out.

He was far enough forward that the guard would only be able to see him if he happened to lean out and look down. The sight before him was so unexpected he had trouble comprehending what he was seeing. There was a stout fence, a manned guard tower and now Japanese soldiers with long rifles slung over their backs, walking the perimeter of the fence line. Beyond them, there were buildings, mostly thatch huts, but he thought the biggest one in the middle was lumber. *What the hell is this place?*

He watched the camp, acutely aware that his squad would be wondering what the hell had happened to him. He was about to back his way out when he heard another voice that wasn't in Japanese.

From around the corner of the big building a man dressed in rags and thin as a rail was pleading with a Japanese soldier. O'Connor couldn't tell what he was saying, but there was no doubt it was English.

O'Connor squinted, trying to see better. The man in rags dropped to his knees with his hands together like he was praying, or begging. The Japanese soldier yelled and spat in his face then thumped him with the butt of his rifle. O'Connor heard the dull thunk of the wooden stock smashing into the man's nose. The man yelled out and fell to the ground. The Japanese soldier kicked him in the ribs and yelled. The man struggled to get up, but he kept getting kicked.

The front door of the building swung open, and two ghost-like wraiths scurried to the down man, and lifted him by the armpits. They dragged him through the door. The Japanese soldier yelled at them the entire time. When the door shut, another Japanese soldier yelled something from where he was walking the fence line, and both men laughed.

O'CONNOR INFORMED Sergeant Carver what he'd found, and the squad retreated into the jungle to decide how to proceed. O'Connor thought they'd stumbled across a prisoner of war camp.

While the men were spread out in a defensive circle, weapons facing the jungle, Carver and O'Connor discussed their options. Sergeant Carver said, "Our mission is to find the road, and my guess is it isn't far from this POW camp. The Japs wouldn't build this place in the middle of nowhere. They must have road access nearby. I bet the Japs have a slick little escape plan in case this place is discovered, and it would be easier to build the place if they could haul supplies in rather than hoofing it over the mountains."

O'Connor nodded. "So we go around it and find the road?"

Carver shrugged and looked around at the men who were trying to listen in. "Yeah, I think that's our best option." O'Connor stared at the ground. "What's the matter? You wanna bust 'em out of there, don't you?"

O'Connor looked him in the eye. "Those men are walking skeletons. The fucking Japs are starving them. I doubt they'll live much longer."

Carver punched the ground and seethed. "Goddammit, don't you think I know that? Don't you think I wanna go in there guns blazing and blow the holy hell out of 'em? Make the mother-fuckers pay? Of course I do, but dammit that's not the mission. They probably wouldn't make it back to the hill anyway. We'd be hauling them along and probably end up KIA or captured and what good would that do?"

O'Connor nodded, knowing he was right, but not liking it one bit. It never crossed O'Connor's mind that Sergeant Carver was opting out because of cowardice. He respected him as a warrior and a leader, and while he didn't like leaving fellow soldiers in the hands of the Japs, he also would never doubt Carver's orders. "How you wanna proceed?"

Carver bit his lower lip. "Take me there. I wanna check it out for myself."

O'Connor nodded and whispered to the radio-man, Private Palmer to pass the word. He motioned Carver to follow, and moved to the edge of the ring of soldiers. They crouch walked for thirty yards, then went to their stomachs and pulled themselves along the stinking jungle floor until they heard voices. Carver went up beside O'Connor who pointed.

Like O'Connor, it took Carver a second to realize what he was seeing wasn't more jungle, but an enemy camp. It was as though the Japanese had hacked it directly out of the jungle. He noticed the thick canopy protecting them from aerial spotters. They also hadn't cut the jungle back from the fence line, which allowed them to get close, but also served to keep the camp hidden. They'd only found it because they almost tripped over it.

Carver took the scene in quickly. He thought it would be easiest to get around by moving across the front side. The back was nudged up against a substantial hill which ended at the start of the Crown Prince Range. He studied the camp for five minutes and was about to turn back to the squad when he heard yelling. It was coming from the center of the compound. It was an agonizing scream full of hatred and pain, and it transfixed Carver as he searched for the source. The scream ended after what seemed an eternity. He glanced at O'Connor who was gnashing his teeth. He pointed.

Carver couldn't see what he was pointing at, until he leaned over. He could see the center of the camp. There was a row of men, most barely able to stand, dressed in rags which were falling off them. They looked to be trying to stand at attention. Every time one of them slouched or stumbled, a Japanese guard would whack them with a bamboo pole.

The real spectacle, however, was in front of the prisoners and was the source of the scream. A Marine was on his knees facing an overweight officer who was yelling in his face. Another older officer stood behind the first with his hands clasped behind his back. The fat officer looked back occasionally, like looking for approval from an especially strict school teacher.

The fat officer had something in his hand, something that glimmered in the morning sun. Carver thought it must be a short knife. From this distance, he couldn't be sure, but he thought it was dripping blood. *The son-of-a-bitch is cutting on him.* The older officer said something to the fat officer who nodded and plunged the blade into the prisoner's shoulder. The prisoner couldn't protect himself with hands bound behind his back. He tried to lean back to avoid the thrust but the short three-inch blade sank into his shoulder, and another agonizing scream quieted the jungle animals and insects.

Carver felt Corporal O'Connor tense beside him and he put a hand on his shoulder. "Easy does it, Corporal."

O'Connor spit, "That fat little fuck is going to kill him."

Sergeant Carver shook his head and seethed, "Savages."

The officer pulled the blade out of the prisoner's shoulder and looked back at the officer again. The senior officer turned towards the line of swaying men and addressed them. They were too far to hear the word's meanings, but they could tell he was speaking in broken English.

The officer paced with his hands clasped. When he was halfway down the line, he lunged out with a clenched fist and smashed one of the prisoners in the face. The man dropped like a rag doll, and two guards were immediately beside him pulling him back to his feet. He swayed uneasily, and the guards retreated. When he started to drop again, another prisoner took his arm and tried to hold him up, but he was too weak and was losing his grip. Another prisoner went to his aid, and together they held the man upright.

The officer turned and walked back to the bound prisoner. He grabbed him by the hair with his left hand and yelled something. With his right hand, he reached across his body and in a smooth practiced motion drew a curved Samurai sword from a scabbard. He held the blade over his head. It glimmered in the diffused jungle light.

O'Connor and Carver tensed. O'Connor put his rifle to his shoulder, but Carver whispered, "No."

Like it was happening in slow motion, they watched the officer step back from the kneeling prisoner. He adjusted his bandy legs at shoulder width facing the side of the prisoner, who was looking at the ground, bleeding from multiple wounds.

He brought the blade down so fast it blurred. The razor sharp blade barely slowed as it sliced through the prisoner's thin neck. His head spun through the air and landed face down. It rolled to the side and spun to a stop. It settled, the cloudy eyes staring at the line of men. A moan went up from the prisoners, and a few bent over and threw up bile and rotten rice.

Carver and O'Connor remained still, but it was all they could do not to rake the Japanese with gunfire. Corporal O'Connor looked at Carver whose eyes hardened. He could see hatred building in them like a stoked locomotive fire. O'Connor nodded. Carver had changed his mind.

17

Lieutenant Taro didn't enjoy beating and humiliating the prisoners he was now in charge of, but he did enjoy the food. He'd seen the hut where they kept the food. He'd seen enough rice and meat to last a long time. For the first time since being on this forsaken island, he wasn't hungry.

The other men whispered out of earshot, poking fun at his weight. He let it happen and pretended not to notice. He was used to it; he'd been pudgy his whole life and teased about it for as long as he could remember. He always looked fat, even after being on half rations for months, he never seemed to lose the fat layer. With this new assignment he was putting on weight, and he couldn't have been happier. Let them tease. They'd all die here anyway, but at least he'd die with a full belly.

Lieutenant Shibata had left after a day of showing him how the camp worked and introduced him to the men. He'd motored off in the sidecar of one of the few motorcycles on this side of the mountain range. Lieutenant Taro didn't know what Shibata's new job would be, but he hoped it got the sadistic bastard killed.

Major Kotani ran the camp with an iron grip. He was hard on the men and expected perfection in every aspect of their jobs. Lieutenant

Taro was afraid of him like he was of most officers, but he was more afraid of Colonel Araki.

When the captain tested him in front of the men that afternoon, he swallowed his disgust and did exactly what he was told. He avoided the young American Marine's eyes as he thrust the knife blade into him over and over again, being sure not to hit vital organs. The screams the man produced grated on his nerves. It was surreal. He knew his dreams would be haunted for the rest of his short life. The feel of the blade slicing muscle and knicking bone was nauseating. He hid the revulsion by snarling and yelling at the Marine. He was as surprised as anyone when Major Kotani executed the prisoner. Lieutenant Taro realized he didn't even know the Marine's name.

They made the Marines bury their comrade in two separate holes; one for the body the other for the head. A final insult heaped on top of their misery. Lieutenant Taro wondered if all the prisoners were to be executed, or would they be sent to the home islands to be used as slaves? He shrugged the thought away. The allies had cut them off from their main forces further north; there'd be no way to ship the Americans. The thought gave him pause, *I wonder how long the food will last?*

He tried to push the gruesome events of the day out of his head. He looked at his watch, it was time for the evening meal, and he wasn't going to be late.

He entered the food hall and went to the officer's low table. The enlisted men shared the canvas food tent, but there was a white silk curtain separating them from the officer section. He bowed to the table of officers. They were all sitting on their knees with pillows beneath.

He was the most junior man of the four other officers. Major Kotani held the highest rank and was the camp commander. Under him was Captain Nagao. He was in charge of the guards and soldiers occupying the camp. The other was First Lieutenant Hara, assistant to Captain Nagoa. As a second Lieutenant, Taro was the low man and as the newest member, despised. His fat body didn't help the other officer's attitudes.

He sat on his knees beside Lieutenant Hara, who scooted over to accommodate him. The pillow Lt. Taro kneeled on was old and tattered. He hadn't sat at a proper table in months. It felt odd and foreign. He felt self-conscious about having his boots on at the dining table but this was war and they had to be ready at a moments notice. Some of the niceties of home got ignored at the front.

A steaming pot of rice sat in the center of the table. Taro's stomach growled when he noticed the pieces of pink meat in the rice. He wondered what kind it was, but thought it best not to inquire.

The pot got passed, and the officers served themselves. Lieutenant Taro wondered why prisoners didn't do the serving. It seemed a fine way to shame them while getting useful work out of them.

Major Kotani noticed his new second lieutenant craning his neck around the room. "Looking for something, Lieutenant?"

Lieutenant Taro's face went crimson. He bowed his head and said, "I was looking to see if prisoners were being used to serve us food."

The other officers scowled and looked to Major Kotani who had a tight smile. "The stench would drive us out of the room and ruin our appetites."

Lieutenant Taro nodded, "I understand, sir."

Major Kotani continued. "We've found the prisoners to be wholly unappreciative of our care. Like a feral dog, they try to bite the very hand that feeds them."

The image of the young Marine's severed head rolling around in the mud passed through Taro's mind. A piece of rice went down the wrong pipe, and Lieutenant Taro couldn't suppress a cough.

Major Kotani looked hard at him. "You find something startling about my words?"

Taro shook his head and got control of his cough. He kept his head down and said, "No, sir. I merely choked…"

Major Kotani cut him off. "You're offended by the killing today? Is that it?"

Lieutenant Taro's appetite left him, the food in his mouth no longer tasted succulent but turned bitter. He knew to speak any more would be folly, so he shook his head.

Major Kotani slammed his balled fists onto the table making his plate jump. "Answer me, damn you!"

"N, No sir. I wasn't offended, sir."

Major Kotani stared at his cowed second lieutenant. After nearly a minute, which Lieutenant Taro visibly shook through, Kotani smiled. "Good. Be careful, the rice has bones in it, yes?" he roared with laughter at his joke. The other officers, taken aback at first, soon joined their commander and the room was full of laughing. Lieutenant Taro looked from officer to officer and let the laughter roll over him. His chuckle soon broke into a laugh. He decided he'd do everything possible to stay out of Major Kotani's way; the man was obviously out of his mind.

18

Sergeant Carver's plan was simple. When darkness came, Private Willy and Private Gomez would sneak close and climb trees that would give them a line of sight to the tower guards. The rest of the squad would be broken up into two teams separated by fifty yards. At exactly 0430 hours, when it was just getting light, the guard tower soldiers would be taken out. That would be the signal for the teams to assault their assigned section of fence with grenades.

Team one, led by Sergeant Carver, would cover team two, led by Corporal O'Connor. Team two would capture and occupy the nearest guard tower. They'd turn the Nambu machine gun inward and rake the responding troops. Then team one would break into the center building and free the prisoners and get the hell out of there.

The men listened in silence to the whispered briefing. After hearing what happened to the hapless Marine they didn't question the wisdom of assaulting a superior force of unknown size. They were as outraged as O'Connor and Carver. No one asked how they were going to escape with a bunch of malnourished Marines through miles of thick, muddy jungle, but they were all thinking about it.

Once Carver was done briefing them, and the men knew their jobs, they went back to defending their perimeter. Carver could feel the tension in the air; it was thick as jungle fog. The men stayed quiet as they made certain their gear was in order. Once it got dark, the job would be much harder.

O'Connor took Private Gomez and Private Willy to the edge of the camp to scope out likely trees. It wasn't as easy as he thought. There were plenty of trees, but few were easy to climb. Most were huge and towering with their branches starting high up the tree. They finally found two likely trees, but neither was perfect. The one Private Gomez would climb looked to be partially dead. Gomez would have to go slow, careful not to break branches and make noise. Private Willy's tree was alive and thriving, but it was far away from the target guard tower. It would be a hard shot in the best of conditions, and he'd be shooting in low light. It was their best option though, so they tied a rope to the bases and slithered back to their lines trailing the rope. It was exposed, but they doubted it would be discovered by a Japanese patrol in the darkness, and it was the only way they'd be able to find their way back to the trees.

When O'Connor returned, he found Sergeant Carver and sat beside him. Carver was cleaning his Thompson in the fading evening light. "We're doing the right thing. Those Marines deserve better than that."

Sergeant Carver nodded. "Sure as hell no way for a man to die."

"What happens when we get back to our lines? The LT's gonna shit a brick when he finds out you went against orders, especially knowing we're probably close to finding the road."

Carver finished putting the Thompson back together and checked the action. It was smooth, and the sound of greased parts moving in perfect sync was satisfying. He aimed down the barrel and said, "That's a big assumption, us getting back to our lines with a bunch of prisoners." O'Connor spit and grinned. Carver continued, "I'll be happy to face whatever the little prick throws at me. Hell, Leavenworth would feel like a vacation after this place."

O'Connor laughed and started to move away, but Carver grabbed his sleeve. Carver said, "If this shit goes sour, take as many men as you can and get the hell outta here. We're gonna wake up a whole lotta Japs when the fireworks go off. The quicker we leave, the better."

O'Connor smiled, "No shit, Sarge." Carver's face flared for an instant but it passed as he watched his insolent corporal disappear into the jungle. He pursed his lips, hoping he wasn't seeing him for the last time. He'd lost a lot of men and each time it happened it hurt, but Corporal O'Connor had been with him through his darkest hours. Losing him would be hard to take.

THE NIGHT CREPT by as Sergeant Carver went over the plan in his head. It wasn't great, there were a lot of loose ends, but it was the best he could come up with without detailed schematics of the POW camp's layout and defenses. He tried for some sleep, but it was impossible with his mind going a mile a minute.

At midnight he moved forward and found Private Willy. He was curled up, snoring softly. Carver nudged him, trying to pull him out of sleep gently. It was never a good idea to wake a veteran soldier any other way. As soon as he touched him, Willy's eyes opened, and Carver could see him focusing. He whispered, "It's time for you to climb your tree, Willy." He nodded and went from sleep to combat ready in an instant. Carver said, "I'll be right back. I'll find Gomez, and we'll move out together."

Willy nodded and rolled to his knees with his M1 pointed into the jungle. Minutes passed before Sergeant Carver was beside him again with Private Gomez and Corporal O'Connor. Private Willy had to borrow a watch, the one he'd taken off the wrist of a dead Japanese soldier no longer kept accurate time. Private First Class Daniels had two, so he let Willy borrow one.

The four of them moved through the rest of the squad. No one was sleeping. They found the ropes and followed them to the first tree. They were ten yards from the POW camp's fence line. The guard tower was twenty yards to the right. This was the most dangerous tree because of the proximity and all the dead branches. Gomez was the better climber, so this was his tree.

Gomez flashed a toothy smile and without a word scampered up. The others watched him climb, ready to cover him if he drew the attention of the tower guard. Their fears were unfounded. He got into position in the crook of a large branch without making a sound.

They went back the way they'd come, found the second rope and followed it to Willy's tree. He took a deep breath and blew it out slowly. He wasn't nearly the climber Private Gomez was. He wasn't looking forward to the climb.

Sergeant Carver hadn't picked him for his climbing prowess, but for his uncanny ability with the M1. He slung his rifle and O'Connor weaved his fingers together and leaned down to give him a step up. Willy put his muddy boot in O'Connor's hands and whispered a one, two, three count, and lunged to the first branch. He pulled himself up and looked down. They could barely see him tip his helmet. They watched as he climbed. He was slower and less sure than Gomez, but he made progress and eventually was out of sight.

When they didn't hear him anymore, they followed the rope back to the squad. By the time they got back, it was time for the squad to break into teams and move into their assault positions.

Sergeant Carver was in the center of the men. He could barely see them. He whispered, "It's crucial we get in and out quickly. When you hear those rifles, blow the fence and get inside. Hopefully we'll catch the Japs with their pants down. Any questions?" The men were silent. "Okay then, let's move out."

O'Connor took point as usual. He moved with caution. The last thing they needed was to tip off the sentries and lose the element of surprise.

They were in position at 0345, forty-five minutes before the snipers would take their shots. Sergeant Carver sent O'Connor, Daniels, and Grant forward with three grenades and a small spool of wire.

The three soldiers left their rifles with the squad. They belly crawled up to the fence. The nearest guard tower was thirty yards to their left. They were under the sentry's line of sight. They were invisible unless the guard decided to look down the length of the fence beneath him. They hoped the late hour would put the guard off his vigilance.

There was nothing but the sound of the jungle. O'Connor strained to hear the guard priming his Nambu machine gun, but it didn't happen. He reached down and pulled the single grenade and worked the pin out, careful not to release the lever. He could hear the other two doing the same, but ignored them. If anyone messed up, they'd all pay the price.

He placed the end of the wire, which he'd bent into a lasso shape, around the lever and placed it next to the fence. The lever faced away from him; he had the wire running beneath the grenade. The wire was four feet long. At the end, he'd shaped another loop and tied thread they'd borrowed from the medical kit to it.

He looked for the others and could barely see them in the gloom. The night was changing to morning, but full light was still a half hour away. He backed away, careful not to snag the line and accidentally pull the wire. He moved into the jungle until he could hide behind the base of a tree. He was mere yards from the grenade, but the jungle was thick, and the tree stout. He hoped it was enough to protect him from shrapnel.

The entire plan depended on the grenades opening a hole in the fence. They only needed a small hole to dash through, but if it failed, they'd have to cut through with knives while the Japanese woke up. There was no use worrying, it would either work or it wouldn't.

He watched the other two men slink into cover. They played out their lines like they were hand fishing for trout. *TNT trout,* he grinned. He checked his watch, twenty more minutes until show time.

PRIVATE WILLY WAS WORRIED. He sighted down his rifle trying to pick out shapes in the distant guard tower, but the darkness made it impossible. Willy looked at his watch for the hundredth time, twenty more minutes. If it didn't get significantly lighter, he wouldn't be able to see his target. He patted his ammo belt. *If I can't see it, I'll lay so much fire on him, he'll be too scared to open up with the MG.*

He was happy with his spot. It was a little far from the tower, but he was in a good firing position. He was laid out on a thick branch with the barrel of his M1 resting in a perfect natural notch. The thick leaves would make it almost impossible to be seen. It was a perfect sniping tree.

As the minutes ticked by, the jungle turned from dark to semi-light. Willy barely noticed the change until he sighted down his weapon and lo and behold, he could see the Japanese sentry. *Had he always been there, or was he up and moving around now?* He decided it didn't matter, he could see his target, and was confident he could take him down.

He took the watch off and put it in front of him. He could barely see the luminescent dials ticking towards 0430. With only five minutes to go the watch moved slightly. He wondered if he'd imagined it, then it moved again and was threatening to fall off the tree. He lunged, but it was too late, the watch slid off and ticked its way through the branches to it's resting place in the mud. Willy cursed under his breath. He noticed a large centipede moving along the branch where the watch used to be. He flicked the damned thing off the branch. He thought about the time and convinced himself it had been five minutes until showtime. He started counting to three hundred.

He pulled the stock tight into his cheek and regulated his breathing with his counting. When he got to two hundred fifty, he let his finger feel the trigger a fraction more. The sentry was as still as a statue. Five seconds, he applied pressure, and the M1 jumped in his hand. He fired off three more shots in quick succession. He was confident his first shot had put the soldier out of commission.

To his right he heard Gomez firing, *damned spic better not miss at that range.* There was a quick series of dull thuds, the grenades blowing the fence. He kept his sights on the guard tower. Satisfied that he'd taken out his man he pivoted the barrel towards the camp.

There was a thin layer of wispy fog on the ground. Nothing moved inside, and for an instant, he wondered if the Japs left during the night, but then a soldier with no shirt on burst around the corner of the prisoner barracks, his long Arisaka rifle leading the way. He looked disoriented and swung his rifle looking for a target.

Willy grinned as he put his sight on the man's chest and pulled the trigger twice. The Japanese soldier's chest exploded, and a plume of red mist exited his back. His rifle flew into the air; he was dead before it landed on top of him.

More targets came from the back of the camp. Private Willy moved from target to target putting soldiers down with each shot. He heard the machine gun from the tower to his right open up and for a second the sound of the dreaded Nambu struck fear in him. He relaxed when he saw the yellow tracers streaking not at him, but into the camp. He watched as Japanese soldiers spun and were flung back as the machine gun swept over them.

He laughed out loud, *like shooting fish in a barrel.* He looked for more targets, but the MG had taken care of most of them. Movement from the corner of his eye got his attention. He moved his rifle back towards the guard tower. Two soldiers were scrambling up the ladder. He took a breath, let it out and shot the top man through the neck. The soldier held on for a second then fell backward into the man behind him, who peeled off the ladder and went down with the dead man on top of him. Willy emptied his clip into the pile and thumbed in another.

He could see more soldiers at the corner of a thatched building getting ready to make a run for the tower. He was about to open fire when three soldiers went prone and started hosing his tree down. Bullets buzzed and smacked into the tree all around him. He put his head down but realized they'd make the tower and fire on the squad if he didn't get the best of them.

He steeled himself and sighted down his rifle ignoring the bullets knocking leaves and debris onto his back. The three soldiers were prone, but exposed. He willed himself to take his time and fired off all eight rounds in quick succession. The clip pinged telling him he was dry.

He ducked down and inserted another and went back to firing position. He couldn't tell if he'd killed the three, but he did see a soldier disappear into the tower. There was another halfway up. Willy shot him off the ladder with shots to his legs and gut.

The machine gun barrel move his way. He had a decision to make. He'd be filled full of holes if the gunner let loose at his tree. He leveled the M1 and fired off five rounds before he saw the muzzle flash aimed at him. He pushed back to the trunk of the tree and held the M1 to his chest. The tree seemed to come alive as it filled with 7.7mm rounds.

He held his breath as countless rounds whizzed by him. As

suddenly as it started, it stopped. The Nambu had found another, more urgent target. Private Willy took a breath and felt his heart trying to pound its way out of his chest. He peeked around the trunk and saw the heavy MG sweeping towards the squad who were making their way to the prisoner barracks.

The squad was working the cover, bounding forward while others covered. Any second the MG would open up on them. He lunged to his firing position trying to find his shot. The branches and leaves had made a mess, and he couldn't see clearly. He could make out the barrel swinging, but it passed over the squad and was aiming into the camp. *Has it been captured? I didn't see anyone get that close.* Then he realized what was about to happen. The MG was going to open up on the prisoner barracks.

Private Willy struggled to clear the branches. The MG opened up, and he watched the bullets slam into the wooden sides of the barracks. The gunner swept back and forth. The stout wood stopped most of the bullets but great chunks were flying off, and he had no doubt men were dying inside.

He pulled the last branch out of his way and sighted down the barrel. The MG was blazing away, and he could see the gunner's head just above the tower wall. He fired three shots, and the head dropped out of sight. The MG barrel aimed to the sky and stopped firing.

Private Willy's hatred for the Japanese threatened to boil over. He searched for more targets wanting just one more kill, one more act of revenge, but there was no one alive. He covered his squad as they busted down the door of the barracks and ran inside. Soon they were coming out with men draped over their shoulders, bleeding men.

He saw a flash of someone in a white tank top near the back of the camp. The soldier was wearing an officer's cap and was holding a pistol in one hand and a satchel in the other. He was bigger than most Japanese Willy had seen. *Thought these bastards were starving?* The angle wasn't good, so he adjusted his body to bring the M1 to bear. He was about to shoot when the officer moved to the corner and disappeared. In frustration, Willy fired off two rounds where he'd been.

He cursed and decided it was time to get out of the tree and back with his squad. He went down the tree much faster than he went up.

He nearly fell the last ten feet and was only saved by a lucky branch grab. He ran along the fence line until he found the breach from the grenades. It was a sizable hole, enough for the entire squad to fit through at the same time.

He ran with his rifle at the ready and crossed the open ground to the door of the barracks. He stepped aside as Private Grant moved past him carrying a wounded prisoner. He put his hand on his shoulder. "Anymore inside?"

Private Grant shook his head, "No one alive."

Willy went in anyway. The stench of the place almost made him gag. The rot mixed with the cordite and blood was almost too much. He put his arm over his nose and walked to the center. There were bodies sprawled in grotesque death poses. Some were still in their filthy bunks their dead eyes staring. He thought about the gunner purposely gunning them down. *That fat fucking officer, that's who ordered it.*

He stumbled outside feeling sick to his stomach. Sergeant Carver was getting the survivors ready to move. There were only four that hadn't been wounded or killed by the MG. The wounded were in bad shape. Private Willy had seen enough combat to know when a man was past the point of no return and these gyrenes weren't going to make it very far. *That's for Carver to figure out.*

He put his hand on Carver's shoulder. "The officer that ordered the MG to open up on them got away. I saw him moving that way. I'm going after him."

Carver looked at Willy's red eyes and nodded, "Take Gomez and Hans, but make it quick, were leaving in the next ten minutes." Willy nodded, grabbed Gomez and Hans and went looking for the officer.

WHEN THE SHOOTING STARTED, Lt. Taro awakened from a fitful dream involving the headless Marine stalking him. He lay on his back listening to the noise, trying to figure out what he was hearing. It continued, and he sat up in the cot and swung his feet onto the dirt floor. There was a flash from the fence line, then he heard the distinct sound of bullets smacking into wood. His eyes went wide as he realized the camp was under attack. His first instinct was to hide. He looked around the sparse thatch hut, but there was no decent cover.

Colonel Araki's voice exploded in his brain, 'do not fail me again.' He was scared to fight the enemy but terrified to fail Colonel Araki. He steeled his nerves and pulled on his boots. The gunfire got more intense as he heard a type 92 machine gun firing. He hoped it stopped whatever force was attacking.

He pulled the pistol from his belt. He didn't have time to put his khaki shirt over the white tank top he'd been sleeping in, but put on his soft cap with the lieutenant's bars, as he left the shack. It was just getting light, but he could still make out muzzle flashes near the front of camp. He was about to charge that way when he remembered the documents Colonel Araki had sent with him. *The Americans are after the documents.*

He stopped in the dimness and tried to orient himself. He'd only been in the camp a few days and wasn't completely comfortable. The machine gun opened up again, and he realized it wasn't shooting at the attackers. He watched as three soldiers spun and dropped, their bodies spouting blood and gore. He raised his pistol and fired a shot that had no chance of hitting anything but air. It gave him courage, and he ran to the headquarters tent.

He tripped on a line holding the canvas tight. He picked himself off the ground and ran through the front flap. No one was there. *Have they fled?* He heard yelling coming from the battle and recognized Major Kotani's voice. He was waving his pistol exhorting his men to attack. He could see three soldiers run out and throw themselves on the ground shooting at something he couldn't see. Then two more soldiers took off like Olympic track stars to the guard tower. He silently cheered them on as they went up the ladder. The first one made it but the second suddenly jolted and fell off the ladder screaming.

He watched, wondering if he should join the fray. *No, I will stay here and guard the documents.* He felt relief at his decision. He wasn't a warrior; he'd only get in the way. He searched the room and found the satchel. He lifted it, but it felt empty. *Is it my place to look inside?* He heard the second machine gun fire. The soldier was giving the enemy a dose of their own medicine. He looked around then opened the top of the satchel. It was empty. He looked on the table and saw a map laid out with lines, dates, and units. He'd never been a good tactician, but he could recognize a battle plan when he saw one. *This must be the document. I'll keep it out unless the battle turns against us.*

He went back to the tent flap and realized he didn't have his pistol. He ran back into the tent and saw it on the table. He cursed his stupidity and returned to watch the battle.

He heard Major Kotani yelling and trying to get the attention of the machine gunner in the tower. The gunner stopped, and he could hear Kotani ordering him to shoot the prisoners. Lieutenant Taro gulped against a dry throat. If the major was ordering them killed the battle must be going worse than he thought.

The chattering of the second machine gun stopped. Most of the firing was from M1s and the occasional hammering of a Thompson and the zipping of the first Nambu. *Are the men dead?* The thought made his bowels loosen. He could still hear Major Kotani exhorting soldiers into the fray.

Lieutenant Taro decided it was time to secure the documents particularly now that he knew their contents. It would be disastrous for the Americans to get their hands on the plans. He scooped up the documents and folded them into the satchel. He threw the long strap over his shoulder and ran away from the battle.

In his hurry, he went the wrong way. He came to the corner of the prisoner barracks and tried to stop. He skidded into the open. He could see American soldiers running towards the barracks. He stood transfixed then shook himself from the trance and sprang back behind the corner as bullets slammed past the spot he'd been standing. He leaned against the building and closed his eyes at the close call. He felt the weight of the bag. He had to get out of the compound.

He remembered the troop truck he'd seen parked under cover in the far corner. He'd inquired to Lieutenant Shibata about it, and he'd told him it was not to be used until the attack started. They didn't want to tip the Americans off that they'd built roads on this side of the mountains. If he could get to it, he could drive through the front gate and be away from the enemy in minutes. This far behind their lines there was no way they'd pursue him. When he showed up on Colonel Araki's doorstep with the saved plans, he was sure his use of the truck would be forgiven.

With the plan in his head, he took off running to the other side of the camp and the truck. Within a few feet he was breathing hard, and sweat was pouring off him in tiny streams.

~

PRIVATE WILLY LED Private Gomez and Hans to the back corner of the barracks where he'd last seen the Japanese officer. He went around the corner, his rifle leading, but the officer wasn't there. He signaled the men to follow. He doubted he'd gone far.

They trotted down the back of the camp searching between each thatch hut before moving on. Private Willy had the feeling the officer wanted to get away, not make a last stand. He didn't look like the suicidal kind, so he didn't bother searching the huts. He was coming to the end of the camp though, and he'd seen no sign of the officer.

He went to the final hut and standing in the doorway was a Japanese soldier looking the other way. Willy instinctively dropped to his knee and fired two shots into the soldier's back. Gomez and Hans had their weapons ready, but no more Japanese appeared. Willy thought maybe the guy was guarding something. He scooted to the front door and heard grunting. He made eye contact with Gomez and Hans and indicated he'd go in on the count of three. One, two, three, he went into the hut and fired at moving shapes. He fired from the hip, and moved left allowing the others to come through. They came in firing blindly in the dark room.

When their eyes adjusted they saw two officers on the ground the older one, a major had a short sword sticking from his gut. His chest was seeping bright blood from a bullet wound. His eyes were dead. The other officer clutched his own gut. His hands covered in blood and bits of flesh. His bowels, the color of maggots, were threatening to spill through his fingers. He chewed his lower lip as he watched the Americans approach.

Private Gomez raised his rifle to put the officer out of his misery, but Private Willy pushed his barrel to the ground. "You see what he did to the prisoners? Let him suffer." He searched the rest of the building and said. "He's not here."

Private Hans asked, "Who?"

"The officer I saw at the barracks, the fat one, he's not here." An engine started nearby. Private Willy ran to the door pushing his way past Gomez and Hans. "That's gotta be him." He ran out of the hut and turned the corner to the back of the camp. He saw a big troop truck pulling out from a camouflage cover. He saw the fat officer at the wheel. He was concentrating and didn't see Willy and his rifle.

Willy drew a bead on the officer's head and was about to pull the trigger when he heard Sergeant Carver yelling, "Don't shoot, don't shoot!"

Willy looked over his shoulder and saw Carver running full speed at the truck. Willy pulled his gun down and watched Carver flash by him and close the distance to the truck in seconds. Carver jumped onto the side step next to the driver. The Japanese officer's eyes went wide and he tried to bring his pistol to bear, but Carver punched him with a brutal right cross. Carver grabbed the pistol and threw it out, then opened the door and kicked the reeling officer to the passenger side. He slammed the brakes, and the officer's head slammed into the dashboard, knocking him out.

Carver kept the engine running and yelled at the gaping Private Willy. "Get the rest of the squad and the prisoners; I just secured our way out of here."

19

Sergeant Carver sat in the window seat of the Japanese troop transport with his Thompson between his knees. Beside him, Private Willy was grinning like a crazy man. Corporal O'Connor was at the wheel studying the clutch and gears. It looked to be like any other truck he'd ever driven, only bigger. The rest of the squad along with five freed Marine prisoners and one unconscious Japanese officer trussed up like a hog, sat on the bench seats under the canvas top in the back.

Sergeant Carver couldn't believe their luck. He hadn't lost a single man during the attack. The only casualties were the prisoners. There weren't many left. Four emaciated Marines killed along with the lone native. Two of the others were mortally wounded, and Carver doubted they'd make it far.

O'Connor looked across the cab at Sergeant Carver. "Where to?"

Carver pointed straight ahead. "I don't think we've got much choice. There's only one road, and I'm sure it runs straight into Japs. We'll get ourselves away from this area then head out on foot."

O'Connor nodded and gunned the engine. The big diesel revved like it was eager to go. O'Connor pushed the clutch in and put it into what he hoped was first gear. It groaned and shrieked but finally notched into place. O'Connor let his foot off the clutch, and the big rig lurched forward. He steered straight ahead toward the front gate area. O'Connor motored towards it and looked over at Carver wondering if he should stop or bust through. The answer came when a Japanese soldier sprang out from behind a hut and fired his snub nosed machine pistol. A few rounds found the truck and thumped into the metal siding, sounding like a ball peen hammer.

O'Connor yelled, "Hold on!" and mashed the gas pedal to the floor, shifting into second gear. A second later the truck smashed into the stout front gate. The impact yanked the truck to the left as the gate swung open. O'Connor corrected, trying to keep the truck on the road. He thought they'd careen into the jungle, but the gate ripped off the hinge point and shattered, releasing its grip. He got control and could hear the men in back firing at the lone soldier. There were no mirrors to see if they'd hit him.

The road was narrow, barely able to accommodate them. There were few straight sections, and each corner O'Connor expected to plow into a Jap vehicle. "How far you want me to go?"

Carver considered, "We'll go a mile or so." He looked at his watch. "We'll stop in three or four minutes, that'll be about right."

Two minutes later the truck maneuvered around a corner and before O'Connor could react, slammed into a Japanese soldier on a motorcycle. The soldier was as surprised as they were. He only had a half a second to react, but it was too late.

O'Connor didn't slow, and the motorcycle slammed into the metal bumper, launching the Japanese soldier into the grille. The truck lurched and bounced as it rode over the carnage.

Carver yelled to the men in the back. "Brace yourselves we've got Japs coming down the road."

O'Connor looked at him. "We do?"

Carver pointed, and sure enough, there was a jeep with a mounted machine gun coming straight for them. O'Connor had no place to go. There were no turnouts, so he did the only thing he could do, he pushed the pedal to the floor and shifted into third. The jeep skidded to a stop, and the soldier in the back stood behind the machine gun and primed it. The driver's eyes went wide when he realized he was about to be rammed. He dove out the side into the jungle. The gunner was bringing the muzzle to bear. O'Connor knew he would get a few shots off before he rammed him. "Get down!" he yelled.

He ducked but kept the truck pointed straight ahead. The sound of the machine gun was like a buzz saw. Bullets thumped into the grille, and the windshield shattered, raining down on them. The impact with the jeep sounded like the end of the world as metal mangled and crushed.

The sudden deceleration threw them into the dashboard, and they fell to the floor in heaps. The truck rolled to a stop. The only sound from the engine was the ticking and hissing as the radiator fluid spilled onto it.

O'Connor was the first to lift his head. Through the shattered windshield he could see the barrel of the machine gun pointing to the sky. A thin stream of smoke wafted into the jungle canopy. The gunner was nowhere in sight. He slapped Willy on the shoulder, "We've gotta get outta here in case there's fire. Get Carver and come out my side, that driver's still out there."

Private Willy shook the cobwebs out of his dazed head, and he nodded. He shook Sergeant Carver who brushed him aside. "I heard, I heard. I'm coming." He held his head, "Feel like I got slugged by a giant." His hand came away wet with blood.

Private Willy asked, "You okay? You're bleeding."

Carver looked at him and smiled through blood stained teeth, "No shit."

O'Connor had to kick the door three times before it finally opened. He slid out with his M1 ready and waved the others out. Willy was halfway out when Carver grabbed his shoulder. "What's this?"

Willy looked behind him. Carver was holding up a satchel covered in blood. Willy shrugged then remembered. "The fat Jap officer was carrying that. He must've stowed it under the seat when he tried to drive outta here. Forgot all about it." His eyes went wide. "It's probably important; we should bring it."

Carver sneered, "No shit."

O'Connor went to the front of the truck to survey the damage while Willy and Carver went to check on the men. O'Connor nearly fired his weapon when he saw what must have been the machine gunner. He was plastered to the front of the grille. His shoulder firmly wedged into the grille slats and the side of his face caved in partially enveloping one of the slats. His bulging eyes were rolled to the back of his head. He hardly looked human.

He was brought back from his trance when he saw movement in the jungle beside the jeep. He remembered the Jap driver and brought his M1 to his shoulder.

There was a flash of uniform running straight away through the jungle. He centered his back in his sights and was pulling the trigger when the soldier dropped out of sight. His shot missed. He waited for another chance, but he never saw him again. He contemplated chasing him but didn't relish hunting a man who was scared and probably armed. He heard Sergeant Carver calling for help. He took one last look and jogged to the back of the transport.

THE CRASH HADN'T DONE wonders for the men in the back, particularly the prisoners. The two seriously wounded Marines were dead, and the other three looked shell-shocked. The squad members had fared better, but Private Palmer and Private Crofter were both holding bandages to their heads. Corporal Dawkins, was wrapping their wounds.

"How are they, Doc?" Sergeant Carver asked.

Dawkins didn't stop working. "They were sitting in front and slammed into the cab. They'll be okay but will probably have terrible headaches." He glanced at Carver who had a similarly gushing head wound. "I'll get to you next, Sarge."

"I'm fine. Head wounds bleed a lot."

Dawkins nodded, "They always do, but I'll wrap it, keep it from dripping into your eyes."

Carver shrugged and nodded. "Just so it doesn't hold us up. I'm sure that was only the first part of a reaction force, more Japs'll be coming any second. We gotta be long gone by then."

Dawkins worked fast while the men got themselves ready to move.

Private Grant called. "What about the Jap? Should we kill him or take him with us?"

Sergeant Carver had forgotten all about him. "Leave him, we've got what he was carrying." Carver held up the satchel. The officer was sitting in the truck bed trying to clear his head. He was woozy and swayed slightly side to side. When Carver held up the satchel his eyes widened, and he tried to get up, but a rifle butt knocked him back down. Carver grinned. "We've gotta get this back, it's obviously important, that Jap's about to shit himself."

Private Willy came up beside Sergeant Carver, "No use letting him live; he'll tell his buddies which way we went." Carver scowled at him. *This man is pure hatred.* "I'll do it quiet if you like." He reached for his K-bar knife.

Carver shook his head. "I'm not killing a prisoner. Make sure he can't get loose, gag him and put something over his head." Private Willy's eyes lit up. Carver barked, "Something he can breathe through."

Willy turned away and spat. Private Grant did as Sergeant Carver ordered. When he finished, the officer was bound up tight. He couldn't talk, see or move. If his comrades didn't find him, he'd die of thirst and heat exhaustion within the hour. Carver took one last look at him and shook his head. *Thought these sons-of-bitches were starving. This one looks like my cousin Peter.* An image of his overweight cousin jumping into the lake during a warm summer day flashed through his mind. It seemed like it happened on another planet in another century.

O'Connor was watching the road with his rifle ready. He yelled over his shoulder. "Which way, Sarge?"

He pointed east. "We'll head east and hopefully find our old path. We'll be able to move faster once were on familiar ground. Find us a good way off this road, Corporal."

O'Connor nodded and jogged down the road. He found a break in the jungle and motioned the squad. The three Marines had sidearms, but they were so weak they couldn't hold them. They stuffed them into their waistbands, happy to have a way to defend themselves.

Sergeant Carver signaled for O'Connor to wait and went to the back of the truck to take one last look at the Japanese officer. He was sweating profusely but hadn't moved. Private Grant had done a good job.

He knew it wouldn't take long for the Japanese to find their trail, but he didn't want to make it any easier for them.

Back with O'Connor, he pointed at Private Willy. "Take point." O'Connor looked at him like he'd lost his mind. Carver addressed O'Connor. "I want you to stay back and set those grenade traps. It'll slow those bastards down, give us more of a chance."

O'Connor smiled like a devil. "I'll collect the squad's grenades…good idea."

Carver motioned the men to follow Willy. He put the three Marines in the middle of the squad with men on either side of them for support. Carver hadn't heard them say more than a few words; they seemed to be in shock with the whole situation.

Sergeant Carver took one last look down the road and signaled Willy to move out. Willy nodded, licked his lips and moved into the jungle.

20

Colonel Araki glared at the newly arrived Lieutenant Shibata. He knew no one would disturb his sleep unless they had a damned good reason. He sat up in bed and scowled at the bowing Lieutenant. He was new, which automatically made him the bearer of bad news.

Colonel Araki rubbed the sleep from his eyes then his aching leg. He could hardly walk unless he rubbed his leg a few minutes to get the blood flowing. Every time he felt the pain his hatred for the Americans grew hotter. He growled, "What is it, Lieutenant?"

Lieutenant Shibata came out of his bow and held out a piece of paper. "This just came over the radio. It's urgent, sir."

"Just tell me what it says, damn you."

He bowed again and opened the paper. He'd heard the transmission and didn't need to read it. "It's from Major Kotani at the prisoner camp. They're under attack." Colonel Araki's head snapped up. "He doesn't know the force size, but he's in danger of being overrun."

Colonel Araki was standing. He found his cane and walked to the door as fast as his injured leg would allow. He took the paper and quickly scanned it. "Get a reaction force assembled immediately."

Lieutenant Shibata turned and ran to get men ready for combat. He was glad to be away from the fuming colonel.

Colonel Araki went back inside and put on his uniform and boots. He slammed his fist on the rickety desk. *Do the Americans know about the battle plans? No, impossible. They're trying to free the prisoners. They're on another one of their Hollywood quests.* He planned on throwing everything he had at them. Losing the prisoners wouldn't be a problem, but losing the battle plans could prove disastrous. He had to make sure they were safe.

Once dressed he went outside. The men were hustling around trying to get their gear ready. He saw Captain Tagami yelling and giving orders. Colonel Araki called to him, and he stopped what he was doing and went to his commander and saluted. "How close are you to getting a reaction force to the camp?"

Captain Tagami replied, "The main force will be ready in minutes. I have two troop trucks. I can have thirty soldiers there in twenty minutes. I've already sent out a three man squad on a motorcycle, and a jeep with a mounted machine gun. Lieutenant Shibata volunteered to be the gunner. If the Americans are trying to escape the squad will be able to stall them until we arrive in force."

Colonel Araki nodded. "Good. I want you leaving in the next five minutes."

Captain Tagami saluted and went back to organizing his force. Minutes later the trucks were filled with troops and trundling along the newly constructed road towards the camp. Colonel Araki called for his jeep; he'd follow along and oversee the operation.

CAPTAIN TAGAMI WAS in the lead truck beside a sergeant and the driver. Even though the road was new, it was already full of ruts and muddy puddles, despite not being used often. He urged the driver ever faster, and the men held on the best they could.

He figured they were a couple of Kilometers from the camp when they came around a curve, and the driver stood on the brakes. The truck following was a fraction too late and slammed into the back. The soldiers were first thrown forward then flung back. The two men in the back of the first truck were flung out and landed on the hood of the second truck.

Captain Tagami had been studying a map and started to cuss the driver until he saw the carnage blocking the road. It was obvious what had happened. The jeep he'd sent out was crumpled against a troop truck. Smoke still wafted into the air from the dead vehicles. He jumped out, and his feet sank into the mud. He yelled for the men to disembark and set up a perimeter.

He waved a squad forward to investigate. He walked with them, his Nambu pistol drawn and ready. There was no sign of the motorcycle he'd sent, and he only saw one body. He studied the man planted in the truck grille and realized it was Lieutenant Shibata.

There was yelling from the back of the wreck. They'd found something. He jogged past the cab and glanced inside. It was covered with shards of glass and blood. He continued to the back and watched as two soldiers hauled a bound and gagged man from the back of the truck. He had a bag over his head. The man grunted and strained as the soldiers struggled to move him.

Once they had him out and on his feet, Captain Tagami ripped the bag from his head. The man squinted at the morning sunlight streaming through the trees. Captain Tagami stepped back astonished, "Lieutenant Taro!"

Lieutenant Taro bowed his head, "Captain Tagami." He bent over; a coughing fit getting the best of him. The men stepped back giving him breathing room. When he was through clearing his lungs, he said, "The Americans attacked the camp, they took me prisoner." His eyes went wide, remembering. "The, the Americans have the satchel, they have the plans." He started to collapse but was caught by the soldiers. He got control and continued. "We have to stop them; they left an hour ago. We must stop them."

Captain Tagami said, "We know about the attack, we were coming to your aid, but it appears we're too late. Which way did they go?" Lieutenant Taro shook his head. He'd lost a lot of fluid languishing in the back of the truck and felt light headed and sick.

Captain Tagami ordered his men to search the surrounding area for tracks leading into the jungle. The sergeants led two groups along either side of the road. He had the soldiers holding Lt. Taro untie him and put him on the ground. Once he was situated, he asked, "What plans? What satchel?"

Lieutenant Taro looked up at the Captain towering above him. "There was a satchel with battle plans, I think. I was trying to escape with them when they captured the truck," he moved his head to the crashed truck, "I had the satchel in the truck, and they took it. Before they gagged and blindfolded me I saw one of them with it."

Another vehicle skidded to a halt behind Captain Tagami's troop trucks. Tagami saw the unmistakable gait of Colonel Araki coming around the wreck. He approached, and Tagami braced and gave him a crisp salute.

Colonel Araki returned the salute. "Report."

Captain Tagami told him what he knew and what he was doing about it. Colonel Araki gritted his teeth when he heard Lt. Taro was involved. He limped to where Lieutenant Taro was still sitting on the ground with his head in his hands. Colonel Araki recognized his generous frame and stepped in front. Lieutenant Taro saw the shiny boots and looked up to see the last person he wanted to face. "Colonel, Colonel Araki," he spluttered getting to his feet. The sudden move sent him into a dizzy spell that he couldn't control. He got halfway up and had to sit back down. He felt the bile rising, but it was too late to stop it. He spewed partially digested rice and meat onto the ground beside the colonel's boots.

Colonel Araki didn't move but kneeled in front of him. "Tell me everything starting with the attack."

Lieutenant Taro wiped his pale mouth and relayed everything he could recall about the past few hours.

When he was finished, Colonel Araki stood. Lieutenant Taro willed himself to his feet and swayed. Colonel Araki lashed out with an open palmed right hand and slapped Taro, knocking him back to the ground. Lieutenant Taro looked up at him, confusion and fear in his eyes. "The Americans now have the plans for our spring attack...down to the very last detail!" His eyes seethed. "Because of your incompetence!"

Lieutenant Taro was horrified to think he'd let his commander down again. He spluttered, "Sir, I tried to get them away, back to you, but they attacked the truck." He shook his head, "there was nothing I could do. There were too many of them."

Colonel Araki looked down at him and spat. "The Americans weren't looking for the plans. How could they possibly know about them, you fool? They were trying to free the prisoners. They took the truck to escape. If they'd come for the plans, they wouldn't have left before finding them. By running away with the satchel, you gave them the plans!"

Lieutenant Taro felt sick again as he realized the truth of it. The world started to spin, and he couldn't keep himself from falling onto his side and emptying the rest of his gut.

Colonel Araki had every intention of shooting him in place, but at that moment there was a muted explosion, followed by shouting and screaming. He left the sick lieutenant in the mud and limped to the commotion. Captain Tagami trotted past him with his pistol drawn.

A Kilometer down the road Sergeant Chida was pulling a body from the jungle onto the road. Behind him, two men helped a screaming soldier, and sat him down beside the dead man.

Captain Tagami got there first. "What happened?"

Sergeant Chida braced, "We found the American trail, but they set a trap. A grenade rigged with wire, sir." He pointed to the two men. One was dead, his chest wet with blood from countless shrapnel wounds. The other's leg was a mangled mess. Fleshy meat and bone showed through his pants. He rocked back and forth yelling in pain.

Colonel Araki went to the man and smacked him with his cane. The soldier looked up with crazed eyes. Colonel Araki spoke through gritted teeth. "You are a soldier of the empire! Stop screaming like a stuck pig." The soldier swallowed the scream and breathed through pursed lips.

Colonel Araki yelled. "Captain Tagami, take your men in pursuit at once. Leave a trail for more troops to follow. Leave me four men." Tagami turned to leave, but Colonel Araki slapped his cane on his shoulder. Colonel Araki said, "Getting those plans back is more important than the lives of you and your men."

Captain Tagami left Araki with four of his best men and followed the trail into the jungle.

~

COLONEL ARAKI and the four soldiers went back to the wreck. Lieutenant Taro had pulled himself up and was leaning against the back of the troop truck, staring at the two dead Marines. He was still pale and dazed, but when he saw Colonel Araki coming, he tried to stand at attention.

The anger that filled Colonel Araki had subsided. His thoughts were clearer now that the rage had passed. He still wanted to punish his fat lieutenant, but he wouldn't shoot him. He'd be more clever. As he approached, Taro tried to snap off a tight salute, but it came off weak. Colonel Araki didn't return it. In an even voice, he said, "You will be in the first wave of attackers." He walked around Taro, still trying to keep his salute at his brow. He dropped it as Araki passed and closed his eyes. Sweat beaded on his forehead. Colonel Araki limped back to the waiting jeep.

Being at the front of an attack on the American line would likely end in his death, but an attack against an enemy that knew their entire plan would be a sure thing.

He took a deep breath and resigned himself yet again to his death. He'd lived the last few months knowing there was little chance he'd survive the war. Men far better than him had died by the thousands. It was a miracle he was still alive.

When he'd transferred to the prisoner camp, he'd gotten a glimmer of hope that perhaps he'd live, but now there was no chance.

He nodded to himself and walked around the wreck just in time to see Colonel Araki's jeep and two trucks speeding away around the corner.

He went to the destroyed jeep and tried without success to ignore the impaled Lieutenant Shibata. He searched for water and found a discarded canteen.

21

The squad moved as quick as possible through the jungle. Private Willy, while not a natural woodsman like O'Connor, had a lot of jungle experience and was able to get them through some tough terrain without having to backtrack. The vigilance of taking point was taking its toll on him, though. He stopped and kneeled, halting the squad. Sergeant Carver loped up to him, his Thompson at the ready. "What's the problem? Why you stopped?"

Private Willy panted and wiped his brow. "Sorry, Sarge, but I'm feeling dizzy. Just need some water and I'll be good to go. Had to stop for a sec."

Carver gave him a good look. He'd never known him to quit at anything. He looked okay, a little peaked, but they all were. "You hit?" Willy shrugged and touched his lower left side. Carver said, "Goddammit, Willy, show me."

Willy pulled up his shirt. "It's nothing, just a scratch."

Carver noticed blood seeping into Willy's pants. He hadn't noticed it before. He shook his head. "Dammit. You need to have Dawkins take a look at that. You're gonna end up with an infection. That doesn't help our situation." Willy looked down and spit a stream of stringy saliva.

Sergeant Carver sent word back for Cpl. Dawkins to come forward.

He motioned the others to take a ten-minute break while the medic took care of Willy.

Carver went to speak with O'Connor about taking over the point position. "You get the grenades set?"

O'Connor nodded, "Sure did. I put the first one near the start of our trail. I haven't heard it go off, but I think we're too far into the jungle now to hear that one. I figured we'd of heard it if we were within a half mile or so. Guess we're at least that far in front of anyone following our trail."

Carver asked, "You sure they'd trip it?"

O'Connor shrugged, "It's well hidden, and they wouldn't be expecting the first one." Carver nodded. "I set two more. I don't have as much confidence in those, but even if they find them without setting them off, it'll still slow 'em down." He opened his ammo pouch and showed Carver two more grenades. "I've still got these."

Carver said, "Good job. Hold onto those; we may need 'em the closer we get to our lines." He noticed O'Connor looking at the satchel hanging around his neck. "I think once the Japs figure out we've got this, they'll double their efforts to find us."

"What's in it?"

"I've only had a second to check, but it looks like an attack plan. That nip officer sure didn't like me having it. I think it's the real deal."

O'Connor smiled, "Maybe that'll get Lieutenant Swan off our backs."

An hour later, O'Connor had found the trail they'd traveled in on. The muddy boot prints were easy to pick out.

Sergeant Carver called for a five-minute rest. The men immediately went for their canteens and whatever C-rats they had handy.

They hadn't come across any drinkable water. They'd crossed a few small creeks on the trail in, but it was hard to figure when they'd cross them again. O'Connor couldn't remember how far away they were, but he figured they'd be able to refill within the next hour. He'd already drained his first canteen and was well into his second. They'd been in constant motion since attacking the camp, and they were starting to drag. Running out of water would make it much worse.

O'Connor finished eating a stale cracker and took the lead position again. Carver took him by the arm. "We need to hurry. The men are dragging ass, but the Japs can't be far behind, and they may be waiting with a blocking force in front. Move fast." O'Connor knew the stakes and Carver pushed him forward. "We'll stay close." Carver thought, *God I hope I'm not sending him to his death.*

O'Connor took up the path and trotted along at a slow, but ground consuming pace. The others filed in behind.

The Marines were doing the best they could, but the men on either side had to support them more and more. The squad divvied up their food and the Marine's devoured everything. They were careful not to give them too much too soon. Their stomachs and bodies weren't used to the flood of nutrients and wouldn't be able to handle it. The Marines were starving and pleaded with their vacant eyes for more, even though they knew it wouldn't stay down. The soldiers didn't give in to their silent pleas as much as they wanted to.

Moving along the trail was easy for O'Connor. He didn't have to spend his time finding the best path; he'd already done that on the way out. Some of the trail looked familiar to him, a moss-covered boulder, a funny shaped tree, but other parts seemed like new territory, even though he was following his boot prints from the day before.

He came upon their miserable sleeping spot. He was amazed how quickly they were covering the ground. *Don't let your guard down now.* It was never a good idea to return the same way you'd come. It was the first thing they taught you about patrolling; never be predictable.

The fast pace was taking a toll on the men. The sucking mud they sank in with every other step didn't help. O'Connor heard the creek before he saw it. His tongue felt too large for his mouth. It was chalky and dry. He'd been ignoring the building thirst the best he could but the sound of the creek brought it all back. *Oh, thank God almighty.*

It was all he could do not to run headlong into the creek, but he slowed his pace and checked to make sure it was clear. It would be a good place for a Japanese ambush. The men behind him were just as parched as he was, but they held back until he gave the all clear. With that, they waded into the little creek and drank.

The stifling jungle heat fell off them like shedding a thick coat. The clear water tasted like an exotic cocktail, and their bodies soaked it up like a sponge. Within minutes they felt rejuvenated.

Sergeant Carver dipped his canteen and filled it. He took a long pull, his dirty Adams' apple moving like a piston. He drained it and refilled both canteens. He clipped them to his belt and watched the men cooling off. He looked at the trail behind him. They had to keep moving. "Fill your canteens and get the hell outta there. Japs could be right behind us."

The three Marines looked like they'd died and gone to heaven. They drank and drank and scrubbed their lice ridden bodies. The water seemed like a miracle. They had to be dragged out. It was the first time since their rescue that Carver saw a positive change in them. In their eyes instead of loss, despair, and sickness, Carver saw hope.

They were getting themselves together when they heard the muffled sound of a distant explosion. Every man went to a knee on high alert. Carver moved up to O'Connor. "Assuming that was your second grenade, how far away are they?"

O'Connor calculated. "I'd say about an hour behind us? I set that one a just before I took over on point."

Sergeant Carver shook his head. "Dammit, thought we might get out of here scot-free." He rubbed his stubbled chin. "Set another trap on the other side of the creek. Maybe they're just as thirsty as we were."

O'Connor nodded and brought Private Gomez to help him. The job was easier with two, and he wanted to teach Gomez. He'd proven himself a good warrior. Carver didn't wait for them to finish. Private Crofter had been the second man in the patrol. "Crofter, take point." Crofter's eyes went wide, but he gave a curt nod and moved out.

22

Colonel Araki got back to his headquarters and stood in front of the radioman. He closed his eyes and went over what he had to do. He gritted his teeth thinking about the circumstances that had brought him to this dishonor. The image of Second Lieutenant Taro continually assaulted his senses.

The radioman sat in front of the radio with earphones on waiting for Colonel Araki to order him to connect him with General Hyakutake. Sweat formed on the soldier's brow and dripped into his eyes and along his nose, but he dared not wipe it away, not with Colonel Araki standing behind him. "Radio the general, Private."

The radioman jumped with the words even though he knew they were coming. "Yessir!" Moments later he handed the headset and the handheld speaker to the colonel. Colonel Araki gestured for the private to leave. He pushed his chair back, a weathered stump and nearly toppled it in his haste to retreat.

Colonel Araki relayed the events of the past few hours. When he told General Hyakutake he believed the Americans had the plans to their spring attack, there was silence and faint static. He thought he lost the connection, but in another moment the General erupted.

Colonel Araki tensed and tightened his grip on the receiver, threatening to crush it. He stood rigid as a board as each new tirade slammed into him like the relentless tides eroding the beaches.

Finally, the General ran out of insults and the line was silent. Colonel Araki took the time to say. "General, I know I have failed you. I have no excuse, the blame is squarely on my shoulders. I will use all my resources to assure the American raiders don't make it back to their lines."

The voice on the other end lost its rage but was replaced with icy coldness. "I'll expect nothing less, Colonel." The line went dead.

Colonel Araki released his iron grip and placed the receiver back in its cradle. He wanted to hurl the entire radio across the tent, but that would only accomplish destroying a valuable piece of equipment. He was going to yell for Lieutenant Shibata, but the image of him stuck in the grille of the truck flashed across his mind.

"Lieutenant Koga," he yelled. Lieutenant Koga had been waiting for the inevitable call. The colonel would want to send as many men as he could spare to find and kill the Americans. He'd already assembled his platoon. They were formed up and awaiting orders.

Lieutenant Koga strode to Colonel Araki and snapped off a salute. Colonel Araki ordered, "Get your platoon assembled. I have a mission of the utmost importance."

Looking straight ahead, Lt. Koga said, "Sir, I have the platoon ready. We're awaiting your orders."

Colonel Araki stared at Lt. Koga. It was frowned upon for officers to take the initiative. The Japanese Army operated on following strict orders to the letter, and that meant not doing anything until ordered to do so. Colonel Araki would have to remind this petulant officer of his role once this fiasco was over. Now was not the time. Now was the time to act. "Come with me." He entered his tent and strode to the large map covering the table in the center of the room. He found their position and moved his finger along a drawn-in line indicating the newly constructed road. "Here is where the Americans were intercepted. They moved east into the jungle. I'm assuming they will continue east then turn south back to their lines. As you can see, they will have to travel many kilometers to reach their lines.

"I'm assuming they're moving fast trying to get home before we can react, but we have the advantage. Our new road parallels the escape route. We will truck you and your men south eight kilometers then you will cut east and cut them off. Captain Tagami is following the American's as we speak. When they hit your blocking force, Tagami will come from behind, and we'll squeeze the life out of them. Understood?"

Lieutenant Koga's intelligent eyes studied the map. Colonel Araki was getting annoyed. "One question, sir." Colonel Araki raised an eyebrow. "We have men nearer the American lines. Will we be in danger of passing through any of our own troops as we travel east?"

Colonel Araki circled three areas of the map. "Three companies are keeping the line. You will be well west of them. I'll alert them of the situation; they can assist you if the need arises. Any more questions?"

He said it as if it would be better if there weren't, but Lieutenant Koga stroked his chin, then shook his head, "No sir."

Colonel Araki said, "Good. This mission is vital to the upcoming Spring attack. See you don't fail."

Lieutenant Koga clicked his heels and saluted, "Of course sir. I will not fail."

Captain Tagami and his twenty men moved through the jungle following the trail. The Americans weren't trying to cover their tracks. Tagami wasn't moving as fast as he wanted, though, due to the booby trap they'd run into near the road. He'd lost two men, one killed the other injured and out of action.

Since then they'd moved slower, and their caution paid off. The point man found another booby trapped grenade. He'd come close to stumbling over it, but he'd noticed a discoloration in the mud and looked closer. He found the trap that had nearly killed him. He pointed it out to Captain Tagami. They'd exploded the grenade by firing beside it, knocking it sideways and allowing the handle to release. The explosion that followed wasn't impressive, but it would've killed or injured the young private.

Captain Tagami wanted to move faster, but he wasn't willing to risk the lives of his men by charging headlong through such a dangerous area.

Another hour passed without finding more booby traps. The men started to relax and their pace increased. Captain Tagami noticed, but he didn't slow them. They were making good time. The American's tracks seemed fresh. They were gaining on them.

The point man, the same private who'd found the second trap, came to a dense patch of jungle. He inspected the ground. It seemed like a good spot for another trap, and his instincts were urging caution. The men behind him halted and watched as he crawled forward feeling and looking for anything out of the ordinary. The American boot prints didn't falter. It didn't appear anyone had stopped. He crawled for ten meters before he was through the dense section. He stood and waved the men behind him through.

The first man strode to the thick leaves and vines and pushed his way through. Suspended on a vine ten feet above his head a grenade started to move side to side. When he was through, the next soldier was close behind.

He was directly beneath the grenade when it fell and released the lever. The one pound chunk of metal landed on the soldier's helmet and bounced backward. He turned just in time for the explosion that tore through his torso. The man behind him never knew what hit him. One second he was pushing through the jungle the next he was blown off his feet and filled with hot shrapnel. Both soldiers were dead before they hit the ground.

The rest of the men dove to the ground as debris rained down on them. Captain Tagami was the first to lift his head. "Sergeant Chida, report!"

Sergeant Chida, only a few feet away from the shredded soldier jumped to his feet and ran to him. He knew he was gone. He went to the next man. He'd taken the brunt of the explosion, and there wasn't much left. He could see two more soldiers further ahead. They looked shaken but unharmed. He yelled back to the Captain, "Two men down, sir. Looks like another booby trap."

Captain Tagami stood, and the rest of the men did the same. "Pull the casualties to the side. We don't have time to bury them." The dead were laid side by side along the muddy path. When Captain Tagami went past, he closed his eyes. *Two more good men gone. When we catch these Americans, we'll make them pay.*

The pace slowed again, but Captain Tagami urged them on, wanting to close with and kill the Americans.

Only a couple minutes had passed before the point man came to where the trail met another and made a ninety-degree turn to the south.

He stopped the men and moved forward looking for anything suspicious. Once satisfied, he called Sergeant Chida forward. He did an inspection of the area before calling up the captain.

When he approached, he whispered and pointed. "Looks like they headed south from here, back towards their lines."

Captain Tagami pursed his lips, "probably the same trail they came in on. They'll be moving faster, covering ground they already know." He looked around at the men. They'd been moving without much rest for two hours. Their faces glistened with sweat, and their shirts had changed color from tan to wet black. "Sergeant, have the men take a five-minute rest."

Sergeant Chida passed the order on, and the men sat and took long gulps from their canteens. Five minutes later they were ready to move. Sergeant Chida reported to his officer. "The men are running low on water, sir."

Tagami nodded. "I know. Get them moving." Without a word, the men took up the trot. The trail was obvious and easy to follow. Tagami watched his men. They were tired but willing to give everything they had to find the Americans. The cowardly booby traps had served to not only make them more careful, but also bloodthirsty for revenge.

He found his spot in the middle of the formation and took up the same trot. Each step was difficult. So many men passing through made the trail a muddy nightmare. He had to spot each footfall, trying to gauge how deep his foot would sink. It was exhausting, and soon he was gasping for breath. The men around him were similarly huffing, making them sound like chugging freight trains. His legs burned, his breathing was labored, but he would not be the first man to stop. He'd push as hard as his men.

Another hour passed and he felt like his legs might stop functioning. He was about to call for a rest, but the man in front of him slowed and stopped. The soldier was unrecognizable, almost completely covered in black mud. Every soldier looked the same. The mud splattering with each footfall had covered them and anyone close.

Once he got control of his breathing, he heard the sound of water flowing over rocks. He'd never been more thirsty in his life. The men around him licked their cracking lips in anticipation.

The point man started checking for more booby traps, but the men behind him pushed forward to the water. They didn't see the thin line crossing the path.

23

It didn't take long for the bliss of the creek to fade. The hot, clammy jungle with the sucking mud quickly reminded Carver and his men of their misery. The water in their soaked fatigues turned to salty sweat. There was never a point when they were dry. If they didn't get back to their lines soon, they'd all come down with foot rot.

They'd made it three quarters of a mile from the creek when they heard the grenade go off. They hunched down, panting.

Carver didn't wait. He stood and waved them forward. "We've gotta keep moving, they're gaining on us, dammit. Double time!"

A groan went through the squad, but they knew they were in a race for their lives. They were tired, hungry and thirsty, but they dug deep and pushed themselves forward. The Marines were well past walking let alone running. They were carried on the backs of the soldiers, passed from man to man as they fatigued.

Carver took his turn and was amazed how light the Marine was. With each jolting step, the Marine grunted. Carver could feel his breath on his neck, assuring him he was alive, but it seemed stringy and weak. "You hang in there, Marine. You've come too far to die on us now." There was no answer, just the breathing.

The men struggled to keep up with O'Connor's blistering pace. Carver was amazed how easily he seemed to run. He felt like a lumbering ox, but O'Connor looked like he hardly sank in the mud at all. He knew it was an illusion, O'Connor just knew how to move well through jungle and wild country.

It seemed like they'd been running a long time but only eight minutes had passed. Carver called a halt. He passed the Marine to Private Denn and gathered the men. They were breathing hard, swallowing, trying to wet their throats. They pulled canteens and took healthy swigs.

When he could talk, Carver said, "This trail will take us all the way to the beach. There's no one there to pick us up. We need to start veering towards Hill 260." He pointed. They could make out the denuded top of the hill through a gap in the jungle. It was off to the right at a forty-five degree angle. It seemed a long ways off. "We've made great time, but I think it's time to slow down and get to our lines without getting shot up."

Private Willy poked his thumb behind him. His other hand held pressure over his seeping wound. Carver noticed it was bleeding again. Willy said, "What about our friends coming up behind us?"

Carver wiped his brow. "They're a problem. They'll be on us soon, and we have no idea how many they are." He stared at O'Connor. "You think you can get 'em to keep following our trail to the beach?"

O'Connor thought about it. He looked down the trail. "I'm pretty sure there's another creek coming up. I've been expecting it for awhile; can't be much farther. We could lose 'em there, follow the creek downstream. I'll beat down the main trail, give 'em fresh tracks to follow, then double back to you."

Sergeant Carver made up his mind. "I like it. Get us to the creek."

~

O'Connor was correct. He found the creek a few hundred yards down the trail. Unlike the previous creek this one's water was briny and copper colored. The men filled their canteens and dropped halzone tablets in for purification. O'Connor wondered if they'd be alive long enough to get dysentery.

Sergeant Carver squatted next to O'Connor. "We'll split up here. I think you need another trooper with you. I don't think one set of prints will fool them and you could use the help."

O'Connor was going to protest but realized he was right about the boot prints. "Right. I'll take Gomez. Kid seems to know his way around pretty well."

Carver agreed, "That's who I was thinking about." Carver called out, "Gomez, you're accompanying O'Connor on this adventure."

Private Gomez's dark complexion went pale, but he stepped forward and gave O'Connor a nod he hoped looked confident.

O'Connor asked, "Feel up to it?"

Private Gomez nodded. "Hell yes."

O'Connor smiled and slapped him on the shoulder. He spoke up so all the men could hear, "Make sure you stay in the creek. One boot print could give it all away." Everyone understood. They stared at O'Connor and Gomez wondering if they'd see them again. O'Connor grinned and tipped his helmet. "You're not getting rid of me that easily. We'll see you back on the hill." He patted his ammo pouch, "I need another grenade. I'll set it down the trail a ways. If you hear it, you'll know they're following me, and so will I."

Carver gave him one, and reached his hand out, and said, "Don't do anything stupid. I'll see you in a few."

O'Connor clasped his calloused hand and looked him in the eye. "You bet."

It was time to go. O'Connor and Gomez splashed across the creek and stomped around the bank on the other side, making lots of tracks. Then they trotted up the trail, sure to leave heavy boot prints.

Carver watched them go. *Hope the Japs take the bait.* The men stood in the creek waiting for the word to move. "Alright, let's do this right. Single file, don't step out of the creek. Grant, you're on point, move steady but know there's bound to be Japs out here."

Private Grant nodded and waded down the creek bed. The water came up to his knees, and the rock bottom made for easy walking.

The men moved out in single file, taking careful steps. The briny water made each footfall a mystery, but it would also serve to keep their tracks hidden. They were making a lot of noise sloshing through, but soon they'd be around the corner and out of earshot from the trail. Carver figured the Japanese were still at least a half hour behind them, plenty of time to disappear.

~

THE SQUAD MOVED down the creekbed steadily for forty-five minutes until the creek steepened and started moving faster. There wasn't a lot of water, but the increased gradient made the walking tough, and he couldn't tell how long the rapids went. It seemed it was building up to something; maybe a waterfall.

Sergeant Carver stopped the squad. He figured they'd moved far enough downstream. He hadn't heard the grenade trap O'Connor had said he would set, but sloshing through water and now the noise of the rapids made that impossible. He had to assume the Japs followed O'Connor and Gomez. He was sure they hadn't left signs for them to suspect they'd gone down the creek. He wondered how his two soldiers were faring. He shook the notion from his head. He had to concentrate on getting these men home.

Carver signaled to spread out and set a perimeter. He motioned Private Grant to him. "You and Daniels move down the creek. I need to know how far this rapid goes. We may need to start moving through the jungle again." Grant slugged Daniels and signaled him to follow. They moved down the creek and were soon out of sight.

Carver figured they had to be close to Hill 260, but the thick jungle surrounding the creek made it impossible to see further than a few feet.

Minutes later Private Grant and Daniels came splashing up the creek. Carver knew by the way they kept glancing over their shoulders that something was wrong.

Out of breath and wide-eyed, Grant gasped, "Japs everywhere moving along the bank. They're right behind us!"

The rest of the squad heard and looked to Carver for direction. He signaled them to move into the jungle on the opposite bank.

They pushed and struggled to penetrate the jungle. Carver followed Grant into a hole he'd pushed through. Within seconds the squad disappeared into the greenery. He was only feet away from the creek but completely concealed. The sound of the whitewater covered any sounds the Japanese soldiers were making, so he parted the jungle to see what was happening.

The creek returned to its incessant task of moving down the canyon as if they'd never been there. He watched the far bank. He could only see a small section through his hole, but soon enough he saw movement. The far bank wasn't as thick with vegetation, there were gaps, and he could see Japanese soldiers moving. They were moving fast, and he knew they weren't a random patrol. They were searching. Trying to find and cut off his squad.

Carver figured it was at least a platoon. They moved along steadily, not giving any notice to their hiding spot. An officer came into view. He was obvious with his pistol and the submachine gun strapped across his back.

Carver watched him. He moved well. He stopped along with two soldiers. The officer looked at the creek and walked to the bank. He said something to his men and they nodded and continued upstream, but the officer kneeled and dipped his hat. He wrung it out and placed it back on his head. He rubbed his neck and looked across the creek seeming to stare directly at him.

Carver knew there was no way he could see him, but he continued to stare. Carver froze and made a conscious decision not to stare back. He kept the officer in his peripheral vision, not wanting him to feel his stare. He knew the rest of the squad was seeing the same thing and hoped no one did anything stupid.

The officer stood and stretched his neck side to side, still concentrating on the opposite bank.

Private Denn wasn't in a good position when the Japanese platoon showed up. He'd pushed his way into the brush, but he wasn't able to find a solid piece of ground to rest his feet. He'd sat down on thick vines and branches only a few feet above the creek. He'd pulled his feet up and tried to jam them into the brush, but it wasn't solid. He struggled to keep his feet from falling into the creek, but his weight was working against him, and he slid, millimeter by millimeter. He thought he was home-free until the damned officer decided to stop.

Sergeant Carver realized he'd been holding his breath as he saw the officer start to turn back to the clearing. He let it out slowly then gulped it back when he heard a splash upstream from his position. The Jap officer spun to the sound bringing his machine gun off his back in a practiced, smooth motion.

Carver was bringing his Thompson around when Private Denn's M1 shattered the evening. The creek in front of the officer erupted in geysers of water, and the leaves and branches around his head jumped and fell to the ground. The officer crouched and unleashed accurate return fire from his type 100 submachine gun, then took off like a track star into the jungle.

Carver put the Thompson to his shoulder and sent a stream of .45 caliber, but he knew he hadn't hit anything. The officer must have been a trained sprinter.

The rest of the squad fired, but Carver yelled, "Cease fire! Move downstream on the double!"

As one, the squad emerged from the jungle, one man short. "Sarge, Denn's down, Denn's down!"

Corporal Dawkins ran up the creek like a mad man and crouched by Denn's side. Blood mixed with water as the life left Private Denn's body. Dawkins felt for a pulse, but he was gone. He reached into his bloody shirt and yanked the dog tags off his neck, and stuffed them into his pants pocket. He yelled, "Denn's KIA, nothing I can do!"

Sergeant Carver yelled back, "Grab his gun and any ammo and leave him. We gotta go now!" He grabbed Private Crofter as he splashed by, "Take us downstream," he pushed him forward. "Double time down the creek! Hans, Grant, take the rear. Keep their heads down but don't dilly dally."

The rest of the squad splashed downstream, and Carver followed the last man. He was just around the corner when he heard the rear guard's M1s. He stopped and waited for his two soldiers with his Thompson ready. He heard their splashes and the cracks of Arisaka rifles and the zipping of bullets passing close.

They came around the corner running full tilt. The water splashed wildly with each footfall. Around them, bullets added to the churn. Carver urged them to hurry. They ran by him, and Carver waited for a target. He didn't have long to wait. Three soldiers came sprinting downstream. Staying in his crouch, he pulled the trigger and swept the Thompson across their bodies and they toppled like bowling pins. He didn't wait for more but turned and followed his fleeing men.

Bullets zipped and smacked into boulders and water all around him, but none found their mark. He caught up to the squad. They'd come to a narrow part of the creek. Downstream the creek entered a canyon with steep, moss covered walls. Carver had a decision to make, either stay in the creekbed and be trapped in the canyon or move to the bank and try to lose them in the jungle.

The men crouched behind boulders, their weapons aimed upstream past Carver. As he slid in behind a boulder, the squad opened up on a group of Japanese coming downstream. They were exposed and easy targets. They went down and stayed down. No more soldiers came down the center of the creek, but Carver could see flashes of khaki uniforms in the jungle. If he didn't move now, they'd flank him. He took a look downstream and made his decision. He pointed to the jungle, "Into the jungle, now!"

The squad rose and moved to the bank, but immediately met with an onslaught of fire. The Japanese were shooting so fast it sounded like one continuous roar. The first two GIs went down immediately, and the rest dove into the shallow water finding any cover they could. Beside Carver, Dawkins jumped to his feet and took a step towards the downed men. Carver grabbed his arm and held him back. He had to yell to make himself heard over the Japanese fire, "They're gone, nothing you can do!"

Dawkins tried to break away. "How do you know? You don't know that! Let me go!"

Carver held, squeezing his arm like a vise. "Knock it off! They're fucking dead!" he cupped his hand around his mouth and bellowed, "Move downstream, move downstream! I'll cover you!"

The men looked back at him and nodded. Bullets were zinging off rocks and making huge fountains of water. Carver gave one last squeeze on Dawkin's arm and yelled, "Covering fire, now!" He released his arm and came around the boulder and laid down a long stream of .45 caliber fire. Dawkins added his eight rounds of .30 caliber until his M1 pinged and he inserted a new clip.

The rest of the squad ran as fast as they could over the uneven ground. When they were almost out of sight, Carver punched Dawkin's arm and yelled, "Go!" Carver unleashed another long burst then took off after him.

With the steep gradient, they couldn't see far downstream, but they could tell the creek went into a steep canyon. There didn't look to be any way out except downstream. He hoped it didn't end in an impassable waterfall. They'd be trapped with Japs upstream and no exit downstream.

The squad stopped to wait for Carver and Dawkins just inside the beginning of the canyon. The entrance was choked with large boulders that had broken loose from the cliff-side sometime in the last millennium. No more bullets were chasing them downstream. The Japanese were weighing their options too.

Carver slid in behind a large boulder trying to get control of his breathing. He laid his head back and closed his eyes. Private First Class Daniels, spoke into his ear. "I've sent Palmer downstream to figure out if there's a way out of here. Thought this looked like a good spot to make a stand. The Japs can't get to us unless they come straight down the creek."

Carver got control of his breathing, and nodded. "Good job, I think you're right. We'll stop here until Palmer gets back." He looked to the towering cliff walls to either side. "We can't scale these walls. If there's no exit downstream we're fucked."

He looked the squad over. They were exhausted and scared. They'd been fighting and running all day without pause. He noticed the two missing soldiers were Private Grant and Hans. He imagined their bullet-riddled bodies floating upstream.

Private Willy was staring at him. He gave him a nod and Willy nodded back then moved his eyes back upstream. Willy pointed, "Here they come."

Carver leaned around his boulder. The Japs were using the smaller boulders upstream for cover, trying to get as close as possible before engaging. He called out. "How many grenades we got left?" The men called out their status. With the one he had, they had five left.

He watched the Japanese advance. "Hold your fire until they're within grenade distance." He looked at Private Crofter crouched five yards away. "Crofter," he looked at Carver. His face was black with mud and gunpowder, his wide eyes white holes within. "You and I will throw on my command." Crofter nodded and reached back for his one grenade. Carver raised his voice, "Wait for our grenades then give 'em hell."

The squad nodded and settled into firing positions. The Japanese soldiers kept coming, moving from boulder to boulder. When they were twenty yards away, he nodded at Crofter who crouched with his finger through the grenade pin. They pulled the pins simultaneously and hurled them. The Japanese saw the movement and fired, but they were under cover before the bullets slammed and ricocheted off boulders.

There was a pause then a sharp yell from a Japanese soldier, then the blast of the grenades. The sound was loud in the confines of the canyon, making Carver wince. The boulders protecting the Japanese soldiers now became deadly, as shrapnel ricocheted and shredded flesh.

The squad opened up, laying down fire. The Japanese soldiers not behind cover were hit and dropped out of sight. There was yelling and screaming, then return fire. The concussion from the grenades and the withering fire kept the Japanese off balance, and their fire was inaccurate.

Carver could see a group of cowering soldiers trying to stay behind a rock that wasn't big enough for all of them. He yelled to Private Palmer. "Throw me your grenade!" Palmer was lying down. He rolled to the side and unclipped his grenade. He rose to a crouch and tossed it the ten feet to Carver. In one motion Carver caught it with two hands, pulled the pin and arced it into the group of soldiers. It was a perfect throw, landing on the back of the middle man. It blew, and all four of the Japanese soldiers went down.

Their deaths seemed to take the fight out of the remaining soldiers.

They rose up and with arms flailing and legs pumping retreated back upstream.

They were easy targets for the squad. Only a few escaped back to the rest of their platoon. Sergeant Carver met Private Willy's eyes. He was chuckling to himself, enjoying the slaughter. Once again, Carver was glad Willy was on his side.

Private Palmer came up through the rocks and boulders. He was breathing hard. He took off his helmet and wiped his brow. When he caught his breath, Palmer said, "The canyon continues for another three hundred yards. It's steep all the way, no chance to climb out. The creek is steep, kinda like here," he gestured around him, "But steeper."

Carver nodded, "Is there an exit?"

Palmer nodded, "kinda. It ends in a waterfall. I'd say it's a thirty-foot drop or so." Carver cursed, but Palmer continued. "It looks like we can climb down the side of it. It's straight down, but there's thick vines we can use like rope." Carver raised an eyebrow and Palmer nodded. "I think it's doable."

24

O'Connor and Gomez ran along the trail, careful *not* to disguise their tracks. It felt strange and unnatural to tromp along like an elephant.

When they'd gone about one hundred yards, he stopped and Gomez kneeled down watching their back trail. "I'll plant the grenade here," O'Connor said. Gomez nodded and turned to help. O'Connor shook his head, "Keep watching the trail. I'll let you know when I need your help." He got to work scraping out a depression beside a small boulder along the edge of the trail. He cut a vine and wrapped it in a tight spiral in the depression. The rest he pulled across the trail.

He pulled the pin on the grenade and placed it on the wrapped vine with the handle against the rock. He stacked small pebbles along the base to keep it in place. When he was satisfied it was stable, he stepped back and looked at his handy work. He pulled some branches across the front of the rock, hiding the grenade. "Hey, Gomez," Gomez turned. "You see anything suspicious?"

Gomez looked over the area and shook his head, "No, nothing. Where is it?" O'Connor pulled back the jungle branches revealing the grenade. He pointed to the vine running across the trail and smiled. Gomez nodded and stepped over the vine with one careful stride.

Once past, O'Connor said, "Let's make some time."

Before he turned away, Private Gomez slapped his arm. O'Connor turned, and Gomez asked, "How far we gonna go before heading back to the squad."

O'Connor shook his head. "There's no chance we'll get back to the squad. We're on our own."

Gomez looked confused. "What? But you said…"

"Forget what I said, Carver knows the score. If the Japs follow us, our only chance is this way. We can't double back past them," he gestured down the trail. "We'll lead them this way then break off somewhere and head towards our lines to the west. We've gotta keep 'em following us for awhile, or they'll figure it out and head back to the creek in time to catch up with the others." He wiped his brow. "We may need to lead 'em all the way to the coast."

Gomez nodded. "Okay, I understand. Let's move, we're wasting time."

~

CAPTAIN TAGAMI and his men were running down the trail. They'd lost another man back at the creek. But instead of slowing them down it had the opposite effect, infusing them with hatred and revenge. It spurred them along like men possessed, throwing caution to the wind. Tagami let them run. He wanted revenge as much as they did and if they didn't catch up with the Americans, his men had been maimed and killed for nothing.

They came to another creek, and his soldiers stopped as the lead man checked for more traps. While he did so, they drank their remaining water. they knew they'd be able to refill their canteens immediately in the briny creek.

When they were sure there were no traps they moved into the creekbed and refilled their canteens. They didn't worry about purification. Most of them were already sick to some degree.

Captain Tagami watched them fill their canteens as he got his breath back. Despite being wracked with disease and hunger, his troops were good soldiers. They fought hard despite the horrible conditions, and he was proud of them. It made losing them harder. Tagami knew he cared too much but couldn't keep from feeling pride.

Without a word from him, the men finished filling their canteens and continued up the trail. Captain Tagami looked downstream as he crossed the creek. It meandered away, and he smiled. If he were out walking with his wife, she would've insisted on exploring its path, but he had no time for such whimsy. He had Americans to hunt.

They moved fast. They had no idea how far the Americans were, but he thought they must be gaining. He'd just stepped over a rotten log when the now familiar whump of a grenade blast sent him to the ground. Everyone was down, and the leaves and branches rained down on them like light snow.

He was up, running forward past his men. The ground was smoking along the left side of the trail, a soldier lay sprawled beyond.

Captain Tagami slid beside the first man and looked for wounds. The soldier's legs were red with blood, his pants shredded like paper. Tagami ripped them away and could see meat, tendons, and bones. Dark, thick blood oozed and pooled, filling the crevices of the wounds. Captain Tagami didn't know where to start. He pushed on his right leg trying to stem the flow of arterial blood, but it was useless, like trying to stem a river's flow with a napkin. When he thought he'd stopped one, another would look worse, and he'd move his hands to the new one.

He silently moved from one wound to another until the blood stopped flowing and the soldier stopped moving. He felt hands on his shoulder, and Sergeant Chida looked down at him. Tagami looked at him as if from out of a haze. His teary eyes made Chida looked fuzzy and wrong somehow. He shook his head and wiped his eyes spreading thick blood across his face.

Captain Tagami came back to the present and stood. His men formed a semi-circle around him. His arms were caked with sticky blood up to his elbows. The men stared, not used to an officer showing emotion. It embarrassed them, and when Captain Tagami looked at them with blurred eyes, they lowered their gazes in respect.

Captain Tagami looked at each man. They needed a strong leader, not a simpering child. When he got to Sergeant Chida's face, he addressed them. "These cowardly Americans take life without honor. They hide and set traps like children. We will overtake them and destroy them. We must avenge our fallen comrades. Their deaths will not be in vain. They must pay for their cowardice!"

He ordered the body taken to the side of the trail. Again there was no time for burials. He wondered how long it would take the jungle to consume him. He pictured him full of maggots. A sight he'd seen many times since this war began.

He waved them forward once again, hoping he wouldn't have to see more of his men blown up.

~

It didn't seem like much time had passed when O'Connor and Gomez heard the soft thump of an explosion. They stopped and crouched. They looked at one another, and Gomez licked his dry lips. "They're close."

O'Connor nodded. "Say quarter mile back? Maybe five minutes if they're sprinting, which they must be."

Gomez looked down the trail then back to O'Connor. "How far to the coast you figure?"

O'Connor looked up at the canopy over their head and the glimpse of sky. "I don't know, but I bet we can get there before dark." Gomez looked to the sky, and for the first time noticed it was evening. He felt fatigue come over him as he realized he'd been fighting and running the entire day.

With shaking hands, he unscrewed the lid of his canteen and took a swig. The briny, chemical taste normally would've made him gag, but the coolness wetting his throat and tongue made him coo in pleasure.

O'Connor drank too and savored every drop. He pulled out a K-rat bar and gnawed an edge, ripping off a chunk. He handed it to Gomez who did the same. They washed it down with another swill of briny, Haldane infused water.

Without a word, they took off down the trail again. They pushed hard, trying to put distance between themselves and the men trying to kill them. They'd gone ten minutes when O'Connor slowed. They were both ready to collapse. The K-bar and water had helped, but they needed more calories. Their bodies were threatening to shut down.

The ground hardened beneath their feet, some of the only solid ground they'd found along the trail. O'Connor remembered the section from the day before. His exhausted mind tried to play back how far the section had been from their insertion point. Everything was fuzzy in his mind. The actions from the day before seemed a lifetime ago.

Through labored breathing, he said, "We're almost there. I remember this section." Gomez only grunted, he didn't have the energy to waste on speech.

O'Connor stopped running and walked, trying to get control of his breathing. Gomez almost ran into him but pulled up short. O'Connor said, "listen, we're close to the coast. We need to get off the trail and let them pass. We don't want to get in a firefight with our backs to the water."

Gomez gasped, "We don't wanna get in a firefight at all, mano. We're outnumbered."

O'Connor leaped off the trail and landed on his feet without causing damage to the surrounding jungle. Gomez followed, trying for the same, but he stumbled and rolled, flattening the foliage. He cursed and tried to get the jungle back to its original state. He watched O'Connor slithering through the jungle. He looked back at the mess he'd made and decided it wasn't as bad as he thought. He followed O'Connor into the jungle not wanting to lose sight of him.

CAPTAIN TAGAMI'S squad moved like men possessed. He felt his legs would give out with each step, but to his surprise, they moved forward. The ground hardened the further they traveled. There was still mud, but it was getting less soupy. Soon the trail turned to hard ground, and the squad had to slow down. It wasn't as easy to follow the American's tracks.

Captain Tagami ordered them to return to a normal patrol pace. To Sergeant Chida he said, "Speed means nothing if we lose the trail. Tell the men we're approaching the coast. We'll find them soon or not at all." Chida looked at him, questioningly. Tagami smiled through his barely controlled breathing. He exaggerated sniffing, "I can smell the sea." Chida nodded and passed the word to slow down and stay alert.

The evening was progressing towards darkness. They didn't have the supplies for an extended patrol. They had enough food for one night. They were already on half provisions, so missing rations for an entire day could prove disastrous. Captain Tagami planned on finding the Americans before morning. If he lost them, he'd be forced to retreat or risk losing men to dehydration and exhaustion.

Tagami was lost in thought when the column stopped and crouched. He bumped into the man to his front. He crouched and pulled his pistol, ready for trouble. Sergeant Chida shuffled through the line and whispered, "We've found something strange."

Tagami followed his sergeant forward. Two soldiers were facing west, crouched with their weapons ready. Sergeant Chida pointed, "See how the jungle's laid down there? It looks like they may have gone that way, but it also looks like some continued this way."

Captain Tagami looked over the situation. "They split then. Can you tell which path most of them went?"

Sergeant Chida shook his head. "The path we're on is most used, but…" he trailed off.

"What is it, Sergeant? We're wasting time. It'll be dark soon."

"The path we're on is older than the one moving west. Private Sai and Tsukada agree; no one's used this trail for at least a day. And one more thing: the boot tracks are going the wrong way."

Captain Tagami stood and stared down at the two privates. "You men are experienced trackers?"

They stared up at their superior officer and nodded, "Yes, sir, we have some experience."

Tagami grit his teeth. "Have we been following a false path? Has the main force split off, and we're following a ruse?"

Sergeant Chida stood and looked down, "It appears so, sir."

Captain Tagami felt the blood rush to his head. He scowled at the privates who stared at the jungle floor. They seemed like cowering dogs waiting for the whip. He wanted to yell, to scream, to demand why they hadn't noticed earlier, but it would do no good and waste more time.

Instead of yelling he took a deep breath and looked at the trail leading west. He thought about the briny creek they'd crossed, the one his wife would have wanted to explore. *That is where they deceived us.*

He pointed, "We will follow the decoys and destroy them. It's too late to double back and find the main force. They'll be close to their lines by now."

He slapped the two privates on their backs. They flinched. "Can you follow this trail to the Americans?" They nodded like children asked if they wanted ice cream. "Do it." They stood and moved into the jungle following the fresh track.

25

Lieutenant Koga gazed into the canyon where he knew the Americans were trapped. He'd sent an assault squad, but they'd been shot up badly. The Americans were well concealed. Sending men headlong into the teeth of the canyon would result in more heavy losses.

He spoke to his sergeant. "We will wait for darkness and assault again. Sneak close, no noise, then attack them with grenades. I want them all killed, and the maps returned."

Sergeant Higashi nodded his understanding. "We will make it so, sir."

"We must assault as soon as it's dark enough, I don't want them slipping out the back-end of this canyon."

Sergeant Higashi shook his head, "I know this canyon, it ends in a large waterfall. There's no escape."

Lieutenant Koga continued. "Send five men overland to set an ambush below the waterfall. Tell them to be ready to kill any stragglers trying to escape."

Sergeant Higashi bowed and trotted away to pick five men. Getting around the canyon through the jungle would be difficult. He chose his strongest men. He made sure they were clear on their mission and sent them away as the canyon shadows spread.

An hour later Lieutenant Koga deemed it dark enough to start their sneak down the canyon.

The bulk of the platoon stepped out of the jungle and into the creekbed. They hunched and moved over the uneven creek bottom with caution. Lieutenant Koga was amongst them, his submachine gun hanging across his chest, ready for action.

As they moved down the creek and into the canyon, the darkness closed on them. The canyon walls were lighter higher up, still holding a slight evening glow, but the bottom was dark. *We'll catch the Americans by surprise.*

Sergeant Higashi led them. He moved with caution and the platoon was silent as the night. The canyon walls closed in becoming magnifiers for any sounds.

Higashi's steps were sure and silent. He stopped and crouched straining to see into the gloom of the canyon. The Americans were only yards ahead unless they'd moved. Sergeant Higashi looked behind him and found Lt. Koga staring at him. Koga nodded and waved his hand forward. The platoon continued downstream. Koga let a few men flow by him, then rose and moved forward another ten yards.

Lieutenant Koga halted them and signaled to use grenades. Sergeant Higashi was ready. He passed the order, and the soldiers in front pulled grenades from their ammo pouches. In perfect unison, the leading six men pulled the pins, slammed the tops onto their helmets, arming them, and threw the grenades into the darkness. Four seconds later six earsplitting explosions reverberated down the canyon. The canyon walls lit up like broad daylight for an instant leaving anyone watching temporarily blind.

The Japanese soldiers rose from their crouched positions and ran forward firing their rifles and submachine guns.

SERGEANT CARVER DIDN'T like his predicament. His squad was in a good defensive position, but seven men couldn't withstand the platoon that was bearing down on them. They'd given the Japs a bloody nose, but they were out of grenades, and they'd shot through most of their ammo. He figured as soon as it got dark the Japs would make their assault. It's what he would do.

Keeping two men watching upstream he gathered the others. "I figure the Japs are coming at us as soon as it gets dark. We're down to a couple of clips apiece. I've got three magazines for the Thompson. We're out of grenades." He patted the satchel that had become a part of his body. "This has gotta be the real deal or they wouldn't be coming at us this hard. We've gotta get it back to HQ. It could save a lot of American lives." The men stared at him blankly. They looked tired and ready to drop.

He shook his head. "The only lives I give a rats ass about right now, though, are yours. If I could give this to them," he touched the satchel, "In exchange for letting us go, I'd do it in a second, but we all know that ain't happening. Japs don't deal, and they don't take prisoners." He looked from man to man. "If we stay here and fight, we'll kill a lot of Japs, but eventually we'll run out of ammo, and they'll run over us. The way I see it, our only chance is down the canyon and out the other side." The men nodded their agreement. "There's a waterfall, but Palmer said there's a way down along the side. We move out in ten minutes. Fill canteens and eat what grub you can find."

Ten minutes later they were moving downstream. It was still light on the canyon walls, but deep in the canyon, shadow turned to darkness.

Private Palmer led the way. It was further than Sergeant Carver thought. Before they got to the lip of the falls, explosions at the mouth of the canyon erupted and rolled down the canyon like flood water. The squad sank to their knees turning towards the threat.

Carver was up, moving to Private Palmer. "How much further?"

"Guessing fifty yards. It's hard to tell in the dark."

Carver slapped him on the back. "Keep moving. Go." Palmer stood and splashed his way downstream. No use being quiet now. Carver stopped Private Crofter and Curtis, who were watching their rear. "Find cover and slow the Japs down when you see 'em, then get the hell outta there." The two soldiers looked at one another then back at

Carver and nodded. "Take two shots each then move. It's fifty yards from here. We'll cover you when you get close. No heroics, two shots and run. Got it?" They nodded and spread out to either side of the canyon. They leaned against bulky boulders and disappeared.

Carver took off downstream hoping he didn't twist an ankle on the slippery rocks. He came up on the squad forty yards ahead and nearly had his head taken off by jittery soldiers with fingers on triggers. Private Willy's teeth gleamed in the night, "Almost got your head blown off, Sarge."

Carver ignored him. "I've got Curtis and Crofter up there. When you hear 'em fire, it means the Japs are damned close. What're you all standing around for? Let's get down this damned falls."

Private Palmer stood on the left side of the canyon on the lip of the waterfall. The water rushed off the grooved edge like a thick funnel. It fell twenty feet before the laws of physics took over, and the funnel spread out then crashed into the pool with a constant roar.

Carver leaned over the edge trying to see the pool. He was sure the scene would be beautiful if he didn't have a platoon of Japanese soldiers chasing him.

The roar of the waterfall surrounded him, and a sudden dread filled him. "Daniels," the young private turned almost stumbling. "Move upstream twenty yards and listen for the Crofter and Curtis's shots." Daniels nodded and lumbered through the creek.

Sergeant Carver went to where Private Palmer was making his way over the cliff edge. He had his M1 slung over his back, and he was slipping over the first ledge to a narrow lower ledge six feet below.

He slid on his butt, moving along the wet slippery slope. When he'd gone three feet, he started to slide. He yelled out as he lost control and dropped the final three feet onto the ledge. He collapsed only inches from rolling off the edge. He looked up at Carver and gave him a thumbs up.

He reached out and pulled on a thick vine that snaked over the second ledge. He yanked hard testing its strength. It pulled away from its attachment but arrested again and seemed to be solid.

Carver cupped his hand over his mouth, "Does it make it to the bottom? Can we climb down it?"

Palmer leaned out and tried to move the vine back and forth to distinguish it from all the others. He looked up at Carver and shrugged his shoulders. He yelled up, "Can't tell, but looks good. It's our only choice."

A second later Carver heard yelling and turned upstream to see Private First Class Daniels sprinting through the water, "They're coming! They're coming!"

Carver unslung his Thompson and moved upstream. Daniels stopped beside him, his eyes wide. Carver stopped him, "Get the men over the side." He pointed to the ledge the squad was hovering around.

Private Willy came out of the darkness beside Carver. He was limping and pale. In a calm voice, he said, "I'll help you cover Crofter and Curtis."

Carver nodded and yelled at the rest of the men. "Get over the side. Now!" He and Willy moved upstream and found cover. Stepping away from the roar of the falls, the sound of gunfire filled the canyon walls. There were flashes of muzzles lighting up the night. Ricocheting bullets zinged and buzzed in the canyon. Two dark shapes were coming towards them, running as fast as their legs would carry them.

When they were almost on them, Carver stepped out, and Private Crofter lost his balance and fell into the knee deep water. He fully immersed and came up spluttering. "Jesus Christ, you scared the hell outta me, Sarge." He got to his feet and pointed upstream. "Pretty sure we hit one or two of 'em. They're right on our asses though."

Carver slapped him on the shoulder. "Good job, the others are on the left edge of the waterfall, follow 'em down. We'll cover you." Curtis and Crofter looked around and saw Willy's teeth shining from the shadows. They nodded and left them.

Carver aimed down his sights. "Let 'em get close enough for my Thompson." Carver could sense more than see Willy nodding his understanding.

They didn't have long to wait. The Japanese soldiers came down the middle of the creek moving from boulder to boulder. They weren't running but moved steadily in the darkness.

Carver had his Thompson to his shoulder. He crouched in the

water with the barrel resting on a boulder. His sights were on the first silhouette. He knew Willy would be targeting the soldiers further upstream with his more accurate M1. Willy was waiting for Carver to open up.

When the first soldier was fifteen yards away and filling his sights, he squeezed off two shots. The soldier dropped out of sight, and Carver was on the next target, a soldier behind and to the right of the first. He squeezed off another round sending the soldier sprawling and splashing.

It was impossible to discern officers from enlisted men in the darkness, but Willy picked his first target based on his position in the group. He was in the middle and moved like he was in charge. It was a gut instinct. When Carver opened up, Willy fired. The soldier went down hard, and he shifted to the next. He fired in quick succession working his way from left to right until the Japanese were behind cover. He was sure he'd hit three others.

Carver and Willy leaned back under cover waiting for the return fire. It came a second later. The air buzzed and snapped as bullets whipped by and smacked into water and rock.

Carver yelled over the gunfire. "We've gotta give 'em a few more minutes to get down the cliff."

Willy didn't answer but leaned out and fired into the canyon. The Japanese fire stopped momentarily then concentrated on Willy's muzzle flashes. Carver leaned out and aimed at the closest muzzle flash. He fired three times, then leaned back as the boulder shook with incoming rounds. *There's too damned many of 'em.* "We gotta go, Willy. Count of three, I'll cover you."

Willy's voice came back to him in a conversational tone, but he could make out the words. "I'll cover you, Sergeant Carver. You go first."

His voice sent alarms through Carver. He looked to where he knew Willy crouched, but could only make out a dim silhouette against the canyon wall. "You hit?"

Willy's voice disconnected and far away. "One, two, three." Willy leaned out and fired at the multiple muzzle flashes; walking his fire with deadly precision.

Sergeant Carver cussed but pushed off and ran downstream with bullets chasing him. He dove behind another boulder and spun around to cover Willy's retreat, but Willy continued firing until Carver heard the 'ping' of an empty clip. He called, "Willy!"

The Japanese heard the emptied weapon too and lunged downstream. Carver aimed but before he could pull the trigger he heard Willy's M1 bark again, and the Japanese dropped into the water. *It must be his last clip.* He yelled one more time, "Willy, now!" but Willy kept firing.

Carver took the opportunity and ran to the edge of the cliff. No one was in sight. He skidded and slipped, almost going over the edge. He crouched and looked down at the smaller ledge. Private First Class Daniels was aiming his M1 at his head. Carver put up his hands, "It's me, it's me."

Daniels waved him down. "Come on. The others are halfway down."

Carver took one last look back up the creek. Willy was still firing. *Must have a hidden clip.* His shots were sporadic, like he was conserving every shot. *Hope he saves the last one for himself.* The Japanese would do unspeakable things to him if he were captured. It reminded him of his three Marines. "Where are Kendrick, Sparks, and Paulson?" He didn't wait for an answer. He slung his Thompson over his back and shimmied down the slope on his butt until there was no more grip, then fell into Daniels who kept him from toppling over the edge.

"They're almost down. They went first with Dawkins and Palmer." He looked to the ledge Carver had just come from, "Where's Willy?"

Carver shook his head, "Saving our bacon." He pointed with his thumb and for the first time realized what Willy was doing. "He's holding the Japs off till we're clear. He, he's sacrificing himself for us."

Daniels stared into Carver's eyes and was about to speak when the side of his head exploded, spraying Carver with blood, bone and gray matter. Carver stared, not comprehending what he'd just seen. A bullet sliced into his cheek and burned him out of his trance. He dropped to his belly as more bullets smacked into the cliff face behind him. Daniel's lifeless eyes stared at him, and his dead body slowly toppled off the cliff and out of sight.

Sergeant Carver could see winks of muzzle flashes in the creek below the waterfall pool. *The Japs are waiting for us.* He shook his head trying to clear the image of Daniels dying. His cheek burned like fire. His hand came away bloody when he probed it.

Jap bullets were smacking all around him. *They haven't spotted the others. They're only shooting at me.* He decided it would be best to keep it that way. From a prone position, he lifted the Thompson and aimed it in the general direction of the enemy, and squeezed off a couple of rounds. The Thompson kicked like a mule, slamming his cheek, making him wince, but his muzzle flash had the desired effect. The Japanese renewed their efforts, shooting at him and not the rest of the squad.

The roar of the waterfall and the smacking of close bullet impacts was all he could hear. *How long till the Japs get past Willy and poke their heads over the side?* He aimed his Thompson at the ledge waiting, but nothing came. Back on his belly, he slithered to the edge and peered down. He could see his men only yards from the bottom.

He squinted searching for the enemy beyond. They'd stopped firing, seeing if they'd hit anything. He looked at the black pool of water far below. He could see the whitewater as it plunged into the pool. There was no way he was going to use the vines to climb down; the Japs could see him. He only had one choice.

The ledge he was on stuck out four feet from the wall and extended fifteen feet towards the waterfall, but the pool was another twenty feet out, at least. He couldn't judge how far it dropped, but it looked like he could make the pool if he got a good enough push off the ledge. There was no telling how deep the pool was. He might be jumping to his death even if he made the pool.

Still on his belly, he pushed his way back until he couldn't go any farther. He got on his knees, took off his helmet and pack, made sure the satchel was in place, then got to his feet. The Japs hadn't started firing again, but they'd see him any second. He took a deep breath, and gripping his Thompson, ran as fast as he could along the ledge. He concentrated on the edge, he'd have to time it perfectly, or he wouldn't get a good push, and he'd die in the rocks below.

He noticed the winking of muzzle flashes, the Japs had seen him.

He planted his right foot on the edge and pushed off with everything he had left, and he fell through dark, empty space. The wind rushed through his hair, and he kicked his legs reaching for all the distance he could muster. He knew he was about to die, but it was peaceful. He was flying and he knew the crushing weight of gravity would end his war without pain.

PRIVATE WILLY COUNTED to three then leaned out and fired at the muzzle flashes that seemed to be everywhere. He was calm, his breathing steady as he squeezed off eight rounds. He couldn't see his bullets hit their marks, but he knew his shots were accurate. The clip 'pinged' and as fluid as the water flowing past his bloody legs, he pulled and inserted a new clip.

The Japanese soldiers heard the distinctive 'ping' too and took the opportunity to rush him. They'd only gotten a few steps when Willy leaned out again, and this time he saw his targets crashing into the creek. *Chalk up three more dead Japs.*

The return fire was intense, and he leaned against the boulder feeling its cool hardness against his cheek. He felt warmth down his side and knew he was bleeding again.

He'd never stopped bleeding. Dawkins had patched him up as best he could, but there was nothing more he could do out in the jungle. The medic thought he'd only been grazed, but when the wound kept oozing through the bandage, he'd taken a closer look and realized the bullet must've nicked a small artery near his right kidney. He was slowly bleeding out.

Dawkins wanted to tell Sergeant Carver, but Willy put his rifle barrel against his jaw and made him swear not to. Dawkins promised, saying, "You don't need to be such an asshole about it, Willy. Just ask for Christ's sake."

Running down the creek to the waterfall had been the hardest thing Willy had ever done. He'd resigned himself to die in the canyon during the night, but it wasn't to be. Sergeant Carver wanted to move. He'd stood up and swayed for a full minute before finally being able to follow the squad. Each jarring step sent daggers into his side. It was all he could do not to yell out, but he wouldn't allow the weakness to show through. Dawkins kept giving him glances, but he had his hands full with the emaciated Marines and couldn't help.

Looking over the edge of the cliff, he knew there wasn't a chance in hell he could climb down the vines. He could hardly hold his rifle, let alone support his body weight. He saw covering the retreat as a way to do some good and kill more Japs.

He hugged the rock and flinched as bullets chipped away at the front. Every instinct told him he should move, if only a few feet, but he felt weak, like a child. He heard Sergeant Carver yelling for him to follow. He leaned out and fired at another muzzle flash. He tried to yell out for him to run while he had the chance, but it only came out as a squeak.

Bullets smacked with renewed vigor. He looked up at the night sky. The canyon walls kept the jungle from forming a complete canopy and Willy could see the intense pinpricks of light from a thousand stars. *Not a bad place to die.*

Splashing from upstream brought him back to reality. *Not yet, Willy. Not yet. Gotta give 'em more time.* He rolled out from behind the boulder in a prone position. Two soldiers were running straight at him only feet away. He angled his muzzle and pulled the trigger. He could hear the bullets impacting and lancing through them like they were made of paper. They toppled. One slammed into the boulder and slid backward. The other fell in a soaking splash beside him then slowly drifted downstream. More soldiers further back. He fired in their direction keeping their heads down.

More muzzle flashes and more bullets filled the air. He didn't have the strength to roll back to cover, so he leveled the M1 and fired back. He felt an intense heat in his left shoulder, and he couldn't keep the barrel lifted. He hefted the M1 with one hand and fired at a figure dashing from cover. The soldier dropped out of sight the same instant he realized he'd fired his last shot.

Out of ammo, he dropped his M1 and pulled his K-bar knife from its leather sheath. He planned to fight to the death. No torture for

Private Willy. He heard the soldiers coming, splashing towards him. They knew he was empty or wounded or both.

Willy pulled himself to his knees. He kept his head down, partially submerged. His left shoulder felt shredded, and his right hand was hidden under his belly, hiding the knife. He could feel his body shutting down. *One final burst is all I need.*

The Japanese soldiers formed a circle with rifles aimed down at him. Willy heard the guttural gibberish of his hated enemies' language. *Little closer.* A soldier put his boot on Willy's right shoulder to push him over.

Like a cobra snake striking, Willy rose up. The soldier lost his balance and Willy used his final ounce of strength to leap on him and sink his knife into the soft skin beneath his chin. The soldier's mouth was open and Willy could see the knife in his throat reflecting his grimace back at him. It was the last thing he saw.

Bayonets sank into Private Willy's back. Over and over they lunged into him, screaming their hatred and fear. It took the strong voice of their lieutenant to stop them.

26

O'Connor had no reason to believe the Japanese were following him and not the trail to the coast, but he couldn't shake the feeling of urgency. The darkness made travel difficult, but he kept a good pace.

Private Gomez was tired, but the brief stop for calories and water had energized him, and he wasn't having trouble keeping up. He asked O'Connor, "Where we headed?"

O'Connor stopped and turned, breathing hard. "We're angling towards the coast. If I'm right, we'll hit water well west of where the Japs will. I'm hoping there'll be some beach, and we'll be able to get out of the jungle and move faster back to Cape Torokina."

In shock, Gomez said, "Cape Torokina? That's a long way west." O'Connor nodded. Gomez sighed. "We've got a long walk ahead." He looked where they'd come from, "Sure hope the Japs aren't following us."

O'Connor took his helmet off and wiped his brow. "I've got a bad feeling about that..." Gomez looked him in the eye. O'Connor said, "You too?"

Gomez nodded. "Can't shake the feeling." They were both silent, then Gomez asked, "What should we do?"

O'Connor looked around the jungle. The terrain seemed to be rising like they were slowly ascending a hill. "Only way to know for sure is to lay up somewhere and wait." He pointed. "We'll keep going this way until we find a good spot."

Gomez looked nervous, "If they're able to follow us through this shit, they'll find us, no problem."

O'Connor nodded and worked the problem. "We'll double back on 'em. I used to do it to my hunting buddy all the time." He moved ahead continuing to talk. "Need to find a good spot to move ninety degrees off the trail. Look for hard ground or a boulder field. Something that doesn't leave tracks."

Gomez nodded and pointed back the way they'd come. "There was a spot like that back about fifty yards."

O'Connor nodded. "I remember it." He turned, "Let's get there. It's even better doing it this way. While they're trying to figure out where the hell we are, we'll get back on the trail and run out of here." He followed Gomez. "Careful, they could be closer than we think."

Gomez got to the spot. It was a piece of hard ground with medium sized boulders strewn amongst smaller rocks. He stopped and waited for O'Connor. They both crouched and surveyed the area. O'Connor said, "This'll work. You go first." He pointed where he wanted him to go. "I'll follow and make sure we don't leave any tracks. Be as light on your feet as possible."

Gomez tensed and looked down the trail. He clutched O'Connor's arm, "Someone's coming," he whispered.

O'Connor didn't hesitate. He pushed Gomez off the trail and onto the rocks. He followed close behind checking for any sign of their passage. It wasn't perfect, but he didn't have much time before he heard the footsteps of Japanese soldiers tromping down the trail.

The rocks and boulders only went ten yards before turning back to spongy jungle floor. They made it the ten yards and went prone, facing back the way they'd come. They couldn't see the trail, the day had given way to darkness, but soon they saw dark shapes.

The soldier in front was moving in a crouch following their trail carefully. O'Connor held his breath as he walked past the spot they'd left the trail. He hadn't noticed anything.

It took three minutes for the rest of the patrol to pass. They waited another two minutes before O'Connor whispered to Gomez. "We have to get back to the trail and get outta here. That tracker knew what he was doing. I don't think we'll fool him long."

Gomez nodded and moved to the rocks. He kept his feet light, sure of each step, leaving no tracks in the dirt beside them. O'Connor was right behind him. He was sure they hadn't left a trace.

When they got back to the trail, Gomez let O'Connor lead, and they took off. The thought of the Japanese only fifty yards up the trail pushed them forward. Even though almost twenty men had beaten the trail, it was still tough to follow in the dark.

O'Connor almost missed the original trail from the coast but recognized it in time to turn and keep Gomez from crashing into him. Gomez looked at him with wide wondering eyes. O'Connor looked to the left, the direction Carver and the rest of the patrol was, then right, the way to the coast.

He pointed right, and Gomez shook his head. "We need to catch up with the rest of the patrol. This is our chance."

O'Connor shook his head. "We'll lead the Japs straight to 'em" he looked to the right again. "We need to move to the coast. Besides, they're probably already home."

Gomez didn't like it, but nodded, wanting to go one way or the other. "Okay, but what do we do when we get there?"

O'Connor shrugged then turned to trot down the trail. He looked over his shoulder. "We'll figure that out when we get there."

It was dark, and the trail they followed was barely visible. O'Connor was moving by instinct and what he remembered from the trip in, which wasn't much. They moved like men who'd gone far beyond the point of exhaustion, but they kept slogging, foot by foot.

O'Connor stopped and unscrewed the cap of his canteen and took a sip. He shook it and figured he had two more sips at most. In a voice he didn't recognize, he croaked, "Need to find water."

Private Gomez only nodded in the dark. "Shouldn't we be covering our tracks?"

O'Connor shook his head. "Hopefully the Japs won't figure our little trick out until morning. By then we'll be at the coast." He screwed the lid back on the canteen and attached it to his belt. "Figure we can swim either direction. Japs won't have a clue which way we went. Find a good spot to come inland, find some water and hole up and rest."

"Rest sounds good."

O'Connor slapped him on the back. "We'll be there soon. I keep getting whiffs of the ocean."

Ten minutes later the jungle ended, and there was an enormous black expanse spreading out forever. It took O'Connor a moment to realize he was looking at the ocean. They'd made it to the coast. He looked at his luminescent dials on his battered watch. "It's 1 A.M. We've been on the move for almost twenty four hours."

Gomez couldn't hold himself up any longer and fell to his knees in the soft jungle. There was a short drop to a sliver of sand. He crawled to it and sat on the jungle floor with his legs dangling. His muddy boots touched the sand. "I've gotta rest awhile."

O'Connor looked the way they'd come. It was black jungle. They'd been traveling through it for hours, but now it looked menacing and deadly. He could picture Japanese soldiers bursting through with bayonets leveled. "We can't stop yet. We've gotta get away from this spot. It leads straight to us."

When Gomez didn't move, he grabbed his hand and hefted him to his feet. Gomez moaned and swayed. "You've gotta dig deeper Gomez. You can't quit when we're so close. Come on." He pulled him into the water and stopped. He looked each way. "They may expect it, but we'll move west towards our lines. We'll wade, covering our tracks. I don't remember seeing the sand when they dropped us off, guess the tide's out, which means it'll come in and wash everything away, but we'll stay in the water to be safe." Gomez nodded, and O'Connor wrapped Gomez's arm over his shoulder and helped him along.

They moved two hundred yards splashing through the shallows.

They'd both fallen multiple times and O'Connor was worried about their weapons in the salt water. *If we need 'em, we're fucked anyway.*

They came to a point where the sand formed more of a beach. It poked out from the main island like a short tentacle. They moved along the shallows until the beach ended at the side of a river.

At first, O'Connor didn't recognize what it was, thinking it some odd ocean current. When he realized it was fresh water, he fell to his knees and drank a mouthful. It took every ounce of his will to spit it out. "It's freshwater," he rasped. Gomez dropped and put his head in, taking gulps. O'Connor pulled him up by his hair. "Put it in your canteen and add the tablets or you'll be sick by morning."

Gomez shook his head, "Fuck it."

"Goddamit." He pushed Gomez, and he fell on his back in the sand. "You'll be useless to me if you're puking, shitting and dying tomorrow. Now, do what I say."

Gomez's eyes flared, but he knew the corporal was right and pulled himself to a sitting position. He filled his canteen and O'Connor dropped in one of the tabs. Waiting the few minutes would be more torture. "Tell me when to drink," he sneered.

Finally, they drank. They drank and refilled, drank and refilled. Their parched bodies soaked up the life-sustaining water and made them feel human again.

O'Connor stood and looked the way they'd come. The night was dark, lit only by the magnificent expanse of stars filling the sky to the horizon. Even in his exhaustion, O'Connor took a moment to take in the night's beauty. It looked like they were completely alone, no sign of Japanese soldiers following them, but that would change come morning.

The river flowed into the sea as it had done for thousands of years and would for thousands more. It didn't care about his predicament. It didn't care about the war, it didn't care about anything but the passage of time and the cycles of life.

He remembered the maps they'd pored over before the mission. There were several rivers he remembered seeing, some little more than creeks and at least two that were more substantial. He didn't remember seeing any on their boat ride in. He tried to picture which river this one was, hoping it might help him decide how far friendly lines were, but it was useless. He felt like his mind was running through thick taffy.

Gomez stood beside him and put his hand on his shoulder. "Do we cross?"

O'Connor nodded, "I think so. We'll lay up somewhere on the other side. We'll hear anyone coming across." Gomez nodded, and O'Connor waded in.

The bottom was sandy until he was a third of the way then it changed to gravel and rock. O'Connor looked upstream searching for anything that looked like a log coming downstream. He'd seen what a saltwater crocodile could do to a man. He hadn't seen any on this island paradise, but this looked like perfect habitat.

They made it to the other side without incident. The water went up to their waists, and the strong current had pushed them downstream a couple yards. They were panting like they'd run a hundred yard dash. They walked up the rivers edge to hide any footprints, then angled into the jungle.

O'Connor stopped a few feet inside its expanse, unwilling to venture further into the darkness. The ground felt springy but dry. He looked side to side, cleared some brush and sat. "This'll do." He put his rifle across his bent legs. "I'll take first watch. Get some sleep." Gomez nodded and laid down clutching his M1 like a lover. He was asleep in seconds.

O'Connor could hear his soft breathing and wanted nothing more than to slip into oblivion, but he bit his dry lips and fought the urge. It was a long two hours.

CAPTAIN TAGAMI WAS IRRITATED. They'd been stopped for ten minutes while his trackers searched for the American trail without success. He'd let them work, keeping his distance, but he'd had enough. He strode through his lounging men until he reached the head of the column. Sergeant Chida stood with his arms crossed while the two trackers moved about on their hands and knees. When he noticed

Captain Tagami in the darkness, he stiffened. Tagami barked, "Why can't these men find the trail, Sergeant?"

Sergeant Chida stared straight ahead and in a clipped tone responded, "They are having difficulty finding sign in the dark, sir."

Captain Tagami barked at the men on the ground. "Stand up." The two trackers shot to their feet and stood at attention. Even in the dark Tagami could see they were scared. "Where have the Americans gone?" Neither spoke, each waiting for the other. Tagami flared, "Answer me."

The nearest soldier sputtered, "The trail stops. They, they must have doubled back and left from another spot, sir."

Tagami questioned him, "Why can't you pick up their trail?" He knew why the moment he said it; he and the rest of the men were standing on the trail they would have doubled back on. He gritted his teeth and addressed Sergeant Chida. "We probably walked right past them without noticing. They could be miles away in any direction." Sergeant Chida didn't respond but nodded once.

Captain Tagami looked at the men sitting on the trail eating and drinking, taking advantage of the temporary stop. They were dark shapes against the night, but he knew they were exhausted.

He made a decision. "Sergeant, find us a suitable place to lay up for the night, somewhere dry. We'll rest and search for the Americans with fresh eyes in the morning."

Sergeant Chida said, "Hai," and sent the trackers in opposite directions to find a suitable sleeping area.

27

Sergeant Carver was as surprised as anyone when he hit the water at the base of the waterfall and knifed through ten feet to the muddy bottom. His legs hit hard, but the water cushioned him enough not to hurt anything. He opened his eyes, and the darkness was complete. The briny water and night combined to make the world inky black.

The waterfall smashing into the pool right behind him buffeted his body. The roar was constant but soothing. He stayed crouched on the bottom of the pool holding his breath and wishing he'd died. If the pool had been shallow, he'd be dead already and done with all this killing and fear. He wished he could stay under and drown peacefully, but his men still needed him.

He pushed off the bottom, but instead of rocketing to the surface, he stayed stuck. He pushed again, but his right foot wouldn't budge. The mud had him in a death grip. He yanked hard and felt it move slightly. He felt panic growing like a cancer in his gut. He pushed and yanked and twisted, but he couldn't get loose. His lungs started to burn like fire.

He still held the Thompson in his hands. He reached the barrel down to his foot. He jabbed it into the mud over and over trying to loosen its grip. It worked, but not enough. He felt his body shutting down. In desperation, he flicked off the safety and put the barrel beside his foot. *Will it fire?* He pulled the trigger. The sound was deafening, and he felt the pressure of the bullet leaving the barrel. He gave one more pull, and his foot came loose. He shot to the surface and took in a gasping lung-full of precious air.

He moved to the edge of the pool, stroking as best he could weighted down by the Thompson and the satchel. He got to the bank and pulled himself up. He heard a shot and saw a muzzle flash. He remembered he was in the middle of a battle.

He laid low, catching his breath. When he had control, he assessed the situation. Using the boulders for cover, he brought the Thompson up, aiming where he'd seen the muzzle flash.

He was still breathing hard trying to keep his muzzle up and ready. When he didn't see anything, he put the barrel down and rolled onto his back looking up at the stars gleaming through the hole in the jungle canopy. He heard shots; they were faint against the roar of the waterfall.

He lifted his head and saw muzzle flashes coming from the side of the waterfall. His men were down and firing. He ducked realizing he was in the middle of the firefight. *Be a hell of a thing to be killed by my own men.*

Bullets whizzed and zinged above his head traveling in both directions. One smacked into the rock above his head, and he knew he needed to get out of there. He pushed back into the pool and walked along the bottom with only his head above water. He moved to the right until he could come out of the water without being seen. He slithered to a nearby log which looked like it must have come down the waterfall during high flows. He propped himself against it and peered over the top. There were more muzzle flashes from downstream. His men returned fire from the waterfall.

Carver centered his muzzle where he'd seen the flashes. He was about to fire, but it would be a long shot. Once he fired and gave away his position, the Japs would shift their attention to him. He got to his belly and positioned the satchel, so it laid on his back. He pushed the

Thompson in front and crawled under the log. The muzzle flashes erupted again.

He moved closer using the boulders for cover. The fire from his men was the real danger. He hoped he was far enough off to the right to stay out of their fire. He ran five feet up and slammed his back into a boulder. He peered around spotting another boulder. It would give him cover from friendly fire and put him ten feet away from the Japs.

He took the satchel off and placed it at the base of the boulder. He needed to have free movement.

He took a deep breath and blew it out slowly. He counted to himself; *one, two, three* and ran to the boulder. He slid into cover waiting for the bullets to come but instead, he heard the whispering of Japanese soldiers. There was a shot and the sound of another bullet being chambered.

He pulled the magazine from his Thompson and felt the weight; it was nearly full. He pushed it back in quietly, waiting for another shot. When it came, he slammed the magazine home, pulled the primer back, and stepped from behind the boulder with the Thompson on his shoulder. The dark shapes of soldiers were only feet away. No one noticed him. They were too busy watching the waterfall. He squeezed the trigger and walked his fire from right to left. The flames from his muzzle nearly reached the writhing soldiers. Their faces lit up in terror and surprise, and they shook and danced as the bullets tore them apart.

Carver burned through his entire magazine, making sure they were dead. He stood above them, his feet spread apart, the muzzle of his Thompson smoking and glowing a soft orange.

The bodies sprawled in front of him were indistinguishable from one another. The darkness robbed him the sight of gore seeping from their dead bodies. He was thankful for that.

A voice from out of the darkness brought him back from his stare. "Sarge? Is that you?"

~

THE AMERICAN SOLDIER at the creek had put up an impressive last stand. Lieutenant Koga respected the warrior spirit that must have flowed through the American. He'd fought Americans many times and knew they were dangerous and unpredictable fighters. He'd stopped referring to them as cowards long ago. He'd seen them kill too many of his men not to respect them. The dead GI at his feet had taken many of his men, even wounding Sergeant Higashi.

"Sergeant, take the men downstream quickly. Find the rest of them and destroy them."

The burly sergeant nodded and splashed downstream exhorting the men to follow. He no longer cared about being careful.

The single American had been sacrificed to allow the main force to escape. They were in full retreat and wouldn't be waiting to gun him down.

Running in a creekbed in the middle of the night was tough, but he managed to keep his feet. He heard other soldiers trip and fall behind him. He almost didn't stop in time before falling off the edge of the waterfall. He stopped himself on the brink and yelled for his men to stop. They skidded and slipped, but none went over the edge.

Sergeant Higashi peered over, but he couldn't see anything except dark shapes that looked like boulders. He aimed his submachine gun at the surrounding walls, but they were steep and impassable. He wondered if the Americans had fallen over the edge.

One of his soldiers called out, "There, down there," pointing to the area beside the waterfall. Sergeant Higashi squinted and saw movement. The boulders were moving.

Lieutenant Koga saw the movement at the same time his sergeant did. He pointed and yelled, "Fire. Kill them."

The remainder of his platoon spread out along the lip of the waterfall and hastily aimed at the Americans. First one then another fired until the entire platoon was shooting as fast as they could cycle their bolt actions. Though dark, they could see men falling and diving for cover.

There was return fire coming from further downstream. Lieutenant Koga saw some of his men lurch and topple forward off the cliff. One soldier fell into the rushing water beside him and went down the spout of water. Koga lost sight of him as he entered the pool below.

He aimed his submachine gun at the muzzle flashes and squeezed off a long burst. The American fire stopped, and he hoped he'd killed him, but there was return fire coming from the base of the waterfall. His men had to lean out and shoot almost straight down. He watched another soldier shudder as bullets sliced through him and he fell forward into the darkness. "Pull back from the edge, pull back," he yelled. The men followed his order and looked at him. Lieutenant Koga pulled a grenade from his waist. "Grenades."

The men pulled grenades and held them at the ready. Koga judged the five-second fuse would be perfect. He counted down from three and fourteen grenades hissed their way towards the base of the falls.

Sergeant Carver saw the Japanese soldiers on the lip of the waterfall. They were in perfect silhouette against the night sky. Their first volley of shots had stopped his men from moving. He was sure he'd seen at least two of his men go down, but he couldn't tell who.

He crouched and fired his Thompson. He shot in short two and three round bursts. He saw soldiers falling off the cliff. He pulled back at the same instant bullets slapped into the water and boulders. He yelled, "Stay in cover. They're on the cliff!" He knew his men couldn't hear him through the roar of the waterfall and the rifle fire. He inched around the boulder and could still see the Japanese on the ledge. No one seemed to be shooting at him, they were leaning over and firing down on his men.

Need to get closer. Carver sprinted upstream for twenty yards and threw himself behind another boulder. He had a good view of the cliff, but no one was there. They'd pulled back. He rested his muzzle on the moss covered rock and watched the edge. He saw his men start to move away from the boulders aiming up. Carver yelled, "Move out! Come on, it's clear."

They could hear him and see him waving his arm. They broke from cover at the same time Carver saw the Japanese reappear on the ledge. He aimed and fired. He hit a soldier, and he fell backward out of sight.

The rest stood on the ledge hurling something. He yelled, "Grenades! Get down, grenades!"

The squad made it ten yards when they heard Carver yelling over the sound of the falls, to take cover. They dove and covered their heads. The grenades dropped around them like deadly raindrops, then exploded.

Carver ducked as the explosions erupted. Before the dirt settled, he was up and firing into the silhouetted Japanese soldiers. They dove back, but not before he toppled another. "Come on, move out, move out." He saw his men trying to get to their feet. The boulders had shielded them from most of the shrapnel, but the close concussions had rattled them. Carver fired, keeping the Japanese from coming forward. He fired his last shot and swapped magazines with an adept and practiced motion. He fired a short burst and ran from cover, towards his men.

The squad looked like drunks as they swayed and swerved, trying to make their bodies work. Carver got to the first man, Private Palmer and pushed him forward, "Go," he yelled. Corporal Dawkins had one of the Marines on his back and was lunging forward, grunting with the exertion. Bullets zinged off a boulder near Carver's head, and he kneeled and fired another burst at the cliff.

His men streamed past him as he kept up a steady stream of suppressing fire. He counted five men, not enough. He pictured the men who'd passed and realized he hadn't seen Private Curtis.

Private Crofter was the last man to pass and Carver yelled at him, "Where's Curtis?"

Crofter had another Marine on his back. He looked back and shrugged. "He's back there." Renewed fire from the cliff made them all take cover. Bullets smacked and splashed into the water.

Carver didn't let them get the upper hand. He leaned out and fired. The big .45 caliber bullets slammed into the cliff wall exploding the rock. Another soldier dropped off the cliff and shattered on the rocks. He yelled, "Get to the jungle". He moved backward keeping his muzzle on the cliff. He had a good view, and whenever a Japanese soldier moved forward, he fired.

The squad was nearly in the spot where he'd killed the first group of enemy soldiers. The squad disappeared behind the boulders and Carver turned to run. He'd taken his first step when the air around him erupted in buzzing near misses. The Japanese had crawled forward and were lining him up for the kill.

He ran hard, weaving in and out of boulders as bullets chased him. There was firing from the boulders to his front, and the fire coming from the cliffs lessened.

He dove behind cover, his chest heaving with exertion. Dawkins dropped from the boulder he'd been shooting from and nearly landed on Carver. "You hit? Where you hit?" he pawed and poked at him searching for the holes he knew must be there. He saw the gash on his cheek, but the dried blood told him it wasn't a fresh wound.

Carver hadn't caught his breath but pushed him away and gasped, "Get off me…I'm not hit." Dawkins didn't believe it and kept groping him. "Dammit, I'm not hit.".

He looked at him in wonder. "There's no way they didn't hit you. They were firing everything they had at you." He shook his head. "You're one lucky son-of-a-bitch." He looked around like he'd misplaced something. "Where's Willy?"

Carver shook his head and looked down. "He's gone. Gave us the time we needed to get down the falls."

The firing continued, but it was sporadic as each side tried to snipe the other. Corporal Dawkins sat down hard and pushed the front of his helmet up. "Never thought the Japs could kill that tough old bastard." He shook his head, "Too damned mean."

Carver nodded, "What happened to Curtis?"

Dawkins looked Carver in the eye. "I was right beside him. A grenade landed between us. Would've killed me, him and the Marines for sure." He looked away reliving the moment. "He didn't hesitate, jumped onto it." A bullet smacked the rock they were behind, and they both flinched.

Carver shook his head. *Where do these men come from?* He was wasting time. Wasting the sacrifices of the dead. He clutched the sopping wet satchel bag. "We've gotta get the hell outta here before the Japs decide to flank us." He slung his Thompson over his shoulder and rummaged around a dead Jap soldier until he found one of the Arisaka rifles. He found ammo pouches and took them too.

A plan formulated. He raised his voice. "We've gotta get outta here, but I wanna make those sons-of-bitches pay." He gestured toward the cliffs. The men looked back at him with blank stares. They were dead tired. "No more shooting even if you see them. We'll wait awhile until they think we're gone. If they start down the cliff, that's when we'll open up on 'em." The men nodded, happy for some time to rest and eat.

Carver felt he needed to explain himself. "If we leave now they'll be hot on our tails and probably catch us before we get to our lines. If we stay and kill them on the cliff face, they'll be forced to go back upstream and come the long way." The men nodded and sat behind the boulders and ate whatever they could find.

Sergeant Carver took the first watch, resting the Japanese rifle on the boulder. He could see movement on the cliff, but he didn't fire. As the minutes ticked by, it was all he could do to keep his eyes open.

28

Lieutenant Koga's jaw hurt from clenching. He'd lost half his platoon tracking these Americans down, and he still hadn't killed them all or recovered the satchel. He lay on his belly at the lip of the waterfall. He and his men had learned the hard away about kneeling and standing. Their black silhouettes were easy to spot.

There hadn't been any shooting from the Americans for awhile. He had his men shoot, but there was no return fire. He made a decision. "Sergeant." Sergeant Higashi rose to a crouch and shuffled to Lt. Koga's side. "The Americans got down this cliff. Find out how. We need to pursue them before they slip back to their lines."

Sergeant Higashi nodded. "It looks like they went down the vines on the left side. They must've used them like a rope."

Lieutenant Koga looked at his sergeant's bloody arm. He was hit in the left bicep. The medic said it went straight through without breaking bones, but it bled profusely and had to be excruciating. Sergeant Higashi never let on that he was in pain. He carried out his duty as if nothing had happened. "Will you be able to climb, Sergeant?"

Higashi looked embarrassed. "I will make it, sir." He gathered the men and sent them to investigate the route down. Five minutes later he reported to Lt. Koga. "There's an outcropping we can climb to, then we use the vines to the bottom. It looks slow but effective."

Lieutenant Koga nodded. "Good. I want three men covering our descent in case the Americans are only in hiding."

Sergeant Higashi nodded and said, "Hai."

SERGEANT CARVER SAW movement on the cliff. He tracked them with the Japanese rifle but didn't fire. There was a group forming on the side of the falls. They'd figured out how to descend the waterfall.

He whispered to the men. "Get to position. The Japs are making their move." They stood, stifling moans as they pushed their aching bodies back into action. They found their firing positions and tracked the targets on the ridge. "Don't fire until I do. I want to pick as many off as possible, but none can make it to the ground." The men nodded. "When we don't have any more targets we disengage and move downstream."

Sergeant Carver watched the dark shapes of soldiers climbing to the outcropping. It was difficult to see them once they were off the ridge. He wished he had a flare gun, but they were traveling light. He squinted trying to see through the gloom.

The soldiers on the outcropping were visible only as blobs of darkness. He wondered if he'd be able to see them at all once they started descending the vines. He didn't want to shoot too early and leave soldiers on the ridge, but he couldn't risk any soldiers making it the creek bed either.

He took his eyes off his sights and looked to his men. They were well concealed, waiting for his signal. The three Marines had captured Japanese rifles and were ready as well. He decided he'd wait until he saw at least two soldiers start descending. He'd shoot them first if he could see them.

More soldiers climbed down to the outcropping. He started to see the vines moving as they took the soldier's weight. He pulled the rifle into his shoulder and centered it on the back of the lead climber. *Hope the previous owner zeroed his rifle.* He squeezed the trigger and the rifle bucked into his shoulder. He cycled another round with the bolt action. He was pleased with the ease of the action and happy to see his target fall from the vines.

The rest of the squad opened fire, and the dark shapes writhed and fell. Muzzle flashes winked from the top of the cliff and Japanese bullets slammed into the boulders. The men ducked away.

Carver swung his rifle to the ridgeline and waited for another muzzle flash. It came a second later, and he adjusted his aim and fired. He quickly recycled the bolt and fired again and again until the five round clip was empty. He had no idea if he hit anything, but he drew their fire. He ducked back as bullets ricocheted off the rocks. He yelled, "Take the climbers. I'll keep the ridgeline pinned down." The men leaned into their rifles and fired at the shapes still on the outcropping. Carver reloaded and fired at the winking flashes. He thought he saw one soldier's head snap back, but he couldn't be sure.

He pulled back as another volley of fire came at him. The 'ping' sound of empty clips up and down the line told him his men were empty. He used the pause to yell. "We gotta go. Reload and fall back down the creek."

The squad moved away from the boulders keeping cover between themselves and the Japanese. There was firing coming from the top of the falls but nothing from the outcropping. Corporal Dawkins shouldered his rifle and went to where the Marines were still firing. He touched Kendrick's shoulder, and he looked back. He had a smile that seemed to reach both ears. Dawkins said, "Come on, we gotta go."

Kendrick nodded but fired the round he had chambered. He turned back to Dawkins and said, "Finally giving some back to those sons-of-bitches."

Dawkins nodded and repeated, "We gotta go."

He turned away and crouched waiting for Kendrick to get on his back, but the Marine shook his head. "I can make it, Doc." He looked to Private Sparks and Paulson who were beside him. They were grinning.

Sparks nodded. "No sweat, Doc. We can make it."

Dawkins turned and looked to Sergeant Carver who'd heard the exchange. "Keep 'em in front of you and move out." Dawkins nodded.

Carver pointed at the Marines as they struggled to their feet. "If you slow us down we'll have to carry you again." The Marines nodded. They stood on shaky legs. Dressed in rags and holding impossibly long Japanese rifles, Carver thought They looked like pictures he'd seen of children hit hardest by the great depression.

The determination on their faces told him they'd die before being helped again. He took one last look at the dark cliff face. There was still firing coming from the ridge, but nothing from the outcropping. He ducked and moved out, following his men. The occasional bullet chased after them, but he was certain the Japanese couldn't see them in the darkness.

LIEUTENANT KOGA DUCKED when the Americans started shooting from the creek bed again. As he feared, they'd laid in wait until his men were exposed. His men on the cliff edge immediately returned fire, but the American fire continued, and his men on the outcropping were falling. There was no cover. They returned fire at the winking muzzle flashes, but it was only a matter of time before they were all hit and down. The men still on the cliff were prone and returned fire in greater volume.

He moved the rest of his platoon away from the cliff edge but left three men covering. He noticed one soldier wasn't firing. He looked to be sleeping, but the hole in the back of his head told him otherwise.

He crawled forward and peered over the edge. He looked down at the men on the outcropping. There was no movement, only dark shapes intertwined in death.

He couldn't count how many there were. He clenched his jaw. He wanted to attack, to descend on the American squad and kill them all slowly. They'd inflicted terrible damage, and he had nothing to show for it.

He didn't like it, but he knew what he had to do. He turned from the carnage and in a tight voice ordered, "We move back upstream and circle to the creek bed." The men were crouched and staring. Lieutenant Koga erupted, "Now!" He clenched his fists as the soldiers jumped into action and started retracing their steps.

Sergeant Higashi shouldered his rifle and winced in pain. His bicep wound had stopped bleeding but the pain increased. He channeled it away, redirecting it as hatred toward the Americans.

THE GIs MOVED FAST DOWN the creek for two hundred yards. If the Japanese decided to try the cliff again, Carver wanted to be far enough downstream that they'd have a hard time catching up.

He called to Private Crofter in the lead position. He was splashing and cursing as he slipped on wet rocks, but he finally heard Carver's rough voice. He stopped, and Private Palmer cussed at him when he collided. "Shaddup, Palmer. Trying to hear Sarge."

Carver slogged through the knee deep water until he was beside Crofter and Palmer. "It's time to slow down. I figure we're close to our lines, but we can't see shit at the bottom of this valley. Find us a good spot to get out of the creek and move south." He motioned to his left. "We need a rocky spot, somewhere we won't leave any obvious tracks." He checked his wristwatch and noticed the face was cracked and unreadable. He looked around at the six remaining men. "Anyone have a watch that works?"

Corporal Dawkins, his medic, and ranking soldier, pulled back his sleeve and squinted at his wrist. "It's 0315, Sarge."

Carver nodded. "Okay. The sun's gonna be up in a few hours. I want to be somewhere we can get our bearings by then." The squad stared back at him. Their blank stares reminded him they'd been awake for more than twenty-four hours; fighting for their lives the whole time.

The Marines looked like wraiths with their sallow cheeks and shredded uniforms. "We're almost out of this nightmare. We're gonna make it. Just need to push for a few more hours."

Dawkins asked, "What about O'Connor and Gomez? Aren't they supposed to meet us?"

Carver pinched the crown of his nose and shook his head. "Yeah, that was the plan, but he knew it was unlikely. He and Gomez are probably already back on Hill 260 sleeping like babes." Everyone grinned wanting it to be true but knowing it wasn't.

Carver pointed with his thumb, "This group of Japs we're dealing with came from downstream. We haven't seen the original group, so O'Connor and Gomez were successful in drawing them away. I'd put my money on those two against any size Jap force any day of the week. O'Connor's a damned mountain man, for chrissakes." He knew he was trying too hard, but it made him feel better. "Now move out and find us a good spot to get out of this creek."

PRIVATE CROFTER FOUND a suitable spot another three hundred yards downstream. He stopped and waited for Sergeant Carver's approval. Carver nodded, "Looks good." He raised his voice. "Drink what's in your canteens and fill 'em back up. Don't know when we'll get another chance."

When they finished, Private Crofter led the way out of the creek. Carver stayed back, pointing his Thompson upstream. He had one magazine left, and once used it may as well be a club. He had the rifle slung across his back along with the satchel hanging at his side. He felt like he was a heavily armed delivery boy for the morning paper.

Once the last man left the creek, he stepped out. He stepped from stone to stone until there were no more. He could see where the others had jumped out as far as they could onto the mossy ground. He jumped too and landed softly. He crouched and felt around for the boot print he knew he'd find. He did his best to cover and conceal, but doubted he'd fool anyone that was looking; especially in daylight.

Private Crofter led them away from the creek, heading due south. The ground gradually sloped upward. The jungle went from nearly impassable to tolerable.

After an hour, Crofter stopped and crouched. The men were exhausted and slow to react, but they bent tired knees and searched the area for enemy soldiers.

Sergeant Carver shuffled by them and crouched beside Crofter.

Crofter didn't speak but pointed. He was at the edge of a cliff. In the darkness, it could be twenty feet or a thousand. Carver whispered, "Shit, is there a way around it?"

He could sense Crofter's shrug. Crofter pointed. "Look at that."

Carver followed his arm and saw the soft glow lighting up low clouds. Carver grinned in the darkness and slapped Crofter on the back. "By God, that's Mount Bagana. She's spewing hot tonight." Crofter nodded not understanding the significance. "Bagana's northwest of Hill 260. We're closer than I thought."

"What about this cliff? I can't keep moving south. We have to skirt it."

Carver took a deep breath and blew it out. He took a look at the sky and made his decision. "We'll move away from the cliff and wait for daylight. I think we'll be able to see Hill 260 from here. I'm betting it's right there." He pointed into the gloom. "I'll bet the Torokina river's at the base of this cliff." Crofter looked at him with a blank stare. "It's the river that runs near the front of Hill 260. We can follow it upstream. It'll lead us home." Crofter smiled. "Find us a good place to sit for another hour. Should be light enough by then."

THEY SAT in the jungle for forty minutes. Everyone except Carver and Dawkins slept. Carver stood on aching legs. "Stay here, I'm going to the cliff, see what I can see." Dawkins nodded and looked downhill, the way the Japs would come when they did.

As he came out of the jungle, the day brightened significantly, and he looked out over the green expanse of Bougainville Island. It was beautiful despite being deadly.

He peered over the edge and caught a glimpse of water moving past vines. He felt relief flood over him. They were almost home.

He followed the river upstream and saw the bombed out husk of Hill 260. He thought the ugly little hour glass shaped hill was the prettiest thing he'd ever seen. He figured it was a mile away as the crow flies. The terrain between himself the hill would be tough going though. He figured they had two hours of hard walking, but at least they knew there was an end in sight.

He hustled back to the squad. Dawkins looked at him with raised eyebrows. Carver smiled. "Get the men up. We're a mile away from hot chow and a nice safe foxhole."

Dawkins pushed himself to his feet. He moved as if made of wood. He kicked the nearest man's boot. It was Palmer. It took a number of hard kicks before his eyes flickered open. It was the same for all the men.

Carver helped the Marines to their feet. They swayed like thin willow branches in a strong wind, but they weren't ready to give up. They shouldered their captured rifles because they were too weak to hold them in their arms.

Carver led the squad to the edge of the cliff, and they walked along it, moving east. He moved slow, not because the men were tired, but because he figured they had to be smack dab in the middle of Japanese territory. *If the Japs behind us don't kill us, we'll surely run into others that will.*

The cliff descended toward the river, and without anyone noticing when it happened, there was no more cliff. They were walking along the river's edge.

Carver stopped and crouched, watching the water flow past. The rest of the squad crouched. Carver looked downstream. The morning light danced off the surface burning his aching eyes. He pulled his helmet lower and looked upstream. The river's edge was sloping sand. It looked inviting. He wanted to slip off his boots, wade into the fresh water and float downstream on his back. He shook his head. He desperately needed to sleep.

He took a deep breath and waved the squad forward. *Won't be long now.* Their eyes looked hollow in their red sockets. He moved out and heard them follow.

There was the unmistakable sound of a rifle firing, and the sand in front of Carver erupted in a geyser. The men dropped to the jungle floor.

Carver spun to the sound of more firing coming from above and behind. He couldn't see where it was it was coming from, but knew they were exposed. He pushed himself up and raised his Thompson to his shoulder. "Run, get around the corner," he yelled.

They ran past him, ducking bullets that smacked the ground around them. Carver still couldn't see where it was coming from, but he fired towards the ridge. The thumping of the heavy caliber sub-machine gun felt good. He sprayed bullets along the ridge they'd left. He could see rock and soil exploding as his bullets slammed the ridge. He burned through half his magazine before his finger came off the trigger.

Private Palmer ran past him, the last of the beleaguered squad. Carver didn't wait, he pulled in behind Palmer and ran. His ears were ringing, but he could still hear the crack of Japanese rifles.

The squad followed the river. It curved to the left, and soon the shooting stopped, but they kept running.

Private Sparks tripped and went down hard. Palmer stopped and bent to help. Carver got on the other side, and they lifted the Marine. Carver gasped, "Bend down I'll put him on your back." Palmer bent, and Carver threw the Marine onto his back. Carver marveled at how light he felt. *Like bones covered in skin.* Sparks grunted as Palmer started running again. The rifle on Spark's back thumped and gouged him with each jarring step.

The squad veered towards the river and were soon out in the open running on the hard sand. Carver didn't like how exposed they were, but they were moving fast and right now getting to their lines fast was all that mattered.

They were low on ammo. Carver had half a magazine for his Thompson and two clips for the rifle. The others were worse off than him. They wouldn't last long if they had to stand and fight.

They came around another corner and Carver got a glimpse of Hill 260. The river continued turning away from the hill. They'd have to cross it, or they'd be moving in the wrong direction. Carver yelled to Private Crofter in the lead. "We've gotta get to the other side. The hill's across the river!" Crofter was lost in the headlong retreat and didn't respond.

Carver yelled, "Cross now. I'll cover you." He waited until he saw the squad heading for the river. It was larger than the creek they'd fought in, but the current was slow. It looked like it would be up to their waists at the deepest. He hoped they wouldn't have to swim. He doubted they had the energy.

The squad splashed into the river and started wading across. Carver was crouched where the jungle turned to sand watching their back. There hadn't been any signs of pursuit since they'd made the corner, but he knew the Japs were close.

He glanced back at his squad. They were halfway across. Palmer still had Sparks on his back and Dawkins had the other two Marines at his side, helping them along. A couple more feet and he'd move across too. He heard yelling coming from downstream, and his mouth went dry. He yelled, "Here they come, hurry your asses up!"

He saw a figure dressed in the greenish uniform of the Imperial Japanese Army run from the jungle onto the sand. He saw the Americans crossing and went down to his knee and brought his rifle to his shoulder. Carver stepped out from cover with his Thompson firm against his shoulder. The enemy soldier saw him and tried to adjust to the new threat, but Carver was already firing. The soldier flew backward as plumes of red mist erupted from his chest. A second and third soldier burst from the jungle. They'd also seen the Americans and couldn't stop in time before seeing Carver.

They skidded and slipped, and Carver emptied the rest of his magazine into them. They bucked and writhed as the .45 caliber bullets tore into them.

The Thompson was empty. He slung it and unslung the Arisaka rifle. He worked the bolt action and chambered a round. He saw movement in the jungle and fired. The bolt action was slow, but he got in a rhythm, and emptied the clip. He retreated back to the jungle as he fumbled for another. He heard yelling and screaming coming from the jungle.

The squad made the other bank. Private Palmer and Dawkins were waving him to cross. The Marines and Crofter were prone with their rifles up. They were firing, giving him cover and a chance.

He didn't hesitate. It was now or never. He threw the rifle down and secured the satchel and took off like he was running a fifty-yard dash race. The hard sand was easy to run on, but when he hit the water, he needed to high-step to keep from tripping. His progress slowed, and he knew he'd be shot in the back any second. *Will I feel it?*

He kept churning forward knowing his luck would run out any second. His squad was firing, but they seemed too far away. He was too easy a target. He would die in seconds.

Over the sound of rifle fire and river splashing, he heard another sound; like someone whistling a long drawn out note. He thought maybe his exhausted mind imagined it, when he felt the thump of a mortar round slamming into the river bank he'd just left.

He was halfway across, up to his waist and moving slowly. The current pushed him, coaxing him downstream. He turned as another mortar shell landed in the jungle. The explosion looked small, but he saw a body flung forward.

More explosions followed. He stood in the middle of the river watching the spectacle. There was splashing to his front, and he saw Corporal Dawkins high-stepping through the water with his M1 rifle held high. Carver shook his head and waved him back. "Get back. I'm alright, get back."

Carver pushed forward, and the water shallowed, and he was running again. Dawkins met him halfway and tried to assist, but Carver pushed him away. "I'm fine. Let's get outta here."

The mortar fire continued. The fire from the Japanese stopped. Carver and his squad were in the jungle moving towards Hill 260. They were breathing hard. Carver couldn't get control of his breathing, none of them could. *Are we dying?*

There was another voice to their front and it took Carver a moment to realize it wasn't one of his men. "Halt. Identify yourselves."

The squad exchanged confused glances. They had no idea what to do. None of them figured they'd make it back alive. The soldier challenged them again. "Identify, or I'll shoot."

Carver took a deep breath and got control. He managed to say between gasps, "Don't shoot…we're Americans. Able Company, 164th Regiment, Americal Division.

29

O'Connor jolted awake. For an instant, he thought he was back in the forests of Oregon, but the trees were wrong. *Where are the towering ponderosas and craggy scrub oaks?* The war and jungle of Bougainville came rushing back when he saw Private Gomez looking at him with his rifle across his lap. He whispered, "Morning, Corporal."

Corporal O'Connor wished he was back in Oregon, but he'd woken from a dream into a nightmare. He pulled back his sleeve and wiped the face of his watch. It was 0500. He'd gotten a few hours of sleep. He did a silent assessment of his body, there was a general fatigue and soreness, but he felt a little better. He rolled to his side and pushed himself onto his elbow. The ground was wet, and he was too. He sat up and had to stifle a groan as his muscles protested. "Did it rain?"

Gomez nodded, "yeah, hard, but only for a few minutes. You slept right through it."

That was a first for O'Connor. *Must be more tired than I thought.* "We gotta get a move on."

Private Gomez shrugged. "You know where we are? Where base is?"

O'Connor nodded and pointed northwest. "Our lines are that way. We should move out before it gets too hot again."

"How far you think it is?"

"Couple miles maybe." He looked southeast, the way they'd come. "The Japs will pick up our trail in the daylight.

"We don't have much food left, but we've got plenty of water." He gestured to the stream flowing past.

O'Connor dug into his small pack and pulled out the food he had left. Even combined with Gomez's, there was barely enough for one person to live on for more than a day or two.

They split what they had and decided to eat before moving out. Watching the river flow by as the sun brightened the sky reminded him even more of Oregon. He wondered if he'd ever see his home again.

Private Gomez tore off a chunk of chocolate bar and pointed the way they'd come. "Beautiful the way the rain washed our prints away. Japs would have to stumble onto us."

O'Connor thought he was right. The rain had turned the strip of sand perfectly flat. It looked as though nothing had walked upon it since the beginning of time.

He looked around the piece of jungle they'd chosen. It was thick with a tiny view through to the river and beach beyond. It was like looking through a green tube. It was a good position, they had a view a long way down the beach, and they were completely concealed.

Gomez finished swallowing his half a candy bar and stood. The sun was barely above the horizon, and steam was rising from the jungle floor.

O'Connor hated to leave such a good position, but they had to keep moving. If he wasn't pursued by Japanese troops, he could live off the jungle. Their entire Regiment was trained to live off the land if it came down to it, but the Japanese presence was the main threat, not starvation.

O'Connor leaned over to push himself up when Gomez's body went rigid. O'Connor heard him take in a sharp breath then lower himself down. He whispered, "Japs."

O'Connor looked through the peek hole and saw figures moving down the beach. They were still a long way off, but he knew it had to be Japanese soldiers. He counted four. They walked close to the jungle, probably looking for any signs of their passage.

Gomez looked at him with wide eyes. O'Connor needed to make a choice. He looked northwest towards freedom. He went over their options in his head. If they moved, they'd leave fresh boot prints in the wet ground. The Japs were searching every inch and would find their tracks. If they stayed put, they could stay hidden, and the patrol might move past them, but then what? They'd have the Japs between them and their lines. He made his choice. He signaled they were staying.

They were fifteen yards off the beach. They'd burrowed deep into the underbrush, and the fresh rain had invigorated the plants they'd trampled returning them to their stout selves. Unless the Japanese stepped directly on them, they'd never find them.

O'Connor pulled his ammo pouch off his belt and set it beside him. He had six more clips for his M1; forty-eight shots. Gomez had seven clips. If they had to fight, they wouldn't go down easily.

Captain Tagami had his men up an hour before the sun. They ate what little food they had and did their morning duties. Every soldier had the runs. Having a solid shit was a distant memory for all of them.

He gathered them in the lightening jungle. "We will find the lost trail and kill the Americans this morning." The men nodded taking it as fact as if it had already happened.

An hour later, the trackers figured out what the Americans had done. "They left the trail here." The taller of the two pointed to a rocky outcropping. "Once we passed they got back on the trail and went back the way they came."

Captain Tagami nodded and pointed. "Go." The trackers trotted off with their rifles slapping their backs.

When the trackers got to the fork in the trail, they studied the ground. The brief cloudburst rainstorm the night before made everything muddy. The taller tracker stood to his full height and pointed, "They went this way, sir."

Tagami nodded. "South, towards the ocean. They'll be easier to track if they're on the beach." He bellowed, "move out."

It took another forty-five minutes to reach the beach. The trail stopped. Both trackers looked around, desperate to find the trail, but there was nothing. Captain Tagami towered over them with his balled fists on his waist. "Well? Which way?"

The taller soldier looked to his comrade who spoke. He had an annoying nasal voice. He stuttered, "S-Sir the trail stops at the beach. It looks like they used the beach, but the rain washed away any sign. There's no way to know which way they went." He lowered his head expecting it to be lopped off.

Tagami sighed and nodded. "Sergeant Chida." The stout sergeant was at his side standing stiff as a board. "Take two men southeast along the beach. I'll take the others this way." He pointed. "The American lines are this way, but they've been clever and may try another trick by going a way we wouldn't expect." Sergeant Chida nodded and picked out two soldiers. As they stepped onto the sand, Captain Tagami said, "Don't go more than a mile. If you don't find anything join us. If you do, come get me immediately."

Captain Tagami watched them move down the beach. There was a small strip of sand. Sergeant Chida walked on the firm sand while the two others were in the jungle moving slow, checking for any sign.

Captain Tagami led the remaining soldiers northwest. He dropped to the strip of sand and looked out to sea. The water color was green and inviting in the early morning light. There were no ships on the horizon. He didn't expect to see any, but he longed for the days when he wouldn't have been surprised to see a Japanese naval vessel cruising along. He wondered if he'd ever see another friendly ship.

Since the landings, the main American forces had moved beyond the Solomon Islands, leaving himself and every other Japanese soldier on the island to wither on the vine, like a fruit tree without water. The image saddened him. He knew he'd die on this island, maybe today.

He let the men pass in front of him. Two moved along the strip of sand with their eyes towards the jungle. The others moved off into the jungle. If the American's had moved inland, they'd find their tracks.

With the early morning deluge of rain, any tracks would be hard to find, but it was his only chance. His mission to recover the satchel of maps had already failed. He knew the men he was pursuing were a diversion from the main body and the satchel. He wondered if he'd made the right decision, but he was committed. Finding and killing the Americans would help him feel better, but would do nothing to make his mission a success.

He pictured Colonel Araki's face turning into a mask of rage at his failure. Perhaps bringing the Americans in as prisoners would alleviate his rage. He decided he'd try to keep at least one American alive.

As they moved down the beach, the strip of sand widened. It was perfectly flat, like a blank page of paper. As the strip widened, the sand softened. The gentle lapping of the green sea and the peaceful sounds of the jungle made him feel like he was walking along a beach back in Japan. No, this sea was warm and gentle unlike the cruel sea of his boyhood.

An hour passed and the men saw no signs of human activity. It was as if they were the first humans to pass this way in millennia.

Ahead he saw a river mouth. Most of his men were still in the jungle moving in line with him, searching the ground. When they came to the river edge, Captain Tagami called them down to the beach.

No one had anything to report. He looked across the river. It was bigger than he thought it would be. The flowing water would be easy to cross.

"Fill your canteens. We'll take a break before crossing." He looked upstream. There was a heavy mist clinging to the water and jungle. "Private Sato. Watch for Crocodiles." Private Sato nodded and trotted upstream a few yards and took his rifle off his shoulder. The rest of the men waded in and dipped their canteens. Some scooped handfuls of water and dumped it over their heads. The cool water washed away the sticky heat.

As the men cooled off and replenished, Captain Tagami looked back the way they'd come. His footsteps disappeared on the horizon. He wondered if Sergeant Chida had been successful. He doubted it. He looked at his surroundings. He decided to wait for the rest of his squad.

Corporal O'Connor and Private Gomez watched the Japanese soldiers moving relentlessly towards them. They moved slow, in search mode. O'Connor decided the soldier nearest the lapping waves was an officer. He didn't have any insignia he could see from this distance, but the way he carried himself made it obvious.

He got Gomez's attention and pointed at the officer. Gomez was sitting in the rifleman's shooting position with legs crossed, elbows resting on knees, holding his rifle steady. He took his eye from his sights and glanced at O'Connor. He shifted his aim and centered the sights on the sauntering officer. He was still a long way out, but he would be the first man to die if it came down to it.

The officer stopped at the river's edge and yelled something. Japanese soldiers materialized from the jungle. There were more than O'Connor originally thought. He counted thirteen including the officer. It was too many to take on by themselves. Their only chance was staying hidden and undetected.

O'Connor was relieved when they didn't cross the river. It looked like they were taking a break. Having the enemy so close didn't allow Gomez and O'Connor to relax, but it delayed their fates.

Gomez lifted his eyes from the sights. They didn't dare move. Their body positions would be their positions for the foreseeable future.

After twenty minutes O'Connor's legs were numb. He flexed his toes, then his calves and quads. He felt the pins and needles of blood returning to starved muscles. It reminded him of Elk hunting with his father in the high mountains of Oregon, except in this case he didn't want the quarry to get closer.

Two hours passed and O'Connor thought the Japanese might just set up camp. Then he saw why they were waiting. More soldiers were coming down the beach. O'Connor guessed they must have gone the other direction, and when they didn't find anything, rejoined.

The officer was the first to stand. The other men followed and started hefting bags and weapons. There were sharp, clipped orders and the men hustled around getting ready to move out. When the three stragglers formed up, the officer had words with another soldier.

He spoke then listened and nodded. He pointed to the river, and they waded in and dipped their bodies. One soldier floated on his back and let himself drift downstream.

Gomez and O'Connor were sighting down their rifles again. There were sixteen enemy soldiers a mere fifty yards away. It would be an easy thing to open fire, but O'Connor knew they wouldn't kill them all even if they waited until they were crossing the river.

The three stragglers cooled off for another few minutes before joining the main force. One of them spoke with the officer and nodded his head, then barked something to the others. O'Connor signaled to Gomez; that soldier, a noncom, would be the second to die.

The first Japanese soldier waded into the river and started to cross. The others followed, careful to keep their spacing. O'Connor and Gomez barely breathed.

30

When the Marines realized they'd made it to friendly lines, they collapsed. They wept and shook as they realized their ordeal had finally come to an end. Private Crofter and Corporal Dawkins bent to pick them up, but they were pushed back as litter bearers picked the Marines off the ground and placed them on stretchers. They moved them like they were made of glass.

There were stretchers for the rest of them too, but they looked at the stretcher bearers with daggers, and they backed off. Sergeant Carver explained, "We've come this far, no way we're quitting this close to the end." Crofter, Dawkins and Palmer shouldered their rifles and filed in behind Sergeant Carver.

The soldiers from Able Company lead them along the jungle trail and up through the hill defenses. There was no more shooting from the Japanese. Either they'd been killed or retreated to the jungle.

As the bedraggled squad filed past the foxholes, the soldiers occupying them gawked. They were only gone a couple of days, but to the men who stayed behind, they looked like they were from another planet. They couldn't help notice how few there were. They nodded, and some took off their helmets as if in the company of angels. Carver recognized most of the faces and nodded back.

They went to the command bunker. One of the escorts ran inside, and in seconds Lieutenant Swan ran out. The returning squad members snapped off sloppy salutes, and Swan stared with an open mouth. He looked from man to man, stopping at Sergeant Carver. He finally spoke. "Welcome back."

Carver reached into his pocket and pulled out a bloody jangle of dog tags. He extended them and Lt. Swan took them. Swan's mouth drooped, and he hefted them feeling their weight. Carver said, "There's a few I couldn't recover."

Lieutenant Swan spread them out reading each one. "Jesus," he murmured. He closed his fist around them and shut his eyes.

Carver slipped the satchel off his shoulder and held it out. Lieutenant Swan reached for it, "What's this?"

"It's what those dog tags paid for."

Lieutenant Swan opened the satchel and pulled out a damp, cloth document. It was a map with arrows and Japanese writing. He looked at Carver with undisguised joy. "Is this what I think it is?"

Carver nodded. "Pulled it off a Jap trying to escape with it. The way they've been pursuing us, I'd say it's important."

Lieutenant Swan stuffed it back in the satchel and turned back to the bunker. "I need a debriefing. I need to know everything."

Carver didn't move. Lieutenant Swan stopped and looked over his shoulder in confusion. He was about to repeat the order, but Sergeant Carver spoke first. "Are Corporal O'Connor and Private Gomez here?"

Lieutenant Swan looked confused and touched the wad of dog tags jangling in his pocket. Carver shook his head. "We split up. He got the Japs to follow him while we escaped. He headed to the drop off point. He'd try to get back here on foot."

Lieutenant Swan shook his head. "You're the first we've seen. I'd know if they showed up anywhere along the line."

Carver's eyes flashed. "You don't need a debrief from me." He put his meaty hand on Cpl. Dawkin's shoulder. "Dawkins can tell you everything." Dawkins nearly collapsed under Carver's hand. He looked at his sergeant with uncomprehending eyes. "These men need food and rest, and I need a ride to Puruata Island."

Lieutenant Swan wasn't happy, but he knew Carver wouldn't rest until he'd done everything he could to get O'Connor and Gomez back. He sent Sergeant Milo and Private Bennett with him.

Private Bennett drove along the jungle road like a race car driver. He seemed to hit every bump and hole. Carver tried to eat K-rations but gave up after losing half of it on the floor of the jeep.

Sergeant Milo raised his voice over the engine. "The Japs attacked a transport truck along this section day before yesterday. It's best to do it at speed. He'll slow down in another mile." Carver nodded, wishing he'd told him that before he tried eating. Sergeant Milo continued, "Sounds like you had a hairy time out there."

Carver didn't bother answering. He could feel every muscle in his body screaming for sleep. Holding onto the side, he closed his eyes. He was on the edge of consciousness. Awake just enough to hold on. When they were beyond the danger zone, Private Bennett slowed slightly, and Sergeant Carver went into a jolting sleep. Sergeant Milo leaned from the back seat and held Carver's shoulder so he wouldn't fall out.

They arrived at the main lines fifteen minutes later. There were two soldiers on either side of the road. They waved them forward when they saw they weren't Japanese.

Private Bennett drove through the tent city that had sprung up around the headquarters and past the lines of artillery pieces dug into the muddy ground with high walls of sandbags surrounding them.

He skidded to a halt beside the small dock. Puruata Island sat across the narrow channel. Sergeant Milo hopped out the back and slung his Thompson sub-machine gun over his shoulder. He slapped Sergeant Carver on the shoulder, and his eyes snapped open, taking in his surroundings. "We're here," said Milo.

Carver shook his head until the cobwebs cleared. He stumbled out of the jeep, catching his foot and nearly falling flat on his face. Milo reached out and held him up. "Jesus Christ, Carver, you can barely function. This is bullshit. You need rest."

Carver shrugged Milo's hand off, "I'm fine. Just waking up." He took steps towards the small boat moored to the dock. There was a sailor sitting beside it with a fishing rod in his hand. "You. Sailor. Cast off, need a ride to the island."

IT WAS A SHORT TRIP. Carver thanked the sailor, who shrugged his shoulders and asked, "You want me to wait for you?"

Carver shook his head and hopped off the skiff onto the dock. It swayed under his feet. He noticed all the PT boats moored alongside the dock except one which was hanging from a crane. There were sailors without shirts working on the hull. As he approached, he noticed the small holes running in a line along the entire length. The sailors were filling them in with caulking and replacing some sections with new boards. They saw the GI walking with purpose towards their boathouse and stared.

Carver burst into the same airy room he'd gotten Commander Hawkins' briefing only a few days before. Three sailors were talking in a corner. They all turned when they heard his sudden entrance. Carver didn't waste any time. He walked up to them looking for rank insignia, but they wore dirty t-shirts. He didn't recognize any of them and assumed they were part of the repair crew. "Where's Commander Hawkins?"

The sailors looked him up and down. The taller of the three asked, "Who wants to know?" Carver was in no mood for bullshit and leaned into the sailor's chest. He glared until he backed away. The sailor looked for help from his buddies, but both backed away, seeing the crazed look in the crazy infantry sergeant's eyes. "I-I'll go see if I can round him up for you, Sarge."

Carver nodded, "Tell him Sergeant Carver wants a word and be quick about it." He pushed him, and the sailor almost tripped over his own feet trying to get away.

An uncomfortable minute passed. The remaining sailors stood back wondering what this dirty, crazy sergeant wanted with their commanding officer.

Commander Hawkins entered the room and looked him up and

down. "Sergeant Carver, it's good to see you're back safe." Carver snapped off a salute and Hawkins returned it. "At ease." He gestured to a chair, and Carver reluctantly sat. "What's this all about, Sergeant?"

Carver gave him the nuts and bolts of the mission. He ended by telling him. "O'Connor and Gomez were following the trail we took in. They're heading back to the drop off point. We need to take one of your boats out there and pick them up."

Commander Hawkins looked at his watch. "We don't do daylight missions, too much exposure to Jap Zeros. The Japs don't either for the same reason."

Carver squinted. "I haven't seen a Zero since I've been here, sir. The fighter jocks cleared 'em out." He pointed, "My men are out there somewhere, and your boats are the quickest and best way to get 'em out. Those men saved our asses. I can't leave 'em out there to die."

Commander Hawkins looked at the floor then back to Carver. "You don't even know if they're alive. I can't risk the lives of my men and these boats for a mission that might be for nothing."

Carver shook his head. "You're right. I don't know if they're alive for sure, but O'Connor's the best jungle fighter in the whole damned Army. He's alive, I know it in my guts." He thumped his chest with his fist. "I know it in my heart." Commander Hawkins didn't respond, but Carver could tell he was warming to the idea. "It'll be quick. We'll stay well away from the shore until were at the drop off point. We can move in fast, if they're there they'll hear the engines and show themselves. We'll pick 'em up and be back here in a couple of hours."

Commander Hawkins said, "Plans never hold up in battle. I doubt it'll be that easy." He paced a few steps then nodded his head. "Okay, I'll get the men together. They thought they were getting a much deserved day off. They won't be happy." Carver looked at him through exhausted eyes. Commander Hawkins nodded, "we'll shove off in an hour. Why don't you curl up somewhere and use the time to sleep? You look like shit."

Carver nodded and threw him a salute. "Thank you, sir. You won't regret it."

Hawkins gnashed his jaw and shook his head, "I already do, Sergeant."

31

O'Connor and Gomez watched the Japanese soldiers wading across the river. They had their M1's leveled on the officer and the sergeant. They followed their movements with their barrels. The sergeant was in front of the group and the officer in the middle. The first soldier stepped out of the river and onto their side of the creek. He looked around with his long rifle at waist level.

The day was bright and hot, and still morning. It would be another scorcher on Bougainville. Sweat dripped off the tip of O'Connor's nose and pooled on the rifle stock. He wondered if he'd live long enough to see midday.

As more enemy soldiers came out of the water, they spread out, coming closer to their position. The lead soldier stopped on the sand right in front of their hiding spot. He looked at the ground scanning for footprints. O'Connor thanked God the heavy rainstorm had erased any sign of their passing.

O'Connor watched the soldier out of the corner of his eye. He didn't look directly at him, fearing his gaze would alert some hidden sense. He'd seen it happen plenty of times while hunting big game. He kept his rifle pointed at the officer who was coming out of the river. If they were discovered in the next couple of seconds, he'd shoot him first then shift to the soldier standing in front of him.

Long seconds passed as the soldier waited for his comrades to catch up. Once they did, he looked into the jungle and sighed. He mumbled something under his breath and pushed into the brambles.

Their hiding place was in the thickest portion they could find. Hopefully, the soldier would avoid the extra work it would take to push through it. He'd have to come straight at them with a concerted effort to stumble upon them.

O'Connor decided if he did come, he'd drop his rifle and use his knife. It would be quieter and may give them a chance to slip into the jungle without alerting any other soldiers. He had little doubt they'd track them down if they found their trail.

The soldier called out, startling O'Connor and Gomez. O'Connor felt his heart rate increase as his body flushed with adrenaline. He could feel Gomez stiffen in his seated position, but neither made a sound.

The soldier called out again, and this time there was an answering call from the beach. Another soldier was coming to join him. O'Connor wondered how thorough they'd be. If they searched diligently they'd find their hideout, and he had little doubt they'd die.

Once the second soldier stepped into the jungle they exchanged words and the first soldier seemed to point directly at O'Connor. The second soldier looked into the jungle, and nodded. He stepped past the first soldier and pushed into the thickest section, using his rifle to push vines and branches out of the way. With the first soldier watching there'd be no way for O'Connor to kill him with his knife.

He shifted his rifle barrel almost imperceptibly to the advancing soldier. He figured Gomez was doing the same, but they couldn't risk speaking. O'Connor went over it in his head. He'd shoot the closest soldier then the second soldier, then find the officer again.

The Japanese soldier pushed and struggled. He'd advanced to within ten feet. O'Connor glimpsed flashes of the man. His face was dripping sweat beneath his helmet, and he grunted with each step.

O'Connor knew Gomez was waiting for him to make the first move. *Another two steps and I'll fire.* O'Connor put pressure on the trigger. He aligned the barrel with the soldier's chest. At this range, the thirty caliber bullet would barely slow down as it passed through his body. The second soldier was behind but slightly forward. If Gomez didn't kill him first, it would be an easy traverse. If he did it fast enough, he should be able to get a bead on the officer before he could find cover.

The soldier stopped, took off his helmet and wiped his forehead. O'Connor applied more pressure on the trigger. He decided not to wait. The second soldier suddenly yelled, and the close soldier turned to look at him. There was a deep thrumming sound coming from the ocean. At first, O'Connor didn't know what it was, but as the sound grew, he realized it was the familiar sound of a PT boat going full throttle.

The soldiers ran out of the jungle to join their squad on the beach. Gomez looked back at O'Connor with a questioning glance. O'Connor shrugged and took the opportunity to get out of his crouching position. His legs were asleep, and they almost collapsed when he tried to stand. He ignored the pain as blood rushed into them. He leaned forward and pushed vines and brambles away trying to see what was happening.

The sound of the PT boat's engine intensified as it neared. O'Connor could see it was further up the coast, about where they'd been dropped off the other night. *Are they looking for us?*

He looked at the troops on the beach. The officer was yelling, and the Japanese dropped to their bellies. O'Connor could tell the PT boat hadn't seen them, or they would've engaged. He looked back at Gomez and whispered, "That's our ticket out of here. We've gotta get their attention." Gomez nodded, and O'Connor saw the fear in his bloodshot eyes. "We've gotta attack. Once we fire, the Japs will have to shift and engage, and hopefully, the boat will see them." Gomez gulped and gave him a short nod.

O'Connor went to his belly. "We've gotta get to the edge of the jungle for a clear shot. Stay down and follow my lead." Gomez went to his belly without a word, and they slithered forward until they were at the jungle edge. They were six feet apart with only thin vines and leaves for cover.

The Japanese soldiers were facing away, lying flat. Their light tan battle fatigues were perfect camouflage in the sand. They looked like scattered rocks.

O'Connor found what he thought was the officer. He was on his belly faced away from him. He couldn't be sure it was him, but he was in the same area he'd seen him last. From this angle, O'Connor would be shooting him in the ass. The thought made his sphincter pucker.

The PT boat was coming close to shore but hadn't slowed. It was turning ninety degrees towards them, paralleling the beach. The graceful lines of the boat were cutting a white wake through the sea. The waves were lapping up against the shore.

At its present course and speed, the boat would be in front of the Japanese soldiers in another minute. He heard yelling from the beach, issued orders. They were coming from the officer. The soldiers responded by shifting positions and bringing their weapons to bear. They were going to engage the boat when it was close. With sixteen guns, it would be an effective ambush. O'Connor couldn't let that happen.

He gave a low whistle and Gomez looked his way. He signaled that he was firing in five seconds. Gomez nodded once and brought his cheek to the stock of his gun placing the sights on the sergeant he'd kill first.

O'Connor put pressure on the M1's trigger until it fired. He continued firing into the officer's backside. The officer arched and writhed onto his back pushing along the sand. He pushed himself to the river's bank and out of O'Connor's sight. He moved to the next target, the closest soldier, the one who'd nearly stepped on him. The soldier had heard the shot and was looking back over his shoulder directly at O'Connor. O'Connor put a bullet through his eye and found the next soldier. Before he could fire Gomez, put two bullets into his side, and he slumped.

The soldiers on the beach were turning around to face the unseen threat. O'Connor shot two more before the 'ping' of his empty clip sounded. Gomez covered him while he pushed in a new clip.

The return fire coming from the beach was inaccurate, fired in panic. O'Connor put the muzzle on a soldier who was pulling back the bolt to reload. He was exposed and only twenty yards away. O'Connor put two thirty caliber bullets through his head. The soldier's head snapped back then slumped forward.

A bullet whizzed between them snapping leaves and vines. Gomez fired his last shot, and O'Connor covered him while he reloaded. The easy targets were dead or out of commission.

The remaining Japanese were behind the cover of the sloping river bank and were firing into the jungle. They still hadn't pinpointed their position, but they would soon, and then they'd die. Bullets smacked into the jungle all around them. One plowed into the sand and sent a fountain of debris into O'Connor's eyes. He cursed and wiped furiously. "Cover me. I can't see."

He tried to open his heavy eyelids, but it was too painful. He clawed at his side for his canteen. He felt bullets whipping and snapping through the jungle around him. He felt the panic starting to mount, rising up like molten lava to the crest of a volcano. He concentrated on the canteen, unscrewed the lid and dumped it over his eyes. There wasn't much left, but it was enough to clear his vision. He looked to his left and saw Gomez clawing at another clip. Bullets slashed the leaves and vines sending debris onto his back.

He cursed, he hadn't heard the ping from Gomez's M1. He brought his rifle to his shoulder and fired towards the river bank. He could barely see the enemies' heads through the thick layer of gun smoke. A Japanese bullet sliced into his helmet and his head flung back as the helmet flew off. Gomez stopped firing and looked over at him; sure he was dead.

Captain Tagami knew he would die soon. He got shot from behind somehow. Two bullets had sliced up his leg and into his body. He felt them burning from the inside, like hot branding irons. In his initial burst of adrenalin his body had reacted without him knowing how.

He found himself on the riverbank facing back towards the jungle. He had no idea how he'd gotten there, but he could see his blood track soaking into the sand leading straight to him. He thought it looked like a lot of blood. He pulled his submachine gun from under his torso. The sling kept it close to his body. He was glad he still had a weapon. He'd die fighting at least.

He tried to lift the weapon and aim, but a sudden weakness overcame him. He felt as though he couldn't lift a single sand pebble, let alone his weapon. He cursed and forced himself to push it forward. He propped it on the slight rise in front of him, the clip acting as the fulcrum point. He reached up and with great effort depressed the trigger. The machine gun jumped in his hand, and he lost his grip. He cursed and tried to recover, but it was no use. He had no energy.

He rested his head and looked to his right. Beside him he could see his men firing their rifles over and over into the jungle. He could hear them chattering, but he couldn't understand what they were saying. *Good soldiers. These are valiant warriors. It's been an honor.* He wanted to say it out loud, but he couldn't speak. Even words were difficult.

With the last shred of energy, he turned himself onto his back and stared up into the blue sky. He coughed, and it sent wracking pain through his chest. He felt liquid draining from his mouth. *Blood, no doubt.* Movement caught his eye. It was coming from the sea. He lifted his head and tried to focus. The shape of a boat slashing towards him reminded him of the American PT boat they'd been trying to ambush.

He watched as the guns on the boat opened up. Even in broad daylight, he could see the long tongues of flame reaching out to him like dragon's breath. He tried to call out, to warn his gallant soldiers, but he couldn't make his throat work. It was clogged and unusable. A glowing ball of flame raced towards him. Before it destroyed his body, he thought it looked quite beautiful.

SERGEANT CARVER WAS beside Commander Hawkins as they raced towards the jungle. The powerful boat was at maximum speed, slicing through the water like a supercharged torpedo. He was concentrating on the jungle, his Thompson submachine gun on his hip pointing to the sky. "You're sure this is the spot?"

Commander Hawkins nodded but didn't speak. He was concentrating on BM Smitty at the bow. Smitty was watching for shallow reefs. When the boat was on a plane it only needed a few feet of water, but if they came close to a reef, they'd have to turn, and that would require more water.

Hawkins was confident they were in the general area of the drop-off point, but navigating using old maps wasn't an exact science. He hadn't run into trouble during the drop-off, but there was no guarantee they were in the exact same spot. Hidden reefs were always a danger and he didn't want to be stuck near the jungle when night came.

The second PT boat stayed back from the shore. They'd be in support if needed. Commander Hawkins looked over his shoulder reassuring himself of its presence. *Glad we're never alone out here.*

Hawkin's plan was to keep the boat on a plane and parallel the bank from forty or fifty yards out. If the two missing men were nearby, they'd hear the boat and come running. The problem was, they'd also alert any Japs lurking nearby.

When they were fifty yards out, Hawkins put the boat into a steep left turn. Carver reached out to steady himself, never taking his eyes off the coastline. He shook his head. He had to yell over the throbbing engine. "It all looks the same. I can't see the trail."

Commander Hawkins finished the turn then leaned close to Carver's ear, "The river mouth up ahead." He pointed. "That's west of the drop-off point. We're definitely in the same area."

Carver followed the beach and found the river inlet. From this far out it looked little more than a slight intrusion poking into the sea. Carver hadn't studied the maps as Hawkins had. He continued scanning the beach and jungle. He'd have to trust Commander Hawkins knew what he was doing.

Ensign Hanks was beside Carver glassing the coastline with his binoculars. He heard Hawkins mention the river inlet and focused in on the area. The sea was smooth, but it was difficult to maintain a steady gaze through the binoculars. He was about to scan away when he saw something flash. He leaned forward steadying the glasses with two hands. There it was again, this time he could see a wisp of smoke rising. He dropped the glasses squinting then put them back to his eyes.

He stepped behind Commander Hawkins, having to push past Carver, who gave him a hard look. He tapped Hawkin's shoulder and handed the binoculars to him. He pointed, "Something's happening at the river mouth. I saw something."

Commander Hawkins pushed Carver over and took his position, leaving the driving duties to his second in command. He put the glasses to his eyes and adjusted the focus. He concentrated on the spot. He saw a wisp of smoke and then the brief flash of something bright. The boat was cruising down the coastline, the river inlet becoming more clear with every foot. He dropped the binoculars and yelled to Carver, "Something happening at the river mouth. Move forward and tell the gunners to be ready." Carver reached for the binoculars, but Hawkins shook his head, "No time. Alert the gunners. Now."

Carver slung his Thompson and shuffled his way forward, careful to keep his grip on part of the boat at all times. He passed the message, and the gunners primed their weapons and turned their big barrels towards the river.

Carver stayed beside the forward 20mm gunner and unslung his Thompson. He crouched with one arm holding his weapon the other holding the boat. The gunner glanced at him and leaned close. "Move out of the way or the spent shell casings will burn you."

Carver looked at the ejector port beside him. He shook his head. *I must be losing it, stupid.* He didn't say anything but moved to the right and behind the gunner.

As they came within two hundred yards of the inlet, Carver could see beige blobs beside the river. There were occasional flashes and wisps of smoke. He knew there was a firefight going happening. He pulled back the primer on his Thompson. He knew his weapon would be almost useless at this range, but he wanted to be ready. He could see firing coming from the tree-line. *That's gotta be O'Connor and Gomez.* His heart rate quickened as the coming combat raced at him full-speed.

He looked back at Commander Hawkins, who was watching the battle through binoculars. Hawkins leaned toward Ensign Hanks' ear and said something. The boat turned out to sea slightly. Carver realized he was putting the boat more broadside to the coastline, allowing every gun a shot at the battle.

The situation developed quickly, but Carver saw the Japanese on the riverbank firing towards the jungle. If the PT boat gunners opened up too soon, O'Connor and Gomez would be directly behind the line of fire. He yelled trying to get Hawkins's attention, but he was still glued to the binoculars getting ready to tell his gunners to fire. He had his hand up like he was starting a race. When he dropped it BM smitty would relay the order to the gunners, and all hell would break loose.

Carver slapped the 20mm gunner's leg. He ignored it, concentrating on BM Smitty and tracking his barrel along the backs of the Japanese soldiers. Carver was about to stand and get the gunner's attention, but Commander Hawkins' hand went down, and Smitty yelled, "Open fire!"

The rumble of the engines at full throttle was overcome by the powerful hammering of three deck guns firing on full automatic.

Carver watched as the river erupted in geysers and the sand around the beige blobs exploded as if it were an artillery strike.

There were fifteen seconds of sustained fire before BM Smitty relayed Hawkins's call for a cease-fire. The target area was engulfed in dust and water spray. The boat continued at full speed passing the river mouth. The guns traversed keeping their targets covered. Carver strained to see the jungle beyond the carnage, but he only got glimpses of green.

The boat turned ninety degrees out to sea. It traveled forty yards before turning sharply back towards the beach. Carver was straining, trying to see his lost soldiers. He gripped his Thompson cursing the gunners for firing while his men were in the line of fire. The image of their shredded bodies flashed across his mind. He didn't know if he'd be able to restrain himself if Hawkins had killed his men.

As the boat approached forty yards, it turned ninety degrees again and slowed to a few knots. The boat slumped forward sending up a wake that traveled up the river current like the back of an immense body. The waves lapped against the shore, licking the boots of dead Japanese soldiers.

The air cleared, and Carver could see movement along the jungle line. The gunner beside him swiveled his barrel to the spot, and Carver stepped in front. "Those are my men, goddammit. Hold fire." Carver looked at Commander Hawkins, whose face went white when he met his eyes. He didn't have to speak, Hawkins could see the murder in his eyes.

Sergeant Carver saw someone stumble out of the jungle on unsteady legs. Carver didn't hesitate, he launched himself into the sea and started swimming until his feet touched the sloping sand bottom. He waded out of the sea, and unslung his Thompson, ready to kill any Japanese that had survived. He lowered his weapon when he saw the mass of body parts intertwined like a nightmare goulash. He could hardly tell they were human, the only clues, bits of hands, boots, and rifles.

He ran towards the tall figure in the jungle. He recognized O'Connor and couldn't suppress the smile spreading across his lips. He heard O'Connor's voice and saw him waving.

A NEW SOUND joined the fight and O'Connor thought it was the happiest sound he'd ever heard. The heavy thumping of machine guns coming from the PT boat. The Japanese were in full view with no cover. O'Connor yelled, "Stay down, stay down." Gomez stopped firing and buried his head into the jungle floor. The heavy machine guns cut a deadly swath into the Japanese, but O'Connor and Gomez were in the line of fire. Stray bullets from the powerful fifty caliber machine gun would tear them apart the same way it was destroying the Japanese.

The machine gun fire was intense but slackened and stopped after what seemed an eternity. O'Connor lifted his head and looked over at the motionless Gomez. He called, "Gomez, Gomez. You hit?" He dropped his M1 and lunged over to his side. He reached out to turn him over, but when he touched him, Gomez exploded with violence and slammed his fist into O'Connor's cheek. He was about to hit him again, but O'Connor threw himself onto his back. Gomez thrashed around but O'Connor talked him down. "Easy does it. It's over. Easy"

Gomez stopped struggling, and O'Connor could see reason

returning to his crazed eyes. He was breathing hard. He shook his head, "Sorry." He reached out, "You Okay?"

O'Connor touched his cheek and nodded. He pointed to the PT boat which was turning away from the beach at high speed. "Let's get outta here."

O'Connor stood and with his M1 over his head, walked out of the jungle. Gomez stayed crouched trying to shake off the uncontrollable shaking that wracked his body.

O'Connor kept a close eye on the Japanese soldiers scattered around the beach. The PT boat slowed and turned back towards them. Every gun aimed at him.

Someone on the PT boat yelled, and O'Connor saw a big man jump off the boat. He landed in deep water but swam until he could touch, then pushed his way through. He was grinning like a crazy man. O'Connor waved, "That you, Carver?"

32

The boat ride back to base was uneventful. O'Connor and Gomez couldn't keep from grinning. Sergeant Carver thanked Commander Hawkins. Hawkins asked Sergeant Carver, "What would you have done if your men got hit?"

Carver gave him a hard look then said, "Guess we'll never know." Hawkins knew the answer.

They left Puruata Island and found a ride back to Hill 260. The ride back was a blur full of bouncing potholes and muddy corners. They were exhausted, barely able to keep themselves from falling asleep and falling out.

The jeep churned to the top of the hill, and the men rolled themselves out. The driver didn't waste any time. He whipped the jeep around and headed back to the safety of the headquarters compound.

The three ragged soldiers were met by Lieutenant Swan and Sergeant Milo. They stood in a loose formation swaying like grass in a high wind.

Lieutenant Swan looked them over. "Welcome back men. You've had quite an ordeal." They stared at him, barely comprehending his words. "Get some chow and rack time. I'll make sure no one disturbs you for the next ten hours." He stepped forward noticing the gash along the side of O'Connor's head. The blood had stopped flowing, but the side of his head was encrusted with dried blood. "Get that wound looked at first, Corporal." He looked the other men over and noticed Carver's gashed cheek. "You too, Sergeant." Carver touched the gash, and remembered the wound.

Swan continued "Before I let you go, I want you to know the maps you stole from that Jap internment camp are proving invaluable. Intelligence thinks they're the real deal." The men were losing focus; barely able to keep their eyes open. He slapped Carver on the shoulder, "Get some rest. See you in the morning."

COLONEL ARAKI WASN'T EXPECTING to get a report from his errant Captain Tagami. It had been a week since he'd sent him after the American patrol. He hadn't heard anything from them since. Lieutenant Koga and what was left of his platoon, did return, however and reported their failure to kill the American's. Colonel Araki was irate and threatened to relieve the young officer, but officers were in short supply.

He put the Lieutenant through a rigorous debriefing, keeping him in a sweltering tent while his men questioned his every decision. By the end, Lt. Koga was convinced he'd die for his failure.

Colonel Araki was baffled that Koga hadn't encountered Captain Tagami and his men. He thought of Captain Tagami as his most competent officer. Had he lost the American's trail so easily? And why hadn't they returned? They didn't have enough rations with them to survive a week in the jungle. He thought they must have come to some unknowable demise, but not knowing their fate ate at him.

ONE WEEK later Sergeant Carver and Corporal O'Connor were back on regular duty. They'd been through a rigorous debriefing with Lieutenant Swan and the company commander, Captain Flannigan.

Flannigan was convinced the Japanese maps and battle plans were authentic. After the debriefing, he'd jumped in his jeep and shot off Hill 260 with a broad grin on his face. He was delivering the Japanese playbook to regimental headquarters. It was just the sort of thing that advanced an officer's career.

Lieutenant Swan was beaming as well. He'd kept Sergeant Carver and the remaining squad members off the guard rotation for most of the week. Now, however, Carver and O'Connor were back on the line crouched in slit trenches midway down Hill 260. The trenches were well used, they even had drainage ports for the daily torrential downpour that never seemed to take a day off.

The platoon was back to full strength with the addition of men from the beachhead. The replacements were all veterans, and fit in well, but every time Carver saw one, he was reminded of the men he lost. Losing Private Willy weighed on him. Willy was tough as nails, but he'd died just like so many others.

O'Connor stood and peered over the edge of the slit trench. The day was moving towards evening, the sun starting to dip towards the horizon to the west. O'Connor squinted into the jungle at the base of the hill. He looked down at Carver propped with his back against the wall and his feet on the opposite wall. "You think they'll pull us back; now they know the Jap's plans?"

Carver shrugged. "Doubt it. Lieutenant Swan certainly thinks so. That's why he's so damned happy. He hates our position, and I can't say I blame him. We're stuck out here like a tick on a dog. The way they've been resupplying us, giving whatever we ask for, they're keeping us here."

O'Connor continued scanning the empty jungle. "If the Japs do what we think they're gonna do, we're screwed. We'll be cut off and surrounded. How many did it say they were committing again... twelve thousand?"

Carver nodded, "Something like that, but coming over those mountains should whittle them down a bit."

O'Connor spit into the dirt. "That's tough jungle, no doubt." The silence stretched until O'Connor broke it. "March 8th isn't far. Only a couple weeks. If they're keeping us here, hopefully, they'll give us some armor, or more artillery."

"Don't hold your breath."

COLONEL ARAKI STOOD outside the colonial style house in Buni on the southern tip of Bougainville. He'd made the trip along the newly constructed jungle road they'd been using to gather troops and materials for the planned assault on the American lines.

There was a constant flow of traffic even in broad daylight. The jungle canopy so thick overhead kept the hated American fighters and bombers away. Even if they knew where they were, the canopy would explode any bombs and stop any bullets long before they'd reach the ground.

The busy troop traffic made his journey in the opposite direction slow and frustrating, but he felt he needed to make his case directly to General Hyakutake. He hoped delivering his thoughts in person would add weight to his plea.

He'd been waiting inside the foyer of the grand house for over an hour, and he was starting to wonder if he was forgotten. The soldier at the desk hadn't stopped stacking and sorting piles of paper and folders since he sat down. There was a buzzing sound, and the soldier peered through the stacks of papers and said, "General Kanda will see you now, sir."

Colonel Araki stood but squinted at the soldier. "I have an appointment with General Hyakutake."

The soldier pushed his round glasses up his nose. "Yes sir, but General Hykutake fell ill two days ago, and Lieutenant General Kanda is overseeing all his business until he returns, sir."

Colonel Araki gritted his teeth. This runt of a man was starting to annoy him. He barked, "You will stand at attention when addressing a superior officer, Corporal."

The small man nearly fell over backward, but managed to get to his feet and stand stiff as a rail. He saluted, "Yes, sir."

"When is General Hyakutake expected to return?"

Still at attention, the young soldier's brow was sweating, wetting the beige hat he wore. "I do not know, sir."

Colonel Araki slapped the side of his thigh with his hat and clutched his briefcase. "Show me to General Kanda."

The soldier sprang into action happy to be rid of the grizzled old soldier. "Right this way, sir." He motioned him towards a closed double door. He swung the doors open and stepped in while Colonel Araki waited on the threshold. "Colonel Araki to see you, sir."

Lieutenant General Kanda was second in command of the 17th Army. He was known as a tough, by the book leader. His distinctive bald head, which he kept closely shaved, shone and reflected the ceiling fan spinning lazily above him.

He looked up but didn't stand. "Ah, Colonel Araki. What is so important that brings you here, so far from your duties?"

Colonel Araki saluted and waited until it was returned. "General Kanda, I was expecting General Hyakutake. Is the General well?"

General Kanda stood and shook his head. "He's suffered some kind of spell. He's an old soldier. The doctors think he may have had a stroke, but it's too early to tell." He looked at him sharply, "You haven't answered my question, Colonel."

Araki felt sick. He'd known General Hyakutake since Nanking. They'd devastated half of China together and conquered countless colonial islands. He was counting on his close ties to convince him to change the attack plans.

He took a deep breath and decided there was nothing to do but forge on. "I'm here to discuss the upcoming attack on the American positions."

General Kanda smiled, "I have a constant flow of information coming from the front, Colonel. I don't need or want my front line commanders making special trips to brief me."

Colonel Araki shook his head. "I'm not here to brief you, sir. I'm here to discuss changing the timeline and possibly the entire plan of attack."

General Kanda's smile turned to ice. "Why would I do that?"

"I know it's late for changes but…"

Kanda interrupted, "The attack is in a couple of weeks, of course it's too late for changes."

Araki nodded but continued. "It wouldn't have to be drastic

changes. I believe the Americans know when, where and how we're going to attack…"

Again, General Kanda interrupted. "Of course they do, because of your blunders the American's have the entire battle plan, but it won't matter. We're bringing overwhelming forces to the battle, and there's nothing they can do about it. Even knowing everything, they still won't be able to keep our brave soldiers from pushing them off the foothills." His eyes gleamed as he pictured the victory in his mind. "Then we'll rain artillery fire onto their damned airfields, and push them back into the sea."

Colonel Araki knew it wasn't going well and thought he should salute and leave, but the thought of coming all this way without explaining his plan seemed a waste. "If we changed a few things, like attack routes and the attack date, we could save many lives. We could even change the attack routes to hit their forces from the opposite direction they're expecting us and take them by surprise, hastening our victory."

General Kanda clasped his hands behind his back and paced. Araki stood at attention sweating. Kanda stopped, spun to the back wall and peered up at a portrait of General Hyakutake which was below a much larger portrait of Emperor Hirohito. "I have fought under General Hyakutake for many years. He's a worthy commander one who deserves our respect and admiration. This attack is his plan, his legacy. He may not return to the battlefield." He turned back to look Araki in the face. He leaned on the desk. "The attack will commence without changes. Understand?"

Colonel Araki stiffened and clicked his heels. "Of course, sir. Thank you for your time and consideration, sir."

He saluted, and Kanda returned it. "You've come a long way, Colonel. Why don't you spend the night? The local girls are warm, friendly and mostly clean."

Araki shook his head quickly. "Thank you for the offer, but I need to get back to my men. There's a lot of preparation to be done, sir."

"Dismissed," Kanda said. As Colonel Araki limped out, he said, "I'll expect nothing short of victory, Colonel."

Colonel Araki stopped and without turning, nodded "Yes, sir. Victory or death, I will do my duty."

33

For the next three weeks, everyone in Able Company was busy fortifying Hill 260. The bunkers were reinforced with another full layer of sandbags; the slit trenches were widened. An intricate system of connecting trenches were dug, so men could travel between strongpoints without exposing themselves to enemy fire.

There was a constant flow of war material streaming in from the rear. Ammunition was piled high. More .30 caliber machines guns were placed along the line until there were more guns than qualified operators. More men were brought in to man them.

Whatever Captain Flannigan and Lieutenant Swan asked for, they got, including five Sherman tanks. Captain Flannigan kept them out of sight in the jungle behind the hill. There were five dugouts ready for them to pull into once the firing started.

According to the captured Japanese plans, the attack would begin with a sustained artillery barrage, in the early morning hours of March 8th. There would be three prongs of Japanese soldiers hitting three different hills soon after the barrage stopped. Hill 700 a few miles to the west, Cannon Hill in the middle, and Hill 260 were all targets.

Lieutenant Swan thought once the big brass saw the situation they'd pull his men off Hill 260, and put them back into the line. He doubted, even though they knew the exact plan down to the last detail, that their company could hold against such an overwhelming force. The odds seemed too great.

Captain Flannigan and every officer up the chain didn't see it that way. They wanted the Japanese to attack and commit their remaining forces. They'd flounder against a well dug-in foe and withering, pre-sighted artillery.

Lieutenant Swan turned an ugly shade of white when he heard the rest of Able Company wouldn't be on the hill when the steel started flying. He'd be left to defend it with a reinforced platoon.

Sergeant Carver had overheard the conversation and relayed it to Corporal O'Connor, careful none of the other men heard.

"The captain stood there beside the LT with his hands on his hips looking out over the jungle like MacArthur for chrissakes. He told him how much he wished he could stay on the hill with him. It was a good show, acting angry and let down, but it was all bullshit. Told him the rest of Able is being pulled back as a fast reaction force in case the battle doesn't go as planned in other sectors."

Corporal O'Connor shook his head and kept filling sandbags. The attack was supposed to come in the morning. The rest of Able Company had left the day before, and the hill seemed empty without them. "They'll probably have to come save our asses unless the Nips cut off the route."

"We've got a shitload of artillery that's gonna rain hell down on the Jap's heads, not to mention a full airfield of bombers and fighters."

"Think it'll be enough to stop 'em?"

Carver flicked the butt of the cigarette he'd smoked down to a nub and blew out the white smoke. He shook his head, "Doubt it."

O'Connor pointed down the hill. "They're out there right now; every crevice filled with Japs. Why don't we just start bombing the crap out of 'em now? I mean at least take out their artillery."

"The brass doesn't want to spook 'em. Wants 'em to think we don't have a clue to what's coming."

"They've gotta know we stole their plans."

Private Gomez trudged up the hill with two loaded sandbags. "You guys need these? I can't stack anymore. I don't think a direct hit could knock my hole out." O'Connor nodded and directed him to place them on top of the many others. "When the Jap artillery starts coming, you're gonna think about those two bags you gave away."

He grinned, and Gomez slapped him on the arm. "Let 'em come, we'll blow the hell out of 'em." He turned and went back to his hole.

From up the hill, Lieutenant Swan sauntered to their hole. He inspected the layout and dropped in next to them. He checked their fields of fire and nodded in approval. "I want most of the platoon up at my bunker at 1500 hundred hours for a briefing, Sergeant."

THE PLATOON SAT AROUND outside the entrance to the command bunker. Radio wires were bundled and ran out the entrance then split off and traveled underground to different areas of the hill. A lot of sweat had gone into digging the trenches the wire ran through. They'd dug it three feet down, hoping it was enough to keep the vital communications open despite the Japanese artillery. Carver hoped it would work, but thought it would make repairs more difficult. If all else failed, there was always the good old fashioned runner.

Lieutenant Swan stepped out of the bunker with two aides and Sergeant Milo at his back. The men started to stand, but Swan shook his head, "Remain seated men." He stepped forward, and the aides spread out to either side. Sergeant Milo stayed behind him with his burly arms across his chest and a scowl on his face. "Thanks for coming." Private Gomez looked at Corporal O'Connor and rolled his eyes, as if they had a choice. "As you know, tomorrow at 0400, the Japs will commence their attack." He looked at them as if giving the news for the first time.

"They'll start with artillery, which means you have to be buttoned up tight. The brass has decided not to fire counter-battery, so it's gonna be hell up here."

The men looked at one another muttering. This *was* news. Lieutenant Swan put up his hands for quiet. "I know, I know, it sounds crazy, but they don't want to give up the game before the attack starts. Once enemy troops are confirmed in the open, they'll not only hit the artillery but the troops too. If all goes as planned, the Japs will die where they stand, but as we all know that's not likely to happen."

He started to pace. Carver thought he looked much older than the wide-eyed kid he'd first met back on Fiji. "We'll undoubtedly be in close contact. We've got good fields of fire, good artillery support and you're all experienced fighters. I have no doubt we'll break this attack." The men looked unconvinced.

"Make sure you have plenty of ammo and water. Once things kick off, there won't be a chance to resupply easily." He stopped pacing and clasped his hands behind his back. "As you all know this knob sticks out from our lines; we're exposed and susceptible to encirclement. The Japs will be hitting up and down the lines, so if it looks like we're about to be overrun, there may not be help readily available. If I think this is about to happen, I'll pop smoke. That'll be the signal to retreat off the backside of the hill and move to the north knob."

He pointed to the low hill behind him. Hill 260 was shaped like an hour glass, they held the south knob, but also had bunkers and defensive holes on the north knob. He looked around at the hard faces. "I've already talked with the tank crews. The smoke will signal them to move forward and cover a retreat. I'm not expecting to be overrun, but I don't expect you to fight to the death either. We'll fight our way back and retake this damned hill if we have to."

The men were silent. It wasn't the rallying speech they'd expected to hear. Sergeant Carver knew Lieutenant Swan didn't have permission to retreat, but he'd laid out a plan anyway. Carver nodded, *the boy's learned some lessons.*

34

While Lieutenant Swan was briefing his men, Colonel Araki was doing the same with his. There were three prongs to the attack, each aimed at different hills. The highest hill, Hill 700 would be the toughest battle. He suspected it would be the most heavily defended and would require more soldiers. None would be easy, however.

The Americans knew the battle plan and had been building up their forces for almost a month. He was sending his men into a meat grinder, and every one of them knew it. The only advantage they had were overwhelming numbers.

The jungle was teeming with troops. Most had made the hard trip over the mountain pass only a week before. They were used to the comforts of Buin, the village on the eastern tip of the island. Now they were deployed in a swamp, infested with countless insects and rats. They were hard troops, though, despite their previous assignment.

Every soldier on Bougainville regardless of their station had experienced the pang of hunger since the Americans cut off their supply chain. They'd been on half rations for months, and their skinny frames and gaunt faces were evidence of the fact.

The briefing was quick and straight to the point. Every officer knew his job, and Colonel Araki knew they'd perform their duties to the letter. At the end of his briefing, he looked over the crowd of officers and found the man he was looking for tucked in the back of the bunker. Second Lieutenant Taro was responsible for the Americans getting the plans and Araki had a special assignment for him. "Lieutenant Taro," He bellowed.

Lieutenant Taro jumped to his feet when he heard his name. Despite half rations, his face was still plump. Araki wondered how he maintained his body fat under such harsh conditions. "Yes sir," he stammered as he shifted from foot to foot.

"As you know, you're in the Muda unit attacking Hill 260. I am bestowing you the honor of leading the attack." He glanced at Lieutenant Colonel Muda who gave him a slight nod. For the other officers in the room, being told to lead the attack *would* be a distinct honor, but Colonel Araki knew his bumbling second lieutenant would see it not as an honor, but a death sentence. Colonel Araki saw the desired effect as all color drained from Lt. Taro's face, and he nearly collapsed. *I'll soon rid myself of this coward.*

THE NIGHT WAS SPENT MOVING into position. Second Lieutenant Taro felt as though he was in a dream world. He had no doubt he was living his final hours on Earth. He tried to take in the world around him, to enjoy the air, the teeming life, but he couldn't get over the nausea.

He moved with the troops without speaking. He was to lead the assault, but he wasn't in command. This was Lieutenant Otani's platoon. Second Lieutenant Taro was thrust into the unit with the sole purpose of dying. The soldiers around him ignored him. Lieutenant Otani barely acknowledged him. He was considered a coward, responsible for the Americans having their battle plans and many upcoming deaths.

They reached their jump off point at 0100 hours. The thick jungle canopy kept the starlight from the jungle floor. The darkness was complete. Taro sat on the ground, feeling himself sinking into the spongy ground. The scent of rotting foliage rose to his nostrils as he pulled out a carefully wrapped ball of rice. He'd kept it protected, knowing it would be his last meal. Back in Japan, such a portion would barely be considered an appetizer, but here, it was a bounty he intended to enjoy.

All too soon the rice ball was gone. He was near the front of the platoon, but no one sat near him. He wanted to talk, to hear a friendly voice, but he was on his own and hated.

He took a deep breath and hoped he'd be blown up, turned to mist in an instant with no pain. He visualized an American artillery shell landing directly on him, turning him to nothing. One second he'd be advancing, the next he'd be laughing with his ancestors; the transition instant and painless. He smiled to himself. The image gave him comfort.

AT 0400 ON the morning of March 8th Second Lieutenant Taro jolted as he heard the opening salvos of multiple artillery pieces firing at once. The canopy above his head flashed like a great lightning storm was in progress. The thundering booms rolled across him even miles away.

He looked to the west, towards Hill 260. He was still 700 meters from the base of the small hill. Far enough away to protect them from any short shells, but close enough to move up quickly once the attack order was given.

The artillery was firing up and down the line and would last two hours. Taro looked at his watch and strained to see the dials. They'd be attacking at 0700. He had three hours to live.

He pushed himself off the wet ground with a sucking sound. He stretched and put his rifle over his shoulder. He took a step into the jungle to his right, but before he could a hand gripped his shoulder. "Where are you going?" It was Sergeant Inaba.

Lieutenant Taro hadn't noticed him, but he must have been there the whole time. He shook his hand off his shoulder. He was still an officer, "Mind your tone, Sergeant." Sergeant Inaba allowed his hand to be shrugged, but stared unapologetically. Lieutenant Taro flushed with anger, realizing the sergeant was there to keep him from running away from his duty. *The colonel thinks I'm a coward.* Mustering as much contempt as he could, he said, "I'm going to take a shit. Care to hold my hand, Sergeant?" Inaba didn't reply, and Taro ambled into the jungle to take his final runny shit.

THE OUTGOING ARTILLERY was constant and intense. Taro crouched beside a tree with his long Arisaka rifle pointed towards Hill 260. The flashes from the impacts lit up his face and the surrounding jungle despite the heavy canopy. All around him soldiers with hard faces were staring towards the hill. He didn't recognize any of the men. He knew every one of them despised him, but his duty was clear. The simplicity was comforting. He wasn't in command of any soldiers; he was there to die.

The artillery barrage ended as suddenly as it started. The jungle was silent for a full minute, but the sounds of life gradually returned to fill the void. The sky was light, dawn had broken sometime during the barrage, without him noticing.

The soldiers around him stood, and Lieutenant Taro got to his feet. He was near the front, where he'd been told to be. Under the jungle canopy, there was still a layer of darkness. There was enough light to see the facial features of the men around him. They were wide-eyed, ready for the coming battle, ready to die for the glory of Japan and the Emperor.

Taro closed his eyes and took a deep breath. He didn't have anyone special back home, but he had been to a whore house in Nanking that was a particularly good experience. He tried to picture the Chinese woman he'd laid with. She'd been ravenous, a good actress.

He was pulled from his fantasy by the harsh voice of command ordering them forward. He opened his eyes and took the first step towards the American line.

They'd walked half the distance when there was a great whooshing in the sky, followed by an explosion behind him. Suddenly the sky was filled with metal as the Americans fired their hidden Howitzers. Taro cringed and wished he had a helmet rather than a soft cap on his head. The shells weren't aimed at him, though. They were sailing over their heads and slamming into the rear. He assumed the Americans were finally firing at their artillery emplacements.

The pace picked up. They'd started out cautiously, but the enemy artillery quickened their gait. Soon they were trotting. The dense jungle opened up as if the underbrush was trimmed back. Taro was in line with dozens of soldiers. As they entered the more open space, he looked to his left. An explosion erupted and ripped a soldier apart. He stared, not understanding what had just happened. Then another soldier went flying as the ground beneath him exploded. He heard someone yell, "Mines!"

The realization hit him, and he nearly lost his bowels. They'd walked into a minefield. He stopped and looked at the ground to his front. He was pushed from behind and nearly fell forward. He heard Sergeant Inaba curse him.

The jungle canopy he'd emerged from flashed and exploded. The American artillery was directed at them now. The blasts shattered the trees sending deadly shards of metal and wood splinters onto their heads. Men fell by the dozens.

A yell went up, and the soldiers surged forward. Sergeant Inaba pushed him harder, and he ran forward, thinking every step would be his last. Explosions erupted all around him as men stepped on mines.

The whistling of mortar shells added to the artillery and there were geysers of dark dirt spouting up on every side of him. Men were dying all around him, but he gritted his teeth and kept moving forward. His legs moved as if they weren't his own. His mind screamed for his survival, to stop and find cover, but his body moved him into the fray relentlessly.

He kept his sights on the next step. He'd given up looking for mines. If he tripped one, he wouldn't be alive long enough to notice. He was getting close to the first incline of Hill 260. The dirt and debris falling from the sky obscured his vision, but he could see he was nearing the base of the hill.

A shriek then a loud thump flattened him onto the ground. One second he was up, the next he was face down staring at the stinking jungle floor. His head pounded and every part of his body screamed in pain. *This is it. This is my death.*

He waited for the dark shroud of death to come, but instead more pain. He lifted his head and watched men streaming past him. There was no more sound. *My ears are shattered.* The soldiers seemed to falter against something a few meters ahead, like the ocean meeting a solid wall of rock.

Artillery continued to pound into the jungle behind him and the clearing. He panicked for an instant when he realized he didn't have his rifle. He looked side to side, but it was gone. He looked behind and saw the smoking crater that must have flattened him. There was a mound of bloody flesh there too. Sergeant Inaba stared at him. He was moving, pulling something from his side. Both his legs and left arm were missing, but he still lived. Taro watched in horror as he saw the pistol emerge in Inaba's hand. He centered the barrel on Taro. Taro accepted what was happening. The sergeant's orders were to make sure Lieutenant Taro died, and he was completing those orders.

With his last ounce of energy, Sergeant Inaba leveled the gun and pulled the trigger. The hammer came down and ignited the bullet's primer, but the pistol barrel had been mangled in the attack, and instead of the bullet traveling out smoothly, it exploded in place and shredded the pistol. Three of Sergeant Inaba's fingers were sliced and dangled at odd angles. Inaba's blazing, bloodshot eyes drilled into Lieutenant Taro for an instant, then the life force within him left, and he slumped to the smoking jungle floor.

The world around Taro was still silent. Soldiers continued to stream past him. Artillery and mortar shells still erupted and shredded them at random. He pushed himself to his feet and took a step forward. The soldiers to his front were stacking up on an obstacle he couldn't understand. He watched as soldiers struggled then lurched and erupted with holes. He realized they were being shot down. They were within range of the American front lines.

He staggered forward without a weapon, and lined up behind the growing queue of soldiers. He saw an intricate web of barbed wire, mangled by the artillery barrage. There were shredded soldiers hanging from the wire. It reminded Taro of a spider's web full of house-flies. Men struggled to pass through, but the Americans had interlacing arcs of machine gun fire that cut them down by the dozens.

Lieutenant Taro slumped against a tree facing back the way he'd come. His hearing was coming back as a loud ringing. The sound of battle was more felt than heard. The clearing was still full of soldiers running across. The artillery continued to drop amongst them, but they ran into the fire anyway. Lieutenant Taro's chest filled with pride. These men were fearless.

He remembered his pistol and pulled it from the holster and stood. He moved in behind the line of men firing into the American lines. They were held up by the barbed wire, they had to push their way through or they'd die where they stood.

He looked for an officer, but only saw enlisted men. He gritted his teeth and tried to bellow an order, but his throat was dry as sand and nothing came out. He swallowed and tried again. "Knee mortars, knee mortars." The men around him looked at him. All they saw was an officer taking command. "I want ten men with knee mortars here." Soldiers pulled off their packs and pulled out their 37mm knee mortars. They moved to where he'd pointed and laid on their stomachs. "Target the machine guns," he said, pointing at the winking flashes. "Put the grenades in front, ruin their vision." The men quickly dialed in the range and loaded and cocked. He directed the other men, "Grab a body and use it to span the wire." The soldiers looked at him in surprise. "Do it. It's the only way to get over the wire."

Soldiers slung their rifles and grabbed dead comrades. They were littered all around and easy to find. Taro watched as the men struggled to lift them, but their dead weight was too much. "Two men per body," he yelled.

When they were ready, he yelled, "Covering fire, Go!" Every soldier not carrying a body rose up and fired their rifles at the machine gunners. Soldiers died as they were cut down, but most kept up the fire. The knee mortars thumped and arced grenades up the hill that exploded all around the well entrenched machine gun pits. "Go, go, go!" he yelled.

The men with the bodies ran forward and hurled their loads over the wire, then stepped onto their backs and advanced to the next layer.

"Next wave," he yelled, and another group of body-carrying men moved forward. The first wave fired up the hill covering the next wave, and the knee mortars continued to land grenades around the machine gunners. The machine guns never stopped firing, but they were firing blindly. Soldiers died by the dozens, but they were making progress.

The men had the flow, and they moved across layer after layer of wire. The Americans had placed mines between them and Lieutenant Taro watched as a duo of soldiers holding a dead comrade in front, erupted in a red mass of tangled limbs and body parts.

The scene enraged him, and he stepped forward and fired his 9mm pistol up the hill. He screamed and ran forward. He felt like a man possessed. He was watching his movements from above as though detached. The soldiers around him picked up the yell and followed their officer over the backs of mangled comrades. The knee mortars continued to cover them, and soon they were at the final layer of barbed wire. The machine guns buzzed, hacking men down all around him.

There was a large bomb crater on the other side of the final barrier. He ran forward with every intention of throwing himself over the wire. He'd be the bridge for his men, but before he could hurl himself, another soldier stepped in front and threw himself down. Bullets shredded his body as he landed. Lieutenant Taro didn't hesitate and stepped on the man's back and leaped across the remaining wire and front somersaulted into the bomb crater.

His men followed and streamed to either side, seeking cover. The machine gun fire cut more down, but now they were in a better position to engage the machine guns from cover.

Lieutenant Taro rose and emptied his clip. He could see more foxholes and bunkers and realized they had a long way to go and a lot of defenses to break through before they took the hill.

He sat and reloaded his pistol. A soldier slammed into the crater beside him. His face was blackened with dirt and gunpowder, and he'd lost his helmet somewhere. His eyes were wild as he looked side to side like a cornered animal. Lieutenant Taro spoke, "Pull yourself together. We must continue the attack."

The soldier looked at him and focused on his face. "Taro?" He squinted at him. "Lieutenant Taro? You led the men through the wire?"

Lieutenant Taro looked him up and down. He realized with a shock, it was First Lieutenant Otani. He didn't salute but nodded, "Yes, it was me." He purposely didn't end with the obligatory 'sir.'

Lieutenant Otani didn't seem to notice, but took a deep breath and got control of himself. He didn't have a weapon, and his clothes were shredded and burnt. "What's the situation?"

Second Lieutenant Taro reached across to a discarded rifle and handed it to the officer. He explained the situation, pointing out defensive strong points. Lieutenant Otani nodded and slapped his shoulder. "Excellent work Lieutenant. I'll be sure to relay your actions to Colonel Araki."

Taro nodded and grinned through his fat cheeks. *Does he think we'll live through the day?*

35

The artillery barrage was heavy and seemed to cover every inch of Hill 260. Sergeant Carver hunkered in his hole with Corporal O'Connor and three other soldiers. He held onto his helmet as dirt and dust filtered down over him. He watched the debris collect on his shirtsleeves then bounce off with a near miss. With eyes closed, he concentrated on his breathing. The barrage seemed to move across the hill in waves, starting low and sweeping to the top and over the other side, then back down.

His hole was halfway down the hill and connected to five other holes through a network of slit trenches. He was in the third line of foxholes from the bottom. He was flanked on either side with .30 caliber machine guns. Behind him, there was a bunker full of ammunition and a radio. Trenches snaked away from it leading to fighting positions. Behind that, there was a well dug-in trench with four, 61mm mortars, surrounded by more troops and more machine guns. Beyond that was the top of the hill where the command bunker was barely discernible behind mounds of sandbags.

Carver knew the layout of the defenses like he knew his mother. He wondered what it would look like when the barrage finished.

He thought his hole had enough cover above to sustain a direct hit, but he hoped he wouldn't have to test the theory. Their defenses were strong, made to withstand the thrashing they were receiving, but he couldn't help thinking what it would be like if one of those big 105mm shells landed directly on top of him.

Some of the men hunkered nearby moaned and even screamed, but Carver continued to breathe and silently pray. He hadn't even realized he was doing it. He hadn't actively prayed in years, but he found himself comforted by the calming phrases he'd learned as a kid in church.

After an eternity the shelling stopped. He held his helmet and kept his eyes closed until he was sure it was over. He shook himself, dirt and dust cascaded off his helmet and body. He pulled the wooden block that opened the viewport and looked down the hill. The ground was torn and shredded. The few trees left on the hill before the barrage were gone. There were smoking craters everywhere. He listened for moans or screams from wounded, but his ears were ringing too badly.

"Shelling's stopped. Move to your firing ports. The Japs'll be coming soon." The men shook their dazed heads and pulled the blocks from the firing ports and pointed their M1's down the hill. The shelling had started when it was still dark, but it was light now with clear skies. The jungle seemed to shimmer in the morning light.

It wasn't long before outgoing friendly artillery arced over his head and slammed into unseen targets to the Japanese rear. They were finally getting around to silencing the Japanese artillery.

There was a slight breeze coming from the west, blowing the smoke away in wisps. Carver put binoculars to his eyes. Through a gap in the smoke, he glimpsed movement in a small clearing a couple of hundred yards from the first line of trenches. There was an explosion, then another.

"The Japs are in the minefield." He pulled the handheld radio from the ground and was about to call it in when he heard the roar of more artillery flying overhead. He watched as shells slammed into a horde of Japanese soldiers emerging from the jungle. They flew away as if made of grass. "Artillery's giving them a good thrashing."

The air filled with outgoing artillery. The Japanese soldiers continued to stream out of the jungle into the scything shrapnel. He watched in morbid fascination as dozens of men died, but they kept coming. "Jesus, Joseph, and Mary, they're still coming."

Minutes later the forward-most line of bunkers and trenches opened up. The .30 caliber machine guns chattered along with M1s and Thompson submachine guns. He couldn't see what they were firing at, there was a small depression blocking his view, but at least some Japanese must've made it through the artillery storm. "They're at the base of the hill. Hear that? Our guys are firing on them."

The second line of defenses started firing. Corporal O'Connor put his cheek to the stock of his M1 and scanned for a target. It would be a long shot, but it was downhill, and he was a skilled marksman. He glimpsed a greenish blob crawling forward. He put the muzzle just below the soldiers head and fired. The rifle shot within the confines of the covered trench made everyone jump.

Carver shifted his binoculars and saw the soldier O'Connor had targeted continuing to move forward. "You missed, try again." O'Connor adjusted his sights a fraction, blew out a breath and squeezed the trigger. Carver watched the soldier jerk as a spout of blood erupted from his holed helmet. "Bullseye. You've got another target further down the hill about ten yards. He's to the right of the last guy. See him?"

"Got it."

He fired and Carver watched the bullet slam into the dirt. "Adjust right a fraction and take him out." O'Connor fired and Carver saw the soldier's back erupt. The soldier arched and pushed himself down the hill and out of sight. "You got him."

The other men in the trench were eager to join in and began firing. Carver yelled at them. "Make sure you're not hitting our guys. You're firing over their heads, be sure of your shots."

He watched the Japanese soldiers struggling to get up the hill, but they entangled in the intricate layers of barbed wire he'd helped string. They were sitting ducks and died tangled and bleeding.

The Jap artillery had done a number on the wire. The long rows were mixed in a jumbled mess that made it even more formidable than before. Beyond them, troops continued to die in hails of shrapnel, but now they had more cover, the bomb craters themselves. More and more soldiers were making it to the wire.

He grabbed the private firing through the port to his right. He looked at him annoyed at being interrupted. Carver barked, "Go back to the mortar pits and tell them to hit the base of the hill just beyond the barbed wire barrier, then hurry back."

The private, the name above his chest said, 'Bauer,' took off in a low crouch with his M1 pointing the way.

The firing from his line was sporadic. He doubted anyone besides O'Connor was hitting anything but dirt. He scanned the barbed wire and saw an officer pointing and yelling orders. He tapped O'Connor, "there's an officer down there. Fifteen yards back from your first kill. See him waving his arms around?"

O'Connor squinted. "I see movement, but there's a tree or something in the way."

Carver moved back, "come to this port." O'Connor moved and settled in. "See him?"

O'Connor said, "yep." He blew out a breath and was putting pressure on the trigger when there was a sudden geyser of dirt blocking his view. He fired anyway. "Shit, the view's blocked. Doubt I got him."

Carver pushed him out of the way, and O'Connor went back to his shooting port. Carver peered through the slit, but he could no longer see the barbed wire section. It was obscured by explosions blowing dirt up in front of the machine gun pits. He watched the machine gun barrels continue to fire, but they'd slowed down, not able to distinguish easy targets. "Japs are getting smart, blocking the gunner's view."

O'Connor had stopped shooting. "Can't see shit down there."

"Hope Bauer got the word to the mortar pits." Carver got brief glimpses through the dirt geysers and relayed what he saw happening. "They've breached some of the wire. They're using their dead to bridge over. They're getting close to the first line, dammit, where's the mortars?"

As if in answer he heard the distinctive whistle of mortar shells arcing over their heads. He watched through the dust and debris as the big shells impacted beyond the wire. He could see men dying, hurtling through the air, missing pieces of their bodies. "That's put a crimp in their giddy-up, but they have a path through the wire. Hope our guys can hold." He put the binoculars on the dirt notch beside his knee and picked up his Thompson.

O'Connor took his eye from his sights and said, "Where you going?"

"I can't hit shit from here. I'm moving up to the second line, lend 'em a hand." The men in the trench looked at him with wide eyes. They were replacements from the Headquarters company. They'd seen combat, but nothing like this. They looked like scared first graders. "You men stay here and hold this line. Do whatever Corporal O'Connor tells you to do."

O'Connor shook his head. "I'm going with you, Sarge."

Sergeant Carver wanted Corporal O'Connor beside him. He was the most competent fighter he'd ever known, but he was needed here. "No, stay here and keep them alive." When O'Connor showed no signs of backing down, Carver said, "That's an order." He slapped his shoulder as he went past. "I'll be back before you know it."

SERGEANT CARVER MADE his way along the trench works but was stopped by a section that had taken a direct artillery hit. Beyond it, he could see a group of soldiers firing out the tops of their hole. The near miss had torn the sandbagged roof off.

Carver looked down the hill. The mortars were wreaking havoc, and the artillery was still flashing in the jungle. He saw a flash to his right and noticed gull-winged corsairs circling the area looking for targets of opportunity. He watched as two of them pitched over and sliced towards the distant jungle. Rockets erupted from their wings and lanced into the jungle with explosive force. He thought they must be targeting Japanese artillery. They turned away at the last second, low against the jungle canopy. If they'd turned towards the battle, they'd risk flying into friendly artillery. They were cutting it close as it was.

He tore his eyes from the scene and leaped over the churned up ground. The two seconds of exposure were terrifying, but he didn't draw any enemy fire. He dove into the bottom of the fighting hole, and one of the soldiers jumped and started to bring his rifle around, but stopped when he recognized Carver. "Jesus, Sarge you almost got your head blown off."

Carver pushed himself to a crouch and adjusted his helmet while resting his Thompson on his knee. "Not gonna die by your hand, Gomez."

Private Gomez grinned and crouched beside him. The soldier next to him looked over his shoulder at the new arrival. Gomez punched him in the ass. "Keep firing, hermano."

The soldier sneered, "Speak English, Gomez." He sighted down his M1 and fired.

Gomez ignored him. "What brings you to these parts, Sarge?"

"I'm making my way to the front trenches, looks like the Japs are getting close to our lines."

Gomez nodded. "They are. Got through the barbed wire, but we've stopped 'em there. Crazy bastards are using their own dead for cover. The mortars are doing a good job on 'em though."

The soldier beside him pitched backward and slumped in the back of the pit. Carver put his Thompson against the bank and moved to his side. The man's helmet was pushed over his face. Carver pushed it back, "You Okay…?" his voice caught in his throat as he saw the soldiers pulped face.

Gomez gritted his teeth. "Sons-of-bitches." He sprang into his firing position and pulled the trigger until the clip pinged.

Carver found a slot and brought his Thompson to his shoulder and took in the scene. The next line of trenches and bunkers were twenty yards in front. He could see the barrels of the .30 caliber machine guns spitting fire down the hill in short controlled bursts. He could make out Japanese soldiers still coming out of the jungle and working their way forward using the bomb craters for cover. He saw movement beyond the bunkers and fired a three round burst of .45 caliber. He had no idea if he hit anything, but he felt better finally entering the fight.

A group of ten Japanese soldiers stood and fired at the machine gun bunker on the right. The gunner moved his barrel to cut them down and as he did soldiers jumped up from the other direction and rushed forward screaming with their bayonets leading. The other machine gun was dealing with his own targets and didn't notice the attack. Carver slapped Gomez on the shoulder and pointed. He lined up his sights and squeezed off a short burst, fighting to keep the barrel from rising. His bullets sliced into two attackers and they went down with blossoming chest wounds.

More were cut down, but there were too many, and they got close enough to the machine gunners to keep Carver and Gomez from firing. "Shit, they're overrunning the bunker."

Gomez yelled and sprang from the trench and took off down the hill with a war whoop. The men beside him looked after him then at Carver. Carver jumped out yelling, "Let's go!" he had his Thompson at waist level as he ran to catch up with the crazed Private Gomez.

Gomez ran the twenty yards in record time, leaping over bomb craters and twisted logs. A Japanese soldier was thrusting his rifle into the open firing port of the machine gun nest. He looked up in time to see Gomez bearing down on him with death in his eyes. The Japanese tried to extract his bayonet from the GI's chest but was too late. Gomez shot him twice sending him backward into another soldier. He stood on the sandbagged roof and shot his M1 until his clip pinged.

A pile of enemy soldiers was at his feet, but there were too many. He reached to reload knowing he'd die in seconds, but Sergeant Carver came in a crouch and hosed the attackers down with a sustained burst. The four men with him crouched and joined the slaughter.

When there were no more targets, Sergeant Carver grabbed Private Gomez by the shoulder. "Don't ever do that shit again, soldier." Gomez looked at him blankly. Carver pushed him down as bullets started smacking around them. The soldier to Carver's right grunted and grabbed his throat. Blood squirted out from between his fingers as he tried to stop the flow. Carver pulled the wounded man down and shoved him into the trench beside the machine gun nest. He pulled Gomez next and the rest of the men dove for cover.

Gomez came crawling over with blood streaming down his face. "Is he alright? Is he okay?"

Carver put his hands over the wounded man's neck and felt the hot pulsing of arterial blood. Soon the flow slowed and finally stopped, and the man's eyes went blank. Carver pushed Gomez towards the unmanned machine gun nest. "He's gone. Get on the thirty caliber or they'll overrun this position." Gomez hesitated, wanting to help the soldier. Carver spit, "Now!"

Gomez pushed his way into the machine gun nest. He shoved the two dead soldiers out the other way and called, "Gus, be my loader."

Gus stopped firing his M1 and scooted into the covered machine gun nest. He checked the belted ammunition and tapped Gomez on the helmet. "It's good, fire."

Gomez sighted down the smoking barrel but couldn't see anything. There were too many Jap bodies blocking his view. He yelled, "Clear the port. I can't see anything."

Carver peaked over the edge and saw the problem. "Cover me." He jumped out of the hole with his Thompson at hip level and fired down the hill. He dove the ten feet to the base of the firing port and pulled a Jap body down the hill. The soldier rolled, spilling entrails from his belly. Bullets whipped and snapped as he fast crawled back to the trench. He yelled, "Fire."

Gomez didn't waste any time. He saw looming shapes sprinting towards him. He depressed the trigger and felt the .30 caliber bounce and rock on the tripod. He swept the barrel back and forth across a wide swath. He couldn't see anything but his own piece of ground. He hoped the rest of the platoon was holding their end of the line.

The Japanese attack faltered, and soon there were no more targets. He stopped firing and looked past the red hot barrel. The bodies were stacked three deep. The sight made him sick, but he swallowed the bile rising in his throat.

Gus Hansen, his loader leaned over and looked out the gunport. "Holy shit. You knocked the crap out of 'em." He pointed at the glowing barrel. "I think you fried the barrel though. Is there another?"

Gomez looked around the smoke filled space. He saw a gunny sack on the floor. It was splattered with blood from the previous gunners. Dust and dirt clung, making the blood look like jelly. He lifted the bag. It was heavy and awkward. "Here it is. Let's swap it out before they come again." He pulled the barrel into the bunker. "The damned thing's still too hot."

The sound of their artillery and mortars had ceased and the battlefield took on an eery silence. It didn't last. The sound of arcing incoming mortar shells made them duck. Sergeant Carver yelled, "Incoming! Take cover!"

THE MORTARS CONCENTRATED on the lower section of the line, sweeping back and forth. Carver pushed his way into the cover of the machine gun nest. The trenches to either side weren't covered, and the mortars were threatening direct hits.

Carver watched Private Gomez and Hansen struggling with the .30 caliber barrel. Gomez held the main gun while Hansen gripped the barrel, using the gunny sack as a hot pad. They grunted and twisted trying to remove the melted barrel. It didn't budge. Through labored breathing, Gomez gasped, "it's fused. It's not working."

The final mortar rounds landed spewing white smoke instead of shrapnel. Carver said, "smoke, they're shooting smoke. Get that gun going." He moved back to the open trench and sighted down his Thompson. The soldiers to his right dusted off and peered over the edge. The smoke was thick, wafting along the ground like fog. "Can't see shit." He looked into the darkness of the machine gun nest. Gomez and Hansen were still struggling. "Forget the thirty-cal, grab your weapons, they're coming."

Up and down the line there was sporadic firing, but Carver couldn't see what they were targeting. He strained to see through the smoke. All at once shapes appeared like dim silhouettes. A roar went up from the charging Japanese that made his skin crawl.

There were suddenly too many targets to count. He fired short bursts, and they dropped but were replaced by three more. He heard the .30 caliber further down the line chattering. Without both firing, he doubted they could hold.

The Japanese were bursting through the smoke fifteen yards from the line. 61mm mortar shells burst amongst them leaving gaps which quickly filled in with more troops.

He shot through the rest of his magazine and pulled another from his ammo pouch, and slammed it into place. The Japanese were close. They had to disengage or die in place. He made the decision, "Fall back, fall back!" Two soldiers to his right stood and leaped over the trench. They took two steps and were cut down. Carver yelled, "Use the trenches for cover. Go, go!" he stood and swept his Thompson across the line of charging soldiers. The heavy slugs threw them back, but it wasn't enough. A screaming Japanese soldier leaped into the trench, his bayonet leading. Carver spun and depressed the trigger sending bullets into his chest. Another soldier dove at him. He didn't have time to shoot, so he used his Thompson to parry the rifle and bayonet. The diving soldier sprawled on the bottom of the trench and Carver slammed the butt of his weapon into his face with a sickening crunch.

Up and down the line he saw soldiers struggling to get out of the trench. He grabbed Gomez by the shoulder and pushed him towards the exit. Hansen followed, and Carver followed him. They ran, staying low. Japanese soldiers screamed and fired all around them, cutting men down. A bullet slammed into the wall beside him. He spun and saw a screaming Japanese soldier running towards him. He fired his Thompson from the hip and stitched him from his kneecap to forehead. The soldier snapped backward, dead before he hit the ground.

Another soldier was behind him. He leaped over his fallen comrade and Carver depressed the trigger, but nothing happened. He didn't have time to reload. He sprang to the side avoiding the lunging bayonet and, holding onto the hot barrel, swung his Thompson like a baseball bat. The wooden stock slammed into the back of the soldier's head and he fell. Carver stomped on his head, and ran to catch up.

He fumbled in his ammo pouch for another magazine but brushed across a grenade he had hanging from his belt. He pulled it free while running. He could feel more enemy soldiers coming up the trench. He was approaching a turn. He went around the corner and tossed the grenade back the way he'd come.

He took off, running as fast as his legs would carry him. Five seconds later the grenade exploded, and he heard screams above the shooting and yelling. He turned and aimed down the trench, but no one rounded the corner.

Bullets smacked beside his head, and he ducked down and continued running. The trench made another turn, and as he came to it, he yelled out, "Friendly coming." His feet went out from beneath him as he rounded the corner and looked into the maw of an M1 barrel. The soldier's grin disappeared as his eyes focused on something behind Carver. He watched the barrel rise and the soldier fired three times in quick succession, but then was thrown back as a bullet explode his chest. Private Hansen looked down at the wound in surprise. His eyes rolled to the back of his head, and he went down.

Carver rolled onto his back and held his Thompson, ready to shoot, but there was no one there. He remembered he hadn't reloaded. He cussed under his breath and swapped the empty magazine for the full. He pulled back the charging mechanism, checked the safety, and went into a crouch. He put the Thompson to his shoulder and was about to stand when he felt, rather than heard .30 caliber bullets flying close over his head.

He got back on his belly and crawled along the trench until he was out of harm's way. Then he stood and ran in a low crouch the rest of the way to the second line of bunkers and trenches. He threw himself into the covered trench and sat against the wall gasping for air. No one noticed, they were too busy firing down the hill.

He closed his eyes, shaking his head. *Keep your shit together soldier.* He remembered hearing those words a thousand times from his drill sergeant back in basic a million years ago.

A hand touched his shoulder, and he opened his eyes. Private Gomez was there looking at him from beneath his dark eyebrows. "You okay, Sarge?" Carver nodded. "I'm gonna find Hansen."

Carver reached out to stop him. "Don't bother. He's gone. Saved my ass, but he took one in the chest."

Gomez ground his teeth for a moment then gave a quick nod and went back to his firing position. Carver stood and peered through a firing slot. The Japanese were still coming, but they were taking heavy losses.

The Artillery opened up and fell on the base of the hill and around the first line of bunkers and trenches, now occupied by the Japanese. Enemy soldiers were flung into the air and ground into the dirt.

Enemy mortar rounds landed around the bunkers. Carver was relatively safe with a thick layer of sandbags over his head, but he didn't feel safe. Gomez punched his shoulder and pointed.

Carver looked and saw a thin, grungy soldier coming his way. "I told you to stay put, Corporal."

Corporal O'Connor spat a thin line between his teeth and kneeled beside Carver. "I got bored. If you wanna put me on K.P. duty back at H.Q. it won't bother me a bit."

Smoke rounds exploded in front, and soon a thick layer of white smoke hung in the air. Private Gomez cursed in Spanish and sighted over his barrel. "Last time they did this, they overran us."

The soldiers stopped firing as they could no longer pick out targets. The .30 calibers stopped their incessant chattering. The only sound was the constant pounding of artillery and 61mm mortars. The enemy mortar barrage had stopped.

36

Second Lieutenant Taro leaned against the back of the American trench breathing hard. His men had pushed the Americans out of their positions, but they'd lost a lot of good soldiers and had only conquered the first line of many. A soldier he didn't recognize kneeled beside him. "Sir, Lieutenant Otani says to hold your position, and prepare to repel a counterattack. He's bringing up reinforcements." American Artillery shells still exploded around them but most of it was hitting the jungle beyond.

Taro nodded his understanding, and the soldier shuffled back the way he'd come, stepping over American and Japanese bodies.

Taro watched him go. All he wanted to do was rest, but there was no time. If the Americans threw them out of their positions, all the brave men who'd been ripped to shreds would be for nothing. He couldn't allow that to happen. He owed them. He spotted a sergeant a few soldiers down the line. He didn't know anyone's name. He croaked through a parched mouth, "Sergeant." He didn't respond, "Sergeant," louder this time. The soldier beside him nudged the soldier beside him and passed the message along.

The sergeant ran hunched over and kneeled at Taro's side. He snapped off a quick salute, "What are your orders, sir?"

Lieutenant Taro was gratified to see he'd gained the men's respect. "We need to prepare for a counterattack. I want the machine gun crews set up on either flank, with at least a squad of soldiers around them. The rest of the Nambus interspersed along the line."

He stood and peeked his head over the trench. The smoke still clung, obscuring his view of the second American line. He knew it was only fifty meters away.

The ground was strewn with bomb craters and dead and dying Japanese soldiers. He kneeled down and addressed the sergeant. "Move men into the trench system that connects with the next line. I don't want a surprise attack coming through there." The sergeant nodded and was about to leave, but Taro continued, "Make sure the men drink water and resupply ammo. We're holding here until Lieutenant Otani brings reinforcements." The sergeant nodded and Lt. Taro watched him go, wondering if he forgot anything.

THE COUNTERATTACK NEVER CAME. Lt. Taro thought the Americans must be licking their wounds too. The situation reminded him of an equally matched dog fight.

The artillery continued but seemed to be harassment fire. Taro could still hear fighting coming from the other two assaults to the west.

He was glad for the respite. He used it to drink water, replenish ammo and check the line. Despite the horrific losses, the men were upbeat.

Colonel Araki had put him in this frontline unit to be rid of him. He understood that, but by luck, he'd survived and now was part of this highly decorated unit. For the first time in his military career, he felt a kinship with his fellow soldiers. Each soldier he passed nodded, recognizing his rank and the fact that he'd survived the last few hours, just like they had. He was one of them, and his chest swelled with pride.

An hour passed with only the occasional shot, as snipers began to square off. Lieutenant Taro sat in an abandoned bunker with a small group of enlisted men and enjoyed nibbling off the dried fish they were passing around. He was surprised to find he wasn't as hungry as usual. He wondered why.

The same runner from earlier burst into the group and threw a salute to Lt. Taro. He saluted back, "Report."

The Corporal handed him a note. Lt. Taro read through it and smiled. The men watched him, trying to glean any information. He held up the note and shook it. "Good news, good news indeed." He sent a private out to find his sergeants. Soon they were gathered around him. "We are getting reinforcements. They will be here within the hour, three more companies and…" he paused for effect, "Tanks." The men smiled and nodded. They wouldn't have to charge into machine gun nests. This time they could follow the tanks up the hill.

Mortar fire signaled the arrival of the reinforcements. Smoke covered their advance from the jungle. Men ran and Lt. Taro watched for the promised tanks but was distracted when he saw a streaking fighter diving towards the clearing. He pointed, and his men shifted their positions. The fighter was too far away, but it was getting closer and would be in range if it stayed on course.

The soldiers in the clearing picked up their pace trying to reach the cover of the trenches. The fighter's machine guns opened fire and sounded like a ripsaw. Great geysers of dirt tore up the ground obscuring the reinforcements in dust and debris. The fighter pulled up, but continued on course.

Taro had his rifle at his shoulder aiming at the ever-growing silhouette of the gull-winged Corsair. He fired when he thought it was about to hit him. Rifle fire rippled along the line. Taro pulled the bolt action to reload. For an instant, he could see the pilot. He wore goggles and cloth headgear. Taro thought he saw bullet holes emerge along the cockpit. The sound of the engine changed and the fighter pulled almost straight up. It was out of range before he could chamber another round.

The soldiers around him cheered and talked excitedly like children, each sure they'd hit the streaking American. Taro watched the blue devil disappear over the hill. His smile faded when he saw the devastation the strafing run had caused.

Soldiers still ran across the clearing, but there were new bodies strewn amongst the bomb craters. He still didn't seen any tanks.

Lieutenant Otani came panting down the trench and sat beside Lt. Taro. Taro snapped off a salute and Otani returned it. Otani caught his breath and said, "Report."

"The Americans haven't moved since we chased them out of here. Some sniper fire, but no casualties. The artillery hasn't stopped, but it's been sporadic, sir."

Otani nodded. "Excellent," he studied his watch. "We attack in thirty minutes, inform the men."

Lieutenant Taro looked at the clearing. There was a trickle of soldiers still coming, but most had made it to the shelter of the trenches. "Sir, you mentioned tank support."

Lieutenant Otani squinted, "Yes, they are coming, but they're too valuable to spearhead the attack. Our men will lead, and once the Americans are on their heels, the tanks will rout them." He pointed to the clearing. "They sit just inside the jungle line, out of sight. When we attack, the Americans won't notice them until it's too late."

Lieutenant Taro was disappointed they wouldn't have the tanks for cover, but he understood the decision. They were cut off from resupply. What they had on Bougainville Island was all they were going to get. Their losses couldn't be replaced.

First Lieutenant Otani continued. "You've done well so far, Lieutenant. You were supposed to die but instead have served honorably. I want you to lead the assault, not because I expect you to die, but because you're the best man for the job. The men will follow you."

Lieutenant Taro gave him a curt nod of gratitude. "Thank you, sir. I won't let you down."

DURING THE THIRTY MINUTES, the American lines were hit with mortar fire. Lieutenant Otani told him their heavy artillery pieces had taken a beating from counter-battery fire. The remaining pieces were pulled back and were only used for the more important assaults on Cannon Hill and Hill 700.

With five minutes before the attack, the mortars blanketed the area with more smoke. Lieutenant Taro was in charge of the same platoon he'd attacked with before. They'd been reinforced with men from the other companies. It was easy to distinguish the replacements. They were wide-eyed and shell-shocked from their dash across the clearing. They gawked at the devastation around them.

First Lieutenant Otani was further down the line, leading one of the fresh companies. Taro wondered if he still thought he'd survive the day.

He watched the time wind down on his watch. With ten seconds left he took a deep breath and readied himself. He heard a whistle, the signal to advance. The men he'd sent into the connector trenches stood and started peppering the American line with covering fire. They couldn't see the Americans through the smoke, but they had a good idea where to shoot.

Lieutenant Taro jumped out of the trench. He had his rifle slung across his back. His pistol was out, and he waved the men forward, but they were already advancing, picking up speed. He was relieved to see the smoke still blocking the Americans. If they could get close enough, they'd overrun them quickly.

Every step was uphill, and the shredded underbrush, mud, and rocks made each step difficult. Taro tried to keep pace with his men, but he wasn't in good shape, and he slowed to a labored walk. He wondered what happened to the flow of adrenalin he'd experienced before. He needed it now, but all he felt was a searing pain in his chest as he struggled to get enough air to his screaming muscles.

The Americans woke up all at once and the air filled with bullets. He felt them whiz past his ears like angry bees, but he didn't seek shelter. Getting hit now would be a blessing, removing him from this misery.

Soldiers started falling around him. The smoke was dissipating and the American .30 caliber machine guns were tearing through them. He kept advancing, putting one foot in front of the other.

Through dripping sweat, he saw the American line. He realized with surprise; he'd made it halfway. He raised his pistol and fired three quick shots. He had no idea where his bullets went.

He stopped walking and looked around. His men were advancing against withering fire. They were being cut down, but they were making progress. He wondered how it was possible that he could stand here and not die. He wasn't trying to take cover, yet he was unscathed. *Maybe I'm already dead. I'm a spirit. My body is somewhere behind me.* He searched for it, but couldn't make out anything specific. There were too many bodies.

He trudged forward firing his spirit pistol. He was twenty meters from the line, and in front. His slow walk had outpaced all the others. He emptied his pistol. When it clicked on an empty chamber, he carefully re-holstered it and pulled his rifle off his shoulder, continuing to shuffle forward. He was sure he was a spirit now. *Bullets must be passing through me.* His men continued to follow him despite the heavy fire. More died, but others lived and kept coming.

He stopped and raised his rifle to his shoulder. He aimed at the muzzle of an American rifle barrel sticking from a firing port. He fired, and the muzzle dropped as if the soldier holding it had dropped it. He smiled, *my spirit rifle is still in their world.*

He saw the muzzle of a thirty caliber machine gun spitting fire from a bunker. The barrel was sweeping towards him like a scythe. *It'll fire right through me.* Bullets whizzed closer as the barrel lined up on him. He took a step forward and was falling. He hit the bottom of the connector trench and lost his breath. He gasped, watching the white puffy clouds crossing the blue sky.

37

The smoke was clearing, and the scene out Carver's firing port made his heart race. The Japanese were charging up the hill. Every gun opened fire at the same time chopping through them. Bullets continued to thump into the sandbags.

Carver leaned into his Thompson and fired at a soldier making progress up the hill. He went down and out of sight in the battle debris. He moved his barrel to the right and fired another burst, dropping his target. There was another soldier directly behind that one, and he put .45 caliber bullets into his chest. Despite the massive casualties the Japanese were taking they kept coming, chewing up feet and yards towards the bunker line.

The confines of the trench were filling with smoke. Carver's eyes burned and watered, but he kept firing. Each soldier he shot blended with the previous. There were too many targets, but he concentrated on each shot, making them count. He wondered if they had enough bullets to kill them all.

He used his Thompson like a rifle, expending one bullet per target. He may not kill them, but a .45 caliber slug does considerable damage to bare flesh. He moved his barrel side to side, firing and moving to the next man.

The bodies were stacking up providing cover for the soldiers beyond. It became harder to find targets, but plenty more leaped over the bodies.

The machine guns were blowing huge holes in the Japanese lines. He knew they'd have to swap out barrels soon or risk destroying the precious guns. He hoped it didn't happen all at once.

The Japanese were only yards from the line. Sergeant Carver wondered if they'd be overrun again. He thought about the trench works leading to the rear. He knew there was one ten yards to his left. He looked down the line at the men firing frantically. Some were on the ground, wounded or dead. Despite the cover they were taking casualties they couldn't afford.

He slapped the soldier beside him. O'Connor looked at him over the stock of his M1. "Grab Gomez and follow me." He didn't wait but stepped away from the firing port and moved to his right. The men along the line continued firing, not noticing them passing behind.

As he passed the connector leading up the hill, he glanced down it. It was intact. If they got overrun, it would be the safest way to the next defensive line. Beyond that, there was the top of the hill and the command bunker. If they overran that, they'd have to retreat to the north knob.

O'Connor yelled, "Where we going, Sarge?"

He glanced back but kept moving, "To the downhill connector trench. I'm worried the Japs might push through and get into the trenches. Be nice to find a damned officer too."

Another fifteen yards brought them to the turn downhill. The junction had been closed off with sandbags, and there was a machine gun crew firing. Carver slid in next to a rifleman reloading his M1. "How you guys doing?" O'Connor and Gomez stood and added their fire down the hill. There were still a lot of Japanese coming, but the steady tide seemed to be slowing.

The soldier slid the clip into his rifle, careful not to pinch his thumb. "They're pushing hard, but we've stopped 'em so far. They used the trench to get close and hurled grenades at us." He glanced behind him at two shredded GIs. "We stopped 'em though."

Carver slapped his shoulder and moved to the machine gunner. He yelled over the chattering gun. "You need anything? Got enough ammo?"

The gunner stopped firing and looked at him with dark, gunpowder encrusted eyes. He looked to the loader who's face was also black with gunpowder. The loader looked behind him at stacks of metal ammo cans full of .30 caliber belts, and gave a thumbs up. "We're good, Sarge."

Carver nodded and found a spot beside O'Connor and Gomez. He aimed down his barrel, found a target and fired. The two round burst caught a soldier across the legs, and he dropped out of sight screaming.

O'Connor slapped Carver's arm and pointed down the hill. "Shit, they've got tanks."

Carver stopped firing and looked. At the base of the hill, he saw at least ten tanks rolling up the hill. They weren't firing, too many friendly troops to their front, but that would change.

Carver dropped from his firing position and alerted the machine gunner of the new danger. He knew the .30 caliber bullets wouldn't have much effect against armor.

He hoped Lieutenant Swan saw the tanks from the command bunker. He needed to direct artillery fire onto them, or they'd be overrun. There were a couple of anti-tank teams, but the bazookas were notoriously inaccurate, and they didn't have enough of them. The brass hadn't expected Jap armor.

The tanks rolled up the hill crunching over obstacles. When they had clear shots, they opened fire with their 47mm main guns and front-mounted machine guns. The effects were devastating. The first volley exploded along the trench line. A direct hit into a .30 caliber machine gun nest, silenced the gun and killed the crew.

Sergeant Carver yelled down the line. "Bazooka teams, we need bazooka teams!" soldiers looked back at him with fear in their eyes. Carver slapped Gomez. "Go find a bazooka. We can use this trench," he pointed at the connector trench leading downhill, "to get beside them and hit 'em from the side where their armor's thin."

Gomez nodded and took off. Carver watched as the tanks ate up the ground. Japanese soldiers rose up and joined the advancing tanks with renewed energy. Another volley of 47mm shots tore up more of the trench sending GIs sprawling. Carver leaned over the trench and fired at a group of soldiers hustling to get behind a tank. His shots lanced across them and sparked off the tank's armor.

With each foot of ground the tanks advanced, their accuracy increased. They'd taken out two machine gun nests and destroyed large sections of the trench. If the tanks weren't stopped in the next few minutes, they'd be forced to retreat and may not be able to hold the hill.

The welcome sound of artillery made Carver look up. He watched as rounds flew over and impacted on the slope. The first volley landed behind the tanks sending up plumes of black earth and jungle debris.

The tanks increased their speed trying to close with the trench line before the artillery could adjust. Carver slid down to the bottom of the trench as the next volley landed amongst the tanks, but almost on top of their own positions. He saw Gomez scurrying in a crouch towards him with two wide-eyed soldiers following. One was carrying a bazooka tube on his shoulder, the other a bag of rockets.

Carver yelled, "Bring that stovepipe and follow me." He moved along the trench, back to the machine gun crew. They hunkered beneath their helmets. Carver slapped the gunner's shoulder and yelled into his ear. "We're moving down this trench to get beside the tanks." He looked at him like he'd lost his mind then saw the bazooka team and understood. "After we've shot, give us some covering fire, but give yourself time to get the hell out of here."

Carver nodded at O'Connor, Gomez and the bazooka team. "Let's go." He leaped over the sandbags covering the machine gun nest and dropped into the trench leading down. He didn't wait for the others. He ran in a crouch down the trench with his Thompson muzzle leading the way.

He stopped and poked his head over the side. The tanks were coming despite the artillery fire. One tank was burning. Flames leaped from a gaping hole in the front plate. A direct hit. The other GIs slid into him. He pointed further down the trench. "Gomez, head down there and make sure no Japs come up." Gomez nodded, holding his helmet as dirt rained down. He moved ten yards, went into a prone position and put his M1 to his shoulder. Carver pointed to the bazooka team. "Those tanks will be beside us in a minute or two. Load that pipe and get ready."

The loader nodded and put his ammo pouch on the ground. He opened the flap and pulled out an M6 rocket. The gunner put the launcher on his shoulder but stayed beneath the lip of the trench. The loader slid the rocket into the back of the tube and armed it. He carefully pushed the rocket until it latched into place then unfurled the firing wire and wrapped it around the contact spring. He tapped the gunner's helmet.

The gunner looked to Sergeant Carver. "Ready, Sarge." He licked his dry lips and tried to swallow. "Let me know when they're beside us."

Carver nodded and peered over the edge. The tanks were only thirty yards away. The artillery had moved down the hill, continuing to kill and maim Japanese. A bullet slammed into the ground in front of him, and he ducked down. "In ten seconds he'll be right beside us. It'll be a broadside shot, you ready?" the gunner mouthed a prayer and nodded. "I'll give you covering fire while you're shooting, but make it quick, they're onto us."

Carver counted down, "five, four, three, two, one, now." He and O'Connor rose up and fired at the Japanese soldiers following the nearest tank. The bazooka gunner rose up to his full height and leveled the tube at the tank. It looked huge. He aimed for the turret joint and squeezed the trigger. There was a flash and a whoosh as the rocket left the tube. It streaked at the tank and hit below the turret and exploded. It penetrated enough of the thin side armor to ignite the inside with hot metal and fire. The tank slewed to the side and stopped. Smoke and flame spit from the hole.

The smoke trail from the rocket left little doubt where the shot had come from, and soon the air above the trench was alive with bullets. At the same moment, Gomez yelled and fired in quick succession. Carver swung his Thompson down the trench line as Japanese soldiers came running up. He shot over Gomez who was on his belly reloading. The sides of the trench exploded with the heavy slugs and hid the devastation of the dying Japanese. O'Connor stepped to the side of Carver with his M1 on his shoulder and added to the deadly fire.

Carver burned through his magazine and as he reloaded yelled at the bazooka team to move back up the line. They scurried away, back up the trench. They stopped after fifteen yards, and the gunner put the tube back on his shoulder. The right side of his face was dark red from the blast of heat from the bazooka tube.

The loader pulled another M6 rocket and pushed it into the breach. When wired and ready he tapped the gunner's helmet. The gunner took a deep breath and rose up searching for another target. There was another tank further away but farther up the hill, almost to the bunker line. He leveled the tube and was about to pull the trigger when the back of his head exploded in gray matter and blood. He pitched back into the loader who caught his falling body.

At first, the loader thought he'd tripped, but the blood and gore told a different story. He looked down the trench and saw Carver and O'Connor coming at him full speed. Gomez walked backward firing intermittently, covering their retreat.

Carver saw the dead gunner and pointed at the loader, "Check the gun, I'll fire." The loader stared, frozen in shock. Carver slapped him hard across the jaw. "Pull your shit together or you die, soldier."

The GI shook his head and gritted his teeth in anger. "You son-of-a-bitch, no need to hit me."

Carver ignored him and slung his Thompson and lifted the bazooka to his shoulder. He'd fired one a few times in training. He remembered they weren't very accurate unless you were close.

O'Connor said, "I'll pop up and shoot from down there," he pointed down the trench, "draw their fire away from you." Carver nodded. O'Connor moved down the trench a couple of yards and said, "Now." He rose up and fired until his M1 pinged. He ducked down as bullets whizzed and slammed around him. At the same instant, Carver stood and saw the backside of the tank he would kill. He only had a second to align the shot or he'd die. He blotted out the tank and pulled the trigger. The heat from the tube was intense, and he flung it away as he dropped behind the trench.

The rocket sliced into the back of the type 97 tank at its thinnest point. The engine exploded sending shards of hot metal into the fuel. Within seconds the tank was engulfed in flame. None of the five-man crew emerged.

Carver didn't know he'd killed the tank; he valued his head too much to look. He moved up the trench holding the bazooka by the fore grip. The loader yelled. "The launcher's fried, Sarge. Leave it." Carver dropped it and noticed the bullet holes along its length. He didn't remember taking the hits. He continued moving up the trench.

He yelled out to the machine gun nest so they wouldn't mistake them for Japs, but when he rounded the corner, there was no sign of them. He looked up to the top of Hill 260 and saw a plume of smoke spouting like a massive, white thundercloud. "Shit, that's the signal for retreat. We gotta hurry, or we'll get caught back here."

They leaped over the sandbags and looked down the trench line. The only GIs he saw were dead. A Japanese soldier came around the corner, and his eyes went wide. Carver shot him with a short burst, and he went down.

The connector trench leading up the hill was just ahead, it would provide them with cover if they could get to it. He didn't think they'd live long on the surface.

He pulled a grenade from his belt and pulled the pin. He charged towards the entrance to the connector. He could see movement in the overrun machine gun nest beyond. He threw the grenade, hoping there were no GIs still alive in there. He yelled, "Grenade!" and dove to the ground holding his helmet. There was a soft whump as the grenade went off in the close confines of the bunker. He sprang up and ran the few feet to the connector trench. The others were right on his tail.

THE CONNECTOR TRENCH WAS OPEN, and Carver led the way. Gomez and O'Connor took turns covering the rear and the loader, Private Tavers moved behind Carver. They had yet to come across any friendly troops. The thumping of mortar rounds crashed around them, covering the American retreat.

Carver came to a corner and slid to a stop. He peered around and jerked back. He signaled to the others. They nodded, and he moved away from the corner. Private Tavers and Corporal O'Connor filled the space and pulled grenades from their belts. They pulled the pins and threw them around the corner then pressed their backs against the wall. There was a brief yell of surprise, then the explosion. O'Connor went around the corner with his M1 and fired into the smoking bodies, but they were already dead. He gave the others a thumbs up, and Sergeant Carver moved past him taking the lead.

He slowed his pace. There was still shooting, and the thumping of mortars, but the fire coming from the friendly lines was almost non-existent. It seemed Lieutenant Swan had them in a headlong retreat.

He could see the command bunker ahead. Barrels were sticking out spewing fire down the hill. Carver was glad to see it. He poked his head over the trench. They were ahead of the Japanese. *Must be clearing out the next line of bunkers.*

He looked for the tanks and noticed the burning hulk of the one he'd taken out. He wondered how it would be to die in such a flaming horror.

The rest of the tanks were making their way up the slope. It was more difficult the higher they went because the ground steepened, and there were more obstacles they had to maneuver around rather than over. They were making headway though.

Behind each tank, dozens of Japanese troops struggled over the ground. Carver wondered why they weren't using the trench system. Whatever the reason he was glad they hadn't figured it out yet. It allowed he and his men to move back to their lines without being exposed.

He slowed when he came to another corner. The command bunker was off to the left. He recognized this as the final turn before it spilled into the main trench system. The others crouched watching the rear.

Carver leaned around the corner and immediately pulled back as bullets slapped into the dirt walls, sending dust and debris into his face. He spit out dirt and yelled. "Friendlies, friendlies! Ceasefire. Sergeant Carver here." He waited, but there was no response. He tried again. "You hear me? Friendlies coming out."

A dim voice called, "Who you say you were again?"

"Carver, Sergeant Carver." Bullets sprayed down the line and Carver covered his head. When it stopped he yelled, "Goddamit, you sons-of-bitches, knock it off."

The voice yelled back, "Carver's dead you Jap sumbitch."

"Dammit, you moronic fuckhead, cease fire. I'm not dead."

No fire came, but the voice questioned, "Sarge?" Carver extended his hand around the corner. When it didn't get shot off, he moved his body into the line of fire with his Thompson aiming to the sky. "It is you. We thought you were dead. The machine gunners said they saw you go down trying to kill those damned tanks."

Sergeant Carver didn't waste time talking but waved the men forward. As Gomez passed him, he caught movement coming up the trench. He went onto his belly bringing the Thompson to his shoulder. A surprised Japanese soldier with a snub-nosed burp gun filled his sights, and Carver unleashed a steady stream of bullets into him. The soldier convulsed backward into more troops. Carver emptied his magazine then pushed himself around the corner as bullets slammed into the wall. He was on his hands and knees crawling towards the sandbagged safety of his lines. O'Connor was there sighting over his head waiting for the first Jap to show himself. He saw a dark object hit the wall at the corner and he dove for the dirt and yelled, "Grenade."

Carver went flat, and the grenade exploded mere yards away. He winced as he felt hot metal slice into his leg. O'Connor was up and helping Carver to his feet. Yelling alerted him and he watched as a Japanese soldier slid around the corner with death in his eyes. The Jap had the drop on him, but before he could fire there was a chorus of shooting from behind and the soldier dropped with multiple gunshot wounds.

Gomez sprinted to the other side of Carver, his gun smoking. Together they hefted him over the sandbags. Once clear, the GIs guarding the trench opened fire as more Japs came around the corner.

They got to the top of the hill as bullets whizzed through the air. The rest of the GIs retreated behind them, and the machine guns in the command bunker stopped firing and pulled back.

The Japanese were in full attack. Their objective was in sight, and the thought of victory had them crazed. The GIs retreated, covering one another as they went. Sergeant Carver was between Gomez and O'Connor. Private Tavers covered them with his M1 Garand. The tanks crested the hill and fired into the command bunker. One 47mm shell went through a firing port and exploded inside. Debris and fire shot out the gunport slits.

As they retreated, Carver thought they'd be shot in the back any second. They passed the dug-in turret of a Sherman tank and Carver remembered Lt. Swan mentioning them covering their retreat. True to his word the Shermans were waiting to blast the oncoming Type 97 tanks.

As enemy troops spilled onto the top of the hill, they were cut down by the .30 caliber Browning machine guns poking out from the middle of the Sherman's. The main 75mm gun fired making Carver flinch. The immediate clang behind them signaled a hit. Carver couldn't turn around, but he could feel the heat of the exploding Type 97 tank.

Gomez and O'Connor continued helping him down the hill. The tanks fired, and machine gunned the oncoming Japanese forces but were forced to pull back as enemy tanks worked to flank them.

The GIs got to the bottom of the hill and threw Sergeant Carver into the back of a troop truck. It was full of wounded and started churning down the muddy road, retreating towards the north knob. O'Connor hoped it wouldn't be targeted by any Japanese tanks.

Three of the five Shermans were backing down the hill with their main guns and .30 calibers firing. They were driving blind, not willing to turn their lighter armored backsides to the guns of the Type 97s.

One of the Sherman's backed into a tree which shuddered but stopped the momentum of the tank. The treads struggled, continuing to grind into the obstacle but the tree wasn't moving. The driver reversed direction, but the treads dug into soft ground. The top hatch opened, and the tank commander popped up grabbing the handles of the fifty caliber machine gun mounted on top. He primed the weapon and sent a stream of bullets into a Japanese tank. The enemy tank sparked as the heavy bullets chipped at its steel front.

The front machine gun of the Japanese tank slewed in his direction and fired a long stream. For five seconds the two machine gunners exchanged fire until the Sherman tank commander lurched and fell back into the tank. The 75mm gun on the Sherman took aim while the Japanese tank did the same. Both fired simultaneously, and both took hits. The Sherman's shell hit the Type 97 in the turret joint, and the tank's turret popped off the base like a children's toy. For a brief second O'Connor could see the surprised face of the suddenly exposed driver before the turret slammed down and crushed him.

The Sherman was spewing smoke and fire from the gaping hole the Japanese shell left. Hatches opened, and men clawed and struggled to get out. Two made it before the Sherman went up in flames. A man screamed as he was halfway out the top hatch, flames burst through and consumed him.

The two surviving tankers ran down the hill following the two remaining Shermans. Their uniforms smoked and smoldered, and their faces were black where their goggles didn't cover.

O'Connor punched Gomez in the arm, "Let's give 'em cover." He ran back towards the hill and crouched behind a fallen tree. He placed his rifle on the trunk and sighted down searching for targets. It didn't take long to find a Japanese soldier leaping down the hill firing at the retreating tankers. O'Connor pulled the trigger and watched as the man took the bullet in the belly and fell forward. Gomez was firing, and Private Tavers joined them with his M1 Garand.

The remaining Shermans passed them and once on the road turned forward. They kept muzzles pointing backward and never stopped firing. The two tankers on foot were running for their lives. Bullets smacked into logs and rocks all around them. O'Connor stood up, waved his arms and yelled. The tankers saw him and sprinted for them.

Japanese were coming down the hill, not taking the time to aim, but firing as they ran. O'Connor dropped one, and Private Tavers hit another. Gomez shouldered his rifle as the tankers leaped behind the cover of the tree. They were breathing hard, sweat and grime dripping from their faces.

O'Connor pointed towards the retreating tanks. "Follow them. We'll cover you." They didn't hesitate and took off down the road. The three GIs fired until their weapons were empty and quickly reloaded. The pursuing Japanese were more careful now.

Bullets thunked into the downed tree. O'Connor pulled the remaining grenades from his belt, and the others did the same. "On the count of three, we'll throw, wait for the explosions then run like hell." They nodded and pulled the pins. "One, two, three." They threw the grenades as far up the hill as they could. When they exploded, all three jumped to their feet and ran after the tankers.

Private Tavers took three steps and yelled out as two bullets lanced through his back and exited his chest. Blood sprayed the back of O'Connor. He turned in time to see the life leave Taver's eyes. He stopped and was about to run back for him, but Taver's body was raked over with more bullets. Gomez grabbed O'Connor's arm and pulled him up the road. "Leave him. He's gone."

38

Lieutenant Taro stood atop Hill 260 with his arms across his chest. He watched the Americans running like scared sheep. He shook his head at the image, *deadly sheep*. They were retreating, but they'd left a swath of destruction. The hillside was littered with dead and dying soldiers. The tank units hadn't gotten off easy either. He could see at least three burning hulks from his vantage point.

Lieutenant Otani joined him. He was breathing hard, and his uniform was shredded, as if he'd lost a fight with a lion. Lieutenant Taro noticed blood dripping off his fingers. "You're hit, sir."

Lieutenant Otani glanced at the blood in surprise. He shrugged, "I hadn't noticed." He followed the blood trail up to his shoulder and winced as he felt the deep gash. He kept his hand on the wound and looked down the hill towards the north knob.

Lieutenant Taro waved and got the attention of a medic. Lieutenant Otani barely noticed when the medic cut his sleeve away. He bit his lip when he felt the needle and thread sewing the gash together. "It is a minor wound compared to the horrors our men went through."

Lieutenant Taro nodded, "Many good men died. I have no idea

how many." He looked to the clouds. "I convinced myself that I too was dead. I thought I must be, so many bullets missed me."

Lieutenant Otani looked at him. "You led the men to victory. You were their example." He put his bloody hand on his shoulder. "You restored your honor a thousand times today."

The sounds of war from the other hills grew intense. An American artillery barrage arced over their heads, screaming towards Hill 700. It reminded the two officers that they need to fortify their new positions and take cover. It wouldn't be long until the Americans counter-attacked.

Lieutenant Taro pointed towards an abandoned and burned out bunker. It was the biggest of the bunkers and was undoubtedly the American's command center. Japanese troops lingered around the entrance smoking cigarettes that smelled like Lucky Strikes, an American brand. "We can occupy the American's old headquarters. It's been cleared and is still relatively intact."

Otani nodded and walked to the entrance. He peered inside. The dead had been removed, but the stench of burnt flesh was unmistakable. Otani looked at the men around him. It was time to get back to work. "Clean this bunker out and set up radios. Follow the American lines and splice into their wires. I want to have contact with HQ within the hour." He turned to Lt. Taro. "I want the trenches dug and reinforced. Use the downed timber for cover. The Americans will come, and I want them to pay dearly for every inch. We have to hold until the other hills are taken. We won't get reinforcements until then." Taro nodded and went to work assigning jobs.

WHEN EVENING CAME, Lieutenant Taro and his men were exhausted. He'd dug and struggled beside them, making their defenses as strong as they could in the short time.

The Americans hadn't fired artillery onto Hill 260. Taro knew it was only a matter of time. He could see them scurrying around the top of the north knob a few kilometers away, no doubt digging and reinforcing. Taro had no illusions about attacking them. They barely had enough men to defend what they'd taken. They were in defensive mode, and he felt good about that. He didn't relish watching more soldiers die trying to wade through machine gun fire and artillery. It would be the American's turn this time.

As the daylight faded to dark, he could still hear the sounds of digging. His men were going deep, tunneling. The American's would have to pull them out one by one. Taking this hill back would cost them dearly.

The night came, and Taro made one last check on his men before collapsing in a corner and falling asleep. A soldier tried to wake him, offering him food, but he was too tired even for that. He slept three hours and woke feeling worse than he had before sleeping.

He ate what little food he could find while watching the light show coming from the west. The artillery hadn't subsided. He couldn't tell if it was American or Japanese, probably both. He could hear the staccato of machine guns and the thumping of explosions. Occasionally there would be a large explosion that would light up the night. From the sea, there was fire too, as the big American naval guns joined the fight. He closed his eyes happy they weren't aimed at him yet.

IT WAS STILL DARK when the bombs started dropping on Hill 260. Even though Lt. Taro expected it, it still took his breath away. The raw power of artillery shells landing close, shaking the ground, shaking his bones, wasn't something you got used to.

He scurried into a hole along with other soldiers and hoped they wouldn't be buried. The artillery lasted an hour. It seemed much longer.

When it finally stopped, he poked his head out and listened through ringing ears. Debris was falling like snow. There weren't any jungle sounds. Indeed the jungle had been stripped from the hill like it had endured a tight haircut.

The brief silence didn't last. He could hear the unmistakable sound of tanks clanking up the hill. He looked over the edge and in the dim light of early morning saw American Sherman tanks churning towards them.

He clutched the soldier next to him, a young man who looked no older than sixteen. "Go to the command bunker and tell Lieutenant Otani the Americans are attacking from the north knob with tanks and troops." He held onto the man's shoulder and stood to get a better look down the hill. He counted the tanks he could see. "Tell him there are at least five tanks and probably more." He pushed the soldier, and he ran to do his bidding.

Mortar rounds started falling all along the hill. He told his men to remain under cover until they could get good shots. He heard the crack of a rifle off to his right. *A sniper.* In a low crouch, he went to the sound.

The sniper was laying amongst fallen timbers with his rifle perched on a rotten stump. Taro stopped and watched him sighting through the scope mounted rifle. He moved the barrel to the right then centered and fired. The rifle jumped in his hand, and the rifleman smoothly reloaded another round.

Taro peered over the edge of the trench and watched the advancing Americans. They moved cautiously, letting their mortar crews work the hill and using the Sherman's for cover. He could see plenty of targets though, men not able to hide behind the moving hunk of metal. The sniper rifle cracked, and this time Taro saw a green-clad soldier fall. He felt no pity, but pride in his shooter. It was a long shot, but he made it look easy.

Firing erupted up and down the line. His men were done watching and were engaging the Americans. The tanks stopped and fired at the muzzle flashes with their 75mm cannons. The sound of the .30 caliber front mounted machine guns joined in, and soon the air above Taro's head was buzzing again.

He stayed down, hoping his machine gun crews heeded their orders not to shoot until the Americans were close. The tank cannons would make quick work of them once they were spotted. He licked his dry lips hoping Lieutenant Otani's plan worked.

He watched as the tanks rolled past the line of holes the men had dug late into the night. Each hole was occupied with a soldier equipped with a rifle and two precious grenades. Their attack would be the signal to start the mortar barrage. The plan was to pin the Americans down and take out the tanks one by one, once separated from the infantry.

He watched in morbid fascination as the tanks went past the holes. *It was working. The Americans didn't notice them.* The hole covers popped open. The men had timed it perfectly allowing the American infantry cowering behind the tanks to get far enough ahead so they could expose themselves without being seen.

Taro watched two of his men pop up and hurl grenades. They looked like rocks from this far away but the explosions burst in the middle of the American infantry, and he saw many fall. They were back in their holes before the GIs knew what hit them.

More explosions sent GIs flying. The infantry faltered and started looking behind them for the unseen threat. One of his men poked his head up and was about to throw another grenade, but he was seen and gunned down by a soldier wielding a Thompson submachine gun.

The GIs realized what was happening and stopped advancing. Their weapons pointed back the way they'd come. Lieutenant Taro watched as one by one the Americans silenced the holes. The tanks clanked forward leaving the infantry behind. Mortar rounds fired from the reverse side of Hill 260 started landing amongst the tanks.

39

The early morning assault on Hill 260 wasn't what Sergeant Carver wanted to happen, but the brass hadn't asked his opinion. He'd been patched up by the medics and told to occupy a cot in the medical tent. He'd slept for two hours, but that was all he could stand. He hobbled away from the infirmary without anyone noticing. He found his Thompson near the front door and slung it over his shoulder.

He limped across the North knob, each step burned and ached. The medics thought they'd gotten all the shrapnel out of his leg, but it still burned like fire. They'd told him he was lucky there weren't any pieces lodged too deep. He didn't feel lucky.

He'd gone to the biggest bunker on the hill trying to get information. He was just about to enter when he heard yelling. Someone was getting chewed out. He stopped and listened. Captain Flannigan was giving someone hell. He couldn't hear any replies, but he would bet money the officer receiving the dressing down was Lt. Swan.

He only caught bits and pieces, but he heard a lot of words like, 'retreat, orders, hold the line, insubordination and court martial.' The brass wasn't happy they'd retreated off Hill 260.

Carver's blood boiled. Flannigan made it sound like there was another choice. He grit his teeth. *There was another choice…death.* He clenched his jaw and was about to burst into the bunker and be court-martialed himself when a voice beside him said, "Thought you were in the medical tent."

He looked over his shoulder and saw Corporal O'Connor. Carver knew he'd been awake since before the attack, but he looked as ready to go as he always did. "No cute nurses." He stepped away from the bunker. "I've been out of it, know anything?"

O'Connor nodded. "You didn't hear? Flannigan wants us to take the hill back in the morning."

"Shit."

SERGEANT CARVER DIDN'T CHECK in with Lt. Swan before the attack. He simply lined up with everyone else. His leg ached, and he had a distinct limp, but he wouldn't be left behind. He was happy to see they had tanks to walk behind.

At first, he wondered if the Japanese had left Hill 260. The tanks with the infantry close behind met no resistance. That fantasy shattered when the man in front of him dropped from a sniper's Bullet. The grinding of the tank's engine and treads muffled the shot, but there was no doubt about the results. The GI was dead before he hit the ground. "Sniper," he yelled and the men got as close to the hulking Sherman's backside as they could.

They moved slowly up the hill. The tank treads churning against the soft ground. The hill was covered with downed trees and blasted ground. They had to choose their routes carefully or risk getting stuck.

Carver peered around the edge of the tank. They were almost a quarter of the way up the hill. *Maybe most of them have bugged out.* He shook his head knowing it was bullshit.

An explosion erupted amongst the men behind the tank to his right. He hadn't heard artillery or the screaming of mortars. Whatever it was, it killed and maimed a number of soldiers. They screamed and thrashed clutching their wounds. Another explosion and more men were down. *What the hell's happening?*

He instinctively kneeled, letting the tank move ahead. He searched three hundred sixty degrees around. Something caught his eye behind him, and he spun bringing his Thompson to bear. A Japanese soldier materialized from the ground about to throw a grenade. Carver flicked the safety off and pulled the trigger, walking .45 caliber slugs up his body. The soldier fell back into his hole, the grenade following him, leaving no doubt.

Carver watched as more holes opened with more Japanese hurling grenades. He yelled a warning and motioned to take cover. The GIs dove to the ground. Carver yelled, "they're behind us in holes."

The next Japanese to pop up was gunned down by the waiting guns. The infantry advance had stopped. Carver watched as more holes were uncovered and the grizzly work of killing the occupants continued.

Enemy mortar rounds started whistling down amongst the tanks. The tankers were oblivious to the Japs in the holes and continued grinding up the hill. The mortar fire walked down towards the infantry, and they had no choice but to hunker down. The tanks got further away from the GIs.

Sergeant Carver realized their mistake and urged the men forward. "We have to guard the tank's flanks." He stood up to move forward, but the pain in his leg and the flying shrapnel kept him down. He watched in horror as more Japanese in hide holes between him and the tanks emerged and charged with satchels clutched to their chests.

He leveled his Thompson and fired into one of the attackers. The soldier fell but got back to his feet and made it the final few steps to the back of a Sherman. There was an explosion, and the soldier and the tank disappeared in flame. There were similar explosions amongst the unprotected tanks.

When the smoke and debris cleared, six of the ten Sherman tanks were blazing pyres.

The shock from the devastating suicide attack pulsed through the GIs like a lightning bolt. They stared in awe, then sprang into action running forward to protect the remaining tanks, despite the mortar fire.

Carver willed himself to keep moving despite his aching leg.

Mortar rounds exploded around him, but he pushed through and made it to the back of one of the Shermans. It was stopped, it's 75mm gun firing as fast as it could be loaded. The .30 caliber machine gun raked the hill searching for more hidden Japanese. The burning hulks spewed black smoke making Carver choke.

He reached for the radio on the back of the tank, hoping it was still operational. More troops were at his side using the tank for cover as they fired up the hill. Carver keyed the side of the radio and heard static. "Tank crew, this is Sergeant Carver. You need to move forward. We're with you the rest of the way. We'll keep the Japs off your tail."

The reply was curt, "Roger." The tank lurched forward. The others followed, and they advanced up the hill.

Bullets zinged and ricocheted off the front of the tank. Carver looked at the other tanks and was dismayed how few soldiers he saw clustered behind them. They'd lost a lot of men over the past twenty four hours. There hadn't been any reinforcements besides the tanks and their crews. The platoon was whittled down to an almost ineffective force and they were being asked to root out a dug in enemy.

The only thing evening the playing field was the fact that the Japanese had taken even more casualties. Carver wondered how many were waiting for them.

They were halfway up the hill when the tanks stopped. Carver nearly bumped into the back-end. He lifted the radio and listened. He nodded and signed off. "There's an airstrike coming, followed by an artillery strike. Find some cover."

Under cover of the hammering machine guns and cannons of the tanks, the men spread out and started scraping out depressions in the jungle floor. There was plenty of cover with all the fallen trees and churned up ground. Bullets whizzed and snapped over their heads as they dug in.

Ten minutes passed before the air filled with diving fighters. Carver kept his head down but watched as they dove and dropped their two hundred pound bombs. The top of the hill erupted as wave after wave passed. The ground shook and he had the sensation of holding on so he wouldn't fall off the world.

When they ran out of bombs, they strafed until their guns were empty, then arced out over the sea and lined up for the Cape Torokina Airfield six miles away.

Carver lifted his head. The top of the hill was covered in dust and debris. New fires dotted the landscape spewing black and white smoke. There was no movement, no firing, but he knew the Japanese were there, waiting.

A few minutes later the air filled with artillery shells. The fire concentrated on top of the hill. Carver doubted the command bunker Lt. Swan operated out of yesterday, was still standing.

The thought brought him up short. He'd been concentrating on getting into the fight with his men. He realized he had no idea where Lt. Swan was. As the shells thumped into the Japanese line, he leaned over and saw Corporal O'Connor laying on his stomach with his arms over his head. He was covered in a layer of dust and bits of jungle fauna. He yelled over the din of the artillery, "Hey O'Connor, you seen the lieutenant?"

O'Connor lifted his head and gazed through slit eyelids. Carver had the impression he'd woken him. O'Connor nodded and pointed down the hill, "He's leading from the rear as usual."

Carver nodded and yelled back. "As long as he keeps the artillery coming, I'm okay with that."

The artillery fell like rain for another ten minutes. When it stopped, there was an unnatural silence. The brief calm was broken by the revving motors of the four Sherman tanks moving forward.

40

Lieutenant Taro sat beside the battered body of Lieutenant Otani. The American air attack and artillery had been deadly. He had no idea how many soldiers were dead. He only knew the officer in charge was dead, which meant he was in command. It was beyond comprehension. How had he survived when so many others died?

He gazed down the smoking trench line. It was filled with pieces of soldiers and ruined equipment. The smell of burnt bodies and cordite burned his nose. They'd dug deep, but the relentless bombing had collapsed most of the holes along with the soldiers. *Am I the only one left?*

He picked up his rifle. It was crusted in dirt and mud. He ran his hand over the cold steel barrel. He sighed, wondering how much longer he'd have to heft it around. He looked over his shoulder. The Americans rumbled up the hill, despite losing tanks to the heroic suicide bombers.

The occasional bullet smacked into the ground in front of him; probing fire. He took one last look at the dead eyes of his commander and clawed his way to the lip of the trench. The Americans were less than a kilometer away. A blackness descended over him. He wanted to end this misery once and for all.

He pulled his legs beneath him and sat cross-legged. He rested his elbows on his knees and brought the rifle to his shoulder. It wavered despite the solid position. His arms shook and he struggled to keep it steady. He looked over the sights searching for a target. He saw tanks, but no soldiers. He leveled the barrel and fired at the metal behemoth. He watched his round spark off the front. He pulled the bolt and snicked in another bullet. He fired until he ran out of ammo. The tank didn't seem to notice him, despite hitting it with each shot. It rumbled forward, clanking and spouting smoke from the exhaust.

He was too tired to reload, so he dropped the rifle and pulled out his pistol. It was heavy, and his shaking hand could barely grip the handle. The tank was close now, looming large like some blocky monster.

He fired his pistol, and it bucked like a wild beast trying to free itself. The front machine gun moved in his direction, but before it made it to him, another machine gun opened fire. It was the unmistakable buzzsaw of a Nambu. He saw the back end of the tank spark as bullets found their mark. He heard screams from men behind the tank.

The Sherman stopped only a few meters from his position and the turret swung towards the Nambu. It adjusted and fired. The 75mm shell slammed into the machine gun nest, silencing it instantly. The boom nearly knocked Lt. Taro's hat off.

The threat gone, the turret swiveled until the main gun centered on Lt. Taro. He stared into the dark maw of the muzzle, waiting for it to deliver him from this hellish world. Instead, soldiers came from behind the tank with their weapons centered on his chest. Fear heightened his senses as he contemplated capture for the first time. He drew the only weapon he had left, his fighting knife. It was rusted from infrequent use. He held it at his side, waiting for the first soldier to come close. He pictured himself thrusting the blade into the GIs gut.

The first man to him was a long lanky soldier holding an M1 rifle. He seemed strangely familiar. He looked young but hard. A combat veteran. He kept his distance. Taro thought his eyes looked predatory. Another soldier limped up beside him. He had sergeant's stripes on his shoulders and held a submachine gun. He was shorter than the first soldier but looked like chiseled granite. He thought he knew the man somehow, but couldn't remember how. He became Taro's new target.

Other Americans streamed past, but these two remained. The tall one spit a long stream, never taking his eyes off him. He said something to the sergeant who shook his head. The sergeant kneeled and pointed at the knife and spoke. Lieutenant Taro was tired, so tired he could hardly keep his head up. He stared back at the sergeant. His vision blurred and tears he didn't know he had, streamed down his face.

He felt the knife drop from his hands and the lanky soldier was on him in a flash lifting him from his seated position and facing him towards the sergeant. He expected to be shot or run through with a bayonet, but instead, the sergeant spoke, and the lanky soldier released him. The young soldier gave him a hard stare and walked away.

The wounded sergeant motioned for him to follow and without knowing how or why his feet moved down the hill towards the American lines. Lieutenant Taro's war was over.

41

EPILOGUE

The battle described did not pan out the way I've depicted here. Hill 260 was real and was attacked by overwhelming Japanese forces on March 8th. The Japanese pushed the Americans off the hill and held onto it for many days. Each of the other Japanese objectives was also achieved, however they took such massive casualties (est. 8000 KIA) that they had little chance of holding the ground and no chance of achieving the ultimate goal of taking over the allied airfields. Despite their losses, the Japanese soldiers held the hills until every man was either killed or captured.

The 164th Regiment was one of many units involved in the battle. The 164th was integral in the defense and particularly in the re-taking of Hill 260.

The American presence on the island ended soon after the battle and Bougainville was occupied by the Australian Army until the end of the war. The Japanese on Bougainville Island were never defeated. They surrendered along with the rest of the Japanese Empire, on September 2nd 1945.

Join my WWII readers list and receive updates on upcoming books, discounts and freebies.

It's completely free to sign up and you'll never be spammed. You can opt out at any time.

Visit chrisglatte.com to sign up for free.

If you enjoyed this book, it would be great if you'd leave an honest review.
Reviews help me gain visibility and they can bring my books to the attention of other readers who may enjoy them.
Thanks
Get the next book:

Bleeding The Sun